Dark Grid

David C. Waldron

DARK GRID

ISBN: 1-468-07915-8

ISBN 13: 978-1-468-07915-9

Cover art by David C. Waldron and Deborah Kolstad.

Edited by Dancing Out Loud Multimedia

First printing, December 2011

Second printing, August 2012

For my wife, Lia.
I will ALWAYS come for you.

Chapter One

June 14, 2012 – 3:14 am Eastern Daylight Time

Eric Tripp had been out of the military for six months and usually slept like a rock. Still, he was extremely glad he had told his girlfriend how to wake him up the first night they'd stayed together. She hadn't believed him when he'd told her to go to the end of the bed, grab him by the big toe, and say his name. Thankfully she'd humored him that first time and become a firm believer when he'd come up all but swinging.

Sure, the barking dog next door was annoying, but that didn't explain why it had woken him up. After two tours in the sandbox he'd learned to sleep through mortar fire, as long as it wasn't falling directly on him.

Slowly, so as not to disturb Karen, he rolled out of bed and went into the kitchen. Now that he was up, he'd need a drink--and water just wouldn't cut it. He'd learned a long time ago that OJ was just the ticket in the middle of the night, especially good OJ--sweet, with lots of pulp, it was like drinking an orange and he didn't even have to peel it. When he'd been deployed he'd made do with pouring Tang powder directly in his mouth--but real, honest-to-goodness OJ, you just couldn't beat it.

Now why is that dog going nuts? What time is it anyway? Eric thought. *And how did I miss that the power is out? Man, I grabbed the juice out of the fridge and didn't even notice the light was off? I paid the bill, and they don't turn the power off in the middle of the night either way. No thunder, so no storm. It's really not that hot, so the grid shouldn't be overburdened. So how come the power's out?*

And then he looked out the window and saw something he'd been missing since his one and only tour in Alaska ended, and thought he'd never get to see again. *No way! Aurora borealis in Tennessee?* Followed immediately by, "KAREN! Get up, getup getup getUP GETUP!" Either he was in the middle of his most vivid dream ever or NASA may have been right after all.

June 14, 2012 – 3:13 am Eastern Daylight Time

Sheri Hines wasn't a night person, but at least working the graveyard shift gave her an excuse to skip out on girls' night at the bar. One less potential miserable failure at a relationship and one less night going home alone while all the other girls had picked up, or been picked up by, someone else. Ok, that wasn't entirely fair--if she'd been a slut, or hadn't had any standards, she could probably have been picked up more often than not, but she was the one who had to look at herself in the mirror every morning.

Oh blech, please not this again! Sheri thought. *There is only one of me inside this head and I cannot listen to this diatribe even one more time. If the only thing all of your failed relationships have in common is you, the mirror is where you need to be looking! Maybe your standards are a bit too high, girl! Maybe you need to quit looking for Mr. Right and accept Mr. Right Now--I did just say that, ok, I'm nuts.*

Red blinking lights at the Nashville Hydro Electric Power Generation Facility were not a good thing--in fact, they were the quintessential "bad thing". Bad enough to break Sheri out of her reverie to stare at the control panel with a sudden stab of panic. There had been a drill only three weeks ago and, anyway, they were always warned about drills ahead of time. This didn't feel like a drill.

The Nashville plant was capable of generating 214 MW of power at peak production. That would be enough to provide power to, on average, 107,000 homes all by itself. It was currently generating and providing power for not only Nashville, but as far away as Cookeville and Jackson, Tennessee; Bowling Green, Kentucky; and Athens, Alabama. It was part of "The Grid".

The load Sheri was monitoring should not, could not, have dropped by over 85 percent and yet that's exactly what the meter was reporting. That was like turning off most electrical appliances within a 75,000 square mile area, and shutting down this and every other hydro and coal powered plant within three hundred miles!

Then the blinking stopped: fat, take your leave of the frying pan and meet the fire. While blinking red lights were bad, steady red lights were infinitely worse. Steady red lights were overload, and just as Sheri reached for the radio the numbers sank in. While the needle was buried at 250 percent--and hadn't that amused her to no end when she had first seen it--the digital readout was climbing past 780.

The load on the long haul lines was currently at 780 percent--what the weakest link in the chain was currently rated to support. For the rest of her life she'd wonder how high the number would have gone. After all, it was a three digit display and technically could have read 999. Ironically, at 812 percent capacity on the high voltage lines, the power went out at the Nashville Hydro Electric Plant.

June 14, 2012 – 3:17 am Eastern Daylight Time

Joel Taylor sat up in bed trying to finish waking up and place what was wrong. *What time was it, anyway?* He squinted across the room to read the clock. *No green numbers. Power's out...again.*

Joel rolled out of bed, giving up on falling back to sleep until he took care of some business. He'd successfully navigated the obstacle course that was their footboard, dresser, and ironing board when the incessant barking of the neighbor's dog finally registered. He and Rachael had dubbed it the Jack Russell Terrorist and were convinced that it didn't actually walk or run, it just vibrated from place to place as it barked.

Standing at the sink, hands lathered up with Summer-Apple foaming soap, it was several seconds before it sunk in that no water was coming out of the faucet. He wanted to blame the prescription sleep medication he'd taken earlier that evening...but, no, this was just him being him. Come to think of it, he couldn't hear water running to refill the toilet tank either. He grabbed the nearest towel--which turned out to be one of the froofy, decorative ones that Rachael kept on the rack--and wiped off his hands, more concerned about what was going on than with facing his wife's wrath in the morning. He eased back onto their bed and gently shook his wife, "Rachael, hon, wake up."

Rachael Taylor wasn't usually a woman of extremes, but waking up in the middle of the night was one of the exceptions. It was either a long, drawn out task involving a great deal of falling back to sleep, or else she woke up screaming because you'd inadvertently scared the hell out of her. Joel had been accused of the latter many times when he himself had still been asleep, and twice when he hadn't even been in the room--go figure.

Joel realized, almost too late, that Rachael was waking up badly, and a little freaked out. "No, shhh, it's okay, shhh, it's just me. Sorry about that, but I'm a little weirded out. I think 'Jack' woke me up. The power's out, which I guess is nothing new, but the water is out too. Power I get—but, water?"

Rachael looked around as her heart rate came back down to normal and realized that the lights for the smoke detector, cordless phone, and alarm system were all dark. The ever-present glow from the strip mall that had sprung up a few miles away last year was missing too. "From the sounds of it, Jack isn't the only dog in the neighborhood going crazy, either. At least Millie only seems to be pacing and whining downstairs." Joel said. He could hear her claws clicking back and forth on the entryway and kitchen floors. "Thank heavens Golden Retrievers aren't yappie like Jack." Rachael's attention, however, remained fixed on the smoke detector.

"Um, you're the 'techie guy'; don't the smoke detector and the alarm system have batteries?"

"Yeah, and we just replaced the batteries in April, when the time changed, why?"

"Well, shouldn't the little green light still be on then? Even with the power out?"

Joel looked up, following Rachael's gaze, trying to remember if the light would stay on if it was just on battery power or if the light would blink every so often. After thirty seconds it was clear that it didn't matter, it wasn't going to blink even if that was what it was supposed to do.

"Ok, like I said, definitely not normal." Joel's attention turned to the window at the back of the house as he thought he caught movement or color out of the corner of his eye. "What was that?" Joel walked cautiously to the window and parted the sheers to get a better look outside.

"What was what?" Rachael asked nervously from the foot of the bed.

Joel swallowed. "C'mere."

Rachael quickly put on the robe she kept next to the bed for midnight kitchen runs and joined him at the window on his side of the bed. "Joel, since when do we get the Northern Lights this far south?" She asked.

"Since never. I sure hope we didn't just miss the Rapture because if so we may be in trouble."

Chapter Two

At a quarter to four Joel decided to get some ice from one of the local convenience stores.

It was several blocks before he realized he'd gone through two dark intersections that should have had blinking yellow traffic lights, and that the only lights on the roads were headlights. The street lights had never all been out during a power outage before either, come to think of it. Joel turned the radio on and was greeted by static on both the FM and AM presets. He got so busy fiddling with the seek button on the radio that he was startled when an oncoming driver flashed his high beams and lay on the horn. Heart racing, Joel swerved back into his own lane just in time to avoid an accident.

Wake up, Joel, pay attention! 4:00 am doesn't mean you're alone on the road. The near miss, the total lack of even backup power to the traffic and street lights, and the aurora finally combined to convince Joel to turn around and head home. The gas station would have a generator. If the power was still out when the sun came up, and it was light out, he'd make a quick trip then.

When he got home, Rachael was asleep on the couch. *Great, I get to stew about this all by myself.* Joel thought. As quietly as he could, Joel went through the house checking the doors and windows and looking to see if any of the smoke detectors, or anything electronic, seemed to be working. Cleaning a 2,600 square foot house may take forever, but checking it over only took ten minutes. To Joel, that just didn't seem fair.

The clock radios were all dead, even with new batteries, as was anything that had been plugged in and turned on. Both of their laptops booted up fine since they hadn't been plugged in; but with no idea how long the power would be out he didn't leave them on for long since there wasn't any Internet to connect to. All three cell phones in the house were on, but none of them had any signal. Thankfully, both the car and the SUV were almost full, as were the two five-gallon jerry cans they'd bought during one of their just-in-case phases--not that an additional ten gallons of gas would get them far in either vehicle.

Millie followed him around the house for the first half of his tour but gave up once she realized he wasn't actually going to do anything but walk from room to room. Finally, Joel went out into the front yard to watch the sky.

"Can't sleep, huh?"

Joel jumped about six inches and spun to his right to see his next door neighbor leaning against his own house and looking up at the sky.

"Don't DO that Carey!" Joel snapped.

"Do what, talk to you? Ok." Carey said.

"That isn't what I meant and you know it, Carey."

"I don't know, you started off telling me what I did and didn't know when I first moved into the neighborhood. Apparently you haven't changed much," Carey replied.

"Yeah, you scaring me at 4:45 in the morning is my fault. Whatever."

Ignoring Joel's response, Carey went on, "It's the end of the world you know," and nodded up at the sky.

"Aw geez, no it isn't, it's the aurora borealis. It's a magnetic phenomenon." Joel wasn't even trying to hide his disdain for his neighbor at this point.

Carey's reply was equally full of sarcasm. "And do they not also refer to them as the *Northern* Lights?"

"Yes, they're normally seen further north, but it's an atmospheric thing, Carey. We do have an atmosphere this far south you know; it does extend to cover the entire planet. Besides, if it was the end of the world shouldn't you have been raptured?" That was a low blow and Joel knew it, but he'd had all he could stomach of the current conversation.

"Piss off, Taylor!" Carey spat and went inside.

Nice. Good going, Joel. With a last glance at the sky he turned and went inside, and wondered what the rest of the day would bring.

...

Eric had been a Cryptologic Linguist in the Army: which is just a fancy way to say that he used multi-million dollar equipment to find, identify, intercept, and decrypt foreign communications. Most of that equipment had been satellites, or "birds", and as such he'd done as much research on them as possible. Eric had read everything he could get his hands on, from maintenance manuals to the highest levels of classified documentation he was allowed to read on their inner workings and programming.

He was intelligent, actually he was a genius, literally, with an IQ of 143--but that wasn't a problem. It hadn't prevented him from being a soldier and taking or giving orders; it hadn't even prevented him from following stupid orders. What it *had* done was prevent him from ignoring the fact that he couldn't change a broken system as a grunt, and he wasn't 'political' enough to make it as an officer. So when his fourth hitch was up he'd made one of the toughest decisions he'd ever had to make. Frustration warred with responsibility until frustration won out and he left the Army.

Prior to leaving the Army, though, Eric had learned all about threats to his birds, which had been threats to other birds (since birds were birds...basically). If his birds were hardened against all kinds of damage and they were still vulnerable to weird "space weather", less hardy birds would be even more vulnerable.

He'd also dealt with land lines, both communications and power, and there was some crossover there with the threats he'd researched. Now it looked like at least one of the reports he'd read from NASA might not have been too far off. Granted, he was making a SWAG based on the power being off and auroras being as far south as Tennessee, but the auroras made it a lot less wild of a guess.

Now he had to distil 25,000 pages of technical reports and four years of research and on the job training into layman's terms to explain why he'd yelled GETUP in "drill sergeant voice". Being intelligent wasn't the same as being good with words. Eric had been dating Karen for five years and they had been living together for--let's see--four years, nine months, and thirteen days. See, very intelligent, did that off the top of his head. But he still hadn't found a way to ask her to marry him. Now he couldn't explain why he'd yelled to get her up.

"Ok sweetheart, work with me for a couple of minutes, ok?" They were sitting at the kitchen table, looking at each other under the flat light of a couple of Coleman LED lanterns.

"Remember about three years ago, when I was working weirder hours than usual and I couldn't talk about it? Ok, sorry, bad example. Man, I am so bad at this. Let me try this one more time." Eric had to take a couple of breaths to calm down and order his thoughts. Thankfully, Karen was the understanding sort.

"Right, ok, further back, back in 2006 there was this report that NASA put out about how the sun has cycles. The long and short of it is that at points in the cycle there is massive sun spot activity and the sun sends out a bunch of 'stuff'. Particles, electro-magnetic waves, plasma…stuff. It's called a 'Coronal Mass Ejection' or CME." Eric was calming down. He'd explained it to a Lieutenant once, after all, and Karen was much smarter than he'd been.

"Normally there isn't a problem with either the amount of material or energy that gets released during one of these events. The report, however, was predicting that sometime in 2012 one of the worst, and by worst they mean massive, events in recorded history should occur.

"The reason this event has the potential to be so bad isn't necessarily due to the magnitude of the event but due to the level of technology we've attained, and specifically our power distribution system. There was a plan that was supposed to be put in place that would protect everything. The problem is it required a certain amount of notice, and the notice is based on how long it takes the CME and its associated matter and energy to reach us.

"It looks like NASA might have been off by about three months, but if what's happening is what I think it is, the entire northern hemisphere just lost power. Not only that, but everything that was plugged in and turned on is toast. Anything that has a soft power switch, like a computer in 'stand-by', or our cable box, is fried." Karen's eyes were starting to get big. *Uh-oh, time to calm her down.* He thought.

"However, and this is a big however, sweetie, anything that wasn't plugged in is probably ok. The main power distribution system may be shot--and when I say shot I mean completely down for months, if not years, if not for good as we knew it--but if we can get a generator and, say, a brand new microwave from the store and plug it in, it should work." *Whew, that was close.*

Eric, unfortunately, had thought about this a great deal back in 2009 and 2010 when he'd had to harden his birds. Microwave ovens weren't the big problem. In fact, they weren't even "on the radar", as it were. The problem was much more fundamental than that.

Society as we have come to know it is a very fragile thing. New Orleans didn't fall apart after hurricane Katrina because of the government and their lack of response.

The reason that society came unraveled in New Orleans after Katrina--and why Eric was so concerned for himself, Karen, and a few people he'd come to know in his short time outside of the military-- was a simple lack of preparation. That and the knowledge needed to survive in the short term, and the willingness to use that knowledge however necessary.

Ok, Eric, fine--be that as it may--what are you going to do? You are here right now with Karen. You have the Taylors down the street. They were the first people to welcome you to the neighborhood and treat you like you didn't have two heads. There's Sheri Hines across the street from them, who met Karen at the 'Y' and has become a really good friend and neighbor too. Good folks, who've treated us really well, and who I really care about already. So...self, what are you going to do?

Just as Eric was taking a breath to tell Karen they needed to tell a few people what he thought was going on, she beat him to it.

"Eric, if it's that bad, and if you're this worked up about it then it's probably that bad, we need to tell Joel, Rachael, and Sheri, soonest."

"Where have you been all my life?"

"Well, for the last four and a half years or so I've been following your sorry butt all over the country waiting for you to propose," Karen had a twinkle in her eye you couldn't miss even in the crappy lantern light, "but seeing as how we're now in the middle of a crisis and you're a gentleman and you wouldn't want me to feel like I had pressured you into it, it'll probably have to wait at least a little while longer."

He couldn't help but smile, both because he knew she was right and because he knew there was an engagement ring in the fire safe in the bedroom.

"Ok, I'm awful. You sure you want to keep me? Wait, don't answer that just yet, you might want me to shoot a deer or lift something heavy in the near future. So, do I go over now or do we wait until later?"

"Well, I'm pretty sure Sheri's got graveyard right now. She mentioned how glad she was she didn't have to go to another girls' night out; or, as she referred to it, the 'get Sheri laid party'. The Taylors are probably sound asleep still, so I say we wait until the sun is up." Karen was looking over his left shoulder now--she always did that when she was deep in thought--her gaze drifted from the person she was talking to, to just over their left shoulder.

"We should probably get some ice for the coolers since those stay cold longer than the freezer. Does the convenience store sell dry ice or just regular ice?"

Eric smiled but shook his head, "Just regular ice, unfortunately." "They restricted dry ice to grocery stores everywhere but the back hills and bait shops back when I was a kid, when dry ice bombs became popular—not that they ever went out of style." Dry ice would keep things colder for much longer than regular ice and when it melted, and wouldn't create puddles of water in the cooler. It was also lighter than frozen water. They'd used it a couple of years ago on a backpacking trip to keep some ice cream frozen for dessert.

"I'll head over to the mini-mart and grab some ice, probably ought to take cash, and I'll rummage around for anything else that catches my eye as a must have."

Chapter Three

The first thing Eric noticed at the convenience store was the humming of the generator; second, the lack of lights; and third, that the sliding doors were already all the way open--not a good sign. *Right, okay…get the goods first and then the conversation.*

Inside, a few emergency lights flickered dimly. Eric was amazed at the kind of beating those systems could take and keep on working. He bought six 10lb bags of ice, two bottles of rubbing alcohol, a bottle of aspirin, a bottle of ibuprofen, a bottle of acetaminophen, a bottle of Benadryl, and four six-packs of 20oz water bottles--which came to nearly fifty-three dollars before tax and earned him a very strange look. He mentioned the generator and lack of power in the store.

"Yeah, really weird, man! The lights dimmed real low and the coolers made a funny noise, then all the lights got real bright--brighter than they should have, you know? Every last one of 'em. Tubes, regular bulbs, even the neon ones for the beer."

"And then they popped--burned right out. I was afraid a couple of 'em were gonna start a fire at first, specially the neons. Started to stink really bad. I had to have the front and back doors open for a while. I even went to turn on the fans to blow the smell out." He chuckled at that for a second and then continued, "How dumb's that?"

"Not dumb at all, man, I went to grab some OJ out of the fridge and didn't even notice the light wasn't on until the fridge was closed again. Just habit, I guess." Eric was still hoping to work the clerk around to the generator. Apparently he didn't get many visitors and was enjoying the company, or the dark was getting to him--or both.

"Well, the generator comes on automatically and I figured the power would be on fairly quick, except it isn't. I reset all the breakers, the ones that'll reset that is. A couple of 'em won't budge. Looks like they got cooked pretty good when the power blew. The main is ok, and most of the others look good too, but nothing's turning on."

"Have you had any calls? Cell phone, anything?"

"Nope, regular phone's out and my cell isn't getting any signal. How 'bout you?"

"Nah, both the girlfriend and I have the same provider and neither of us have any signal either. She's probably freaking out a little as a matter of fact; I ought to be getting back. Hang in there."

On the way back to the house Eric decided he would definitely be at the Taylor's door at sunrise.

…

Joel could see it was Eric through the windows set to either side of the front door.

"Morning, Eric, I'm going to go out on a limb here and guess this isn't a social call since I don't see Karen or a bottle of wine. Come on in. I'd offer you coffee but, as you can see, the power's out. We've got cold Diet Coke and Diet Pepsi though. Rachael swears cold caffeine is better than no caffeine but I told her Diet anything is worse than…yeah, never mind, have a seat please."

"Thank you, I'm good." He was starting to feel bad for giving Joel the shock he had. He hadn't realized how hard he'd knocked on the door until he'd seen them jump on the back porch. *I guess I'm still wound a little tight, probably will be for a while too.*

"So, what brings you over so bright and early?" Joel stole a glance at his wife whose gaze was fixed on Eric. Oddly enough, Millie hadn't barked at all when Eric had hammered on the door, and came over to have her head scratched once he sat down.

"Well, um, now that I'm here, I feel kind of funny bringing it up. I know you folks haven't known me for all that long--only a couple of months--but Karen and I really like you guys, and the kids--we feel like you're family. This is going to sound crazy, but…"

It took about fifteen minutes to go over the same information he'd gone over with Karen earlier. When he was finished, Rachael was the first to say anything and that was after several seconds of silence. "Everything you said, taken one at a time, sounds perfectly logical, Eric. When you put it all together, though, this conversation sounds like something from 'Coast to Coast AM'. Are you sure the power isn't just 'out'?"

Eric didn't answer right away. He wasn't sure what he was expecting but being compared to a tinfoil-hat-wearing nut job hadn't been it. "Yes, I am." Eric sighed, "Yes it sounds insane--that's fair--but the power isn't just out, it's Out with a capital O."

"So help me, Eric, if I have to admit to Carey that he was right earlier this morning, I will never forgive you," Joel muttered.

Eric snorted. "I don't think I want to know."

"Not right now, no," Joel replied.

"My point is that I'm really not one of those end-of-the-worlders you hear about. I don't just have a 'bad feeling' about this. It's based on some pretty heavy-duty past experience and research." Eric stopped and looked around for something that he could use as an immediate example to prove his point.

"I see you have the coolers out. Did you go and get ice this morning?"

"Well, I tried at about 3:45, but turned around when there were no street lights and no traffic lights. The ice is just from the freezer right now."

"I must have missed you by about ten minutes. Humor me for a sec, ok? Did you try the radio while you were out?"

"Yes."

Eric waited for more and when Joel didn't go into any further detail, he prodded for additional information. "Did you try more than one station, and did you try both FM and AM?"

Joel didn't answer right away but eventually responded with a curt, "Yes."

"Joel, this isn't an interrogation. I'm not waterboarding you for crying out loud, I'm trying to make a point! I bet your cell phones don't have any signal either do they? If you've got laptops that were turned off and unplugged then I'm sure they boot up just fine because the batteries are ok. If you have an inverter in the car you can charge them without a problem. Unfortunately, the Internet is down. For the first time in recorded history when someone says 'Hey, the Internet is down' they're actually right. The whole thing is really and truly down!"

"Calm down, Eric." Joel said.

"I am calm, Joel, I really am. I've just spent too much time being a sheep dog and you two are too intelligent to be acting like sheep." Rachael was about to take offense to the last remark and Joel was fast on her heels with, "Now just a minute", but Eric kept right on going.

"I wasn't trying to offend you, although anyone with a brain can see I just did. *That* wasn't my point at all but I'll let myself out now. I was trying to get you to entertain for a minute that you might not have all the information. I'm done, I've said my piece. If you don't believe me maybe you should ask Sheri when she gets home."

Eric got up from the kitchen table and headed for the front door, passing Joshua, the Taylor's sixteen-year-old son, on the way out.

"Hey, Mr. Tripp. You're out and about awful early." 'Awful early' actually came out 'awwwuuul uurreeeee' as Joshua had yet to learn not to speak through a yawn. Sixteen years old and he hadn't learned to cover his mouth while yawning yet either, apparently.

"Morning, Josh--you have no idea." As he passed Josh, Eric looked over his shoulder at Joel and Rachael with raised eyebrows while moving his eyes between them and their son. He didn't say another word but the message was clear: If I'm wrong, so be it; but if I'm right, what about your kids?

Eric let himself out and Rachael brought over bowls of cereal for Josh and Maya, who had also come down just as Eric was leaving. They had to use the milk while it was still cold, and they were using the ice to keep frozen foods as close to frozen as they could. Josh and Maya were both kids, there were no two ways about it, but they were fairly mature for their age

As they ate, Joel and Rachael looked at each other across the length of the table each willing the other to make the first mention of the night before. Finally, Joshua broke the silence and the tension.

"Ok, what's up, what did we do? Did you guys find Maya's Playboys?" For which statement, Josh was rewarded by a kick in the shin from his sister.

"Eww, as if! You are so gross!"

Rachael rolled her eyes and Joel stifled a laugh, which was a welcome if short-lived change.

"No, and let's just not go there, Joshua Michael Taylor. It isn't anything you've done. Although, if there's something we should know, now's the time to spill it; I seriously doubt your mother and I could be any more surprised about anything than we think we are right now."

"No," Joel repeated, pausing to take a breath, "It's about why Mr. Tripp was over so early this morning. Maya, do you remember waking up and seeing the aurora borealis last night?"

Chapter Four

"Ten-to-one the radio doesn't work." Sheri muttered to herself after the lights went out. "Figures." This they had actually drilled for--a lot. Not to this catastrophic level, but a power plant losing power isn't as impossible as most people might think. All it takes is one idiot pushing the wrong button and the outside world keeps getting their power just like always, while everyone inside is in the dark. Ok, technically it takes three idiots, a manager, two switches in different rooms, and five minutes--the point is that it's possible.

The emergency lights came on after about a two-second delay and Sheri reached into her left-hand top desk drawer for her three D-cell Mag-Light. She didn't carry a purse to work--she had a wallet--and her keys were on a carabineer on a belt-loop. *Ok, now for the radio.* Dead, of course; it was plugged in. The surge would have knocked it out. *Hell, that surge would have knocked out Superman!* Sheri thought. *So, what just happened? Had a nuke gone off? It hadn't been a bomb inside the dam, they would have felt an explosion. Cutting the lines, all of them, even simultaneously, wouldn't have shut the power off inside the facility. Aliens? No, they only blow up national monuments...usually. Sheri, you are sick.*

"Is everybody OK?" Sheri asked of the other seven technicians and engineers in the control room. If this had been a drill, there would have been supervisors on shift within shouting distance of the entire plant, but there was only one on site tonight, and he was in the cafeteria. One more nail in the coffin of the idea that this had been a drill.

Nobody was stepping up to take control of the situation; not that there was much to control except getting everyone out of the control center. They were under almost one hundred and fifty feet of concrete, steel, and water. Without the air pumps they had about thirty minutes before the air got stuffy.

"HEY!" *That got attention, if only for a couple of seconds; now to get people moving.* "Ok, folks, we've only got about thirty minutes before the air is going to get stale down here. Who knows why they put the control room at the *bottom* of the dam but they did. Jack and Pete, help Carol up the stairs, but bring up the rear." That got her a sour look from Pete. So be it. Carol was pregnant and Pete was able-bodied; he could deal with it. "We need to get up top, let's go people. We've done this a hundred times if we've done it once. When the power comes back we can do most of what we need to from half a dozen different places up there and come back down later. You've got two minutes to grab your stuff."

The key is not to let anyone think you aren't in control; if you question yourself or let them question you it will devolve into chaos and someone will get hurt. Let them write me up for ordering my peers around after everyone is safe.

It didn't take quite sixty seconds once everyone snapped out of their initial shock. Sheri was right, they'd done this at least a hundred times; it had simply caught them flat-footed.

The emergency lights in the stairwells were working, which was both a good sign and a testament to the design and construction of the backup system. Sheri wondered idly if the transfer switch had started to kick in during dip or at the beginning of the spike. Oh well, another one of those things she figured she might wonder about for a while.

They heard voices up ahead as a couple of technicians were climbing out of the dam and picked up Chuck, their supervisor, near the top.

"Sheri, we got anyone else down there? On the way up a minute ago, Jerry said two of the turbines arced over fifty feet between them. He's been doing this for thirty years and he's never seen anything like it."

Chuck was shaking his head, eyes wide, as he continued. "He said that those two seized up while the rest spun down when the lights went out, from what he could see. Those two turbines that seized are shot, Sheri, and if that spike was as big as you said--and don't give me that look, I believe you--I bet the rest are shot too."

Sheri felt some of the supernatural calm of earlier this morning give way to whatever the next stage of shock was. The stage that gave you trembling knees and sweaty hands, apparently. "Super. Now what? I got everybody out, I now defer to you oh great and powerful management-type guy!" Sheri said it with a shaky smile, but she was serious. She'd stepped up to get everybody out of the control room but she really didn't have a clue what to do next.

"Ha ha ha. Well, the manual says we, um, uh, let's see, oh yeah, this isn't ever supposed to happen. We drill for it, sure, but actually having a spike on the grid, that blows out turbines and shuts power off to the plant? Uh-uh, ain't supposed to really be possible short of a nuke, and if we're talking about it they've got hydro plants in the afterlife and/or hell looks an awful lot like an early Thursday morning."

Just then, they got to the door and stepped outside and Chuck swore under his breath. "Charles! There are ladies present and one of them is pregnant. Watch your mouth!" Sheri had been riding Chuck for almost four years about his language, and--truth be told--he'd been getting better. But when he didn't think she could hear, or when he was really caught off guard, he could turn the air blue.

"Sorry, Sheri, but I think I know what happened. Idiots had six years warning, got it wrong by three months, and *still* weren't able to give us the warning they thought they would!"

Sheri gaped as what Chuck said registered. "Wait…No!...Chuck, tell me it wasn't the CME. Please tell me that isn't what happened." She reached out a hand as if to shut off a switch, or bolt a heavy door. Chuck thought about reaching back to comfort her, but changed his mind. It might not seem right, coming from a supervisor.

Sheri continued, "The DoE was sure they would be able to notify us at least twelve hours in advance. There was a plan in place to do a whole Emergency Broadcast System alert. The grid was going to be offline for goodness' sake which was what operation 'Dark Grid' was all about--1,542 pages just for this event!"

Sheri was looking around at the small group of people who had gathered outside of the building. "Hospitals were going to be on generator power, elective surgeries were going to be postponed. Airports were going to be closed and flights cancelled for the day-- just to be safe. They were going to put the astronauts into the Soyuz capsule on the ISS for the duration of the event because they had no idea how much radiation was going to be generated!"

Sheri's voice was rising by this time, and Chuck turned to face her directly. "If this was the 2012 CME and we didn't get a warning we are so..."

"SHERI!" Chuck's bark was part amusement, part command, and part shock at what he was pretty sure Sheri was about to say. "There are ladies present and one of them is pregnant. Not only that, but if you panic all these people I am gonna be so pissed. There's a reason I was cursing under my breath and it wasn't just to avoid your wrath.

"I think we need to send most of these folks home and see if there is anything worth salvaging here. By the looks of the sky, I personally think I know what happened. We're in the know and frankly so are most of the people here right now, but not everybody. We need to figure out a way to let everyone know but not panic them, and then let them go home. We need to secure the dam and then the rest of us should probably head home too."

Chuck paused for a minute, not quite sure how to go on. Finally, a little quieter than he'd been before, "Sheri, do you have someplace to go?"

"Sure, I'm sure the house is still there."

"Sheri, I'm not talking about your house. I'm sure it's still there, too, unless you've got a 10KW electric heater running day and night that was drawing full power when the spike hit. I mean afterwards, do you have somewhere to go--family, friends?"

"Oh, um, I never really thought about it. Wow, I don't know. I don't have family close by. I've got some friends in the neighborhood and I'd like to think we're close but I don't know. Why?"

"Well, I'm not suggesting anything but a hand, but if you need a place to stay or, well, you know, anything."

Was Chuck turning red?

"Chuck, I really appreciate that--a lot. I can't tell you how much that means. Tell you what, let's get this goat rope sorted out and then how 'bout you follow me back to the house, just to make sure everything's ok? Like I said, I do have a couple of close friends there and they know I'm working graveyard. If I don't show up they might start to worry."

"Sure…yeah, good deal."

"OK, people," Chuck turned to the rest of the crowd, "from the look of the surrounding area the power's out and I don't just mean out for a little while. We need to secure the facility and then the following people can go ahead and take off. Don't worry about the rest of the shift, you're covered. I'll need the rest of you to hang back for a few minutes afterwards…"

Three and a half hours later, just as the sun was coming up, all of the now totally unnecessary shutdown procedures were finished and the only people left were Sheri, Chuck, Pete, Carol, and Jerry. Chuck had waited until all the cars were completely out of the parking lot before he pulled those he'd kept behind together. "Everybody know what happened this morning?" Chuck asked, although the looks on everyone's faces pretty much told him everything he needed to know.

"I thought we were going to get some warning," was Pete's response.

"Yeah, like twelve hours," Carol chimed in.

Jerry just shook his head--not in negation, but in resignation.

"How are each of you set for getting by, at least for a while?"

Pete was the first to answer. "I'm getting out of town, like now. My dad's got a spread in Oklahoma and I'll be on the way as soon as I get home. I've got fifty gallons of gas for the truck, a battery powered siphon for the gas stations that I *know* will be without power and the tools to take the caps off the refill ports. I think I'll be able to convince any reluctant gas station owners to part with the gas too. I knew this was coming, damned if I didn't." Pete chuckled at his little joke as he looked at their surroundings.

"Well, I can't just take off. We've been putting everything extra away since we found out I was pregnant, so everything's in the bank-- which of course we can't get to. Scott's never been one for the whole 'prepare now, while you can' thing either, beyond a couple of days in the pantry, unfortunately. I'm not sure what we'll do, but I think we'll be ok. I don't know why, but I really think we will. Scott's a good hunter…" Carol's voice trailed off. She was obviously worried, but she was going to stand by her man.

Jerry didn't say anything right away, just looked at the sunrise. Finally, after several seconds he let out a breath he didn't realize he'd been holding. "I guess I'll be staying here. I've been here ever since they commissioned her; I can't just leave her now." His gaze took in the dam. "My wife and I'll be fine. We've got a good six months or more saved up. My son's a Mormon and every couple of years we get a three month supply of food for Christmas and they last for a couple of years each. I'll let the folks in my area know what's going on best I can; not like in a panicky sort of way--just so they know the power isn't coming back on by the weekend.

Jerry squinted as he looked into the sunrise. "Life's sure going to be different for a while isn't it?"

"That it is Jerry, that it is," Chuck said. They all shook hands, except for Sheri and Carol, who hugged and promised to keep in touch-- then Carol started to cry when she realized what they'd just said. There wouldn't be any more email or Facebook updates and Sheri got misty when she realized she was going to miss the baby's birth. "Chuck?" Sheri asked, "Where are you going to go?"

"I don't know yet Sheri, I honestly don't know."

"Wrong answer, Chuck," Sheri smiled. "You're following me home to make sure my 10KW heater didn't blow my house up when the spike hit, remember?"

With a slightly lighter heart, Chuck climbed into his pickup truck as Sheri climbed into her SUV and they both headed back to the outskirts of Nashville.

...

As Sheri turned the corner and her house came into view, her hand went up to the garage door opener on its own. She held the button all the way to the driveway before she realized what she was doing, and that the door wasn't going to open. If she hadn't been putting the Explorer in park she would have face-palmed herself. *This is going to take some getting used to.*

Chuck pulled into Sheri's driveway but didn't get out. He wasn't sure if she wanted him to wait for her or come inside, and although he was feeling protective, the last thing he wanted to do was make her uncomfortable. So he compromised and rolled down the window. Sheri took a couple of steps towards her front door and then waved to him. "C'mon in Chuck, it'll be a few minutes at least. No sense in you waiting out here."

Sheri had her second 'duh' moment as soon as she opened the door and reached over to punch in the disarm code on the alarm keypad. She got the first two numbers in and then just hung her head. "This is gonna suck."

"You mentioned there were some folks in the neighborhood you wanted to check in with?"

"Yeah, the Taylors are across the street, we'll try them first. It's almost 8:30 so I'm sure they're up. Let me check on the fridge and run through the house real quick, and then we'll head over."

The food in the freezer wasn't quite frozen anymore. The ice-cream was more mostly-firm cream and the chicken and hamburger were starting to thaw. She put the meat into the fridge and threw out a couple of things that just weren't going to make it--not that anyone was going to be coming by to pick up the trash any time soon: old habits die hard.

In her home office there was the faint smell of ozone where the uninterruptable power supply/surge suppressor had shorted out. It was possible it had saved her computer. It had been in standby mode, which meant it was technically on. She knew she should have turned it off when she wasn't using it but she hated how long it took to boot up every time she wanted to use it so she used stand-by instead. She'd invested in as close to a commercial grade UPS as she could afford and it may have prevented the machine from being fried. On the other hand, she was sure the laser printer was toast because it was plugged directly into the wall and it was old enough that it wouldn't go into power save mode anymore.

Why am I thinking about this right now? It's not like the Internet is up and I've got a bunch of email to respond to! Sheri tried to scold herself mentally. *I know what's happened and even I don't want to admit it. This is going to take a long time to sink in.* Everything else in the house seemed to be fine. It was time to head over to the Taylor's.

As they came back outside, they saw that Joel and Rachael were already coming across the street. Sheri wasn't sure if she should be surprised or not, but she was touched. It meant they had been on the lookout for her and that meant a lot.

"Joel, Rachael, meet Charlie Turner. He's my supervisor at the power plant. He offered to follow me home to make sure everything was kosher here and that I got home safe. Chuck, Joel and Rachael Taylor."

After brief handshakes and the obligatory small talk, Joel and Sheri tried twice to bring up the same subject at the same time. Finally, Joel, having been married for almost twenty years, put up both hands in the universal 'I give' gesture and let Sheri go first.

"Well, I see you aren't at work today. Did you go in and come back already or just decide to pack it in sight-unseen?"

"Actually, Eric came over and was hammering on the door at the crack of dawn, literally on both counts. As a matter of fact, if you've got a few minutes why don't you and Mr. Turner come on over and grab a rapidly-warming soda."

"On one condition," Chuck interjected, as they started back across the street, "don't ever call me Mr. Turner again unless I'm dead or the President is on the phone."

"Fair enough," Joel smiled. "I assume you're ok with Chuck, or do you prefer Charlie or Charles."

"I answer to all three, but most people call me Chuck."

"Done. In that case Sheri, can I ask you a question?"

Chapter Five

By that time, they'd made it back to the Taylor's house and were on their way to the kitchen table and Joel had one of those fleeting epiphanies. Why is it that in an emergency we all gather around the kitchen table? We don't go into the living room or the library or the office or the back yard; we gather around the kitchen table. Joel wondered briefly what Og the caveman and his family had gathered around.

Sheri noticed that neither Joel nor Rachael had been much more than cordial when she had introduced Chuck. They hadn't actually been cold or hostile, just not their typical warm and friendly selves. When Joel had asked permission to ask a question it put Sheri's hackles up.

"How bad is it?" Joel asked bluntly.

"Huh?"

"How bad is the power outage?" Joel repeated.

"Why do you ask? The power has been out before and you've never asked me how bad it was then."

"Honestly? I've never had Eric pounding on the door at dawn either." Joel said.

"How bad did *he* think it was?" Sheri asked.

"I'd rather not say until I've heard your unbiased opinion."

Sheri glanced at Chuck, who was looking at Joel and didn't look back at her, closed her eyes, and took a deep breath before answering. "In my professional opinion," Sheri paused, not entirely sure how to continue, "...Joel, the power plant took a spike that was over 800%

of its rated load. The power grid may be down for the foreseeable future."

Joel didn't say anything when Sheri finished. He simply looked at Rachael, who blinked slowly and seemed to thaw a little. Sheri turned to Chuck and said, "He seems to have taken that rather well, don't you think?"

"Crap." Joel said matter-of-factly.

"All right then, Eric wanted to get together once you got home but we kinda called him a tinfoil-hat-wearing lunatic." Joel was leaning back in his chair now with his hands behind his head. "He then accused us of acting like sheep--which we were--and suggested we get your take on the situation--which we have."

Joel sighed. "He'd pretty much put together what had happened and I think he's got some ideas, but I don't think he wanted to throw everything out on the table before he had some independent verification. You do, after all, do this for a living."

"Did," Sheri corrected. "It's entirely likely we both *did* this for a living."

"Have either of you got any suggestions on how to move forward? What to do next?" Joel asked.

"Honestly? No. I'll admit I'd put all my eggs in the DoE basket." Chuck was weighing in for the first time. "I'm no astrophysicist, but it really looked like they had a good plan in place to give us at least twelve-hours warning to get the grid shut down.

"Don't be too hard on yourself, Charles," Sheri interrupted. "You aren't the only one who felt that way and let it go. Let's see what Eric has to say and take it one step at a time."

Chuck nodded. "Man I wish I had some coffee."

"Same here, but I guess you know by now the electricity's out." Joel had always been a bit of a smart-aleck; it was about to get him into trouble.

"Well yes, I had, but do you ever go camping?" Sheri already knew the answer; she'd gotten their mail for them for two weeks last year when they had done just that.

Joel just looked at her for a few seconds until it hit him, "Aw geez, I've been sitting here for five hours jonesing for coffee and all I had to do was break out the Coleman!"

"Hang your head in shame, Mr. Taylor," Rachael jibed. "Not only that, you don't get any until we've all had some."

It took about ten minutes to get the stove set up on the patio table and the coffee brewed, and by then Joel had steeled himself for the walk of shame over to Eric and Karen's place. When he got there his first instinct was to ring the doorbell which, of course, did nothing but rub Joel's face in the fact that he was in the wrong. After taking a deep breath and shaking his head, he knocked on the door a couple of times and waited for Eric or Karen to answer.

"Morning, Joel," Karen said after a few seconds. "Everything alright?" Assuming Eric had told her what had transpired at their house, Karen was being polite enough not to mention it.

"Morning, Karen, yes…well, no. Sheri's home, is Eric around?"

"Sure, just a sec. C'mon in."

Joel waited in the entryway while Karen went to get Eric instead of yelling for him to come to the door. Yeah, she knew what had happened. About a half a minute later Eric came around the corner looking like the world's biggest idiot. He had an aluminum foil hat in the shape of a colander on top of a string mop he was using as a wig.

Joel folded his arms and leaned against the wall in the entry hall and shook his head. "I came over to tell you that Sheri's back and that her analysis of the situation seems to bear out your initial take on events," Joel said. "That does not, however, dismiss the fact that you are stark raving mad, I want you to know that. You aren't just wearing a tin foil hat, you're doing it while wearing a mop, which I assume is supposed to make you look like a sheep dog."

Joel was shaking his head. "I've heard of being crazy like a fox, but never crazy like a dog. Do you want a formal apology or will this suffice?"

"I don't need an apology, Joel, formal or otherwise," Eric replied. "I am glad I didn't have to wear this all the way over to your place, though. I get enough funny looks from the rest of the neighbors as it is. Although, maybe I *should* wear it just to see what Rachael says."

"However funny it might seem at the time it won't be worth undoing the good that Sheri has done so far."

"Right. Gotcha. Since everyone else is already at your place do you want to head back over there, and do I smell coffee?"

"Sure, and yes. Sheri reminded me that we have a camping drip coffee maker. We just finished brewing a fresh pot before I came over and you're welcome to it, but take that stupid get-up off your head!"

...

Introductions all the way around took a minute and then everyone took a seat around the kitchen table.

"Where to begin? Sheri, Chuck, was it the CME?" Now that Eric had gotten past it the first time with Joel and Rachael, and he knew that both Chuck and Sheri knew what he was talking about, he was fine talking shop without beating around the bush.

"We don't know for sure, but it looks like it." Chuck was the first to answer. "With the way the power readings behaved, the auroras last night, the blackout, no radio, etc.--it really does seem that way. Is there anything you know that would lead you to believe otherwise?" Chuck asked.

"I'm afraid not. I went to a convenience store early this morning and they had a generator running but nothing was on inside of the store. The clerk said that all the lights blew at the same time, and that some of the breakers wouldn't reset even though the mains were ok. It's just one more nail in the coffin."

"I think we're agreed then. Sheri, we're looking for work."

"I needed a vacation anyway. I was sick of working graveyard."

"Ok then, the question is how long is it going to stay bad and what do we do until it gets better?" Eric said. "The grid is down, power is out, and people are going to panic. Food is going to get and stay scarce for a while. Until some sort of communications system gets set back up, there's no central government--it's going to be everyone for themselves."

"I get the feeling you have a suggestion, Eric, or a couple of them. Go ahead, we're listening." Sheri prodded.

"Well, the Army--and I assume the other branches of service--had a couple of plans for this depending on how the population around the base or fort reacted. If the civilians were 'docile' we would basically supplement the local police force, secure the surrounding area, and start re-energizing the area with generators from on base. Let's just say there's a lot more mobile power generating capacity on a military base than it needs at any given time."

"If it was feasible, the surrounding area would be under power restrictions but still have at least some power while portions of the normal generating capacity were repaired and brought back online. Connections to the rest of the grid would be severed and the town, county, whatever, would become an electric 'island' that would expand as generating capacity increased."

"That's if the area was 'passive' or 'docile'--I hate those terms. Makes it sound like they were talking about dogs." Eric shook his head and then moved on. "If the surrounding area was 'aggressive', 'hostile', or the population became violent--the base was to become an island unto itself and defend itself at all costs. I won't go into what that means, other than there are men, women, and hospitals on base; end of story, but not end of civilization. Nobody ever actually thought it would go that far but the think tanks are full of nerds who read nothing but science fiction-- heavy on the fiction."

"Everything they had that I read is way too large scale to implement with us, or even as a neighborhood. I don't know of anyone in the neighborhood who even has a home generator, much less something that could power several homes. We might be able to cobble something together with the one from the convenience store, maybe, but we'd have to steal it, and I'd really rather not do that."

"The other option is to take what we can as a group, plus whoever else we trust and would all want to bring along, and head somewhere safe for the time being. I don't know where that would be though.

It's going to get crazy and one place may be just as good, or bad, as another. Here's where I'm open to suggestions."

Chuck shrugged, "One of the guys at work, Pete, said he's heading to Oklahoma. He's got family out there with land, and I guess he's been preparing for the end of the world. He said he already had gas for the truck and means to get it out of tanks at gas stations without power. Didn't strike me as all that odd at the dam, but in hindsight he almost seemed to be looking forward to it."

Chuck directed his question more to Eric than the rest of the group. "Are you more inclined to head for the hills, or just be a little out of the way? Or, I guess a better way to ask the question is how long are you thinking we need to set out to be self-sufficient for? There's a big difference between roughing it for a couple of months and trying to make it through the winter in a tent."

"I don't think it will take more than a month for things to quiet back down," Eric replied. "But for that month, I think we should be a half-day's travel by foot or a couple of hours by car from the nearest someplace if we can manage it.

"Ideally, I'd love to find a summer camp with cabins that people had abandoned by the time we got there, but the likelihood of that is pretty slim. Same with hunting cabins and summer places in the mountains."

Joel and Rachael hadn't been contributing much up 'til now, but Joel had an idea at this point. "Eric, you mentioned that the Army had a plan in place for this. Was the National Guard included in the plan?"

"I don't know, why?"

"Well, we have an armory here in town. If they were included, wouldn't they be implementing the plan? And if so, how quickly?"

Eric thought for a minute before he answered, but the look on his face wasn't very encouraging. "Possibly, probably, but I'm not sure. The problem with the Guard, and I don't mean this in a bad way, is that the majority of it needs to be activated. Short of driving around to pick everyone up there isn't a whole lot they can do to get them together with the phones out."

"I don't recall reading anything in the Army plans I had access to involving any of the Guard units, but that doesn't mean there weren't plans to include them."

"The other potential problem with activating the guard during an emergency is the scope of the emergency. Getting to muster won't be as important to some of them when their family is involved and they haven't officially been activated. I can't say that I necessarily blame them."

"Well then, what's the chance of appealing to their sense of self-interest and taking some of them and their equipment with us?" Rachael asked.

"If I had to guess, I'd say about fifty-fifty. The longer it goes on and there's no communication from higher up the greater the likelihood some might come with us.

"We also need to keep in mind what I said about the electricity. It won't be out forever. With the right plan and people working together, we could be eighty percent back to normal in six months. The military and Government could be--probably will be--back online sooner, if there are spares to be had. For all we know, NORAD never even went offline."

Eric ran his hands over his face and through his habitually crew-cut hair. The silence in the kitchen seemed to last most of the morning, although it was less than ten seconds. It was Joshua who broke it from the hallway. Nobody had heard him and his sister come downstairs shortly after Eric and Karen came back with Joel.

"Mom, Dad, Maya and I think we should go ahead and get out of the more populated areas. Dad, I think we need to break the news to Mom now, too."

With the raise of Rachael's eyebrows, Joel responded before she could ask. "Although I agree with you on both counts, Josh, thank you so much for your tact and impeccable sense of timing and decorum. Remind me to thank you properly at some point in the very near future."

"Rachael, as our son has so eloquently stated, there is something you should know. Please wait here. You, young man," he pointed at Josh, "come with me. It's yours, you get to carry it from here on out. When we come back downstairs you will stand around the corner until I tell you to come out and then if there are any questions it is between you and your mother, understood?"

Josh swallowed, "Yes sir." It had seemed like a good time to bring it up; now, not so good. Joel and Josh went upstairs and Rachael heard them go into the master bedroom. She was pretty sure she heard the gun safe open. She was almost positive Joel wasn't going to kill their son--almost--but Joel had seemed pretty upset about being blindsided by something. She couldn't imagine Joel was this mad about a gun; they had a number of them in the house, and Joel was an avid hunter. She didn't necessarily have a problem with guns either; there was a place for them as long as they were handled properly. Rachael noticed that Maya was being uncharacteristically quiet throughout this whole episode, though. She'd have to have a talk with her daughter about exactly which secrets to keep and which ones to let slip in the future.

When they came back downstairs, Joel came around the corner by himself. "Rachael, I ask that you keep two things in mind. One, technically it is simply a rifle--very, very similar to both of my hunting rifles. Two, he researched it and bought it with money he earned himself. He wasn't old enough to purchase it, that's where I had to come in, but it's his. I don't say that to remove the blame…but don't strangle me, please. Come on out, Josh."

Rachael, to her credit, did an academy award winning job of keeping her jaw off the floor. Now she knew why Joel had been so upset at being blindsided. This had been a constant back and forth argument between them since shortly after they were newlyweds, and now her son had snuck out and bought an AR-15 rifle.

"I just have one question. Did you buy one too?" Rachael asked.

At that point Eric started to laugh out loud.

"Joel, I know we've fought this back and forth but at this point, I guess I'm glad that there's one in the house."

"To answer your question," Joel answered, "no, I didn't. Although I really, really wanted one, I mean it's so cool! I figure if push comes to shove I could always be the one up in the bell tower with the 770 and pick 'em off at a distance."

"Sheri, Chuck, Eric, oh stop it, Karen, now that we've aired that dirty laundry what say you? Apparently my son feels he's the spokesman for the Taylor household, again, not that I disagree."

"I'm for a trip. Won't call it a vacation because I don't think it'll be all that relaxing, but I don't think hanging around Nashville for the next couple of months would be all that good an idea." Chuck said.

"I'm with Chuck," Sheri agreed.

Chuck sat up a little straighter not even realizing he'd done so.

Karen and Eric had already decided they'd go with the group but had hoped they wouldn't stay in the neighborhood or near the city. With the decision looking made, Eric weighed in. "In that case, it looks like we're all agreed."

Interlude One

Within minutes of the power going out at the White House, the President was notified of what had happened. Backup power was swiftly brought online and a third of the White House was running in under five minutes. None of the portion that had power was visible from the street, however, as it wouldn't be wise for the White House to be the only building "glowing" at this point.

Within thirty minutes, power was also restored to infrastructure deemed critical, such as the Capital Building, the Pentagon, and a dozen other buildings in Washington D.C. Additionally, secondary communications links were brought online to re-establish links with NORAD, Bolling Air Force Base, the Marine Barracks at 8th & I, and a half a dozen other points in the continental US.

Thirty-eight commercial communications satellites that now no longer functioned, having been destroyed by the recent CME, would cease to exist when they broke apart sometime in the next twenty-four hours. At that time, the same number of much smaller, but fully functional--and until recently fully shielded and offline--military communications satellites would come online. It hadn't been so much a case of cloak-and-dagger as "why not"?

One communications company, who also happened to have a vested interest in military communications satellites, had been approached with a prototype design. The design included a secondary satellite, encapsulated and fully shielded inside the outer satellite and electronically locked there. The electronic lock was very simple: should the outer satellite fail without having the electronic lock permanently locked first, within twenty-four hours the lock would degrade and the outer satellite would literally come apart.

As the outer satellite came apart it would engage, or enable, the inner satellite--which would then bring itself online, determine its position via stellar and camera references, change its orbit if necessary, and begin its life as a military communications satellite.

In one of those rare combinations of planning, technological design, and execution, the first of these satellites, Communication Satellite FNC-8842-- commonly referred to as BERCOMM-4--split as neatly in half as a three-and-a-half-ton satellite can, and SECCOM-4, codename SPARROW-9, took flight. Over the course of the next eighteen hours, all but three of the thirty-eight military satellites would properly come online in similar fashion.

Chapter Six

"Great." Joel had just finished rubbing his eyes when he noticed Eric's posture and the look on his face change. "What's up?"

"It sounds like I might have been wrong about nobody in the neighborhood having a generator. Most likely the portable kind, and it's probably big enough to run most of their house a few pieces at a time for at least a while. Until someone comes and takes it away, that is." Eric was shaking his head.

Sheri raised a questioning eyebrow.

"No, that's not what I meant. I don't mean we should go confiscate the generator. I mean at some point someone else is going to do it."

"That's good to know, and I'm sorry. I didn't mean for it to come across that way." Sheri replied.

"Not your fault, but thank you. We can do our best to let people know what's going on before we leave but some, most, will probably react the same way Joel and Rachael did, if not worse."

"So maybe we have a fourth thing to consider. How do we get the word out?" Karen asked, and then looked at Joel. "Isn't Carey the new HOA President?"

Joel's face was devoid of any emotion or animation whatsoever when he answered. "Yes, Karen, he is."

Karen's eyes widened, "Everything OK, Joel?"

"No, Karen, it is not."

"Care to fill us in?" Sheri asked.

"Not really but at this point it doesn't look like I've got a whole lot of choice in the matter." Joel folded his arms and hunched down in his chair, taking a typical "I'm closed off" pose because he was starting to sulk about this morning again. "It started about a month after Carey moved in, about six years ago. I was the President of the HOA at the time, which I will *never* do again by the way, and Carey had already made a name for himself as someone who didn't like to follow the rules. He'd done a couple of things in his back yard that were skirting the bylaws and had made some changes to the exterior of his house that were in violation of the restrictive covenants. We were in the process of getting a lien on the property since some of the work was structural and had been done without permits--*and* wasn't to code."

"I've noticed he lets his grass get a little long before he mows it." Sheri added.

"He lets it get practically knee high--right to the legal limit!" Joel took a breath. "Ok, so back then he tried to put in a bird bath or fountain or some ugly thing in the front yard, which is just plain not allowed. I'd been referring everything to the management company to let them handle it but he knew I was the president and he knew I was the one making the calls. Every few minutes while he's putting this eyesore in, he's glaring over his shoulder at me while I'm mowing my lawn, and I finally snapped."

"I killed the mower and walked over and told him that what he was putting in wasn't allowed by the CC&Rs. We got into it, he asked me what business it was of mine, I told him I was the HOA president, etc., etc., etc. I really wasn't in his face about it but I did say that he got a copy of the bylaws before he bought the house and whether he read them or not, he was bound to them, and had agreed to them, and that he knew that. He's been using that 'You've been telling me what I know and don't know' line for the last six years."

"And now *he's* the HOA president," Karen said.

"Now he's the HOA president." Joel confirmed. "As such he hasn't done anything…yet. I can't prove it, but I'm sure he's the reason that a couple of things we've wanted to do with the yard and the exterior of the house have been declined, though, since he's been on the Architectural Review Board for a while. The thing is he can be charming when he wants to be, and there's quite the rift in our little community."

Sheri didn't say anything but she was nodding.

"Well, we've only lived here for six months but this table includes just about our entire group of friends. We *know* some other people but as far as welcoming us in and making us feel at home, you're pretty much it," Karen said.

"Yep," Eric said, "and I've noticed the same thing about Carey. That's the first time I've heard the whole story though."

"It's not common knowledge unless he's been talking about it." Joel paused for a few seconds and looked sheepish, "And we got into it again this morning."

Rachael put her head in her hands, "What happened?"

"It really wasn't anything other than Carey being a jerk, again, but I had to go and push it too far. I was out looking at the sky and he startled me. One thing led to another and he threw that phrase at me, again, and said something about this being the end of the world. I fired back with a smart remark about the first wave passing him by and it kinda pissed him off."

"Ya think? You accused him of missing The Rapture, Joel! Nice work. We're lucky he didn't fire bomb the house. I won't claim to understand it, because you're absolutely right about his attitude regarding rules, but one thing the man takes seriously is his religion and you know that."

Joel wasn't upset anymore, he was getting to the point where he was just plain wrung out and it wasn't even noon yet. "Yeah, Rach, I know that, and in retrospect it was a really stupid thing to say but he was deliberately pushing buttons." Joel turned to the rest of the group at the table, "Sorry, folks, it's been a bit of a long morning and I'll admit I'm not tracking real well emotionally right now. Carey and I have pretty much stayed out of each other's way for the better part of a year until this morning. Eric, you and I have gotten on fine, again, until this morning. Chuck, Sheri, should I kick you guys out now so I can make it a clean sweep and apologize to you too, and just hit reset around lunch?"

Eric was the first to respond, "No, Joel, what we need to do first is get each of our places in order and figure out how to spread the word." Eric was starting to take the lead of what was shaping up to be the expedition out of the neighborhood. "I've never checked at the local grocery store but does anyone know if they sell dry ice? Usually grocery stores do but I'm not sure about ours."

"I think they still do," Rachael said. "We had a Halloween party a couple of years ago and I'm pretty sure I got the dry ice there for the 'witches brew'." She turned to her husband, "Joel, you know Mike, the manager, pretty well. Do you want to run up there with Josh and check if they are open even with the power out, and see if you can get some with a check or the cash we have on hand?"

"I'm sure they'll be open. I'll get Josh and head over." Joel started towards the stairs, as Josh and Maya had gone back upstairs once talk had started getting serious again.

"I suggest we all head home to begin organizing, until Joel gets back at the very least, and be thinking about how to break the news to the rest of the neighborhood," Sheri said and proceeded to get up, followed by everyone else.

...

As they were all coming out the front door, Rachael spotted Carey in his front yard. He looked like he had caught himself in mid stride coming back from somewhere when he saw them come out. When he saw Sheri, he headed in their direction.

"Hey Sheri, any idea how long the power's going to be out this time?" He asked.

"Unfortunately, I haven't a clue Carey. This time I really don't." Sheri replied.

"Not even a ballpark?"

Sheri looked at Chuck and then back at Carey, and sighed. "Tell you what, why don't we get everyone we can up to the cabana by the pool at, say, 11:30. That should be enough time to spread the word, and I'll let everyone know what I know. Sound fair?"

"Sounds like a plan. How 'bout you give me heads up now, though, so I don't get blindsided. After all, I am the HOA president. My word I'll get everyone up there at 11:30."

Sheri tried not to snort, "I guess I can tell you anyway." She was watching the rest of the group out of the corner of her eye. She could also hear Joel in the garage getting some coolers packed into their Suburban. "It looks like the power is going to be out for a while. I honestly don't know how long, but it's going to be longer than a couple of days, or even weeks. Chuck here," she inclined her head in Chuck's direction, "is my supervisor at the power plant and he can vouch for what I'm saying, but the grid took a spike this morning that shorted out turbines in the dam."

Carey looked stunned. No, he looked pole-axed. Sheri had heard her grandfather use the term growing up but had never been able to internalize the expression until now. Poor Carey.

He shook his head as if to clear it and then took in the group as if seeing them all for the first time. "Ok, 11:30 it is then. Right. See you at the cabana." Then he turned and went inside his own house.

Just then there was a muted clank on the sides of the garage door followed by "THAT was shiny" from inside the garage, followed by a pinging sound around the middle of the garage door, and then the door slid upwards. "Heh, power's out. Garage door opener doesn't work. Had to disengage the opener trolley thingy before it would open manually."

"Good point. I'd hate to wrench my back when there aren't any doctor's offices open." Eric said.

"Yeah, speaking of which, Rach, hon?" Joel looked at his wife.

"I'll get the Lortab." She was shaking her head and laughing as she went inside and everyone else headed to their own homes.

Chapter Seven

As Joel and Josh left for the store, Chuck let Sheri know he was going to head out to his place and start packing so they wouldn't have to make any last minute detours.

"I feel like the odd man out here and I don't want to be the reason we have to make any changes of plans, that's all"

"Oh nonsense, Chuck. If they hadn't felt comfortable with you, you'd have gotten the cold shoulder as soon as you walked into Joel and Rachael's house. They invited you in, sat you down, and even gave you coffee."

"But I understand. Hurry back, I don't want to have to worry about you. Remember, I'll need you here at 11:30 as an expert witness." Sheri squeezed his arm and turned to go inside.

As Chuck pulled out of the driveway, the sun was shining on her living room window but he thought he saw Sheri watching him drive away through the glare.

It was almost 10:00 when Joel and Josh got to the grocery store, which was, in fact, open—and hand writing receipts for what people were buying. Eric had mentioned getting as much dry ice as they would sell, and to do it on the sly with the manager, if he could, so as not to cause a run on it or get himself mugged as he left the store.

Joel and Rachael had been shopping here for almost ten years and knew the manager, so Joel was pretty sure he would take a check or run the credit card manually. He still waited until he could get him alone and that took about fifteen minutes as the store was actually quite crowded, considering the power was out. Really, it was barely controlled chaos and Joel was pretty sure there was a fair amount of shoplifting going on--but there was no way to be sure, and he alone couldn't have stopped it.

"Mike, I've got a favor to ask but I'm sure I'm not the first one to say that to you today," Joel said.

"If I had a nickel… Heck, if I had a wooden nickel for every time I'd heard that today I could build another store. Whatcha' need Joel?"

"First, would you take a check and second, do you guys sell dry ice?"

"From you, sure, I know you're good for it and the power'll be back on eventually, and yeah, we have dry ice. Surprisingly, you're the first one to ask, too. Do me a favor, Joel, don't clean me out, huh? "

"Deal. You tell me how much you want to keep for you and whoever you want to treat real nice, see?" Joel was doing a really bad James Cagney. "And I'll take the rest, see?"

"Ok, as long as you never do that again," Mike chuckled.

"Done and done."

As it turned out, there was a small cooler of dry ice up at the front of the store but there was a substantially larger cooler in the meat section in back. There was no way Joel and company could have used it all and Mike cut him a deal for $1/lb since the power was out and it was all likely to melt anyway. They pulled around back to load up, so as not to draw attention to themselves, and they hauled off almost 200lbs of it in slabs. Cooling, even freezing, their food was not going to be a problem for the next several days at least.

When they were done, Mike went out into the store and got a brand new combination padlock and locked the dry ice cooler. "I have a feeling that you may have just gotten a really good deal, Joel, not that I'm changing my mind. I just don't want the rest sprouting legs and walking away. This and those idling trucks back there," Mike motioned to the refrigerator trucks in the parking lot behind the store, "might be the only refrigeration for a while, now that I think about it. Honestly, thanks for bringing it up, Joel; I think it'll come in handy."

"Welcome, Mike. Hang in there-- but do yourself a favor and don't hang around too long, man."

"You too, and now I need to get back to discouraging would-be shoplifters. Take care."

When Joel and Josh arrived back home, Rachel and Maya had completely emptied out the pantry and were organizing everything into meals by days and weeks on the living room floor. They were also keeping a tally of how much water they thought they were going to need just for the cooking. Cleaning could be taken care of by boiling but drinking was another matter, if you could manage it.

Joel and Josh manhandled the coolers they had filled into the house and Joel sent his son over to let Eric know how much dry ice they'd been able to get. He then sent his daughter upstairs to sort out some clothing so he could be alone with Rachael for a few minutes.

"Rach, hon…"

"Don't, it's ok. I'm really not mad. It's kind of funny if you think about it. If the gun had been yours, I'll admit I'd be furious. If you'd said you had bought one too, again, you'd be sleeping on the couch. I'm not even mad that you didn't tell me. It's his. It was in the safe. He doesn't even know the combination…right?"

"Correct."

"Then I really don't have a whole lot of room to be upset. Mind you I didn't say any, just not a whole lot." Rachael faced her husband and put her arms around his neck. He put his arms around her waist. "He and I will have a talk, because I'm sure he knows that you and I were still 'discussing it', but I love you and there are certainly worse things he could have spent his money on. It's not like he isn't responsible."

"True. Ok. Can I have one?"

"No."

"I meant a kiss…"

Maya came down just then, "Dad, how long are we, ewww gross!"

Joel put his head on his wife's shoulder, "Do you think she even made it up the stairs?"

"Maybe, but probably not. It is a whole sixteen stairs, honey."

A quick hug and he turned to his daughter, "How long are we what, Punkin'?"

"How long are we going to be gone? I only have summer clothes in my closet. Do I need to get out any of my fall stuff?"

"You know, it wouldn't hurt to make sure you had some long pants and shirts. I think we should be back before winter but you never know, and if we go up into the mountains it can still get cold. Make sure you pack plenty of under...things."

"Daaaddy!" Maya turned and flounced away.

"What? I'm just saying!" I am never going to get used to having a growing daughter! And when the hell did she learn to flounce anyway?

"Dad," Maya stopped and turned around, a concerned look on her face. "Are we really going to be gone a long time?"

"I honestly don't know," Joel said. "Why?"

"Well," Maya paused, "I'm supposed to start Junior High this year. Mom and I went shopping for my new school clothes since I don't have to wear a uniform anymore." Her shoulders slumped. "I can't even post on Facebook where we're going to be."

Joel glanced at his wife and then looked back at his daughter. "I won't even get into the fact that you're supposed to be thirteen before you have a Facebook account, young lady," he said with his arms folded and then held them out for her to come to him.

"I don't know what's going to happen, sweetheart," he said, "but we'll figure it out. It would be better to be prepared and not need it than to need it and not have it though, ok?"

Maya gave him a hug and nodded and then went upstairs to get packed.

"I didn't have a chance to tell you before you left, we're having a neighborhood meeting at 11:30 at the cabana. Carey ambushed us as we were all coming out the front door."

"Now is probably the best time in the world to have told me that. I've got nothing left, so I can't overreact." Joel said.

"Too bad you weren't there. He looked like he'd been hit with a crowbar. He was trying to pump Sheri for information and actually used the fact that he was the HOA president as justification for her telling him before everyone else." Rachael giggled, "And when she did, I thought he was going to pee his pants. He just stood there for a good five seconds before he was able to say anything. I'm really sorry you missed it but it's probably a good thing you weren't there."

"I'm enjoying it vicariously through you, and the imagination is a wonderful thing. I can add the crowbar," Joel winked.

"You are awful!"

"Yes, yes I am. I'm also going to enjoy every minute of this meeting when people look to him for leadership in this time of crisis." Joel got serious then, "But I'm going to feel very bad in the long run if someone else doesn't step up if or when he fails miserably. For their sake, I hope that doesn't happen."

About forty-five minutes later, Chuck pulled up in front of Sheri's house. The bed of his truck appeared to be completely full, and then some, and covered with a tarp held down with bungee cords.

He knocked on Sheri's door and had to wait a minute for her to come and answer it. "You know, you could have just come in, Chuck. I was expecting you."

"No ma'am, I couldn't have." Chuck said. "You might have been expecting me, but I didn't know for sure, and neither of us knew when I was going to get back. I didn't want to presume, and I certainly didn't want to startle you. The alarms don't chirp when the doors open anymore after all."

"Well, I appreciate that and I guess you're right. Thank you for that. Looks like you had a little more than you realized squirreled away in that man cave of yours. What did you decide you just couldn't live without?" Sheri asked.

"I ended up bringing most of my hand tools, including one of my smaller air compressors and the air tools." Chuck said. "We're taking a bunch of vehicles and nobody has mentioned taking anything to repair any of them with. If we end up packing all of them full and one of them breaks down we'd end up having to leave stuff behind. I figure this is something I can bring to the table."

"By the way, do you remember what kind of car Pete drove?" Chuck asked.

"Why? I thought he'd be on his way to Oklahoma by now. He sure sounded all fired up to go when he left the dam earlier this morning." she said.

"I thought so, too. I know he has that old Chevy pickup but I thought he had a restored Mustang too. Yellow, wasn't it?" Chuck asked.

"Yeah, I think so. He drove it to work a couple of times but didn't like to bring it in because of the gravel parking lot-- he didn't want to get the paint messed up," Sheri agreed.

"That's what I thought, too. I could have sworn I saw him over by my house on the way back here, but he lives way over in East View. What would he be doing over by Lockland Springs?"

"His girlfriend lives in East View too, so I have no idea. Why do you ask? Worried?"

Chuck shrugged. "Not so much worried as aware. He sounded pretty sure about heading to his dad's place this morning, and he did make it sound like he wasn't real concerned with observing common civilized niceties where getting there was concerned. It might be nothing. It's not like there isn't more than one yellow Mustang in Nashville."

"Well, there's nothing for it. He's either left already or he hasn't, I don't know that it'll matter either way. Give me a hand getting a few more things into the truck and then I want to head over to the Taylors before we go to this community meeting."

Sheri had done a fair amount of packing while Chuck was gone. She'd completely cleaned out her pantry, including repacking anything that would spill or was in bags that were likely to tear, and Joel had sent Josh over with a box full of dry ice for her two coolers. She'd packed her clothing into a number of duffel bags and backpacks, and thought to include laundry soap and dryer sheets of all things.

"Hey, you never know," Sheri said when she saw Chuck raise an eyebrow at the dryer sheets. "Eric keeps reminding us that the electricity is going to come back on sooner or later, and he's right after all. All we have to do is raid a Sears and we're in business!"

They had just finished packing Sheri's bags into the Explorer when Josh knocked on the front door.

"Dad was wondering if you wanted to head over to the cabana together now that Mr. Turner is back."

"Someone is bound and determined to call me that, aren't they?" Chuck grumbled.

"Oh lighten up, you big grump." Sheri said. "The boy's only sixteen and he's just doing what he's been asked to do. He can't rightly call you Chuck now can he?"

"Lead the way, Josh," Sheri said as she ushered Chuck out of the house and locked the door.

Chapter Eight

The pool cabana was as full as Sheri had ever seen it by 11:30. "I hope this was a good idea," she muttered to herself.

"Don't worry, it'll be fine. Joel, Eric, and I are all packing," Chuck replied from her right side.

That snapped her out of her silent brooding about what she was going to say and how she was going to say it. "What in the world are you talking about?" Sheri looked at Chuck and then quickly glanced at Eric and Joel. For the first time she noticed that Joel had changed his shirt from earlier this morning and what he was wearing was now longer and un-tucked. "Holy crap, you're serious!" she whispered.

"Yes ma'am." Chuck answered. "This is exactly the kind of situation I was worried about. Someone in the know breaking the bad news to someone who's not. You're the messenger Sheri. Yeah, I was your supervisor but they don't know me from Adam."

"Any more good news I need to know before this little shindig gets going?" she asked.

"I don't think so, no. If I think of something I'll be sure to tell you on the way back to your place, though." Chuck grinned.

"Thanks," she elbowed Chuck in the side, "you're gonna be a lot of help I can just tell."

Just then, Carey stood up on one of the tables and started waving his arms to try to get people's attention. That went on for a good ten or fifteen seconds before someone in the crowd whistled through their fingers and cut through the noise. "Thank you, whoever that was." Sheri was pretty sure it had been Joel, but neither of them was going to say anything at this point.

"As I'm sure you are all aware by now," Carey began, "the power is out." A couple of folks started to make rude or smart comments at this point but Carey kept talking and most of the hecklers shut up. "What some of you may not know is that our very own Sheri Hines works for, but let me stress the point that she is *not* responsible for, the power company. As a joke this morning I asked her if she knew how soon the power would be back on--assuming that the answer would be 'sometime between 2:00 and 4:00, assuming someone will be home'," that got a chuckle. "Unfortunately, that wasn't the case. Let me say again that Ms. Hines simply works for the power company and is only sharing what she knows as a favor; but at my request she's going to let us know as much as she knows regarding what's going on."

People were murmuring now. What did Carey mean by 'regarding what's going on'?

Sheri cursed Carey under her breath. Thanks a lot, you moron. I don't even think you realize how bad you just made me look in your attempt to pump yourself up. Saying that I'm only sharing what I know as a favor? Like I was going to hide something? I'm only doing this at your request? Great, now no matter what I say it's going to be tainted by that and I'll look like I'm trying to dig myself out, or cover my own butt.

Sheri stepped up onto the table as Carey stepped down. She looked around at the expectant crowd--now gone silent. She had to swallow a couple of times before she could say anything past the lump building in her throat, and then she looked down at the group she'd spent most of the morning with and began talking.

"Well, a couple of things to get going. First off, I want to let you know that if you have any questions that I know how to answer, I will. I don't mean questions I'm *allowed* to answer--I mean questions I have the technical expertise or know how to answer. If *I* don't know, then my supervisor from the power plant, Chuck Turner over here, probably does. I'm not trying to hide anything."

"So, here's the deal. This morning at the dam it looks like the grid--the power grid--got hit by a spike. It was a big enough spike, and it was preceded by a large enough dip in power, that it got past the safeties and actually blew two turbines at the dam and shut down the rest. The power is out for the foreseeable future; not just here but most likely everywhere, because the entire electrical grid was affected. I don't know how long it's going to take to get power back here or anywhere else. I don't know if it will be days or weeks or months," Sheri paused, "or even longer."

People were murmuring again and a couple of people swore loudly. Sheri raised her voice like she did in the control room to continue to be heard. "I'm saying this to let you know what's going on and so you aren't surprised when there's no power tomorrow morning. I'd love to be proven wrong, but I'll be more surprised than I can put into words if I am."

A couple of the more vocal folks in the crowd were started yelling questions at Sheri along with a few choice derogatory remarks. As things grew rowdier, Carey jumped back up onto the table and yelled for silence. Sheri looked over at Eric, Joel, and Chuck who had formed a subtle, but very real, wall between the crowd and Karen, Rachael, and the kids. They had also lined themselves up to let her get down off the table and behind them fairly easily without being too obvious. Eric had his hand behind his back and Joel had his in his pocket. *Geez, how could it have gotten this bad in less than five minutes?* Sheri thought to herself. At least Chuck just had his arms folded.

"Settle down, settle down! Sheri isn't here for her own good people, what the heck's wrong with you? She didn't do this, it isn't her fault."

Joel stood off to the side of the table with the speakers on it, wondering if Carey had ever taken a course on public speaking in his life. If so, he had apparently misunderstood every bold and highlighted phrase in the textbook because he was doing the world's worst job of crowd control Joel had ever seen. It was like every phrase Carey used was designed to stir the crowd into a mob, and the look on his face showed that he had no idea what he was doing. To do a worse job would have required a Project Manager, actual planning, and weeks of meetings!

Despite what he'd said to Rachael at the house he was *not* enjoying watching the scene before him because nobody was turning to Carey for leadership; they were milling about like a bunch of bulls in Pamplona before the running. He was just about to say 'screw it' and step up onto the table himself when somebody else did just that, and, thank goodness, it was one of Carey's buddies.

"Which part of SHUT UP and SETTLE DOWN did you people not understand?" Rick Gayle bellowed at the top of his lungs as he stepped onto the table. He had seen the mob forming and didn't like it one bit so he figured it was time to step up and put an end to it. Carey looked like he could use a hand too. "Thank you very much ma'am, if you'll step down I think we can take it from here," he said to Sheri, who did just that.

"Now, just be quiet for a minute and *listen*," Rick was addressing the group again. "Go home. Take stock of what you've got as far as food and water and other supplies. We'll get the board together and see what we can do to work through this together. Quit pointin' fingers, it's a good way to get 'em broke."

As the crowd dispersed, Carey, face red with anger, embarrassment, or both, came to talk to Joel and his group.

"I'm sure you enjoyed that thoroughly," Carey sneered.

"Not at all, Carey, and I really wish you'd just let it go."

Instead of responding to Joel he turned to Sheri, "Will you and Chuck be available if we have any other questions?" He asked it like a police officer asks a suspect after questioning.

"I don't see why not." Sheri answered noncommittally.

"Thank you." and Carey turned and walked off with Rick.

"Why is it that every time he opens his mouth *my* blood pressure goes up?" Joel asked.

"Because you're a very empathetic person and you're projecting. It's very sensitive of you, dear." Rachael replied.

"Did she just call me pathetic *and* sensitive?" Joel asked no one in particular.

...

The Taylor's house had become the central meeting point because it was between Eric's and Sheri's and was the largest of the three homes. As such, it was where they all headed as soon as the short neighborhood meeting broke up.

Once everyone was seated around the Taylor's kitchen table, Maya and Josh included this time, Eric brought the question to the group. "Ok, so where do we want to go? We've all mentioned that we don't want to stay in a population center for a number of reasons, and I think the impromptu HOA meeting just sealed the deal. Driving around aimlessly will just run us out of gas, though. Anyone have any suggestions?"

"What semi-accessible wooded areas are there around here? I would think that those would probably be our best bets. Not too far away, because we don't want to use too much fuel to get there, but not too close either, and secluded enough that we wouldn't be too obvious once we got there." Rachael was more thinking out loud than asking a direct question but Sheri answered as though it had been asked directly to her.

"Well, off the top of my head, I can think of Port Royal State Park, north of here--probably a little too close. Bledsoe Creek, northeast of here--also probably still too close. Cedars of Lebanon, east-southeast--about the same distance as Bledsoe but closer to other towns. Everything else I can think of is actually closer than that."

"How about Natchez Trace State Park?" Joel asked. "We were there about a year ago. It's about eighty-five miles west of here on I-40. Once you get into the middle of it you are really in the middle of it, and it's not too close to any other population centers.

"If we get lucky we could even use some of the facilities there. If not, it's large enough that even if all the cabins were booked, and everyone stayed there, we could still primitive camp and not encounter anyone else."

"Let me go get the road atlas and we can take a look," Rachael said.

When she got back she also had the map from the park that they had picked up during their visit and it looked pretty much as Joel had described. It was ten to fifteen miles from any town in the center of the park, and even the permanent park facilities were several miles from where they could set up if they wanted to.

"Looks good to me," Sheri said.

"Same here," Chuck agreed.

"Karen?" Eric asked. When she nodded, he went on, "Ok, I think it's unanimous then--but I'm assuming nobody's going to be ready to leave today."

"Not realistically," Joel said. "We're going to need the rest of the day to finish packing and a good night's sleep wouldn't hurt."

Sheri felt much the same way. "I've also been running on adrenaline since I saw the auroras this morning. I'm going to need some sleep before we head out and I assume that Chuck is going to need some too," she gave him a sidelong look, "unless you were sleeping in the break room when the power went out."

"No! I was *not*!"

"So, tomorrow morning at the earliest then, as it's getting late in the day if we want to make any contact with the Armory. I suggest we get some lunch and start packing." Eric continued.

"On that note," Rachael said, "let's have some lunch with at least a semblance of normalcy to it. We have a ton of lunch meat, thanks to a growing 16 year old, and only so much space in the coolers, so we might as well have sandwiches if that's ok with everyone?"

When nobody objected and everyone offered to help, it was actually more work and chaos than Rachael had thought it would be when offered. It did, however, take everyone's mind off the fact that they would be leaving their homes for the foreseeable future, which was the real reason she'd suggested it.

Chapter Nine

Everyone was going to drive a truck or an SUV. Sheri's Explorer and Karen's Pathfinder were both 2-wheel drive but each could carry a lot while keeping it under cover. The Taylors had a Suburban; which, while a gas guzzler, could tow anything anyone would be driving--even fully loaded. Chuck had an F-350, and Eric had a Silverado--both of which were turbo-diesel crew cabs.

Between them they had seven tents, six lanterns, four 20lb propane tanks from backyard grills, almost two dozen disposable propane canisters, more than enough sleeping bags, coolers for three or four days of food--assuming the dry ice lasted that long--and a couple of weeks of canned goods. Karen had wisely suggested that they pack the vehicles in the garages so as not to arouse any suspicion. They weren't necessarily hiding from the rest of the neighborhood, but there weren't any other folks in the neighborhood that they wanted to seek out and bring with them either.

Packing was going slowly, due in part to the fact that everyone was subconsciously putting of the inevitable departure. At about a quarter after three in the afternoon, Carey knocked on the Taylor's door.

"Carey, what can I do for you?" Joel asked. He wasn't about to invite Carey in, but he wasn't going to be rude either. Frankly it was actually cooler outside than it was inside with the A/C not working.

"We're going to start pooling resources and need to compile a list of what you have so you can bring it to one of a number of central points." Carey replied...straight-faced.

Joel couldn't respond right away and just blinked for a few seconds. "Ok, when do you need the list by, and what are you wanting catalogued?"

"I'm here to make it now," Carey said.

"I'm sorry, what do you mean 'you're here to make it now'?" Joel asked.

Carey was taken aback by the question. "I'm here to make an inventory of what you've got as far as food, water, fuel, and clothing," he clarified-- and made as if to walk into the house. Unfortunately for Carey, Joel didn't get out of his way, so he had to stop.

"We don't have a huge amount of time to screw around Taylor…"

"My first name is Joel, and the hell you're going to walk in and inventory my house. This isn't the Communist Community of Carey Pavlovich buddy! A few hours isn't going to make or break anything; so you can just back off. Maybe you need to be a little more concerned about the fools out there mowing their lawns with what little remaining gasoline there is, or the two or three people who've fired up their backyard propane grills this afternoon to cook a half-a-dozen hotdogs.

"If you want a list of the resources I've got, fine, I'll give you a list. But you're going to give me a list of where you think you're going to put it and how you think you're going to protect it. Where's that list Carey, huh? You bring that with you? No, then get off my porch and get to work doing something useful; and don't come back until you can answer some simple, basic questions." Joel slammed the door in Carey's face.

"It's probably a good thing we're leaving," Rachael said.

"Ya think?"

…

Sheri'd had her windows open and heard the door slam across the street. She got to the living-room window in time to see Carey slam his own door and wondered what was going on when Rachael came out of the Taylor's house and started across the street. *Uh-oh, this doesn't look good.*

She opened her front door just as Rachael reached the porch, and waved her in. "What just happened?"

"I'm not sure if it was Carey's idea or not but apparently there's a plan to consolidate supplies; and for us, at least, it was going to start with Carey himself performing an inventory of our house." Sheri's eyebrows shot up and her eyes got wide at that. "Yeah. Joel read him the riot act about doing something productive and then slammed the door in his face. I swear, if I had more tender sensibilities I'd be all flushed and fanning myself and saying things like 'Isn't this just so excitin', but this is just getting stupid."

"Well, that explains the visit I got a little while ago while I was, um, indisposed." Sheri said. "Chuck answered the door and told the guy that he wasn't someone he thought I was expecting--since it wasn't Carey, Rick, or one of you folks--and never even let the guy finish. He eventually gave up and said he'd come back later. I wonder what Eric said." Sheri and Rachael both grinned like idiots thinking about that.

…

"No."

"Excuse me?" the man at the front door said, perplexed.

Eric simply repeated himself. "No."

"Sir, I don't think you understand the gravity of the situation."

"Oh I assure you I do, more so than you by leaps and bounds. It's you who don't understand. You are on private property. You have no authority here, period. No authority to enter *my* home, no authority to catalogue or inventory *my* possessions, no authority whatsoever once you cross those borders to do anything at all." Eric replied.

"But the board," the man continued.

Eric interrupted, "Doesn't have the right to do what you are saying they've sent you out to do. This is a home owners' association, not a sovereign nation. Are you kidding me? Are you insane? No. It doesn't matter what I have or don't have. If I have something I feel I would like to share then it's up to me to do so. If I run out then it's up to others whether or not they will share with me. Frankly, I have every intention of sharing but I'm not letting you or anyone else into my house to make a list of what I have and then turning everything over to someone else to manage. Not gonna happen."

"But what if there isn't enough for everyone to go around? What if there isn't enough for the kids? That's not fair for one person to decide!"

"Ok, you obviously aren't listening so I'll try it another way. How much food, water, and fuel do you have at your place?" Eric asked.

"What does that have to do with anything?"

"It has everything to do with everything! You want to come in and inventory *my* house but won't tell me what *you* have? Doesn't that strike you as even the least bit hypocritical?"

The guy at the door, whose name Eric still didn't know, was working his mouth like a fish with no words coming out. The word gobsmacked came to mind. "I think we're done here. I'm going to close the door now, bye." Eric was barely able to keep from laughing until the door was completely shut.

…

As the evening progressed, more people were out and about but the mood in the neighborhood was tense. Carey was holding one of his infamous HOA board meetings in his driveway, which made it all the more difficult to hide the fact that Sheri and Chuck, and Eric and Karen, at least, were pooling resources for dinner with the Taylors.

"Are we the only neighborhood that's acting like this?" Rachael asked as dinner was wrapping up.

"Acting like what?" Sheri countered.

"Well, all paranoid and worried and weird. Is knowing that the power isn't coming back on better or worse than not knowing? Are other groups out there freaking out more, less or the same as we are?"

Eric waited a few heartbeats before he replied because nobody else had answered. "I think that the majority of people are starting to freak out, as you say, because it's sinking in that there is absolutely no contact with the outside world. Aside from no electricity there's no phones, no radio, no cell phone, no wireless Internet, no satellite radio…nothing. People aren't used to that level of isolation--even when they go camping."

"How have you been doing, Sheri? I know things didn't go as well as they could have at the cabana today." Karen asked.

Sheri sighed. "I'm exhausted, but I don't know how much sleep I'm going to get tonight." She was looking at the back of the house, scanning it from one end to the other, taking it in and not realizing she was doing it.

Chuck reached over and took another one of the bagged rolls he'd brought back from his house, catching Sheri's eye. "Chuck! Why don't you stay at my place tonight?"

Chuck stopped with the roll part way to his face--mouth hanging open. "'Scuse?"

"Well, you're already packed and here. I have an actual guest bed for when the occasional family comes to visit; and that way we can get out of here as early as possible in the morning. I'll sleep better knowing someone else is in the house too."

A slightly awkward silence followed before Chuck finally agreed. "Ok. I mean, sure, makes perfect sense." Chuck tried to cover his pause with humor, "As long as the pillowcases aren't all lacy and froofy smelling, because I won't be able to sleep if they are."

"Yeah, you know me too well. Froofy-smelling pillowcases--as if." Sheri replied, obviously relieved.

As they said goodnight and headed back to their own homes for some final packing and an early night's sleep they were all recipients of icy looks from the board members still in Carey's driveway. *Tomorrow morning can't come soon enough for me*, Joel thought to himself.

Chapter Ten

Joel was a little surprised to wake up to an empty bed. Occasionally he or Rachael would grab a blanket and go sleep on the couch if the other one was snoring loudly or tossing and turning--but Rachael hadn't taken her pillow downstairs which meant she had gotten up for the day. Joel made his way downstairs and was met by the sound of soft sniffling.

"Rach?" Joel said as knelt by the couch in front of his wife. "Hon? How long have you been up?"

"Not long, only about ten minutes. I had to say good-bye though."

"We're not coming *back* Joel. We've lived here since before Maya was born. There are three guinea pigs and a cockatiel buried in the back yard." Rachael grabbed another tissue. "This has been our home for over half of our marriage, Joel, and we're just going to walk away from it in a few hours...and not look back? I don't know if I can do it."

Joel didn't have a response at first, except to lean forward and hold her. When he did speak, his voice was more raw with emotion than he'd expected. "I really haven't wanted to think about this. You're right, you know. We're not coming back, because I don't think we're going to be able to come back. Once we leave," Joel pulled back and looked Rachael in the eyes, "it won't be ours anymore. Once we're gone, someone else will most likely take it."

Rachael closed her eyes and looked away from him.

"Rach, look at me." It took a few seconds, but eventually she did. "How do you think it makes me feel to say that? I've worked for over a decade to make this house our *home*. I built the gazebo. I built the fire pit. We've put how many hours into keeping that horrible lawn alive?" She barked a small laugh. They were constantly complaining about how they had a thriving lawn full of lush crabgrass and chickweed--but couldn't keep fescue alive for love or money.

"And now, for no good reason, we're leaving it all behind." Joel said. "I don't mean we don't have a good reason to leave--because we do. I mean that some oversight committee, or panel, or appropriations board, or overfunded and under-brained bureaucracy out there knew this was coming but screwed up so thoroughly that nothing was done."

"Now I've started worrying," Joel continued, "about what we're taking. How long are we really going to be gone? Do we have the right clothes and enough of them? Do we need to pack more blankets or towels or knives or ammunition? Should we have tried to get a trailer or a car-top carrier and loaded it too?" Joel's voice rose, "I don't know what I'm doing here, with any of this,...my wagon train always died when I played Oregon Trail as a kid!"

"And you weren't supposed to be awake yet hon. I was supposed to be down here alone being neurotic for a half an hour and get it out of my system." Rachael was smiling just a little.

"I'm glad I was awake though," Rachael said. "I think I needed to see you freaking out."

Joel snorted. "Yay me." He leaned forward to give her another hug and a kiss. "Shall we take another walk-through to make sure we haven't missed anything?"

"Not right away," Rachael said, as she pulled back just far enough to be nose to nose with Joel. "Unless you want to start in our room..."

...

It was almost 8:00 by the time Eric checked in with all of the families and they agreed it was time to go. All three garage doors opened at roughly the same time and the trucks and SUVs started up as if on cue. Joel would be first in line with the Suburban, so he pulled out first.

Out of habit, Joel reached over and turned on the GPS--which would normally take a few seconds to find a satellite--and then turned on the radio. He tried to cover his gaffe by switching to the CD player, but caught Rachael's smile out of the corner of his eye. "Hey, I'm not the one who tried to turn on the alarm."

Rachael snorted, "Ok, that's fair." Then she reached over and, also out of habit, pulled up the state park from the list of past destinations on the GPS. Neither of them expected the semi-robotic, vaguely female voice saying "In point two miles…turn left."

Joel came very near to causing a five-car accident right in front of his house when he slammed on the brakes. Eric and Sheri's tires screeched. He and Rachael were still staring wide eyed at the GPS when Eric came running up to the driver's side window.

"What's wrong?" Eric asked, more than a little concerned.

"I don't know," Joel replied, still looking at the GPS. "I mean, I don't know if it's wrong or not. Just a sec." Joel switched from the CD changer to the radio and was met with static. He tried a number of their FM presets followed by a couple of the AM stations he'd checked the previous morning and was greeted by a different frequency of static--but static just the same.

"Joel, what happened, why'd you stop?"

"Eric, the GPS is working."

"Huh?"

"Eric. The. G. P. S. Is. Working."

"Ha ha ha. Ok, hold on a minute. Karen has a satellite radio in her car; can't remember which one. Let me see if that's up." Eric jogged back to Karen's car and had her turn on her radio. After a full minute of '…Searching…' on the LCD they gave up.

Eric's jog back to Joel's Suburban wasn't quite as quick as his first one. "I was hoping some satellites had made it through. It's possible that the GPS satellites we are using were simply on the night side when the CME wave hit but there are a couple of other more likely reasons GPS is up. Do us all a favor Joel and don't slam on the brakes like that when we're on the freeway?"

"Sorry, it just caught me by surprise. Won't happen again." Joel looked a bit sheepish. It had only been a little over a day but the lack of any communication and sense of connection to an outside world was playing havoc with his sense of normal. As Eric walked back to his car, Joel heard Rachael curse--which she never did--and looked out the windshield. Carey stood in the road in front of the Suburban.

Joel laid on the horn and, although Carey flinched, he didn't move out of the way.

Joel rolled the window back down and yelled, "Get out of the way, Carey!"

"You can't leave Taylor!" Carey shouted back.

"Says who?" Joel was still in the car but he unbuckled his seatbelt. "Says me and the board."

"The board doesn't get to tell me what I can and can't do Carey," Joel said, as he opened the door and climbed out. "I can leave at any time. Get out of the way. Now." Joel was already on the ragged edge and this threatened to put him over.

"We have to stick together, Taylor. We can't have people just running off and doing whatever they want. You all elected me to be in charge, so I'm going to be in charge."

"We elected you to be the president of the Home Owners' Association, Carey; to make sure we didn't spend more money than we took in with dues, and ensure that the lifeguards got paid every summer, and keep people from letting their grass grow up to their armpits. We didn't elect you to be President," Joel made air quotes to emphasize the last word.

"Carey, I'm serious…get out of the way." Joel just wanted to leave and escalating the situation wasn't going to help. Although it was the last thing in the world he wanted to do he needed to *convince* Carey move.

"You aren't in charge like you think you are." Joel said. "Maybe at some point you will be and that will be great and I'm sure you'll do a fine job. Three housefuls of people leaving aren't going to make a difference in the long run either way, but we're going."

"No you aren't; you can't go. I forbid you to leave!"

"Listen to yourself. You can't forbid me from doing anything. Move or you're going to get run over. Truck versus human--the truck wins every time."

Rachael had opened her door by now and stepped out. "Carey, please just move. Please."

"Hon, get back in the truck." Joel said, without taking his eyes off of Carey.

"Better yet, why don't you go back in the house," Carey said, with a distinct lack of respect.

"Don't ever talk to my wife again, period." Now Joel was mad. That was a line you didn't cross. "You have nothing to say to her or any other member of my family, but especially her, ever."

"Right, and I suppose you're going to stand up for the rest of your little brood too aren't you, starting with your daughter? Like mother like daughter? The apple doesn't fall too far from the tree? Learned it all from her mom, the little…"

Joel didn't even remember making the fist but he certainly remembered the satisfying meaty feeling when it hit Carey in the middle of his face. He was also very gratified to see Carey land squarely on his butt almost three feet away with his hands over his nose and mouth. When he pulled them away, already covered with blood, the look on his face was one of purest shock. And then he spoke.

"I'm going to SUE YOU!"

It took almost three full seconds for the words to register with Joel, but when they did he laughed out loud. Exactly the kind of deep, stress-relieving belly laugh he'd needed ever since the power went out yesterday. "Are you kidding me? You still don't get it! You're the one who told me 'it's the end of the world' and you *still don't get it*! Well you were right. There, are you happy? I said it, you were right! You're going to sue me? With what? For what? Where? HOW? It's *over* Carey! I don't trust you or the bulk of the people in this neighborhood in a crisis so I'm leaving with the people I do trust.

Now get out of the way or I'm going to run you over and not even look in the rear-view mirror when I'm done."

Joel turned around and got back in the Suburban and put it in gear. To his credit, he did in fact drive around a scurrying Carey to avoid hitting him. He also looked in his rear-view mirror to make sure nobody else hit him either.

...

Traffic wasn't as bad as they had feared it would be on the turnpikes and parkways by now. Most people had realized there wasn't going to be anything to do at work the previous day and the majority of traffic seemed aimless and sporadic. There were a larger than normal number of police on the road, but that was probably more a matter of ratio than actual numbers. They passed a couple of convoys like their own headed in the opposite direction, each consisting of five or six cars and trucks. One even had a surplus school bus, although Eric wouldn't have wanted to be in that for much longer than absolutely necessary.

The couple of times they saw RVs Joel was openly jealous. "We're going to be sleeping in tents, most likely, and they've got a hotel on wheels…so unfair."

Rachael was a bit more pragmatic in her approach to the situation. "Yes dear, and they get a whole 1.2 gallons to the mile and we have no idea how soon, or even *if*, we're going to be able to get more gas."

Fifteen minutes down the road they passed a fairly large group of vehicles headed their same direction. This group, however, was pulled to the side of the road as one of the cars had a flat tire. Once all five SUVs and trucks had passed, Eric flashed his lights and turned on his turn signal and everyone pulled over onto the shoulder.

At first glance, driving by at over fifty miles per hour, no one had recognized anyone from the group they'd passed. Eric felt it spoke well of the caravan that they hadn't abandoned either the people or the vehicle just because of a flat tire. He suggested it might be worth a few minutes to find out where they were headed …and how others were reacting to the crisis.

Everyone got out of their cars and walked back towards the group with the flat. The area was clear enough that Eric wasn't really worried about an ambush; but given what they'd just left in the neighborhood, and Joel's adrenaline level, he wasn't ruling anything out. In fact, give it a couple more days and he would be looking at every piece of ground with a combat eye: you can take the man out of the Army, but you can't take the Army out of the man. You couldn't, however, pass on twelve years of training and paranoia in six hours--and he couldn't convince everyone else to stay back with the vehicles.

Eric, Joel, and Mille were in the lead in front of Rachael, Karen, and Sheri. Josh and Maya were behind the women and Chuck was bringing up the rear. Just because Eric didn't think there would be an ambush didn't mean he wasn't going to at least try to have some order in the group, and keep the women and children in the middle.

A couple of men from the group with the flat came out to meet them about half way.

Eric stopped himself just shy of asking, 'So, got a flat?' and instead opened with, "Anything we can do to help?" Out of the corner of his eye he noticed Joel pulling back on Millie's leash.

One of the two ambassadors from the flat-tire group, as Joel was thinking of them now--the thinner of the two, --replied, "Not 'nless y'all got an extra 165/75R14 under onea them tarps. Spare's gonna slow us down."

"Sorry, friend, wish I did. I'd be more than happy to give it, too. Everybody doing ok, car ok after the tire went flat? Wasn't a blow out?"

"Nah, juss a slow leak that fin'ly got too low an' it came apart. Ah think we'll be fine."

"Big group, y'all headed out of town?"

"What's with all the questions, huh?" asked the larger of the two from the flat group a bit belligerently. He had a large, footprint-shaped birthmark on the right side of his face that got darker as he grew more agitated. "We're just changing a tire, we're not blocking traffic. You a cop? I don't see a badge. Cops don't bring kids with 'em usually, so why so curious? You headed out of town?" He was looking past Eric and Joel at the women and the kids.

"Calm down Earl, they's juss bein' neighborly; sides, it's a fair question. Yeah, headed down south for a while. Don' reckon' it's too good the 'lectricity's out, plus the radio, an' the phone, an' the cell phone an' everythin' else. Don' wanna be around if it gets real bad."

"Well, we're thinking about the same thing. Headed east most likely, just until things get back to normal. Just wanted to make sure everything was ok with you folks. Like you said, we were just trying to be neighborly. Hate to see somebody get stranded, especially like you said--with the phones out, not like you can call triple A. We'll be on our way and wish you luck." Eric nodded to the two from the flat-tire group and turned and started ushering the group back to the vehicles.

Eric's take on the situation had changed rapidly, especially with the low rumble coming from Millie, but he was glad they had stopped nonetheless. Chuck was the last to turn and let Joel, the women, and the kids get through the group. When Josh saw Chuck hanging back and Eric waiting for him, he sped up to take the lead with his dad.

Good instincts on that one, Eric thought to himself as they headed back to their little convoy.

"I assume you told them we were headed east because you don't want them anywhere near us."

"That would be as near an absolute as possible," Eric replied. "As bad as 'Earl' was, I didn't trust the fake dumb hick drawl on the other guy one bit. Earl got defensive awful quick but his buddy was real nice. No question as to who was in charge there at all. I was hoping it was a good sign that they didn't abandon the car for a flat tire. Now I'm not so sure; but I have no idea what it means, if anything. I didn't like the way Earl was looking at the women and kids either. Apparently, neither did Millie. I think it's a good thing Joel had her on a leash."

"On the plus side, they did give us at least one good idea--aside from staying away from them, that is. Don't turn around, but did you see the CB antennas on all their cars and trucks? I don't know why none of us thought of it before but I'm sure that those would still work, and they would let us communicate from truck to truck."

This time Eric actually did hang his head. He'd been acting, and if not admitting it to anyone else at least thinking to himself, as if he was going to be the leader of this little expedition. Every time he turned around, though, someone brought up something he'd missed or hadn't thought of.

"No, I didn't notice that, and that was a mighty fine catch, Chuck, a mighty fine catch. Based on the cat-that-ate-the-canary look on your face I'm assuming you have an idea of where we can get some as well?"

Chuck shrugged. "I'm willing to bet we'll pass at least one truck stop between here and the Armory, and they've all got CBs and antennas. They may even have some handheld models." Chuck was grinning now.

Eric smiled at this point too. *It would be nice to be able to talk back and forth between cars, trucks, whatever. And if CBs were working, then the truckers must be using them.* Eric thought. "We may even be able to get news from further away." He had kicked back into big-picture mode again and wasn't sulking anymore, at least.

Chapter Eleven

Chuck was right, and less than two miles up the road was a sign for "Frank's Food & Fuel". It had been one of the big chain truck stops until the recession hit a couple of years ago--but apparently 'Frank' was still doing ok. Joel decided not to park right next to the front door, so that they could get five spots next to each other a small distance from both the building and the semis idling in the parking lot.

Once everyone was out of their cars, Chuck suggested they discuss barter before they went inside. Joel mentioned some of the canned goods and Chuck offered up some of his tools. Sheri mentioned that they actually had more dry ice than they were actively using, but Rachael suggested that they just offer to buy it with a check--or if necessary, multiple checks.

With that decided, they tied Millie's leash to the bike rack in the shade, and in defiance of every decent practice of deal making, went straight to where the CB whip antennas stuck up over the aisle tops. As any good truck stop will, Frank's had almost a dozen different types of CB radios--and twice as many types of antennas--on display. There were also a good number of boxes in stock.

The store buzzed with activity, but most customers looked to be truck drivers. The feeling inside was actually quite upbeat; in stark contrast to the tension back in the neighborhood, and their recent run in with the flat-tire group. A petite, brunette attendant with a nametag that read "Laurie" came over to ask if she could be of any assistance.

"Well, I'll cut to the chase," Karen jumped in before one of the men could pipe up. She didn't figure that a woman working at a truck stop would be at all intimidated by a man, that was just stupid...but talking to another woman couldn't hurt. "You folks take a check--or five--or is everything cash with the power out?"

"As long as y'all didn't steal the five trucks you just drove up in, we shouldn't have any problems taking checks. The manager did say it was up to us, but the limit is $250 per person. You looking to get some radios?"

"Yeah, we're thinking one per vehicle and maybe a couple of handhelds," Rachael chimed in. Chuck had mentioned the handhelds during the barter discussion prior to coming in.

"Y'all want all the same kind? We've got a couple that I've got at least five of."

"I think our major criteria are reliability, not too complicated, and plugs into the lighter. We don't want to have to hard wire anything, and I don't know about anybody else, but I don't have much experience with these." It was Chuck's turn to contribute his two cents.

"Well, believe it or not, you don't have to go with the more expensive models with all the bells and whistles to get a decent radio." This was a voice that came from behind and above them. They all turned to see that one of the truckers had taken an interest in their conversation and decided to weigh in. "If all you're looking to do is be able to talk back and forth, and maybe be able to call out to about eight or ten miles, just about any of the lower end models that come with a microphone should be just fine.

"You don't need all the flip switches and knobs and dials. Get one with a digital channel display though; seeing what channel you're on in the dark is a stone cold bi...um, can be rather difficult, otherwise. I'd suggest you just get a magnet mount antenna too. No reason to get a 5 foot whip antenna unless you just really feel the need to compensate...there really isn't any reason for most folks to get a whip antenna." The newcomer was turning red from trying not to put his foot in his mouth in front of strangers.

"Timothy Grace," he stuck his hand out in introduction. "Sorry for barging in like that but I figured you might be able to use a little advice."

"No apology necessary," Eric replied. "Like Chuck here said, we don't have a whole lot of experience with any of this. I used some two-way radio gear in the Army, but I doubt it was much like this." Eric was actually pretty sure it had been a lot like this, but he didn't want to dismiss the trucker and he really did appreciate the offer of help. Someone who used these brands on a daily basis would have a much better idea which ones were worth anything. Tim's experience would be invaluable.

"In that case, I'd probably go with 'D', even though 'B' is on sale. You have five of those, Laurie?"

"Lemme see." Laurie had to check behind a couple stacks but came up with a total of five boxes--one of which was empty. "Looks like it if we sell the display. That should be ok. You folks ok with the display unit? Works just fine. We just take 'em out of the box and put 'em up."

"As long as we can test it right away, I don't see a problem," Eric said.

"No problem with that. Now, Tim mentioned you'd need to get antennas too. He's right about the whips. Unless you're trying to go a long distance you shouldn't need a long whip. Most folks won't suggest a whip unless you are going to permanently mount it, too, as whips have a tendency to hit stuff. You don't want to knock it off, or scratch the paint--and if you hit enough stuff you *will* knock off a magnet mount, no matter what the manufacturer says."

They ended up getting 18-inch antennas for each vehicle as well as the mobile CBs for less than $100 a set, plus $100 for each of the handhelds; then Joel started wandering around. "Hey, Eric, c'mere."

"What'd you find, Joel?"

"DC powered refrigerators."

They both stared at them for half a minute and then Eric shook his head. "As small as they are, I'd rather find a generator and a regular fridge."

"Yeah, I guess so. Maybe we should grab some coffee and sodas while we're here though. Aren't you supposed to make sure you have some kind of treat or snack food during an emergency to keep the natives from getting restless?" Joel said.

"Good point, and we have the room. Man, I wish the fountain machines were working. A can just doesn't taste the same." Eric suggested.

Everyone made a couple of trips through the store, making like 21st century hunter-gatherers in search of the elusive sour gummy this or salty vinegar that or oddly shaped chocolate covered peanut pretzel other thing. Then they grabbed all the twelve-packs of soda they could carry and six bags of coffee.

Tim was standing at the counter chatting with Laurie when they were finally ready to ring up—after carefully dividing everything into piles of stuff $250 or less. He glanced over their piles of CB radios and hoarder-style junk food stashes and chuckled, "So, I guess you guys heard, huh?" Everybody stopped and looked at each other--no one willing to say anything.

"Oh my goodness, people, I drive a truck for a living; I'm not an idiot. Why do you think we're all just sitting here? You're obviously not all related, except for you two married folks and you two kids who I'm guessing 'belong' to you two," Tim pointed at Joel and Rachael.

"You're buying CB radios and you already said you're going to hook up the display unit in the parking lot." Tim said. "You'd be fools not to hook up all five before you leave. I was, and still am, going to offer to help you get them all hooked up. I'm not going anywhere anytime soon. I drive a freezer truck and there isn't a store in the state with power. Where am I gonna go? At least if I keep the truck running the stuff'll stay frozen!"

"When you get the radios hooked up you're going to hear the same thing we're hearing. The power's out. Capital 'O'. Some solar thing which blew some giant fuse somewhere and you can't fix this one by wrapping it in tin foil, so the power is out nationwide. You're getting out of town; you're buying six bags of ground coffee for Pete's sake."

"Dude, you used to be in the military--said so yourself. You must have been a staffer man, because your OpSec sucks. No offense, because all my military experience comes from Space Opera, but c'mon, six bags of coffee in one trip?"

Eric was turning red, and that had led to the 'no offense' remark from Tim, but it wasn't because he was mad. He was trying not to laugh. At 'Space Opera' he felt his diaphragm start to spasm, and by 'in one trip' he just couldn't hold it in any more.

He sputtered; then he snickered; then he was chuckling, and then he was laughing hard enough to bring tears to his eyes. By then, everyone else had realized just how obvious they'd been and were laughing too. Tim was laughing in relief.

"Guilty on all counts. Yeah, we know, or at least think we know, what happened; and yeah, we're on our way out of town. We'd also be grateful, again, for any help with getting these things installed."

"Happy to help, I really am, and I'm just glad you were building up to laugh. I was afraid I'd really pissed you off there for a minute. You were turning purple."

"I really needed the laugh I think." Eric was actually wiping tears from his eyes. "Ok, let's get you folks paid up. Speaking of which, if you guys know what's up how come you're taking checks?"

It was Laurie's turn to laugh. "Frank, and yes that's his real name, is a skinflint and a prick. If things are really going to go downhill and a few folks need to grab a few things on their way out of town, I'm going to do everything I can to make sure they get what they need. If the power comes back on I'm sure the checks'll clear, if it doesn't it'll be the least of anyone's worries.

"I'll know I did right by some folks when it mattered and I'll be taken care of by the folks around me. I'm sure y'all need the radios and the coffee more'n Frank needs a couple hundred bucks, that's for darn sure. And like I said, he left it up to us and then he went home...prick."

"I'd like to make a couple of suggestions if I may, though. I did say $250 per person and I only see five piles of stuff and six adults. I assume that both of your names are on the checks," Laurie looked at Joel and Rachael. When they both nodded she went on, "In that case, and no I'm not just trying to get more money out of you, but do y'all have enough food for the four legged member of your party? We do sell dog food, treats, and biscuits," Laurie finished with a grin.

Joel and Rachael glanced at each other with the remainders of the earlier grins on their faces and then Joel nodded to Maya and Josh. "You heard the lady, go get Millie taken care of too."

Rachael looked back at Laurie once Josh and Maya had headed off towards the dog food aisle. "You said a couple of suggestions. What's the other one?"

"Well, the radios are only good as long as they have power," Laurie replied. "The vehicle units are going to be kinda stuck where they are but the handheld jobs will need to be recharged. If things don't come back to normal real soon then gas is going to get real hard to come by. We've got some solar chargers that I'd be willing to cut you a deal on, say buy one, get one free? They even have adapters for cell phones and most game systems."

Ten minutes and three trips out to the trucks later, they had everything packed up, the radios out, and were plugging them in to make sure that they all powered on. Tim gathered them around one vehicle and gave them a crash course on how to use the rig they had bought. He showed them how to change channels, use the microphone, and more in between rubbing Millie's stomach and scratching her hind end. She'd taken to him as soon as he walked out of the store. Twenty minutes later he was helping them get the antennas situated and cables run into each vehicle. It was almost 10:00 by the time they pulled back out of the parking lot, but now they were able to call each other.

With CB radios nothing is private; it's a completely open system-- unless you have some sort of scrambler. The best you can hope for is that you are on a channel nobody else is monitoring; the next best thing is to get on a channel that nobody else is actively using. They decided to monitor channel nineteen, which was the de-facto trucker channel and should keep them up to date on anything going on around them. If they had anything they wanted to keep private within their group, they would simply get on and say their name and "go daily." Everyone in the group would then change channels to the current day of the month.

Since the citizen band is broken into forty channels, that would work for every day but the nineteenth--for which they would move to channel thirty-nine. If they heard someone on the daily channel they would also move to thirty-nine. It wasn't perfect but it made a moving target--and made Eric feel a little better about his "sucky OpSec". He also hoped it would keep the flat-tire group from hearing his group until they were completely out of range.

Chapter Twelve

Tennessee is The Volunteer State. The nickname is said to have originated during the War of 1812 when thousands of Tennesseans volunteered to fight under Andrew Jackson in the militia. The nickname was then proven again when, during the war against Mexico, the U.S. Secretary of War requested 2,600 infantrymen and 30,000 men volunteered.

It came as no surprise to anyone, then, that the Army National Guard Armory parking lot was virtually full at 10:30 when they arrived. Nobody was even surprised to be greeted by an armed Guardsman at the entrance to the parking lot. Joel had wisely suggested that Eric lead the way to the Armory as he would probably be better equipped to talk to any of the Guardsmen there.

As they pulled up, Eric already had is IRR, or Inactive Ready Reserve, card out and his window down. "I need to speak with Lieutenant Parker, First Sergeant Jensen, or Staff Sergeant Ramirez. It's rather important."

"Yes, Master Sergeant, please wait one moment."

"I'm IRR, take it easy," Eric smiled as the Specialist on guard duty used the radio clipped to his shoulder to call into the Armory proper.

"If you will wait right here for just a minute, Staff Sergeant Ramirez will be right out."

About thirty seconds later a red-headed human fireplug came out of the Armory and jogged over to Eric's truck. Ramirez was taller than he looked--because he was so wide--but absolutely none of it was fat. Ramirez came to attention and bawled, "Staff Sergeant Ramirez reporting."

"Oh cut the crap, Ramirez, I'm IRR and you know it. I'm here hoping to appeal to your better nature and if that doesn't work, your sense of self-interest." When Ramirez kept standing at attention, Eric kept going. "You're fifteen years older than me if you're a day, and anyway you look silly standing like that." When that didn't work either, Eric barked, "What I meant by all of that was AT EASE SOLDIER!"

Finally, Ramirez smiled and stuck out his hand. "Good to see you, Eric. I didn't know how much longer I could keep standing there with a straight face. I was hoping you'd crack first because I was just about to bust a gut. I never was any good at the political BS, why do you think I'm still a Staff Sergeant?"

"Well, let's see; you're good at it, the guys love you, they don't WANT to promote you, and they can't promote you because nobody's died--how about those for starters? Can we get off the street? We need to talk about what's going on and I'd like to introduce you to these folks."

"Sure, sorry, been a little hectic what with no commo today. Thank God we're a Signal Company. Can I hop in?" He was already on his way around the front of the truck.

"Please do, easier than leading this group with you walking." Eric picked up the CB, moved everyone to the daily channel, and then let everyone know to follow him.

Once they had everyone past the zigzag concrete barriers and into the parking lot, they all piled out and Eric introduced Kyle Ramirez.

"Ok, you stressed what both Chuck and Sheri here used to do for a living. I've got a bad feeling we need to go inside and sit down for this little chat you mentioned. We have at least 6 MW of power generating capacity inside of the Armory, but we've only got a limited quantity of diesel so we've only set up one building with power.

Inside, the building was much quieter with the noise of the generator muted. They also noticed the lights! Shining fluorescent and incandescent lights—the first they'd seen in two days. It was amazing how quickly you got used to some things being gone. Kyle led them to a conference room down the main hall and asked them to have a seat inside.

"Eric, I was only partially kidding out there. I know you're IRR, but that still means something." Kyle said. "Before you all get going, if it's dropped in the pot I've got to assume that anybody that's IRR would have been activated which means you'd have been too. That means you'd be a Senior NCO right now. You're here, as in inside the building, for a number of reasons."

"I'm serious about the IRR, consider it Eric. We've had about ninety-percent muster so far." Eric's eyebrows went up at that. He wasn't expecting quite that high a turnout...period--much less so quickly.

"Well said, Kyle, and I'm already thinking about it; but that isn't why I'm here. Chuck, Sheri, is it OK if I start and then we kinda go around the table, as it were?"

"Fine by me, I don't know that I know more about this than you do," Chuck replied.

"Same here, I think we can fill in the blanks but I think you've been plugged into this, no pun intended, longer than we have," Sheri said.

"What about GPS, Eric? You mentioned that you had an idea about that on the way out of the neighborhood a couple of hours ago," Joel interrupted.

"I'll actually get to that, maybe, if I can. I don't know how classified that is, or was. I might be able to sum it up and not get myself in trouble if and/or when the power comes back on and the government is back online." Eric looked at Ramirez, "Actually, Kyle might be able to speak to that better than I can. I'd forgotten that you all were a signal company. You'd probably know more regarding what we could share regarding that."

Kyle nodded but didn't say anything at this point.

"Fair enough," Joel wasn't entirely pleased, but thought he understood the reason.

"So basically, anything that was plugged in and turned on went poof." Eric proceeded to explain the basics of the CME to Kyle with clarifications and additional information from Chuck and Sheri occasionally provided.

"Wow, and I sincerely mean that, like from the bottom of my heart. We should go ahead and start working on the other buildings. Man I wish the Captain was here, or even the LT." Kyle was muttering to himself.

"You mean neither of them is here yet?" Eric was more than a little surprised and it showed in his voice and face.

"It's not like that. The Captain is in DC and the LT and his wife are out of town for their 20th anniversary. C'mon man, they're 'lifers'."

"So, are you telling me that I might actually be the senior NCO here? I might be the senior staff, period, if I activate myself?"

"Calm down, you aren't the senior NCO, the First Sergeant is here; she was here at o'dark thirty yesterday and hasn't slept yet to the best of my knowledge. We just don't have a single officer here, is all. We also don't have any communication with higher yet--although if GPS is up, that should be resolved shortly I would think." Kyle made a face.

"I'd rather not be micromanaged from afar once we get commo set up, and without the LT or the Captain here, I'm afraid that's what they're going to do." Kyle said. "You and I both know why you got out man. They are *NOT* going to leave it all up to the First Sergeant, no matter how good she is."

Kyle turned to Joel, "Mr. Taylor, Joel if you prefer, I'll answer your question about the GPS as much as I, we, can. Suffice it to say that if you are getting GPS signal the military is getting back communications capability as we speak. I can't go into the details, but sometime in the next forty-eight hours we should start getting instructions from higher up and eventually, officially, begin getting recalled. You too, E.T." Kyle looked at Eric.

Great, it's going to get to the point that every time I hear a radio crackle and see someone headed my way I'll have to run and hide. Oh well. Eric thought. Communication *was* pretty important, after all, and at least his 'baby birds' were working. They'd been his brainchild and how cool was it knowing that something the military had conceived, designed, built, and deployed had actually worked right the first time and in a time of need?

Kyle looked at this watch and shook his head, "You all have been here for a little while, does anyone need to use the bathroom or want to get a drink? The soda machine's got power. Ironically it was unplugged when the power went out."

"Actually, yes sir, if I could I'd like to take advantage of both. Maya's been squirming for a couple of minutes too," Josh replied.

"Ewww, gross!" Maya said and slugged him in the arm. Man, he was getting beat up a lot the last couple of days.

"I'm sure you've heard it before but I'm not Sir, I work for a living," Kyle replied. "We save Sir for the officers, none of whom are here right now. Typically we refer to each other by our rank. That's more than sufficient respect, we know how much it means to have attained it and there's no disrespect in not being called Sir or Ma'am. For that matter you can feel free to call me Kyle or Mr. Ramirez if that works for you."

"In that case, Staff Sergeant, I need to pee please."

Kyle couldn't help but laugh at the combination of formality and casual address. "Carry on, son. The bathrooms are down the hallway to the right on the right and left side. The soda machine is at the end of the same hallway. While everyone is taking care of business I'll go get the First Sergeant. If we could all be back here in five minutes we can go through this all over again."

. . .

Everyone but Joel and Rachael had left for either the bathroom or to get a soda or both. "Joel, what's wrong? You haven't said anything since you asked about the GPS."

"You haven't said anything either, why's something wrong with me?" Joel snapped.

"Well, your sunny demeanor aside, you usually aren't this quiet. You were much more involved back at the house yesterday and I doubt you're still dwelling on the Carey situation. Personally, unless I have something specific to add, I'm going to let the men handle things for a while. I don't feel like I'm bringing a whole lot to the table, Joel. I feel like the kids and I are baggage right now--I'd rather not call attention to that if it's all the same to you."

"Well hon, now you know how I feel. The longer we sit here the more I feel the same way. I'm a cubicle dweller. I manage servers all day long for a living. You can at least cook; what can I do? I don't see a whole lot of server consolidation going on in the next couple of months, do you? I can't see myself bringing up a ton of new web servers for the next killer app in time for the Christmas rush either."

"We like to camp--great, super. I'm 38 years old with a bad back and I'm bi-polar, which reminds me I haven't taken my medication today and I think I forgot it last night, which probably explains my piss-poor outlook on life right now. What happens when the three-month supply of our daily meds run out if the power isn't back up? Mail-Med isn't delivering right now and I doubt they'll be delivering without payment. Do we rob a pharmacy and do we do it today before everybody else thinks of it? What happens when I blow out my back lifting a…whatever…and I don't have any more Lortab? What happens when your birth control expires?" Joel shook his head in frustration.

"Hon, what's going to happen to your mom and my dad, both of whom are diabetic? They're practically to the point of insulin dependence--and needing to use those pens. Without refrigeration they're good for what, three months? Then what? I know there's power to be had, but there's no way to get it to people.

Joel slumped backwards in his chair and scrubbed his hands over his face. Rachael knew exactly how he felt; she just hadn't put it into words yet. This was just a microcosm of what was going on or likely to happen. "Joel, that's what you bring to the table. You are thinking big picture and you aren't afraid to voice the concerns that the rest of us keep to ourselves. I've been stewing about some of those same things, especially the birth control, but didn't know how to bring it up. Maybe try to be a bit more tactful but don't keep it all inside."

"Ok, that's fair. It's just that the longer I sat here with nothing to contribute the more like a lump I felt."

"Just don't let it rule your life, Joel; it's still just the second day. I love you and I need you, in all your mood-swingy, sore back, receding-hairline glory."

"Is my hairline really receding?" Joel asked, a bit of a whine in his voice.

"For heaven's sake, you're as bad as a woman--and I should know!" Rachael put her arm around Joel and her head on his shoulder as Karen and Sheri came back in.

"You look to be in a slightly better mood, Joel. Rachael give you a pep talk?" Karen had a couple of Cokes and slid one over to Rachael as she sat down.

"You could say that. I was starting to feel sorry for myself there near the end. I guess all these military types, and Sheri, you and Chuck, were making me feel superfluous." Joel was eyeing Rachel's Coke.

"Open it before you drool on yourself, Og, just leave some for me. Never mind that you should have been a gentleman and gotten up and gotten one for me yourself," Rachael cocked her head slightly to one side and ever so slightly down, looking 'up' at Joel and arching her left eyebrow. In other words, giving him what is known by men the world over as The Look.

"Oh Lord, have mercy on my soul. Civilization as we know it may have come to an end at 3:14 yesterday morning and I'm sleeping on the couch because I didn't get a Coke during our five minute break. I am so doomed!"

"What's this about civilization coming to an end when the power went out at 3:14 yesterday?"

All eyes turned to the open door and it was all everyone present could do not to immediately stand up, just by reflex. First Sergeant Mallory Jensen had been in the Army for thirty-one years, and was one of the full time staff for the Tennessee National Guard stationed at the Nashville Armory. She had a presence about her that commanded not only respect, but immediate, absolute obedience.

"Well, that went well. Now that we have the preliminaries out of the way maybe we can get to the details," Kyle said as everyone continued to walk into the room.

"Can it, Ramirez. I've been up since three-something yesterday morning. The coffee today is worse than usual and hit its peak effectiveness about three hours ago. Good to see you, Eric. I hope that continues to be a true statement."

"First Sergeant, it's good to see you too, although I wish the circumstances were different," Eric replied.

"Wonderful, you're IRR but you're still calling me First Sergeant, not Mallory. What the fu…sorry, kids present, hell happened that has you showing up today and Ramirez coming to find me, then? Wait, before you begin, let's get some introductions out of the way. I think you have all deduced by now that I'm First Sergeant Mallory Jensen. Right now I'm both the senior ranking enlisted staff, or NCO, which means Non-commissioned Officer for those of you who aren't familiar with military jargon, and the senior ranking staff, because there are no Commissioned Officers present. Talk to me, Eric."

"It's a long story, how much do you want and in what order?" Eric asked

Before Mallory could respond, Joel interjected, "And there's a whole lot more to discuss than we got through with just Staff Sergeant Ramirez."

Chuck and Eric both looked over at Joel-- relieved that he'd finally chimed in. "In that case, Eric, why don't you see how much you can debrief me in fifteen minutes, with any additional input, and then we'll get some chow, sorry, lunch. Afterwards, we can reconvene and go into the details."

Fifteen minutes later, give or take twenty seconds, Eric wrapped up his debrief.

Mallory had sat with her elbows on the table and steepled index fingers at her lips for the entire fifteen minutes, except to ask the occasional question for clarification. When Eric finished, she sat there for a full minute with her lips pursed, eyes squinted just a bit, and a thousand-meter stare. "Ok, clearly I'm going to need more coffee. Let's get fed."

As they walked out of the conference room, Chuck smelled lunch cooking and realized just how hungry he was. He was a snacker and this three meal a day business was going to kill him. It smelled like chicken, potatoes, green beans, okra, cornbread and rolls. He thought maybe he even smelled brownies? As it turned out, there were both chicken and roast beef, green beans, peas, fried okra, cornbread, fresh yeast rolls, fresh mashed potatoes (not instant, no sir), fresh baked macaroni and cheese and yes, brownies for desert.

The head cook was a chef and part owner of a restaurant--hence the fresh mashed potatoes and from-scratch yeast rolls. One of the benefits of serving in the guard was that those you served with, many times, did what they did in the guard for a living. The diesel mechanics actually did it as a day job; so they were intimately familiar with the engines on the weekends as well. The cooks were chefs, and made really good food. The communications guys were computer geeks and electrical engineers who could fix and make stuff up on the fly that would blow your mind.

"Excuse me, First Sergeant Jensen, does the Army always eat like this?" Josh asked Mallory.

"No son," Mallory chuckled. "This is one of the perks of being in the guard. Our head cook is part owner of a restaurant. Out in the field we'd be eating MREs, meals in a box, and unfortunately they aren't like Lunchables. They aren't horrible but we miss Sergeant Walker something fierce."

Joel excused himself and went out to the Suburban to dig through the duffle bag Rachael had packed with their immediate necessities until he found the pocket with their medications. Coming down off of most bi-polar and anti-depressant medications was murder-- sometimes literally--especially those that you took twice a day. Missing two in a row would make him, and everyone around him, miserable, right up until they tied him to a chair and gagged him. He took one dose with him and headed back inside. *What are we going to do in a couple of months when our supplies of these run out?* He wondered.

Chapter Thirteen

Back inside, conversations in the mess hall ranged from guardsmen wondering what was going on, to when the Governor would call to officially activate everyone, to how long it would last, to whether or not it would affect this or that sporting event. It was nice to hear normal conversation interspersed with the speculation. The First Sergeant was sitting at their table, but the conversation remained completely casual.

"So you still haven't decided between Sprint and AT&T huh? I'd heard that they both want you, but you keep pitting them against each other. How long do you thing that's going to work, Tripp?" Kyle was giving Eric a hard time about still not having a full-time job.

"I swear, worm poop, that's what it says right on the bottle. No kidding, liquefied worm poop. I might never know how well it works but there are whole discussion boards on the Internet that swear by it. Smells to high heaven though." Karen was telling Sheri and Rachael about her latest foray into home gardening.

"Actually, there are quite a few Sergeants in the Army. You start as a Private, and you have no insignia on your uniform at all. Your goal is to become a Private 2 as quickly as possible because frankly, a Private, or Buck Private is lower than whale crap and that's on the bottom of the ocean, son." It was obvious that Mallory had had this talk more times than she could count but she was still giving Josh and Maya her attention while taking in the conversations around her.

At 12:15 everyone headed back to the conference room. On the way there the First Sergeant disappeared, and when she showed back up she had was joined by three more guardsmen. "I need my platoon leaders up to speed. Gentlemen, please have a seat. I had Staff Sergeant Ramirez brief them at the end of lunch so they may actually be further along than I am.

"Mr. Taylor, you mentioned that there were more things to discuss than just the initial power going out via the grid going down and the collapse surrounding that. The floor is yours, Sir."

"The specifics that need to be addressed that I've come up with begin with medications." Joel looked around the table because he didn't want to appear to just be talking to the First Sergeant. "People, like myself, for example, who are on anti-depressants or who are in chronic pain and on pain killers or who are, and this is where it gets really serious, diabetic or on chemotherapy or immune-compromised and in need of constant antibiotics. In some cases, there is a vast store of those medications sitting in warehouses or even in pharmacies that can simply be given out manually if people present their expired bottle.

"A lot of those drugs--like insulin and chemotherapy drugs--need refrigeration, at least some of the time. Without it we are going to start losing people. Just insulin-dependent diabetics are between two and three million people. That's a ballpark figure off the top of my head from research when we found out my dad was diabetic. Both Rachael's mom and my dad are type 2, but type 1's need insulin."

Joel held up his hand and two fingers. "Next, we have hospitals--which may or may not be on generator power--but even if by some chance the generators are working, and the equipment inside wasn't damaged, and is online and functional, are only going to last as long as the fuel. How long is that rated for? Anyone know? I know our datacenter at work was rated for eighteen hours before we needed to have diesel standing by and constantly coming in thereafter. If it was natural gas, that's great, as long as the pressure stays up, which it won't because there's…dramatic reverb…no power." Joel took a drink of the warming Coke.

"But back to people and medicines. People on chemo won't be able to get it anymore. I have no idea what the long term outlook for those people is but it's obviously not good or they wouldn't be on chemo. Same for the folks needing to be on antibiotics; you don't do that to yourself if you don't need to.

"Like I said, I've been diagnosed as needing anti-depressants and being bi-polar. Maybe if I just exhaust myself with physical labor every day I'll be so tired I'll be fine but there's a bunch of folks out there that are pretty messed up. I'm on a pretty low dose of the stuff I take but there are people out there that take lithium every day. I personally don't want them to miss a dose because when they do they're going to have a psychotic episode."

Nobody was saying anything because everyone seemed fascinated by what Joel was saying, and he was just getting warmed up.

"I would guess that within a couple of weeks pharmacies will be raided for anything they have. It will start with narcotics, dare I say obviously, and in the rush for the *good* stuff a lot of *useful* stuff will get ruined. Within a month the remains will have been picked over fairly thoroughly by people who got desperate when their thirty-day supply ran out. Two weeks after that, if not sooner, if it was a life-sustaining medication, those people will have died. The exception will be people like me and my family who get ours through the mail and have a ninety-day supply, but the end result is the same without the picking over window at the end."

The only noise in the room was the electronic ticking of the battery powered clock on the wall next to the door for a good fifteen seconds. It was, not surprisingly, the First Sergeant who spoke first. "And you don't write horror stories for a living, correct Mr. Taylor? You've been thinking about this for how long? A couple of hours? A day and a half tops? With all due respect, Sir, please remind me never to get you drunk. You have a scary, scary mind."

"First Sergeant," Kyle started.

"No, Ramirez, there is no way out of this Mickey Mouse outfit, don't even ask," Mallory didn't even turn to look at him.

"Right," Kyle said.

Everyone laughed, which was the point.

"Mr. Taylor, you said the specifics *begin* with medications, what did you mean by that?"

"Well, that was what I was originally focused on when I started down this train of thought but the more I thought about it the more things came to mind. For instance, this Armory doesn't seem to be the most secure base in the world--not that you all wouldn't do a fine job defending it but the location just sucks. I mean it's in downtown Nashville for crying out loud!"

"Like the old saying goes: When seconds count, the police are just minutes away, and that's only going to get worse. I think people are going to start counting on the military for protection and this is where they'll turn. If they can't get refuge or relief or whatever it is they think they need here, it might turn ugly; and that's a big perimeter out there to defend against an armed populace.

"Then, going back to the first point I made; well, it's June. We're in the South. If my calculations are right, the first large waves of dead bodies could be in six weeks or so, which would be the end of July. In the South--in the middle of the summer. We're going to have a major health problem on our hands in very short order." Joel looked around the room again. "People who aren't used to the heat without air conditioning are going to succumb like they do every time there is a blackout for more than twelve hours or so, except *this* is going to last for months, potentially. And this is nationwide. The entire country is going through this. Everywhere. Even the people who have windmills and solar power are going to be victims of this, because as soon as the rest of the neighborhood sees the lights on they will become victims of a different kind. It's that old 'Twilight Zone' episode where the only guy in the neighborhood to build a bomb shelter gets it torn down by everybody trying to get inside." Joel had to stop again, his throat was getting dry and he finished the Coke.

"Ok, Mr. Taylor, all good points. I'm going to ask you to stop at this point, not because they aren't valid points, not because they aren't things that need to be thought about or even acted on. We can, however, only do so much at one time and the human mind can only assimilate so much in one sitting. There is a reason that there is a Joint Chiefs of Staff after all, we don't leave it ALL up to one person, really we don't. Yes the President has the football but even he doesn't go around issuing orders just because.

"I would like to continue picking your brain and have you continue to think about it because you are, frankly, quite good at coming up with these things, scary as that is. I would be surprised to find out that all of this hasn't been thought of in infinite, gory detail by some group of eggheads in DC. We may even have an OP Plan here that tells us how to deal with it. It's also probably on the one computer that wasn't on the UPS or it's backed up on a tape drive that will take us two weeks to track down and get access to and print out.

"Change of topic. Are you planning on pushing on to whatever your final destination is today or have you reached your final destination?" Mallory asked, wearing her diplomat's hat.

Everyone was looking at Eric now so he felt compelled to answer the question. "Not necessarily, and no, why?

"Multiple reasons," Mallory replied, "not the least of which is that I'm sure you could all do with some additional rest after the last couple of nights. Joel, you've brought up a very good point about this particular location and one that I would like to address. Finally, there is the nature of the Guard specifically and the Army and military in general." Mallory stopped for a moment to gather her thoughts.

"In principle the Guard is here to protect the civilian population and assist the full time military or, in the case of a natural disaster, local and state law enforcement. It's more complicated than that in practice because people and politics end up getting in the way, but the idea is pretty straightforward. In order to do that, however, we need to be able to function as a unit or units and in order to do that we need to protect ourselves."

Mallory nodded to Joel, "As you mentioned, this is not the most defensible position in the world or even in this city. Staying here is probably not the best long-term solution and thinking long term is where everyone's head needs to be right now. You've left your homes for what I assume is the same reason. Unfortunately, making the decision to leave and actually doing so are a little more involved for a group the size of the Armory.

"For example, we have over two hundred vehicles that would need to be moved to wherever we're going along with all the materiel that goes along with supporting however many people come with us. No matter where we go we will have a huge impact on our destination, assuming that we do in fact relocate." Mallory held up her hand to forestall any interruptions.

"We're not making decisions right here, right now, around this table. That isn't what this is about and please, don't take this wrong, but none of you are in the military chain of command--at any level." Mallory's glance lingered a little longer on Eric than any of the other civilians at the table, but not by much. "It behooves any leader to have as much information as possible at her disposal before making a decision, which is what I'm trying to do but this is still a military installation and as such it *must* remain a military decision."

"All of that being said," Mallory broke off and her head whipped around as a number of things happened at the same time. Mallory, Ramirez, and all three of her platoon leaders were out of their chairs and crouched down in a number of positions that could only be described as tactical with their side arms out. Eric shouted, without actually shouting, for everyone to get on the floor *now* and Joel heard yelling and the echo of gunfire. Finally, there was the sound of boots coming down the hallway and a voice calling for the First Sergeant.

"Top, we have a situation," the voice said.

"HALT!" one of the platoon leaders barked, and the footsteps stopped.

"Sergeant Jackson, Specialist Davis reporting. Zulu duress Sergeant"

If he'd actually said 'zero duress' or 'no duress' they would have known he wasn't alone.

"Proceed at a walk on the far side of the hall, son."

All three platoon leaders had their firearms trained on the door and Ramirez was physically between the door and Mallory. Joel thought to himself, "I never realized how seriously they take this." Then again, he, Eric, and Chuck had once again made a human wall in front of the women and children--even crouched down as they were.

Once Davis came into view he stopped and waited to be recognized, with his hands visible, and the Sergeant who'd identified himself as Jackson did a quick head bob out the door to verify that nobody else was in the hallway. "Come in, Davis. What just happened?!" Everyone slowly got up and Eric motioned his group back to their chairs.

"Sergeants...Top," he nodded to everyone. "We just had another group show up, but this one tried to ram and then shoot their way into the Armory." Although he said it like he was reading the weather report his face told a different story.

Jackson asked, "Any casualties?"

Davis's eyes flicked to the civilian group before answering the question. "None whatsoever from the Guardsmen or their families. Unknown for certain on the, uh…Sergeant, what in the world do I call US citizens who attack the Armory?"

Mallory stepped in before Jackson could answer. "You call them misguided, scared, and in the end you call them to account for what they've done. If you have to put a label on them, though, call them the OpFor. That way they can simply be the other guy without being the bad guy." Jackson nodded, almost to himself, at Mallory's response.

"Fair enough, Top. Uncertain number of casualties for the Opposing Force as they took off when we fired back. We do know that they didn't leave any vehicles or people but we weren't aiming to miss. If anyone was armed and aiming at us," Davis closed his eyes and took a breath, "I'm pretty sure they got hit."

Mallory held up her hand for Davis to stop and turned to Eric. "E.T., folks, I'm afraid I need to be devoted to some strictly military matters for the time being. I can't hold you here but I would suggest that leaving right this minute would be a very bad idea. Before I duck out for a while I would like to offer you a place to stay until tomorrow morning. We've got a number of squad bays and we won't be using them all tonight. I don't know everyone's situation, but…"

Karen came to both Sheri's and Chuck's rescue, "Mallory, if you could designate one 'Female' for Sheri and I, one 'Male' for Eric and Chuck, and I think one 'Family'--assuming that's ok, Joel, Rachael?"

With nods and agreement all around, it was decided.

"Sergeant Ramirez, would you please see to the rooms. This conference room is yours for now as well. If you need anything, one of the guardsmen should be able to find either Sergeant Ramirez or myself."

Chapter Fourteen

Once all the guardsmen left, nobody said anything for almost a minute. As stressful as the last day and a half had been, they'd also been so busy that they hadn't been able to stop and think about what it all meant until now. As a group, they were taking it fairly well. There hadn't been any real panic, yet. Disbelief, and tension, sure, but along with it there was a core of trust that had allowed them to overcome it. Most people didn't have that core of trust on a large scale, and the result had just played itself out at the entrance to the Armory.

"How do you think it's going to go?" Chuck asked Eric.

"Mallory is smart, and she's good at what she does. Part of it depends on whether or not there's any communications capability with higher up yet. If not, it's all up to her, and this little incident will probably help tip the balance towards getting out of Dodge. If she gets micromanaged then all bets are off."

"I take back what I said about defensibility. They obviously did fine." Joel said.

"No, you're still right." Eric replied. "Against a concerted attack along the entire perimeter there's no way to protect this position as it sits. With some time and more people, sure, but I think we just found out that we don't have the former, and how do we trust or train the latter?"

"People really aren't taking this well are they?" Joel asked with a straight face.

"Um, no Dad, they aren't." Josh answered, equally stoically. "The giveaway for me was the whole pulling the guns and everybody getting on the floor while the Army base was under attack. How about you?"

Rachael was really trying not to laugh while Chuck just stared at Josh and Joel. Karen and Sheri shook their heads. Maya summed it up best when she said in that exasperated tone that only an eleven year old can have, "MEN!"

For the second time that day, they laughed until they cried; the stress relief was amazing--even if short-lived. They were wiping their eyes when Ramirez came back in with a number of sets of keys to let them know where they would be sleeping. "Oh, come on guys, she's not always this bad. She grows on you...kinda like a fungus. You get used to her."

"Can it, Ramirez." Eric chuckled.

"Right, anyway, I've got squad bays set up for you folks and if you'd like to follow me I've got keys for you all and we can bring your luggage in as well. You're all parked in a more interior area and you'll have a couple of armed escorts while we have someone watching from the tower."

"Works." Eric said and got up to lead the way.

"Looks like bunk beds tonight, hon." Rachael said as Joel followed her into their unlocked squad bay with the bags he'd carried in from the SUV. "They're even bolted to the floor. Worse than college."

Maya and Josh rolled their eyes at each other as Josh dug through the extra backpack that he'd brought inside. "Since the conference room has power I figured we'd charge the games and the cell phones. No reason to let them go completely dead, and we'll probably use the alarms in the morning again."

"Ok Josh, knock it off, you're making me look bad," Joel said with a mock scowl. "So, what are we going to do for the rest of the day?"

The short answer was...not much. Over the next three hours they wandered around the main areas of the Armory as a group and watched as people slowly trickled in. At one point they saw Sergeant Ramirez walking with a slightly less determined stride from one place to another and took the opportunity to ask a couple of questions.

"Looks like you're getting some new recruits," Joel motioned to the steadily increasing population in the main hall.

"Actually, Top's been sending out groups to pick up Guardsmens' families since yesterday afternoon. We're about halfway through the list of folks that have mustered," Kyle replied. "In a number of cases, bringing them in has been by far the safest thing to do. We're also pretty sure it's what triggered the group who tried to get in earlier this afternoon."

"Any word from higher?" Eric asked.

"Not yet. No communication whatsoever. I'll admit we aren't trying real hard though. Everything's hooked up and we're listening, but we're only transmitting once every six hours for the time being. I gotta run. Give us another hour or so and I'll probably be coming to find you guys." With that, he was off again.

...

It wasn't actually until dinner that they saw Ramirez again and he caught up to them as they were lining up. "Sorry guys, it's been a bit crazy for me today, apparently the power is out." He winked at Karen who rolled her eyes. "I know today's probably been boring as sin for you but, believe me, I think it'll pick up here shortly. Let me fill you in at dinner and then Top wants to get together with everyone if that's ok?"

"Fine by me," Eric said and looked around to nods and shrugs.

At the same table they had used at lunch Kyle gave them a rundown of the day's activities, which included one more recent attempt to raise the local Army base, the Pentagon, and NORAD. "We'll be picking people up throughout the night and into tomorrow afternoon most likely, but we should have everyone who's coming in accounted for no later than tomorrow night."

"Any idea which way Top is going to jump?" Eric asked.

"Possibly, but I'm not going to say anything until she sits down with you guys. Sorry, Eric."

Eric made a c'est la vie face and shrugged.

"Has there been any word from any other source? Like CBs or short-wave from further away?" Rachael asked.

"There has, but it's all been general and it's all been pretty much the same and very fragmentary. The power is out; some folks think it's the end of the world while others are just waiting for it to come back on. Mass panic hasn't set in everywhere yet but its hit in a lot of places, mostly because there is simply no communication with the outside world and that's what has people the most freaked out."

"What's the furthest away you've gotten reports from?"

Kyle made a face for a second, "I think the furthest away we've gotten a relayed report from about the power being out was Anchorage."

Conversation continued until everyone finished and Kyle ushered everyone to the conference room with the exception of the kids.

"Ok, off to bed you two," Rachael said. "Or at least into our room. We don't need to be taking up as much room as we are and we still have some things to discuss."

"Mom, I'm not tired--it's not even 6:30!" Maya complained, and then ruined her case by yawning.

"Uh-huh, fine, you can play your handheld 'global domination magical pet horse trading game' then. I'll come with you and get you and your brother settled in but then the adults still have a lot to discuss..."

...

Mallory came into the room with her three platoon Sergeants in tow again. This time she introduced them to the group. "Everyone, this is Sergeant Bill Stewart, Sergeant Allen Halstead, and Sergeant Douglas Jackson. I lean on these guys pretty heavily when we go on maneuvers; and if we have any planning that needs to be done, I need them here."

At Eric's raised eyebrows, Mallory explained herself. "Yes, I said planning. The decision is still mine, but if planning needs to be done I'm going to avail myself of all possible tools at my disposal. Yes, Eric, I just called you a tool." Mallory smiled as Eric put on a faux-pained expression.

"Joel, you brought up a number of good points but the one that concerns me the most is one I've considered as well, but only tangentially. The fact that a day into this mess a civilian was already thinking of it does not give me the warm fuzzies. You're correct that the Armory is in the middle of Nashville, and that it's really not that defensible of a position--that's because it was never intended to be." Mallory was trying not to lecture but she had to get some basic information out to the non-military people in the room. "The Armory is basically a staging area, a rallying point if you will. We muster here and get sent elsewhere to fight or support if necessary. We don't train here; we hold onto and maintain equipment here."

Rachael came in from settling the kids in at this point and took a seat.

"So, as you mentioned, tactically this position is sub-optimal to say the least. I was not going to have this portion of the discussion in front of your kids though. Frankly, I wasn't going to have it in front of you, either, but you brought it up first, so I'm not going to hide it from you. Stewart, Halstead, Jackson--we are going to need an Advance Area. I want some suggestions on a TOE for a detachment, including size and specific individuals you would send tomorrow morning. Here's the kicker, I need it in one hour." Mallory paused to let that sink in.

Kyle's face fell. "Oh that is so unfair, they get a whole hour!"

"Can it, Ramirez."

"I'm getting a lot of that today."

"Something's telling me you get a lot of that most days," Joel said.

"What can I say, there's a reason I'm still a Staff Sergeant."

"Wrong, there's probably fifty reasons you're still a Staff Sergeant, Ramirez," Mallory rejoined. The mood lightened in the room a little.

"Top, how long do you anticipate the forward deployment being on its own, and do you have any idea where it's headed?" Stewart asked.

"Good question, Eric, I'll start by deferring to you. When I asked you if you had reached your final destination earlier this afternoon you said no. Care to share where you were headed?"

"Absolutely. Love to, as a matter of fact. We were planning on heading to Natchez Trace State Park. Based on the Taylor's previous visits and what we'd been able to piece together from a couple of road atlases, it might do well for what you're thinking. It's about eighty-five miles west of Nashville, and ten or twelve miles from the next largest town. It straddles Highway 40, and has three or four good sized lakes if I recall correctly. It's fairly wooded and I would think that game would be, if not abundant, certainly sufficient for the time being."

Mallory had assumed her 'thinking pose' with elbows on the table and steepled index fingers against pursed lips. She was tapping her thumbs together. "Were you already thinking of getting us out of here?"

Eric didn't answer the question directly right away. "It was Rachael, I think, who brought up the park. She mentioned that the family had camped there a couple of years ago." He stopped for a few seconds and then went on, "Bringing at least some of the guard along *did* come up during the discussion though, yes."

Mallory looked over to where Rachael and Joel were sitting and nodded, "And neither of you were ever in the military, huh? Too bad--for the military, that is. You've both got really good instincts. Both of your kids do too, for that matter--not that I think you need my validation on that--but I actually enjoyed talking to both Josh and Maya at lunch, very mature for their ages."

Joel and Rachael couldn't help but smile a little at the compliment, more so for their children than for themselves.

"That, however, doesn't let my right arms get to their assigned task. Before I start your clocks, gentlemen, no, I don't know how long I anticipate the detachment to operate on its own. Assume two weeks of operations in an unknown--but not a known hostile--environment before anyone else joins you. Also assume that there will not be either the ability or the availability to supplement your rations; I would rather you be pleasantly surprised than hungry. Assume one of you will be leading the detachment, because one of you will. However, one of the many first things to do will be to get communication back to the Armory set up."

Sergeant Jackson glanced over at Kyle and back to Mallory, and she responded in the very next breath. "I have not yet decided if Mr. Ramirez will be part of the deployment. Jackson, if you go, he doesn't--*end* of discussion. You two get in too much trouble where I can actually see you, there is *no way* I'm sending you two out there together eighty-five miles away."

Mallory rolled her eyes heavenward and held her hands palms up, "Please give me strength. I know they think I'm crazy for staying in all these years, but do they really think I'm *stupid*?" She shook her head and looked back at her platoon leaders.

"If there are no further questions...dismissed." All three Sergeants got up, said their goodbyes to the rest of the group and trooped out, already discussing the beginnings of their operational plan.

"Now, Mr. Taylor, I know I'm going to regret this but I'm going to ask anyway. Have you come up with any more disasters for us to deal with?"

Chapter Fifteen

"Actually, yes...fires."

"You are going to be so much fun, I can just tell." She took the sting out of the comment with a smile, but Joel knew what she meant. "Go on."

Joel was taking Rachael at her word; they needed someone to look at the big picture. "There are bound to be fires eventually. Someone will fall asleep with a cigarette in bed or try cooking with a gas grill inside, or some nutjob who wants to watch the world burn will try to do just that."

"Then there are natural fires-- in the city or the surrounding countryside. We get some whopper thunderstorms down here, as you well know, and lightning strikes are common enough. Those can certainly start fires, although depending on how bad the rain is they may not cause too much damage. Either way, fire could become a real problem if it got out of hand."

"You don't seem to think it's going to be as big a problem as, say, disease though, correct?" Mallory asked.

"Basically, yes, for a couple of reasons. Fires are preventable to a large degree, and even if they do occur they typically don't burn down entire neighborhoods. We don't live in the era of Mrs. O'Leary's cow kicking over a lantern and burning down Chicago anymore. Forest fires are the one thing that truly scare me, but we can't do a thing about those so I have to just back off from thinking about them so it doesn't drive me insane."

"Point. Ok, go on." Mallory replied.

"We don't have a huge amount of control over the people who are going to die due to lack of medications either, but the consequences of their deaths are much farther reaching than fires would be. If push came to shove, we could wait until a building was done burning and then go in with a couple of bulldozers and a steamroller and all but level the place. You know where it is, or was, and you deal with it."

Joel was glad the kids weren't here; he really didn't want to have this discussion in front of them. "How do you know where every person in Nashville has died in the last twelve hours, and deal with it before the next twelve hours goes by? It wouldn't take too long to get behind. The germs and bacteria in the dead bodies spread and then people start getting sick, and dying from being sick--you get more and more behind and pretty soon it's a lost cause."

"So disease in the populated areas is a big issue. Next." Mallory looked like she was making a list in her head, literally.

"Well, then there's Napoleon Syndrome. Civilization has come to an end, I've got X amount of personal artillery and I think I'll take over this little piece of Nashville. I always wanted an 8,000 sq/ft house, and at this point it's going to be survival of the fittest. Sheri and Chuck were telling us about one of the guys she worked with at the dam who's heading to Oklahoma. Plenty of gas and tools to open the filler tubes, electric pump on his truck to pump his own gas should he run out, and as he put it, 'sufficient means to convince any reluctant sellers'. Supposedly that was just to get him to Oklahoma, but what if he decides he wants to stay here, or someone, or a bunch of some ones, planned to stay here all along?"

Joel glanced at Sheri and Chuck but neither of them looked like they had anything to add at this point, so he went on. "Neither Tennessee nor Nashville have been real big on restrictive gun laws. Trust me, I know--I have my son's AR-15 in the car right now. By the way, hon, can I have one?"

"No." Rachael didn't seem to be budging an inch on this one. Not yet at least. Maybe he needed to get her when she was even more exhausted.

"Anyway, there are all kinds of AR-15 and AK-47 style weapons out there, in addition to your standard Remington 700/770 deer rifles, and handguns galore--all over the place. If communication can't be reestablished for the general population, the folks who do have communication are going to be seen as attempting to establish and maintain a position of authority. That will cause resentment in those who don't have that capability and all kinds of nastiness could ensue--not the least of which is the breakdown in the relationship between the people doing the protecting and those they are sworn to protect."

"What role do you see the Guard playing in maintaining the peace? We can be called out and activated by the Governor and/or the Army directly but until that point we are acting on our own based on the best information we have in a very small sphere of influence. We also have to assume certain things that will restrict our actions. Things like the fact that the Constitution is still our ruling document, the Bill of Rights is still active...little things like that," Mallory said.

"Unless directed to, and actually it is more like unless *asked* to by a specific law enforcement agency or branch, we cannot perform many basic law enforcement tasks. We can actually be detained and charged for unlawful arrest for holding someone against their will, even if they were suspected of committing a crime."

Joel had no comeback for what he'd just heard. He'd always just assumed that the National Guard could act on their own to expand the local, county, or state police as needed. And they could, possibly, but only to a degree, and in specific ways, and only if asked. They were severely limited in what they could do and how they could do it.

Eric broke into the silence, "Mallory, worst case scenario, the Armory Company takes everything and relocates to a defensible position. Let's call it Natchez Trace for now. We bring in the families of anyone here in the Guard, close friends, people we encounter on the way, and turn it into a mini base. We still have the equipment, we still have the personnel, the structure is still intact, and you--oh all right *we*--are providing our primary role of support and security to the population while still maintaining our integrity."

"We'll be limited in what we can field, Eric, you know that. We have a fair amount of hardware as far as mortars, crew-served weapons, a few tow-behind field pieces, etc. But we haven't got any really heavy artillery, and we don't have any ammunition for the heavy stuff. Our job isn't to hold the ammo for those, it's to hold and maintain the equipment, and train on it occasionally.

"We have plenty of personal weapon ammo, don't get me wrong. We've got literally tons of ammo for everything up to the M60 and the .50, but anything bigger than that and we're hauling it along just to keep it out of someone else's hands for the time being."

Eric pondered that for a few seconds and shrugged. "Keeping it under our control and out of anyone else's hands both work to the same end, and we may be able to get up to the practice range after a while. Once we have somewhere we can defend we can take a look at that in more detail."

Mallory shook her head, "Actually, once you all are on the road in the morning and my brain trust has had some sleep, they'll start looking at it tomorrow." She looked at Rachael and Sheri and nodded, mentally shifting gears, "How are you at directing people--taking general direction and fleshing it out and passing it on, that is? I've known Karen for a few years, so I have a little bit of an idea how she works, but we're going to have a larger group of civilians to handle, eventually, than she can ride herd on alone."

Rachael smiled , "That's pretty much what I do as a mom, I'd say. It may not sound like it, but that's my day, all day, every day. Volunteering at the school, the Y, at Church. Running the house, balancing the budget, making sure Og over here eats and bathes. It sounds like you're looking for civilian analogs to your Sergeants here. I think, no, I know I could help with that."

"I'm not management, but I do OK in a pinch. I'm willing to give it a shot." Sheri added.

"Well said, you've just been drafted. The pay sucks and the hours are lousy, but like you just said, you're a mom so that shouldn't be new to you," Mallory smiled, "At this point, at least, there should be no more messy diapers for you." She gave a sidelong glance to Joel, "At least not for a few more years, anyway."

"Oh thank you SO much...'Ma'am'," Joel shot back with a smirk.

"Touché," Mallory laughed.

Within a minute of their hour deadline, the three platoon leaders arrived, took seats, and presented their deployment plan. Rachael and Joel were torn between being impressed and wanting to roll their eyes at the promptness of both Eric during his debrief and the arrival of the three Sergeants. In the long run they both came to the same conclusion; that in the military, timing was in fact *that* important, and if you got used to being that close on the little things, you would be that close on the big things.

"Suggested TOE, or Table of Organization and Equipment, is based on 1st Squad, 2nd Platoon," Sergeant Halstead began. "Recommended mobile units as follows: 2 HMMV each with mounted M60s and 2500 rounds; 1 M923 5-Ton, also with an M60, with 7500 rounds; 1 M577 for Como, with a full load out; 1 600 GPH ROWPU, or Reverse Osmosis Water Purification Unit plus 1 set of filters and two 3,000 gallon onion skins; 1 10kw Generator and 250 gallons of diesel; Rations for 1st Squad for 90 days plus the attached civilians for same, and standard logistics supplies. We anticipate using satellite communication back to the Armory, and in the event of a loss of primary communication we will have a long-wire already erected. The only exception we suggest to your initial tasking is that none of the three of us needs to be in direct oversight of this detachment. Staff Sergeant Ramirez is perfectly capable of running this, and frankly, Top, you're going to need all the help you can get here getting everything set to move out there."

Sergeant Jackson continued, "We're going to need to move, simple as that. We finally got word from higher, and they aren't giving us specific instructions. They haven't even officially activated us yet. There has been zero official communication from any state government to any military command authority excepting anecdotal comments through unofficial channels. Washington DC seems to be up and communicating with NORAD and a half dozen other locations in and around the capital but that's about it, all using the 'baby birds' that came online yesterday afternoon."

"They had a plan for the event, but that plan called for power to come online six hours later." Sergeant Stewart added. "It's not going to happen and they don't know what to do now. It's June of an election year Top, less than half of the Senators were even in DC, and a number of Representatives were out drumming up votes as well. The President is apparently in the air but that's where he's been for most of the day, they still haven't decided where he's going to touch down."

"How many functional water purification units do we have now?" Mallory asked.

Sergeant Stewart answered, "six 600 GPH and three 3,000 GPH, plus four sets of replacement filters for each unit. We also have fourteen 3,000 gallon 'onion skins'. At last check, two months ago, all nine units were fully functional--including onboard generators."

"How much diesel do we have on site including in the vehicles and what's the current average fuel level in the vehicles?"

"Currently we have 14,000 gallons of diesel and 2,000 gallons of 87-octane unleaded. Average vehicle fuel level is 2/3 of a tank." Sergeant Jackson replied. They were using 'normal' terms for diesel and unleaded gasoline instead of DF2, Mo-Gas, JP-4 and JP-8, in deference to the civilians.

"Who's going to set up the long-wire?"

"Bowersock can do it half drunk in his sleep without the book...in the dark...up hill both ways in the snow, wait, no, that's for something else...scratch everything after 'in the dark', so I figured we'd leave it to him. If anything, he can use his spare foot as the resistor." Ramirez had been Staff Sergeant along with Staff Sergeant Bowersock for almost ten years and been giving him a good natured hard time for pretty much the entire ten years.

"I don't know, Ramirez. He may need that extra foot when he breaks his primary one off up your butt. Remember, if he rears back to kick you don't let him do it with his left foot, that things carbon fiber and it hurts." Stewart shot back.

"Not only that, he's a firm believer in the old axiom 'If you find yourself in a fair fight, your tactics suck.' He's convinced he's too young to die but too old to take a butt whoopin' so he'll just haul off and shoot ya'." Halstead chimed in.

Mallory had obviously been through either this very conversation or one much like it, many times before. These four were starting to feed off of each other and in another minute or so they would reach the point where they were finishing each others' sentences. She gave them another ten seconds to get it out of their system, because it had been a long day, and it was going to be a long night followed by another long day and night combination, setting a pattern for the foreseeable future.

"Well, Ramirez, you know the drill...if he breaks it off you have to clean it before you give it back, so decide if it's really worth all that work. And back on track, this is a lot to plan and deploy in nine hours or so. Ramirez, I want your squad to hit the rack in twenty minutes. One of the other squads will get the gear loaded. You'll still be able to verify prior to moving out." Mallory got up and motioned to Kyle. "Walk with me, Ramirez."

"I want everyone loaded for bear. Its eighty-five miles and it's going to be cool in the morning, so I don't want to hear any bitching about how hot it is. I want full riot gear--Kevlar, lined helmets, and the trucks will have the armor on them going out. At the speeds you should be able to make, it's an hour and a half until you can hopefully stand down a little but we need to get a secure area set up as quickly as possible. I know we'll include chainsaws for this, but grab a couple of extras and I'll see if we can tow a Bobcat behind one of the five tons.

"Think about it as you drift off into the unmolested slumber of the pure in heart and mind so that you can wake up refreshed with inspiration from on high, or from higher up…I'm fine with either at this point."

"You turning in, Top?" Ramirez asked.

"Not yet, I need to sit down and think long term with Eric and Joel, I think. Together, those two are just a bit frightening. Twenty minutes, Kyle, get your guys to bed. It's gonna be an early morning."

"Good night, Top. Please don't wear yourself out. We're gonna need you. We know that, we want you to know that. We want you to know that we're glad you're here, First Sergeant. We'll keep this together, by working together with direction by our senior NCOs-- starting with you. Don't burn out on us because this is gonna suck for quite some time."

"Ramirez. Staff Sergeant Kyle Ramirez," at that he turned to face her, "Thank you. You need to know that I try, I honestly do. Those boys," she paused, "no, those men, you included, are my family. My husband couldn't take it, and he's gone. When he left, you were all still here. None of you judged me and I don't think that was out of fear. None of you treated me any differently because in your eyes I hadn't changed--I just had a bunch of stuff move out of my place."

"But what you just said is the first time it's been put into words that you guys need me and know it, and want me to know you know it. That it isn't all just fear and tradition and respect of rank. I appreciate that Ramirez, I really do. It's another one of those things that makes doing this all worthwhile--because that whole 'Army of One' bull that they were selling for a while is great for sociopaths and people who don't like people, but…."

Mallory stopped and shook her head for a second, then smiled.

"I promise I'll get some sleep, how's that?"

"Better than no promise at all, and a promise from you is golden so I know you'll get *some* sleep. See you in the morning."

On the way back into the conference room, Mallory brought in three battery-powered lanterns, as the squad room circuits weren't live yet. "I suggest we break for the evening and get up at 5:30. Breakfast is 5:45 and I'll have squads packing through the night so you can get on the road by 6:30. Any questions before we turn in?"

"Outside of petroleum products, is there anything here for plans for alternative electrical power generation?" Joel asked. Getting more Diesel might get difficult after an undetermined amount of time.

"Frankly, I'm not sure, but if anyone knows it'll be Sparky. I'll drop that on him right before I send him to bed, too. I'm going to need him fresh in the morning. Anything else let's discuss in the morning."

They said goodnights and headed to the squad bays, unlocked their doors, made minimal preparations for bed and were asleep within minutes; all but Joel, who was thinking up disaster after disaster.. He was still asleep rather quickly; he just didn't recognize the transition from thinking disasters to dreaming disasters.

Chapter Sixteen

Although the alarm that woke Joel up at 5:30 wasn't his own, and the horizon was only just beginning to turn pink, it was comforting to hear after the previous day of little to no technology but cars. He was initially surprised at how well he'd slept in the strange bunk bed, but after some quick math based on getting up entirely too early two days in a row, it made more sense.

"Rise and shine kids--you too, hon," Joel turned on the battery-powered lantern they'd used last night. "Breakfast in fifteen minutes and on the road by 6:30."

Just then there was a knock on the door. "Mr. Taylor, Mrs. Taylor, 5:30."

"Thank you, we're up. We'll be out in a few minutes," Joel said to the still closed door.

"Josh, they dump people out of bunks if they don't get up on time. I'd wager that's going to hurt from way up there." Rachael and Maya were already rolling out of bed, but Josh was exhibiting his typical morning back trouble; he couldn't get it off the mattress. "Let's go son."

"I'm coming. Remind me I never want to be in the Army. The toys are cool, but the hours stink."

They had all slept in their clothes, so it was a simple matter of putting on clean socks, pulling on shoes, and heading over to brush their teeth and splash some water on their faces. The girls ran brushes through their hair and pulled it back into pony tails in an effort to save time, and Joel cursed his dad under his breath for his sparse beard. He'd had to shave every day since he'd turned sixteen to keep from looking like a hipster poser.

On the way to the mess hall they met up with Eric, Karen, Chuck and Sheri--who were running just a few minutes ahead of them with no kids to chivvy out of bed. "I don't even remember my head hitting the pillow," Sheri said as they caught up. "I've heard that phrase before, over and over, but I've never actually said it and meant it. I turned out the lantern and I don't remember leaning back into bed."

"I hear ya," Chuck agreed. "I woke up in the middle of the night on top of the blankets and realized I'd just laid down on the bed and fallen asleep. Thank goodness it's June and there's no A/C. I caught a glimpse of myself in the mirror. I feel better than I look, though, believe me. A couple cups of coffee and I'll be good--at least until we get to the park."

"Well, I, for one, am looking forward to these green eggs I heard about my entire childhood." Rachael's dad was in the Army before he'd met her mom and had continually tried to disgust the kids with stories of field rations consisting of powdered eggs, undercooked bacon, burnt biscuits and the like.

"Sorry to disappoint you, ma'am," the Guardsman at the beginning of the breakfast line chimed in. "The eggs haven't been in the pan long enough to turn green and since we're using freshly frozen eggs, as opposed to powdered, they don't actually turn green on the edges like they used to."

"Oh well, I guess I'll live. I suppose the bacon's completely cooked too."

"I'm afraid so," he smiled. "An army moves on its stomach, and it's awful hard to do that if we're all confined to the latrine, ma'am."

"As much as I'd like to argue with that, I just can't," Rachael replied.

"Staff Sergeant Ramirez said he'd be at the same table you were at last night."

Joel thanked him as they moved down the line and had their plates filled. Once they had food, coffee, juice and the obligatory Diet Coke for Rachael, they made their way to 'their table' to meet Kyle.

"Sleep well, folks?" Kyle was about half way through breakfast already.

"Like a rock. How many more people are you expecting to bring in?" Chuck asked.

"When we've got everyone who mustered in with their families, we figured that we should have between six-hundred-and-seventy and seven-hundred-and-thirty people. That doesn't include the dogs, cats, birds, gerbils, rats, hamsters, guinea pigs, snakes, ferrets, two horses, three cows, twenty-seven chickens, two emu and a pot-bellied pig; all of which are classified as pets by their owners.

"Come November, if we're still 'camping', I'm thinking most of those rodents will have disappeared down the snakes, who will either end up in a stew pot or be fed to the ferrets. Emu is supposed to be pretty good eating too. I can't say I've ever had pot-bellied pig before but I can't think it's much different than any other kind of pig. At least the chickens lay eggs and the cows are the dairy variety.

"I know you brought in your dog too, and I don't begrudge you. She's been fine so far, and dogs and cats are at least fairly low maintenance, it's just that they're one more thing to keep track of and take care of, that's all. Frankly, I wish I had a dog of my own."

"How long have you been up Kyle?" Eric asked.

"'Bout an hour; couldn't sleep with all the noise. They've been loading trucks all night and with the families coming in it's been kinda noisy. I deliberately put you guys at the far end so you could get some sleep. I was fairly sure Top was going to make the decision to move out quick, like this morning, and I didn't want to have you folks interrupted all night."

"What's on the plate for today?" Coffee hit Chuck fairly quickly and he wanted to get back up to speed as quickly as he could. He felt bad for going to bed before everyone else.

"Aside from being out of here by 6:30, we're going be setting up an advance area which is just an assembly area which we will then transition into our main base of operations. I'm assuming that the plans are to make it fully operational within thirty days, but functional in seven to ten, and usable in two to five. We're un-assing the Armory Chuck--and we're doing it yesterday."

Kyle shook his head. "It's not official yet, and the only word we've had from higher up is the military equivalent of 'Your call is very important to us and will be taken in the order in which it was received'." He shifted in his chair.

"Sorry, folks. The official story is that the situation is *completely under control* and that there is no need to panic." He ruined it with the raised left eyebrow.

"Right, and aren't you supposed to say, 'I'm with the Government, and I'm here to help,' so we can say, 'We're glad you're here.' That way the lie can be complete. Who's panicking? Who said anything about panic? I distinctly recall the first, last, and only mention of panic right up until you said it was…you!" Karen was doing her best to cheer Kyle up.

"Right. Ok, so we're going to set up an advance area, we're going to prepare to egress the Armory--and yes, that's the military word for 'run away'--and then we're going to either wait for additional direction from higher authority or we're going to act on our own. That last part is still a bit fuzzy."

"Will it just be us as far as civilians going with you, or did anyone else in your squad bring in family last night that's coming with us?" Rachael was already taking her new assignment to heart and thinking of logistics concerning additional civilians.

"No to the first question, and a combination no and yes to the second question. I took the First Sergeant's order to get my boys in bed last night seriously. All told, we're bringing an additional forty-five civilians…I won't get into pets."

Kyle shook his head again. The pet situation was killing him. "It took until almost 3:30 this morning to get them all here but one thing about the Guard in general, and this group specifically, is the level of readiness of everyone involved. The husbands and wives of our unit took it in stride and when they showed up throughout the night, they didn't show up with the kids in tow and nothing to show for it--neither did you folks, so please don't think that's where I'm headed."

"Headed?" Joel asked, looking from Kyle to Eric and back again.

Eric shook his head and looked to Kyle for clarification.

Kyle shrugged, "We've got a little over a half an hour before we need leave," he said. "We can outfit everybody in a couple sets of BDUs, including you guys," he nodded to Josh and Maya, "including boots and dog tags from ready stores before we take off."

The group looked around the table for a few seconds until Kyle broke the silence. "We need to use them one way or another," he said.

. . .

"Sergeant Ramirez, front and center." First Sergeant Jensen called out.

"Sergeant Ramirez reporting, First Sergeant"

"Have you any questions about your mission or the parameters surrounding that mission, Sergeant?"

"No, First Sergeant. 2nd Platoon, 1st Squad is to secure and establish a forward advance area capable of transitioning into a fully operational forward command base within thirty days. We expect to be functional in seven to ten and usable in two to five. With no direct operable communications coming from higher, and a situation that we have every reason to believe will be unmaintainable within two weeks, we are planning and preparing for our own egress from the Armory, including all hardware, electronics, armor, weaponry, and systems."

"I would still like to register my formal protest to the operation's name. I think that operation 'Walkabout' would have been less depressing that operation 'Exodus'."

"Thank you, Sergeant, duly noted. If that is all, mount up and move out. I will expect radio contact from the TOC in no more than 180 minutes from now, by 09:30. Let's move it, people." At that three dozen diesel and gasoline engines roared to life and headed out of the Armory towards Highway 40.

. . .

The area where they had decided to set up was about three miles into the park off of I-40, and just on the other side of the road from Maples Lake, which would be their initial primary source of water--there had also been some rather detailed satellite information on file at the Armory. They were on a slight rise, which pleased the Guardsmen and would help a little with ventilation for the generators they had brought along.

Prior to leaving the Armory, they had determined they would forego any of the cabins that the park already had in place and go straight to camping. The same thinking that drove the decision to limit the size of the group that left the neighborhood had driven the decision here. They were already of one mind and a fairly single purpose so far, why muddy the water.

The M577 and 5-ton led the way and did any additional ground breaking necessary for the smaller vehicles simply due to weight and size. They would be enhancing the roadway so they could drive as necessary without getting stuck, but it had been nice at first to have the larger vehicles to crush the more reluctant vegetation into submission.

From the civilians' point of view, it was a good thing they'd decided to spend the night at the Armory as there was going to be far more work to prepare the area for use than they had realized. The forward party had stopped a couple of times and scouted ahead for a while and this was the best site they'd found, and they would still need to cut down a number of trees and do some pretty heavy duty "landscaping" to level out the ground. Since they had no idea how long they would be there, and no idea how many people would eventually be a part of the group, they were trying to compromise between immediate usability and future growth. If and when things got back to normal, the Tennessee Department of Parks and Recreation was gonna be so pissed.

From the Guard's point of view, having the civilians along was both a blessing and a curse. This unit had done this specific exercise twice in the last three years--and in this same type of environment--so they knew what they were doing. The guardsmen appreciated having the extra help since they were used to doing it all themselves; what they weren't used to was watching out for kids and animals at the same time.

They had done it once with and once without any heavy equipment, other than the vehicles they rode in on. In this case they had been able to tow in a Bobcat tractor. That was going to make some of the landscaping easier but there was still plenty of back-breaking manual labor that needed to be done. The general layout would put the communications and what would eventually be the civilian population at the center of the encampment, along with a portion of the military headquarters. The overall layout would be in a circle, as that minimized the amount of exposed surface and time to get from one side to the other.

They had communications established with the Armory by 8:45, which was actually a little earlier than Mallory had expected.

"The roads were almost completely deserted once we got out of the city proper, Top. We were able to make top speed for the 577 right up until we got off of I-40." Sergeant Ramirez was handling the reporting back to the Armory for the time being.

"That could be good or bad, Ramirez. How are the civvies at this point?" Mallory was still not entirely sure she'd made the right call when it came to sending the families along with the guardsmen.

Kyle paused for a few seconds before he replied, "Top, I can't say I disagree with the decision to send them along-- after all, Eric and his group were going to head out either way. They stopped by more as a courtesy to us than anything, after all.

"This mixed force for the guard's families is more than a little weird, though." Kyle said. "We've never done anything like this before and frankly, I think there's a reason for that; everybody's mind is in a dozen places right now. Having your family around does different things to the guys. I mean, I keep catching them looking in the mirrors in the trucks, or over their shoulders while they're unloading stuff."

"And I swear, the dogs are driving me nuts. I love 'em, I swear I do, but they are getting in the way and they don't all love each other the way we do."

"You're a smart guy, I'm sure you'll think of something. I know you only have a squad with you but I want someone monitoring the radio at all times. If it means things take longer so be it. Call in once an hour."

"Roger, I'll rotate everyone through. Promised Land, clear."

"Oh wonderful--this is what I get for not going with 'Walkabout'? Advance Area 'Promised Land'? Fine, Pharaoh out." Mallory laughed as she signed off.

"Oops. That's gonna bite me in the butt, I can feel it already," Kyle muttered to himself as he took off his headphones and stepped out of the communications tent.

"Wilson, you're in charge of the radio rotation. Her eminence, Pharaoh First Sergeant Jensen the First, has decreed that the magic box will be manned at all times and to report in hourly," Ramirez told Sergeant Wilson.

"I understood the part about the radio and the First Sergeant, and that's good enough for me. Why do you get her going like that by the way? You two siblings or secretly married or something?" Sergeant Wilson prodded.

"What can I say…"

Both Wilson and Ramirez finished the last half of the sentence together, "there's a reason you're/I'm still a Staff Sergeant." Laughing, Ramirez trotted off to make sure the rest of the squad was operating as the well-oiled machine he knew it was.

Shaking his head, Sergeant Mark Wilson ducked into the communications tent and sighed. "Thank goodness we have Sergeants like him and Top." He got briefed, relieved the Specialist who still had his headphones on, settled down in the chair, and proceeded to be bored for the next fifty-eight minutes until it was time to report in.

Chapter Seventeen

With only minimal use of the heavy equipment and chainsaws, they cleared enough area for all the vehicles in the advance expedition, plus room for a few more by 10:00 am. To do so, however, they had had to cut down seven very large trees and more were going to have to come down. Some of these trees were an absolute tragedy to waste, so Ramirez sought out Eric and Joel.

"Before I run something up the flagpole and see who salutes, I wanted to run it by you guys first. We're going to be cutting down a lot of trees over the next couple of weeks, and some of it looks to be prime timber. I hate to waste it by chopping it up for firewood or letting it rot. I'm thinking of suggesting some more permanent structures to higher,--sorry, First Sergeant Jensen."

"Any of the other squads have any Engineers?" Eric asked.

"Yeah, we have three Specialists who own an engineering firm in 5th Platoon, 1st Engineering Squad. That's who I was going to suggest we have come out to supplement us so it got done right. Problem is I know nothing about wood. It looks like good wood, but frankly I don't know if we could even use something right after we cut it down anyway."

"Well," Joel interjected, "I can help a little bit there. It isn't what I do but it's been an on again off again hobby of mine for years. Plus, I love the New Yankee Workshop. Norm Abrahms is the man! Anyway, you can use newly-felled wood for some things but it's going to shrink and crack as it dries, and some of it will warp. Some wood will obviously be better than others and it depends entirely on what you want to do with the wood."

"If you're planning on planking the wood, shrinkage and warping will be the biggest problem you face. If you want to build log cabin style buildings, shrinkage and cracking would be the big thing. Note that shrinkage will be an issue no matter what. Does the Armory have any milling equipment?"

"None that I know of. Shoot. Maybe this won't work. I just hate to clear cut acres of woods and not do something worthwhile with the lumber if at all possible. It didn't even occur to me until we were cutting it all down."

"Don't throw in the towel just yet there Kyle. Doesn't the U.S. Military have the ability to requisition supplies in a time of crisis? We passed how many 'Big Box' hardware stores on the way here this morning? For that matter there's a Northern Tool & Equipment in Madison and I know they sell portable sawmills. You can even get ones that clamp on to a chainsaw for the rough cuts."

"Joel, I'm starting to like you a whole awful lot." Kyle was smiling from ear to ear. "If you'll excuse me then, I believe I've got a call to make."

"Does he ever stop?" Joel asked.

"Stop what?" Eric replied, grinning.

"Well, I guess that actually answers my question, dunnit?"

"Let's get back to helping the ladies get the families situated. You know, having either wooden floors under the tents or even half walls would be really nice come the first rain. I was so busy thinking 'get out of Dodge just in case' that I didn't think everything through…you know?" Joel was looking up, trying to divine the weather for the next week from the three degrees of sky he could see.

Less than ten minutes later, Kyle tracked them down again to let Joel know he was going shopping. "Looks like you drew the short straw for finding one or more sawmills. Actually, there was only one straw and you were the only one doing the drawing. It felt kinda rigged if you ask me."

"Nice. They are usually sorta heavy though, I'll probably need someone to drive one of these monstrosities," Joel inclined his head towards their impromptu parking lot.

"Yup. You'll be going with KB--that'd be Sergeant Kevin Bowersock. As soon as the 5-ton is empty, the two of you will head up to Madison. Your point about the portable sawmill was well taken. Top said to get as many as you could, literally. She figured they would have at least one of the big band saw varieties and hoped for several of the chainsaw clamp-on type. Top likes New Yankee Workshop, too."

They were walking away from the main group, where Kyle had found Joel and Eric. "He'll be authorized to sign the requisition forms which I'll have ready by the time you take off. There's actually a list of things to get since you're going. No reason to waste a trip; and it's a big truck." At this point Ramirez--because Joel couldn't think of him as Kyle for some reason--looked almost uncomfortable.

"Mr. Taylor, how comfortable are you with handguns?" Ah, that's why, Joel thought to himself.

"Very. You apparently haven't looked in the Suburban. I've been around all kinds of firearms all my life. I'm as comfortable as can be, I would suspect. What handgun specifically are you asking about? Semi-automatic or revolver? Model 1911, like what you're wearing?"

"Yes sir, exactly like what I'm wearing as a matter of fact. How familiar are you with that?"

"Come with me if you would, and I can show you." Joel motioned to Kyle--as he felt like Kyle once again--to follow him to the Suburban.

He opened up the back and pulled out a locked case. From inside he pulled out another, smaller, locked case. From inside of that he pulled out his grandfather's Colt .45 Model 1911-A1 Semi-Automatic Government Issue sidearm. This one had been issued to his grandfather upon entering the European theatre during WWII and was documented as having been destroyed upon his exit of same.

As a matter of fact, his grandfather had been instructed to throw it onto the ground in front of a steamroller to become part of the base of a road on his way out of Germany. Like all good soldiers, he had responded with something along the lines of "Sir, yes sir!" or "Roger, out!" or some such, and proceeded to not only ignore the patently absurd order, but to bend down and pick up another one of the perfectly good side arms that had already been discarded.

This particular .45 was all original, including the barrel and recoil spring. It was Joel's pride and joy. It was the first firearm he'd ever owned or fired, having literally knocked him on his butt at the age of eight, and he loved to tell the story behind it. He was sure he would get the chance to tell Kyle at some point but instead he proved how comfortable he was by ejecting the magazine, clearing the chamber, locking the slide back, ensuring it was safe, and handing it to Kyle.

For his part, Kyle was impressed with how well Joel handled the weapon. That alone didn't necessarily mean anything but it certainly meant that it wasn't the first time Joel had picked it up. Then when Joel handed it to Kyle, he was forced to take note of the GI stamp on it. Upon closer inspection, he noticed the serial number. He set Joel's .45 down on the tailgate, removed his own--which also happened to be a Colt, otherwise he wouldn't have bothered--and proceeded to clear his own weapon and check his own serial number.

"Joel, how old is this?"

"Circa WWII. Actually, it was manufactured in 1936. It's an actual Colt too, not a Springfield or a Singer."

"How many rounds have you put through it?" Kyle asked as he put his own sidearm away.

"Me, personally? I've put probably 5,000 through it, myself. I should probably replace the barrel but I just can't bring myself to do it. It's original."

"Oooookaaaay. I guess I was worried about nothing then. I'll just be getting you a holster." Kyle shook his head. "Here I was all concerned about sending you out there, yes it's just day three, blah blah blah, but I was still concerned. If you've put that many rounds through it I assume you have a decent fifteen-meter score?"

"Yeah, seven rounds only leaves four holes in the paper and you can't see the X anymore."

"I swear I worry about the dumbest things. There's really no good reason other than continuity but you're wearing BDUs so let's keep the uniform complete. Let me get you that holster." Kyle returned his own weapon to his holster and trotted off to where some of the supplies were being sorted.

"Joel, that is probably the closest I have ever seen Kyle come to picking his jaw up off the floor. The whole silent treatment, no story behind it like you did with me, the whole thing. Very nicely done, man--way cool. He will want to know the story now too, by the way. He'll appreciate it. His grandfather was over there as well, so it means a lot to hear about it from other guys."

...

It was almost another hour before the 5-ton truck was done being unloaded, but true to his word, as soon as it was finished Joel and KB were on their way. Thirty seconds into the ride Joel had determined that the 5-ton was not designed to be driven empty for long periods of time over rough terrain.

"I can't imagine being in the back right now," Joel commented.

"I don't have to imagine and I am very glad to have this incredibly uncomfortable canvas seat. Those teak slats suck. So, how'd you get drafted for this? Top rig the straw draw?" KB asked.

"Sounds like she has a reputation for doing that. Yeah, I think that's what happened. I mentioned that I was pretty sure I knew where we could find a portable sawmill and I was a fan of the New Yankee Workshop. I think that sealed my fate."

"Oh yeah, you were doomed as soon as you opened your mouth. I don't mean that in a bad way, don't get me wrong. I think the world of Top. Lucky to have her. Any Platoon Sergeant or higher that doesn't rig the outcome their way isn't worth their salt either."

"Nope, Top, she's #1. What she says goes. Sure we've got the LT and the Cap'n, usually, but everything gets filtered through the First Sergeant and from there to the Platoon Sergeants and on down. If it got to us, it came through her and if it came through her it was worth making its way down. She won't let it through unless it needs to get through, know what I mean?"

"Yeah, I think I do. It actually makes a lot of sense. What I wouldn't have given to have a boss like that most of my career," Joel mused.

"Oh, don't get me wrong, there's plenty of active stupid that works its way around Top. I just meant the important stuff. And in my day job…don't get me started."

They were just turning onto the highway, and Joel was looking forward to a flat surface to drive on. "So, what else do they want us to pick up besides the portable sawmills?"

"Tools mostly, and concrete if they've got it, which I sure hope they will. I'm authorized to requisition whatever I feel is in the best interest of the U.S. Army and the U.S. Government and I've got a whole passel of forms I can leave with anyone who might be there. Assuming the lights eventually come back on--and I think they will--they'll even get paid for whatever we take, with interest.

…

When Joel and Kevin pulled into the parking lot they realized that they might actually have to wait in line. The parking lot was by no means crowded, but it wasn't deserted either. It was amazing how many stores were--if not exactly open as usual--at least populated and doing business of a sort.

It took Kevin almost five minutes to find an employee, although nobody in any form of management had shown up that day, apparently, and it was already nearing closing time. He explained three times, using smaller and smaller words each time, what he needed and would be doing. Finally, after it was made clear that whatever Sergeant Bowersock needed, Sergeant Bowersock was taking, in the name of the U.S. Army--and not just because some dude in fatigues wanted to take some stuff--things started to roll.

"I didn't want to have to kill him and put his dead body out front as a warning to others, I swear I didn't, but man it was a close thing there near the end!" Kevin shook his head as he neared the truck so they could move it around back and load their newly acquired items with the forklift.

Joel had stayed with the truck since the 60 was still mounted. Even though the ammunition was under lock and key, KB was still responsible for the rather expensive piece of hardware and had no intention of leaving it alone. He and Joel had swapped enough hunting stories on the way that he figured Joel could at least strike a menacing enough pose to keep people at bay; and if he heard a shot, he'd be back out before all eight rounds were fired...Joel had one in the pipe after all.

As luck would have it, there were five of the portable band-type sawmills in stock. They requisitioned a total of three, and all of replacement blades for the brand they were taking. They also got six more chainsaws, four dozen replacement chainsaw blades, ten clamp-on sawmills for the chainsaws, three dozen shovels, a dozen picks and a variety of saws, hammers, bolts, nails, screws and hinges. They had most of the hand tools already, but they also had more hands than they were used to. Having more tools meant getting some of the work done quicker.

"I really wish you guys had cement and cinder blocks." Joel told the clerk who was helping them get everything sorted out.

"I can't help you there, but I can help you with mixers. We just got a shipment of them in on Tuesday. If you get the premix, you'll at least be able to mix it."

"Outstanding. KB! Make sure we have room for a couple of cement mixers up there!" Joel shouted up to Kevin over the sound of some jerkoff squealing his tires in the road behind the store.

"Great! Super! Fabulous! I bet those will come in real handy once we get some CEMENT!" Kevin had really expected to find cement, but couldn't hold it against them. After all, they were a Tool and Supply store, not a hardware store.

Joel chuckled, "I'm fairly sure he doesn't hold you personally responsible. Then again, I've only known him for about two hours, so I'm not absolutely positive," he told the clerk.

"Wonderful. I survived almost being run over by a band of looters when I showed up first thing this morning, and being threatened at gunpoint by 'Peter the Great', or whatever he was calling himself, earlier this afternoon. As long as he only yells at me, I think I'll be ok."

"Wait, what happened this morning?" Kevin was all business now.

"Well, I showed up for work--actually I showed up to grab some stuff, but I'm not going to go into that, ok? Anyway, I see this huge caravan in the parking lot and they're trying to jimmy the gates open in back. They didn't break any of the windows out front; I guess they didn't want to attract any attention with broken glass.

"Everybody was still in their cars except for two guys from the first truck and when I yelled at them they jumped back into the truck and tried to run me down. The whole lot of them took off at that point, which I didn't understand since I was just one guy. I went back to my car for about a half-an-hour to make sure they didn't come back while I was inside by myself and then other folks--people I knew--started showing up and, well, it's kinda been business as usual, sorta."

"With maybe one possible exception, early this afternoon?" Kevin prompted.

"Actually, you guys make two exceptions, but yeah--I don't usually have a gun pointed at me around lunchtime. Some dude comes screeching in here in a sweet ride, fully restored Mustang. I don't know what year but it was smokin'. I don't usually go in for the Ford Yellow but this one looked nice. He hops out and he's got a pistol hanging halfway between his hip and his knee.

"This guy is so lit it's not funny. There's beer cans rolling around inside the car, and you can smell the hard liquor rolling off him in waves, and I sincerely doubt he'd been burning incense if you know what I mean. I honestly don't know how he hadn't wrapped himself around a telephone pole hours before, truly.

"But before I could smell the booze or see his bloodshot eyes, I made a smart remark about not shooting himself in the foot trying to draw that gun. Next thing I know I'm staring down the business end of whatever he was carrying--and it looked like Dirty Harry's .44 Mag--trying to just keep my mouth shut. I figured I'd said about all I'd needed to say and by then I could see he was so lit that nothing I could do or say at that point would do any good anyway." Steve, the clerk (based on his name badge), stopped for a few seconds and closed his eyes. A sheen of sweat had broken out on his forehead and he was visibly trying to calm himself down as he recalled the chain of events of a few hours ago. When he opened his eyes he was looking towards the parking lot...but seeing something that wasn't there.

"So this guy, Peter the Great is what he called himself later, says 'Dumb kid for having such a smart mouth,' then he put the barrel of the gun to my forehead," Steve closed his eyes again and took a deep breath.

"Steve, it's ok, I think we got it," Kevin said.

Steve went on like he hadn't heard KB say anything, but kept his eyes closed, "I closed my eyes, and he said 'Ask, no, *beg* Peter the Great to spare your life,' and then he pulled back the hammer. Does a .44 Magnum click three times when you pull back the hammer, Mr. KB?"

"You can call me Kevin; and it depends on the make, son, but yes, it can."

"Ok. Then I did the only thing I thought I *could* do. I begged for my life." Steve said. "I didn't move, but I begged that human shaped sack of crap for my life. I didn't grovel, but I begged, and after what felt like a month the barrel wasn't against my forehead anymore and I opened my eyes. Dick, I mean Peter, was standing there trying to get the gun back into his holster and once he'd succeeded he looked back up at me and said 'Yup, smart kid, just needs to learn to keep his mouth shut.' Then he walked into the store, grabbed who knows what and left."

"I stood there the entire time trying not to piss all over myself and hoping he would just leave. He took off about ten minutes later. I figured I could either go home and have a complete breakdown or try to hold it together for a couple more hours and be around to be of help to some people...and *then* go get very drunk."

Chapter Eighteen

KB shook his head. "Even New Orleans took three full days to begin to falling apart after Katrina. Ok, can you remember anything else about either the caravan this morning or this 'Peter the Great'? I need to let higher know about what's going on, and if there's already folks running around like they own the place, well…"

"I didn't get a real good look at the caravan folks but I remember that one of them had a birthmark on his face, um, the right side. He was a passenger in the truck. It looked like a footprint on his face."

"It just gets better and better. I guess we weren't the only ones to lie about where we were going," Joel said.

"Ok, I'm lost. What have I missed?" Kevin asked.

"It's a group we ran into yesterday morning," Joel said. "The guy with the birthmark's name is Earl, or at least that's what one of the other guys called him. They said they were headed south and instead they came due north. Of course, we lied about heading east because we didn't want to be anywhere near them. It's a little bit of a story but the long and short of it is that the two we met gave everyone, especially the women, the creeps."

"Ok, Steve, go on. Anything else about Pete?" KB asked.

"Not really, about 6 foot, sandy brown hair, stud earring in the left ear that looked like a lightning bolt. Pretty average really. Nothing really remarkable, sorry." Steve said.

"Nothing to apologize for. Remembering anything about him at all is more than most people would have done, especially under the circumstances. Let's finish up here, and head back. You going to be OK Steve, you have someone to go home to? You really need to not be alone for a couple days. Even roommates to get drunk with is better than being completely alone at this point." Kevin didn't want Steve to just freak out all by himself if he could help it.

"Yeah, I do. My girlfriend and I live together." Steve said. "I think I'll be OK."

"Well, I'm not your dad. I can't force you to do anything, but please trust me--today is going to stick with you for a while, a long while, so don't try to downplay it." KB said. "Don't let it rule your life, but don't underestimate the effect it's had on you either."

"I appreciate that, I really do. I'm sure I won't know how much for a while." Steve shook himself and looked at Kevin, "Ok, let's get the portable cement mixers loaded."

. . .

Once they got back on the road, Kevin called in to the Advance Area and reported to Sergeant Ramirez. "We don't really have much on this Peter the Great and we don't know anything about the folks Eric's group met yesterday other than that they weirded everyone out. We do know it's already hitting the fan, though. Over."

"Roger that. I'm going to pull in Chuck, Eric, Sheri, Karen, and Rachael. I want to talk to all of them again about that group from yesterday. Report in to Top and I'll debrief you and Joel when you get back, Ramirez out."

It took five minutes to get the First Sergeant on the radio back at the Armory, as apparently she felt the need to get some sleep at some point in each forty-eight hour period. "I'll have 1st Eng. bring a couple of 7-tons and pull-trailers when they pull out and have them make pit stops at the local big box stores. They usually have pallets of ready-mix cement and cinder blocks. I won't have them waste weight on actual bricks. What I wouldn't have given for an actual defensible position to begin with. How much of what we're doing is going to look like empire building and our own little land grab--which technically it is?"

There was a pause while Mallory looked over something on her end.

"1st Engineering won't be leaving until tomorrow afternoon at the earliest. You'll need time to finish at least minimally settling in and it doesn't make sense to have them plan on the fly when we still have facilities we can use here. You're going to have company tomorrow night, though. A little less than doubling what you've got now since almost everybody coming next is single or newly married. Far fewer dependents coming along this time.

"I need to coordinate back on this end. Call Ramirez back at--I'm gonna kill him for using that name over the air where people could hear it and start using it--'Promised Land', and let him know. Jensen, out."

"He is so screwed," KB chuckled. "She might calm down after she's gotten some sleep; then again, she just might start thinking clearly enough to come up with ways to really make him suffer. Wonder if she'll start calling him Moses?"

Kevin never got a chance to call back to the advance area, however, as the radio squawked just then. After authenticating, it turned out Ramirez needed to confirm a couple of things himself, first. "I need verification on the make, model, year, and color of 'Peter the Great's' car." Kyle said.

"We can verify, second hand, Ford, Mustang, Yellow. We cannot verify year however, as the closest we can come is fully restored and terms like 'pristine' and 'cherry'. Terms that would lead us to believe it was a vintage year and not recent." KB replied.

"Good copy, can you verify description and distinguishing marks?" Kyle asked.

"We can verify, second hand: approximately 6 foot, possibly a little taller, sandy blond hair, stud earring in the shape of a lightning bolt in left ear." KB said

"Roger that, I read you: approximately 6 foot, sandy blond hair, stud earring in left ear in the shape of a lightning bolt." Kyle responded

"Good copy." KB answered.

"This is 'Promised Land', hold one."

"What's going on, KB?" Joel asked.

KB shrugged. "Heck if I know, but it sounds like they've got some tentative ID on the guy and they want us to verify everything before they go any further with the ID process."

"Joel, this is Chuck. It sounds like they ran into Pete from the dam-- the guy who was going to high tail it to Oklahoma as soon as he could get home to his truck. The fact that he hasn't chosen to begin that little trip quite yet is possibly more than just a bit worrisome. Kyle wants to have a war council when you guys get back and start thinking of contingencies for when we run into these groups. We know about a couple now but heaven only knows how many more there are."

"Sounds like a plan, although I probably shouldn't say that. Plans up to this point haven't worked out all that well so far."

Chuck laughed, "See you in thirty, Promised Land, out."

By the time Joel and Kevin got back they'd been telling each other hunting stories for half an hour. One thing that both of them could respect about the other was that neither of them had had trophy walls at home. When pressed, they'd give details on the number of points this buck or that elk had but they'd both been staunch supporters of the "you can't eat antler" camp. You hunted to learn, and hone a skill, and to eat what you shot…not to brag.

As Kevin climbed down out of the truck he was met by Kyle. "Sergeant Ramirez, I have good news and bad news. Which of those would you prefer to hear first?" KB said.

"You can't even wait for debrief can you?" Ramirez said. "Great, good news first--I've learned to build myself up first and then go rushing straight down, kinda like a roller coaster."

"Outstanding. The good news is I think there's only one piece of bad news." KB replied.

Kyle shook his head. "Bowersock, you suck. Ok, go bad news."

"On the way back from Madison we were being followed." KB said. "I saw a yellow Mustang behind us at least a couple of times and the last time he was close enough to see us turn into the park."

"Wonderful. Security requirements--which were not inconsequential to begin with--just got doubled, at least." Kyle called over his radio to get some help unloading the truck and turned to Joel. "I need you and Eric to help supervise getting the mills set up. I don't know how quickly we can get some planks going, and I'm sure that the first things we turn out will end up as firewood, but at least we'll get some practice."

"Now," Kyle said, "I need to get Chuck and Sheri on the horn with Top to discuss this whole Pete business."

…

"Based on the story Steve from the hardware store told, Pete was about as lit as you can be and not be on fire." Mallory had pulled in two of her platoon leaders for this impromptu meeting and wanted to get some of the basic facts straight first. "Chuck, as his supervisor, did you know of any history of drug use? Wait, scratch that, never mind…don't answer that. Let's assume the power is coming back on in ten minutes and everything is going back to normal. I don't want you between a rock and a hard place legally. Sorry about that. Let me rephrase that; have either of you witnessed him using or high before?"

Chuck answered first, "No I haven't--not drugs. He's come to work hung over a couple of times. I don't recall that he's ever shown up drunk though. He's never been drunk on call either that I'm aware of. Sheri?"

"Not that I can think of. There've been plenty of times that he's 'just happened' to show up at a girls' night out, though. And there've been none too subtle attempts to hook up with me when he was plenty wasted--but never on the job. And no, I've never seen him do anything illegal, drug-wise. I've been offered enough…stuff…though, to know it's not hard to get around here--certainly not pot."

"Oh, I wasn't questioning availability. I've had to discipline more than I'd care to admit regarding that. No, I was just wondering what 'Mr. Great' was like. If this was part of his personality or if he's, shall we say, expanding his horizons. Hopefully he'll expand his perceptions to the point he embraces a telephone pole with his frontal lobe, but until then we have to deal with him." There was a sigh from the other end. "Ok, next question, did he hunt?"

Again, Chuck was the first to respond. "He did, yes, but he wasn't a lifelong hunter and he was the opposite of what a lot of the folks around here are. He was a 'shoot it and stuff it' kind of hunter. He wanted everyone to see how big a man he was for shooting a rabbit or a deer or a bear--as if--so he had near 'bout everything he shot stuffed. The first deer he shot, he didn't even get the count right. Bragging to everyone that he got a six-point buck--everyone looked at him like he'd lost his mind. Didn't know you counted all the points on both sides here in Tennessee.

"Sorry, where was I? Oh yeah…hunter, yes and no. Yes he hunts, no he's not a lifer, why?"

"I wanted to know how tight security needed to be around 'Promised Land' and yes, Ramirez, I'm still pissed." Mallory said. "Stupid name for an advance area. Point being if he were a long time hunter with finely honed skills we could be in worse trouble than if he's a drug using alcoholic who's going to come speeding in here and try to run us all over in his Mustang instead of snipe us from the tree line." There just weren't enough people for the security detail needed at that level yet.

"Change of topic, do you remember anything else about the group on the freeway from yesterday?"

"Nothing other than Earl was eyeing all us ladies, and the kids," Sheri replied. "I don't even remember most of what Eric said. I was busy deciding what to go for first, knee, groin, throat, or eyes."

"Chuck, you? Any impressions other than freakiness?" Mallory asked.

"I got the idea for the CBs from them, but that's about it. Earl seemed like he was looking for a fight, but his buddy kept trying to calm him down. That other guy kept playing dumb, too, even though he obviously wasn't. He was laying it on real thick too. The dumb hick was just too obvious. I don't know if he was trying to let us know he was smart and in charge and telling us to back off and leave them alone in his own way, or if he's overconfident or what."

"My concern is that they had one good idea, and that was it." Mallory said. "They didn't seem too coordinated this morning and although going in the back way might have seemed like a good idea, they fled when a single person showed up. They didn't respond with a gun, which, while good for us, shows that they don't necessarily have any long-term plans yet. That might make them desperate and in the long run that's bad for everyone. I don't like dealing with desperate people, ever."

Kyle was nodding as Mallory continued. "It's actually one of the cardinal rules of setting up an ambush. Unless you have a nuke and you are willing to use it, leave the enemy a way out and a means to recognize and use it. If they are well and truly trapped with no means of escape and no realistic chance of surrender, they have nothing to lose and you will be forced to kill them to a man as they will fight to the death out of sheer desperation.

"All right then, Chuck, Sheri, I have some purely military matters I need to discuss at this point, then." It was an obvious dismissal but still incredibly polite.

"Understood, no problem." Chuck held the tent flap for Sheri, and they were on their way.

"Ramirez, you've got a whopping ten guardsmen." Mallory was in logistics mode. "Yes, I planned on security; no I didn't plan on needing security yet. How does the barracks situation look so far?"

"Well, it looks like someone accidentally packed six whole barracks tents; don't know how that could have happened." Kyle was sure that Mallory could hear his smug, self-satisfied grin. At least he hadn't been idle after getting up so early. "So we've got more than we could fill right now. We don't have cots yet but those could come at any time. All the tents should be up within the hour including mess and latrines. Water is all set up and being reverse osmosised-- or whatever,--and the civilian park is completely set up."

"Ramirez, you are forgiven," she said.

"For what?" Kyle asked

"Don't push it." Mallory said.

"Right," he said

"In that case, I'm sending another squad out tonight." Mallory said. "It won't be the engineers I was planning on, I still want them to do some planning. I've actually got two short mortar sections I'm going to send, along with their families."

"I'm sending additional night vision and field security equipment as well."

"They'll have a place to sleep when they get here and we'll put them into the security detail rotation starting tonight. "

"Sounds like a plan. Good work Ramirez, keep it up."

"Roger, Ramirez, out."

"Wow, I think she really did forgive me," Kyle thought to himself. "Nah, musta been a slip of the tongue, not calling us 'Promised Land'."

Interlude Two

The initial plan, codename Dark Grid, involved taking the entire electrical grid down for as long as twelve hours, depending on the amount of notice that NASA had been able to give. The government also had a worst case scenario plan, which allowed for the power to be out for eighteen hours. In addition to both of those plans, the military also attempted to provide a "go to hell plan"--as in 'what are we going to do when it all goes to hell'. These were held in reserve for when Mr. Murphy made his inevitable appearance and even the worst case scenario plan failed to provide for all contingencies.

The government, traditionally, doesn't believe in "go to hell plans" as every contingency can be overcome if you throw enough money at it. Take for instance, uhm, the uh…well, I'm sure there's a good example out there somewhere. The CME of 2012, unfortunately, was not one of them; and as of 5:30pm EDT on Day One, the President and his staff were in the air trying to decide where, or even whether to land. When Day Two broke, the President was still in the air and his staff were still trying to decide where to land.

That they must land eventually was never really in question--the plane couldn't stay in the air indefinitely; but after refueling midair twice, they'd gotten a nasty surprise. Getting refueling planes in the air with full refueling tanks was rapidly becoming a problem. Couple that with the need to minimize the distance the refueling planes had to fly and coordinate the logistics surrounding keeping the plane airborne and suddenly they were in a sufficiently predictable flight pattern that they might as well land. From the limited reports they were receiving now, the entire northern hemisphere had gone dark. Assuming those reports were correct, and there was no reason to believe that any other country had been more prepared than the U.S. had been, the military threat to them was now virtually nonexistent.

Washington D.C. had become less than conducive to anyone's continued safety rather early on. Suffice it to say that word got out that a number of buildings in the Capital either still had power or had it again--nobody knew or cared which. By 2:00 pm, the President and all of the Cabinet that had been in Washington were evacuated from the White House and the Capital Building, and by 3:30 they were aboard Air Force One.

That was a good thing, as a mass riot on the Mall started at 3:41 and there were nowhere near enough law-enforcement officers to keep it under control. It was either the first riot of many over the course of the next week or it was the beginning of a week-long riot, nobody would ever be absolutely sure.

One thing that was known for sure was the time of the first fire. June 15, 4:19pm EDT: a garbage can was lit on fire and thrown through the front window of an interior decorating company. With all the draperies, pillows, fabric samples, stuffing, and cotton-poly blend materials in the showroom the entire place was engulfed in a matter of minutes, and the entire building, with the exception of the stone façade was completely gutted shortly thereafter. Nor was that the last fire in the Capital.

With no electricity to run the water pumps there was no water pressure. The pumper trucks had the ability to pull water directly from lakes and streams, and they did so when they saw a fire and could get to it in time, and there was water available. But that was the exception to the rule. Usually once a fire got started, it simply had to burn itself out.

There are people who just want to watch the world burn. On the downside, they got to get a little carried away in mid June. On the upside, they tend to get sloppy after awhile and get caught up in their own orchestrations and by the end of the week there were several fewer arsonists in the world--or at least Washington D.C.

Chapter Nineteen

The day after they'd been surprised behind the Northern Tool & Equipment, Clint decided enough was enough. The ragtag bunch that had decided to follow him out of his apartment building when the power went out needed direction in a big way. He kept thinking about the group that had stopped while they were changing the tire on the side of the road and how they had seemed to have their act together. The one guy had obviously been ex-military too.

Nah, he'd been former military and Clint was honest enough, with himself anyway, to admit the difference. Not everyone drew a distinction between the two--ex and former. For a lot of people they were the same thing, but for someone who'd received anything but an honorable discharge, well, they weren't. Former meant you'd left on your own, on good terms. Ex held the stigma that you'd been kicked out and told not to come back. Clint was ex-military, OTH or Other Than Honorable Discharge, and to top it off it had been after a very short time.

What had we been thinking, and why was I talking like that? I have a full set of teeth, I don't come from a family stick; they must have thought we were a bunch of inbred hillbilly rednecks waiting for all the tires to just explode. I must have taken my own advice to 'play dumb' too seriously.

Now things were a little different. They'd been trying to get into the back of the Northern Tool to avoid notice when that guy had shown up and he and Earl panicked and tried to run him down. That was on Saturday, June 16th. On Sunday he'd made the decision that he wasn't going to live like a beggar on the streets anymore.

Early Sunday morning, before the sun had quite come up, Clint grabbed Earl and two of the other large guys in the group. "Everybody else stay here. We should be back in about an hour or so. Stay quiet and just keep your heads down and everything will be fine." They left in the largest pick-up truck they had and headed back towards the tool store. They needed some bolt cutters and potentially some drills to get into where he wanted to go.

When they pulled up behind the store it was empty and Clint got out with the tire iron. He fed it through one of the links on the chain and twisted it until it was tight and then had Earl grab the other end. Together they kept twisting until the link broke. There, no more chain and the lock was still in place. Ten more seconds and the gate was open. They went inside and found a pair of bolt cutters, a DC powered electric fuel pump, fifty feet of non-static hose and nozzle, as well as a couple of battery powered drills and drill bit sets. The last thing he grabbed was a couple of hammers and a set of cold chisels.

The other guys grabbed flashlights, batteries, handfuls of Slim-Jim beef sticks, candy bars, and one of them had snagged an inverter and was dragging a 4.5 KW portable generator behind him. Clint hadn't gotten everything he'd wanted but that was ok; he was planning on being back later and taking his time to stock up. He'd be getting several more generators shortly.

On the way out he gave directions to Earl, who was driving, to head out towards the less desirable side of town where Clint had noticed a number of pawn shops the day before. First things first: they had a few guns but not nearly enough to arm everyone, and nowhere near enough of the same type or caliber. They needed to standardize and they needed to get ammunition. This was where they would do just that.

They drove past seven different pawn shops taking glances inside each one and trying to determine if someone was inside and what, if any, firearms there were to be had. On the third pass Clint decided on the second one they had passed and told Earl to pull over. Clint had the bolt cutters for the chain around the metal gate and a hammer for the glass window in the door. The other three all had handguns in case someone showed up to contest their entry.

It took about five seconds to cut the chain, which felt like a full two minutes to Clint as this was really stepping up the breaking and entering. When the handle didn't turn, he smashed the rubberized handle of the hammer through the window. Then he scraped the glass out of the way with the claw end of the hammer, reached in to unlatch the deadbolt and the door handle, and they were inside.

Clint really didn't have a desire to take everything in the shop, and was initially torn between being silent the entire time and speaking out in case someone might be hiding inside. He finally decided to say something. "I'm not here to take everything but I'm obviously here to take *some* things. I cut the chain as close to the lock as possible so that you can re-lock it after we leave. I made as small a hole in the window as possible for the same reason. I'm not a vandal, but I do have people I need to protect just as I'm sure you do--wherever you are. Understand that I'm only here to take what I need and I'll leave...which will include leaving you enough to protect yourself. I'm not trying to clean you out of anything, including the guns." *And I didn't even sound like a dumb hick from the backwaters of stupidville either!*

The guns were behind the counter and they were locked, which meant that Clint had to cut another cable. In this first store they ended up leaving with eighteen rifles of various makes, mainly Winchester and Remington, and five shotguns in a variety of gauges. They also made off with about 3000 rounds of ammunition. True to his word, though, they didn't come anywhere near cleaning the place out of rifles, shotguns, or ammo. They didn't touch the handguns or anything else in the store. They closed the door when they left and then looped the chain so that it at least appeared to be locked from the outside.

As he climbed into the truck and looked back at that first pawn shop something changed inside of Clint. He decided that he wasn't going to explain to the owner of the next two shops he planned on visiting if they happened to be there when he showed up. *They wouldn't hesitate to take it from me without explanation if they needed it, why should I be any different?"*

Their pattern with the next two was a little different as well; any rifle or pistol of the caliber that Clint designated went with them...period. The last pawn shop also had had a number of assault-style rifles. Clint made sure to grab all of those on the off chance that they could be of use in the future, as well as every round of ammunition available for them. By the time they were done with the three shops they had targeted they had accumulated ninety-seven hunting rifles, forty-two shotguns, twenty-nine handguns and thirteen assault-style rifles. They also had almost 40,000 rounds of ammunition. Clint was just getting started.

He had grabbed a phonebook from a phone booth outside of a convenience store and checked it for car dealerships the afternoon before. This was phase two. "Earl, you're driving again. Head to the CarMAX we passed back on Gallatin." While Earl drove he got two of the drills fitted with the carbide tipped bits and the bolt cutters ready. Both drills had been charging thanks to the inverter. Bolt cutters made quick work of the chain on the gate and they were in.

"The goal is to replace every car in our group with a truck or SUV," Clint said as he looked at the three who had come with him. "If there's enough, everyone who can drive gets a vehicle. Nothing smaller than 8 cylinder, 4WD is preferable and automatic is required. I don't want to get stuck somewhere because we ran out of people who don't know how to drive stick. .."

When all three men nodded, Clint went on. "I want tow-hitches on everything, immediate disqualification if it doesn't have a hitch. No exceptions." More nods. "Now, before we get started we have to get these lock boxes off without destroying the windows so I'm going to do something I've always wanted to do."

The something that had started changing inside of Clint on the way out of the first pawn shop had continued working its magic on the drive to the car lot. Clint walked over to a Jaguar XJ8 Vanden Plas 4 door sedan, took a batter's grip on the bolt cutters, and swung for the fences at the driver's-side window. It wasn't the most expensive car on the lot, not by a long shot, but it just *screamed* snob to Clint. *What in the world is a Plas anyway!?* Clint thought to himself.

The feel and sound of the shattering window was deeply satisfying; the sound of the car alarm, after three days of no technology but the cars themselves, scared him half to death.

"Dude!" Shane, one of the guys Clint had brought along as additional muscle this morning, yelled almost as soon as the window had finished shattering.

"Had to get the lock box off the window," Clint yelled back over the noise of the car alarm as he reached in and grabbed the box and then popped the hood.

It took a less than a minute to get all the wires to the battery completely cut and silence the alarm. *It's amazing how quickly you can silence those things when you aren't worried about moving the car afterwards,* Clint mused.

"Did you have to go after a Jag, man?" Frank, the other muscle, asked.

"Why not?" Clint replied, no remorse.

"Because there is a Civic *right next to it!*"

"What's the fun in that?" Clint asked. "Neither of them are of any use to us in their current state but frankly I can't think of anyone off the top of my head who's ever thought they were more important than I was who drove a Civic. This," Clint hit the fender with the bolt cutters, causing all three of the other men to wince, "well, how many times have you been cut off by one of these, huh? Tell me you weren't the least bit jealous it wasn't you swinging just now." Clint raised an eyebrow. When nobody spoke up, Clint shrugged, "Fine…moving on."

Clint had seen the key boxes open before but wasn't sure exactly where the locking mechanism was so he began methodically drilling on the box from the Jag until it opened. Now he knew where the mechanism was…Next! "Since there's only the four of us we can only take at most four trucks with us, and that's assuming we move all the guns. I want to take the keys for *all* of the vehicles we want though. It'll make getting them all that much quicker if we already have the boxes open and the keys in our possession when we come back."

It took almost half an hour to collect all the keys and be back on their way to the RV Park they'd been using for the last couple of days. Each of the vehicles had a little less than a quarter of a tank of gas so that there would be enough for test drives but that wasn't going to be enough for long. That was why Clint had gotten the DC fuel pump and hoses earlier in the day, and he'd be using them shortly.

The approach to the RV Park could have been dicey if they hadn't moved the CB into Clint's new truck but with notice, nobody panicked at the arrival of four new vehicles. With the additional space the SUVs and Crew Cabs provided it was a little easier to pack everything up, get everyone back to the car dealership, and get the remainder of the trucks that they wanted.

A ten-minute ride and the entire group were at the dealership picking vehicles. Two minutes later they were being questioned by the police. The problem centered on the fact that one car driving around inside a closed parking lot is suspicious, but not overly so. Thirteen cars driving around inside a closed parking lot plus almost twenty adults milling around cars that they don't own would make Tommy Chong suspicious.

And then a decision was made. The two police officers, as that's all that had showed up, couldn't help but notice that several members of the group they were questioning were armed. Not everyone looked to be intimately familiar with what they were carrying but there were a whole lot more of them than there were of the officers. The officers were single and had been doing their beats on their own out of a sense of duty, but with no coordinated or centralized management, for almost three days. For all they knew, these guys just might be some of the new law.

"So, are you all looking for a hand?" Officer Robert Cooper asked.

"Depends on just what you mean by that." Clint replied.

"Well, you look to be in charge of this here expedition and it does seem to be going smoothly. I don't know that bucking what appears to be the new system would be the wisest course of action for us at this point. You need some extra hands?"

"In that case, I think provisionally, yeah. You plan on bringing that along," Clint nodded to the cruiser, "or grabbing something here?"

"Personally, I'd rather get something here. Those seats are for the birds and I've got a bad back. Unless you want everyone to be able to pull something, there's a Beemer back there I'd love to grab. But if you prefer, I'll get the Escalade in the back row." Officer Anthony Roach replied.

"Me, I'm getting a 4X4 crew cab. I like the Midnight Blue F350 over there, if that's alright." Cooper said.

"Sounds like a plan," Clint said, slightly surprised but not alarmed at the ease with which the officers had switched allegiance. "Earl has the keys. He's the one with the birthmark on the right side of his face. Let him know you've seen the light, as it were, and to come see me if he has any questions. You going to bring along any of the gear from the car?"

"Absolutely. I'm not leaving that around for just anybody." Cooper replied.

"Good man."

As they were getting ready to leave, a thought struck Clint and he pulled Roach aside. "We have enough people to drive your Escalade back to where we were setting up camp for the night, but it might be helpful to have the cruiser with us for the next little bit as we go to get gas in all the vehicles."

"Wow, good point. We're down under a half a tank as it is. You already have a plan for that?"

"I do. Having a 'Police Escort' for it might keep people off our backs as well. Make it all look legitimate."

Cooper smirked. "Not a problem Mr.?"

"Clint. Just call me Clint."

...

Once everyone who could drive had a truck or SUV the next stop was a gas station, or in this case a truck stop on the outskirts of Madison. It took a few minutes to get the filler cap off the underground tank and another couple of minutes to snake the hose down, but within ten minutes they were filling up all the vehicles with 91-octane. Only the good stuff for this crew, at least to start. Like the pawn shops and the car dealership, the truck stop hadn't had anyone show up today either, so they made a run on the packaged food and the over-the-counter medicines always in such abundance at truck stops. They also outfitted all the new trucks with CB radios and antennas.

It took almost forty minutes to fill the nineteen trucks and SUVs that had met Clint's criteria. By the time they were done, Clint had decided it was time to be a little less visible with all the fairly new rides. They had been car camping at an RV park which had given Clint his final idea before heading out this morning and was the reason for getting only vehicles with tow hitches and big engines.

"Ok, everybody, I'll be in the lead and I don't want any questions once we get back on the road. From this point on it's an all or nuthin' deal. We've got decent rides, we have fuel, and we've got food. Now we're going to get places to sleep that we can take with us. I don't know what we're going to walk into, though, so I want everybody over eighteen armed."

He hadn't mentioned this last leg of the outing to anyone yet, so there were some looks flying back and forth--but nobody asked any questions. That was good, so far. "Grab something you are comfortable with from Earl, Shane, or Frank. They're going to make you load it, unload it, and safe it. If you can't do that, they are going to take it away from you and make you pick something else, aren't you boys?"

"After I hit 'em, durn straight!" Earl yelled.

"So pick something you actually know how to use and don't come crying to me if you get smacked. I want to get going in five minutes and I'd *really* like to do it without having any shots fired." Clint looked over at the two former officers, "Either of you ever hook up an RV?"

...

The Internet had been a wonderful thing; some people had even called it awesome. Unfortunately it had required electricity to run and an ISP to get online. The yellow pages, however, required neither and could *still* be just as awesome in a pinch. In Madison and the surrounding area there were seven RV rental and sales lots, and it took the convoy five tries to get lucky.

The first one appeared to be heavily defended by the owner, his family and friends, dogs, and a number of very obvious firearms. Just because Clint and company *had* weapons didn't mean he wanted to have to use them. The second lot was junk--either because it had already been picked over, because it had seen better days, or because that was what they trafficked in. The next two were mostly all-in-one RVs, fifth-wheels, or pop-ups. The fifth lot was a gold mine, though. They had over one-hundred trailers on site ranging from twenty-eight to thirty-four feet long. It was deserted. It hadn't been picked over.

There were no guard dogs to give them trouble and the sales office even had things like bedding and kitchen implements to outfit the trailers. It was, in a word, perfect. They even had extra ball mounts for the couple of trucks that only had receivers.

"Ok, folks, I don't want to be here forever but at least we don't stand out like we did at the truck stop. Let's take a little bit of time and pick one trailer per truck." Clint said to the group after they had all parked and closed the front gates. "I'm not dumb enough to think that everyone knows how to tow a 30' trailer but we should be able to get a bunch of these back to the RV Park without anybody rolling anything. We'll take it slow and make wide turns and then we'll let the people with some experience park 'em when we get back."

"I also understand that I have husbands driving one truck, and wives driving another, and in at least one case their sixteen year old son driving an SUV. Yes, I want a trailer hooked to all three vehicles. No, Aaron, as far as I know your parents are not going to let you live on your own." That brought a few laughs. "We need to get as much as we can while we can. If the opportunity somehow presents itself to get more trucks or SUVs and bring more trailers along, then even more will come with us. Let's not take any longer than we need to though." Clint had picked a white Dodge Ram 2500 SLT Turbo Diesel when they made the smash and grab for the trucks. It had been the only diesel on the lot and luckily it had more fuel than the other vehicles to start with. They were going to need to get another pump, because they couldn't use the same one for diesel and gasoline without fouling the regular engines. Now it was time to pick his new home.

For him, of course, only the best would do and he ended up picking a 32' Coachman Catalina with *all* the bells and whistles. The only thing it didn't have was a king size bed but that didn't really matter because he was single, 5' 7" and didn't move once he fell asleep. Of course the propane and water tanks were empty, but one thing at a time.

...

"Oh for the love of," Clint trailed off into a mutter. It was the middle of the afternoon and they had been at the RV lot for almost three hours. Clint had been staring at the bulk propane tank for ten minutes when it dawned on him that he didn't have to figure out how to *use* the refilling equipment to fill the tanks for the trailers.

"Earl! C'mere!"

It took several seconds for the bigger man to make his way over to where Clint was standing. "What's up, boss?"

"Grab a couple of guys with trucks, not SUVs but actual pickup trucks." Clint was still shaking his head. "I can't believe I didn't think of this before but just about all of the home improvement stores and a lot of grocery stores have self-serve propane tank exchanges now. You guys are going to serve yourselves."

"I'll go check for a phone book in the office," Earl said. "We'll probably need at least one actual crowbar too, instead of that flimsy thing we used this morning to snap the chain."

"Good point. I want to be back at the RV Park before it gets dark. We're all here so I want to stay together as a group. Safety in numbers and all that, so don't dawdle." Clint thought for a second and then continued, "Get more water, too, while you're out…as much as you can carry. You and five other trucks, I don't want all those propane tanks inside a vehicle."

"Gotcha, I'll get all the full tanks in the immediate area and all the water we can carry. We'll be back in no time." 'No time' ended up being a little over an hour and a half but since they all had CBs at least it wasn't a surprise. By the time Earl and his band of hunter gatherers returned with their booty all of the chosen trailers were hitched and the six set aside for the ones sent out to get propane were lined up waiting to be connected.

"Ok, I lied," Earl said when he got back. "I don't have all the full propane tanks in the area because we didn't have enough room. There were over fifty just at the first home improvement store we went to, it just took a long time to pry each of the doors open. It might be worthwhile to figure out a way to bring a bulk tank like this along too, or at least find and fill larger tanks."

"Well, you only had so much room. How much water did you get?" Clint asked.

"That's why we ran out of space. They had five-gallon water cooler jugs and we grabbed a bunch; forty of them, actually. They've got more, but we can go back once we drop off the trailers."

"I was just thinking we need some *trailer* trailers. Either way I want to get out of here, though. We can always come back, at least for a little while. I'm sure we aren't the only ones who've thought of this and if we want anything else we'll need to get it while the getting's good. You're the last one to get hooked up, so get a move on and let's get going."

Chapter Twenty

"Top, I changed my mind. Can't I please just burn it all down...please?" Ramirez wasn't really that tired yet, but he figured he'd better start the nagging clock early. It was, after all, only Sunday.

"No, for the umpteenth time, using the lumber is a good idea--deal with it." Mallory was so used to the routine she hardly gave it any thought.

"Me and my big mouth. Being this smart is such a burden sometimes."

"Can it, Ramirez."

"Right."

"Here's the deal, though," it was time for Mallory to throw Kyle a bone. "For the amount of space you are going to need to prepare, you do need something bigger than a Bobcat. There are a couple of heavy equipment rental places between here and there. The next group is coming out this morning and they will be making a pit stop."

Mallory could hear Kyle's eyebrows go up.

"I sent Jackson out yesterday and had him tack a notice on the door, so if anyone is checking on the place they should see it. He's tagged a front-end loader, two bulldozers and two backhoes. What ends up coming out will depend on what the drivers are comfortable with."

"I'll admit that will help. Can I at least thermite the stumps?"

"Fine, you can thermite the stumps--but you have to field expedient it, nothing from the ready stores!" Mallory chuckled. "You know, you're worse than a nagging wife and I know, I've been one!"

"Well, you know…"

"Don't say it or I swear you'll be a Corporal before you get to the word 'still'."

"Right."

Back to business, Mallory asked, "Do you have anyone with any over-the-road or wide-load experience?"

"Actually, yes, Garrett and Porter have both had summer jobs hauling, of all things, construction equipment." Kyle said. "They are both under Sergeant Wilson."

"In that case, have Sergeant Wilson, Garrett and Porter rendezvous at 09:30…"

…

The roads were fairly empty, and those few vehicles that were out and about stayed out of the way of the two Humvees. *Must be the 60s on top, go figure,* Wilson thought to himself. On the way back towards town for the rendezvous at the heavy equipment rental facility, Wilson noticed a number of trucks at one of the weigh stations. A quick count--very quick as they were doing about 60 MPH--looked like about three dozen rigs, including some tankers and refrigerated trucks. Interesting. Have to remember that.

As it was, they arrived at the heavy equipment lot just as the convoy from the Armory was pulling in. As Sergeant Wilson got out he saw Sergeant Halstead and nodded to himself. They'd really been pushing the egress of the Armory and he'd wondered how quickly they would be getting someone a little more senior out to the AA.

"Wilson, how are things going at Promised Land?" Halstead asked. He'd been itching to get out there himself and was happy to be on his way.

"Good, for most definitions of good. It's a forest. We're cutting down trees, putting up tents, and eating MREs. Good training, in other words." That elicited some grumbles and moans from the men around them but Halstead laughed and Wilson grinned. They all knew what 'Good Training' was a euphemism for.

"Top mentioned you have some guys with heavy equipment experience, at least hauling. Any idea which machines we should take for starters?"

...

While Garrett and Porter were getting things lined up for transport back to Promised Land he mentioned the weigh station full of semis to Halstead. "From a purely strategic point of view it would make sense to at least attempt to make contact with the group, and if possible get them to join up with us."

"Frankly, I don't like the idea of running around commandeering and appropriating whatever we think we need in the name of 'the greater good'. I'd personally much rather have people join us and bring those things with them but that's not up to me, or at least not entirely. Top isn't like that either, I know that, but like I said, I thought it was worth mentioning."

Halstead thought for a few seconds and motioned for one of the other Sergeants to come over. "Get the Armory on the horn; we need to talk to the First Sergeant soonest." To Wilson he said "I'm pretty sure I know how she's going to want to handle it but I want to be sure.

...

"Hmm, interesting, and it could go either way for us as we know absolutely zero about these folks, over." Mallory said.

"True. On the other hand, we do have CB capable radios and we can listen in and/or radio to them prior to approaching. It isn't like they haven't seen us driving by this morning, over." Halstead replied.

"Point. I don't want anyone going in uncovered though. If we send someone in, I want, let's see..." Mallory was thinking out loud, and both Wilson and Halstead knew that someone, actually a couple of some ones-- if not them specifically-- would be going to see the truckers stopped at the weigh station.

"I'll want two Humvees, I want the 60s loaded and hot, I want the gunners in the slings, and I want you two to be the ones to approach the group. Wilson, you noticed them so you deserve to be there, and Halstead, I need you there as you've got the seniority to make a command decision if someone wants to come in with you. Keep in mind we can't take them all right now though, over."

"Roger. We'll monitor channel nineteen and be scanning the rest going in so that we know what we're going into, obviously. Any idea how many we could bring back with us if any decide they want to come with, over." Halstead was still in charge of this end of the conversation.

"Negative, and you and I both know that Ramirez is going to be absolutely giddy at the prospect of as many as three dozen trucks needing parking spaces." Mallory snorted. "Serves him right, 'Promised Land', I'm gonna…never mind. Over."

"Good copy, we are officially never minding, over."

"Oh, don't you start too!" Mallory laughed. "Thanks, I needed that. Report back in once you've made contact with the group at the weigh station and you know their disposition. Over."

"Wilco, Halstead, out."

"Well, let's get rolling. The bulldozer is loaded and ready to head out, we should do the same."

Halstead took a minute to give orders to the crews that would be taking the equipment back to the AA and detail the Humvees that make the detour to the weigh station. Once they were sorted, they let the heavy equipment roll first and the Humvees that would be stopping took up the rear. They were capable of monitoring a half a dozen CB channels at a time so they were skipping around the dial while keeping an ear on 19.

There was a lot of chatter, which picked up as they approached the weigh station, and they knew they were being discussed specifically about a mile out. They dropped back behind the bulldozer and heard one driver comment, "We either need to meet up with some of the other groups of drivers out there or find out where all those Army trucks are going to and from--if only for our own protection. We can't sit out here forever."

Halstead and Wilson briefly discussed and then agreed that they should maintain radio silence on the CB channels so as not to tip their hand. Less than a minute later they pulled across the median to get into the weigh station on the other side of the freeway, as all of the trucks were on the 'outbound' side.

Once the Humvees came to a stop, Halstead and Wilson got out and walked towards the group of drivers headed their direction. The two gunners stayed aboard, although they pointed the M60s skyward. They were loaded and ready for action, however, should the situation justify it.

"Mornin' gentlemen," one of drivers said as they got closer.

Out of habit, Wilson looked over at Halstead and then behind him and then pointed at himself and said, "You must be using a rather loose interpretation of the term if you were referring to us, and you sure as heck don't mean the two still in the Hummers!"

"A man after my own heart...Timothy Grace," Tim shook hands with Halstead and Wilson. "This here's Alan Saunders," indicating the man to his left, "and Aaron Becker," the man to his right. "Now what a coincidence, we were just discussing how we needed to find another group of trucks or find out where in the world all you Army folks were headin' and here you come to find us. Imagine that." Tim had a twinkle in his eye as he made the comment.

Halstead had the good grace to blush slightly. "As it just so happened, one of our Sergeants noticed you all gathered here this morning and it got mentioned, and then it got discussed, and then it got thought about...you know how the Army works. And on the way in, as it just so happens--yeah, we were monitoring channel nineteen. Always helps to be prepared."

"Well, it's good to know you weren't coming in blind. I'll assume those things are loaded, too. I'd invite you in for a cup of coffee but I don't have any coffee and I don't think you'd take me up on it either way. What's on your minds, then, if we might be so bold?" So far, after brief hellos, Tim was doing all the talking.

"It occurred to us that you might not want to stick around here forever and we're setting up, well, not here. One of the things brought up was how many fuel and refrigerated trucks were parked here. There's reason to believe that the power outage is going to be a long term problem and, as such, things like diesel and unleaded fuel and refrigerated goods--while they last--would be useful and welcome, as would you folks." Halstead said

"I know how that sounds, or at least I think I do." Halstead continued. "That last little bit wasn't rehearsed because there wasn't any time, but even if there had been, I don't know that I'd have been any good at it anyway. I'm not full time and I haven't ever spent time in the sandbox 'pacifying' a city. Folks, we'd love to bring you guys with us, obviously because of what you've got with you--fuel and food--but just because I'm not full time Army doesn't mean that I don't take the oath for the Army seriously. We're setting up where we're setting up because, as I'm sure you know by now, it's probably going to get bad, and we've got to be in a position to take care of as many people as we can."

"We couldn't do that from the Armory in downtown Nashville, so we're setting up elsewhere. We don't want to get you guys to come with us and then kick you out once we have the diesel, that's not what we're doing. I'm sure there're groups out there wanting to do just that--and when I say I'm sure I mean I'm *actually* sure. There's even some moron running around calling himself 'Peter the Great'."

At the mention of Pete, Tim's jaw clenched. "Yeah, we've heard a little about old Pete. I think I'd like to get into a little fender bender with his little Mustang. It'd be a shame to utterly destroy such a fine piece of machinery but it'd be worth it to rid the world of his worthless hide."

"I'll just ask straight out, you folks have a group with you with a former Army fella' named Eric?" Tim asked.

Wilson barked a laugh before he could stop himself.

"I'll take that as a yes. In that case, and keep in mind I'm only speaking for me--I'm not a duly elected representative of this here little band--I'm following you on the way out if that's alright. I made my mind up a couple after they left the truck stop on Thursday that if I ran into him again I'd tag along with him if he was willing."

Halstead stepped in at this point, "Mr. Grace, Sergeant Wilson has apparently confirmed that Eric and the group you encountered Thursday afternoon are indeed with us, but he isn't in charge..."

"Oh, I'm sure of that, and call me Tim, please, but he wouldn't still be with you if you weren't worth sticking with, I'm also sure of that."

Alan spoke up, for the first time since introductions, and it was obvious why he'd let Tim do the talking. He had a slight stutter which was more pronounced around people he didn't know very well. "I'm with th'the other f'fuel tankers." Alan cursed under his breath. "If I say we go, we go. If Tim goes, we'll go."

"Tim, you're laying the humility on a little thick! You know good and well that anyone who doesn't roll out of here when you and Alan do is either asleep or having sex in their bunk and I guarantee that they'll finish quick when they hear us all leaving. There isn't anyone here that hasn't known you fifteen years or more. We're all sittin' here because of you." Aaron said.

"I'll need a list of how many total rigs you have here to make sure there's space ready for everybody." Halstead said.

"Not a problem," Aaron said. "We've also been hearing from a couple of other groups not too far out that would like to join up, and there are some relays going on between people with shortwave/CB combo units. Once you get set up you could get some more company fairly quick," he continued. "There're some neighborhoods that seem to be doing ok for now and might be ok for the long haul but Pete's not the only one out there raising a ruckus." Tim's jaw was clenching again. There was something more going on there than Pete and his delusions of grandeur.

"Based on what you've seen so far last night and today, do you think you'll be ok until tomorrow afternoon?" Halstead asked.

Tim looked at Alan and Aaron, both of whom nodded. "Yeah, I think so."

"My guess is that we'll be in touch fairly early tomorrow, then. I don't know if it will be one of us or someone from the Armory though."

"Sounds like a plan. Sergeant Halstead, is it?"

"That it is, Tim. Until tomorrow, then, hopefully."

They all shook hands again and everyone headed back to their vehicles. "Well, that certainly went well. Sounds like that was the guy who helped Eric pick out the CBs, too. Fancy that." Wilson said as they neared the Humvees.

"Certainly looks that way. I'll phone home and let Top know how this went; you go ahead and prep Ramirez to begin thinking about where to park thirty-four semis. I'm beginning to think we should have just taken over a small town. At this rate that's what we're going to be, and we're starting from scratch."

"Roger that. We're going to need another Reverse Osmosis Unit going pretty quick at this rate too. I'm glad the engineers took the extra day at the Armory. They came up with some pretty sweet field expedients for sanitation and plumbing."

...

"That's good to hear, for a number of reasons." Mallory said. "I'm glad about the people, the materials, and the fuel. Things are starting to break down around here already--which is almost unbelievable. There have already been two fires at night that we could see from the glow, if not the flames, and several more during the day."

"Oddly enough, there have only been a handful of, well, refugees for lack of a better term, coming to the Armory." Mallory continued. "I don't know how much longer that will last, though. The neighborhoods they came from are coming apart fast."

"Any word from higher yet?" Halstead asked.

"No direct or indirect orders and nothing countermanding our current course of action."

"Good copy, I read you, Lima Charley."

"I'm sure you do, Halstead. In fact, I'm absolutely certain that you do."

...

"Yeah, sure, things will go quicker with heavy equipment, but it's a matter of degrees." Kyle said to Wilson. "Anything is an improvement over how slow things were before. But a thousand-fold increase over a snail's pace is still pretty slow! Thirty-four tractor trailers by tomorrow night? At least Halstead had the presence of mind to have *you* tell me so I could swear," which he proceeded to do, profusely and with great relish.

"Fine, ok, one parking lot coming right up," Kyle sighed. "We should have the parking deck done by tonight and the elevator finished in the morning. Too bad Bun-Bun probably killed Dr. Schlock in this universe. Inflatable tech would really come in handy right now." Kyle was muttering now.

"Say again?" Wilson was lost now.

"Never mind, obscure geek web-comic reference. You'll probably never get to read it now unless someone's got a copy of 'Little Evils' lying around."

"Oookay, how about I act like I want to know at some later time?"

Kyle snorted, "Fair enough. How far out are you?"

"No more than five minutes from the exit, I assume the bulldozer's showed up already?"

"Roger, it should be off the trailer by the time you get here. They'll be going back for the backhoe within the hour. See you in ten."

"Wilson, out."

Chapter Twenty-One

Karen had been on the outside looking in as a civilian in a military man's life for the last four years--pretty much ever since she'd started dating Eric. Not that she'd ever had anything against the military, or guys in it; she'd just never dated anyone in any branch of the armed forces before. Then she'd met Eric, fallen head over heels in love, and ended up following him around the country. Truth be told, they'd only moved twice-- but still, she gave him crap whenever she could. That was her job after all.

They'd lived off base the entire time; which, while a bit odd, wasn't unheard of, and made the transition to a completely civilian life a little easier for Eric. It had also, unintentionally, kept a bit of a barrier between Karen and the other NCO's wives. The end result had been to make Karen work that much harder to be included in their circles, as it was important not only to Eric but to Eric's career. That experience was coming in handy again now.

"Rachael, I don't know that this has really ever been done before. We're breaking new ground here so we'll have to make the rules up as we go. Don't get hung up on 'how does the military do this' or 'what does the Army think of that'. Don't get me wrong, the Army is a *very* important part of the group here, but they are only about a fourth of the people here right now."

"We are determining how we're going to integrate everything together, and I think Mallory knew that when she put you, Sheri, and I together to start getting things set up. She knows my background and some of the things I've been through with Eric's postings. She knows that this isn't going to be a military base, and it isn't going to be a town--it's going to be something in between."

"Is it that obvious that's what I'm thinking? You know, I could probably get caught up in what already exists fairly easily." Rachael asked

"It'd be easy to fall into the same trap I did when Eric and I first met. It took me about six months to realize that I wasn't an Army wife because we weren't married, stupid as that sounds. It took me another six months to realize I wasn't an officer's wife, because Eric wasn't an officer--again, stupid as that sounds. Some time in there, I also realized there was this 'glass wall' between me and the other significant others, because we didn't live on base."

"Part of that was because Eric made enough that he wanted something nicer than base housing for us--for me. Part of that was because he wanted something more convenient to my job. Just before we moved, I clicked with a couple of the NCO wives. I'm not entirely sure how or why, but I did, and things started to gel. I was a person to them, I was real, I was a part of Eric's life, and I was someone that they would have to deal with, and that they wanted to interact with.

"Then I got to do it all over again. At least I didn't have the learning curve the second time and it only took a couple of months, which I'm pretty sure is normal for everyone."

"So, what are we going to do, Karen? How do we integrate these two completely different cultures? How do we create this thing that hasn't ever existed before?"

"Well, ok, I lied. If it hasn't existed before, something like it has, but not quite like this. But to answer the first question, look at it like this. Would you ever want a police officer living on your street? A good police officer, the quintessential officer of the law, the epitome of law enforcement, truly one of the good guys?" Karen asked.

"Um, I'm afraid this is a trick question, so I'm torn between answering truthfully with 'Yes' and lying and saying 'pineapple'," Rachael replied.

"Go with your gut, and good answers, both, though I'm not sure where pineapple came from--it can't hurt, especially if it's in season. Yes, you want a police officer on your street. How about, say, a couple of them on your street? Still sounds good, right?" Rachael nodded. "Ok, in a community with a militia--yes, I said a militia--

everyone is expected to muster in defense of the community. But even with a militia, there is still typically a standing Army, capital 'A'."

"In a community such as this," Karen spread her arms out and encompassed the general area, "you don't also, necessarily, have separate law enforcement. That can be the job of the Army, or a portion of it. It has to be spelled out legally, and recognized as such, but it has and can be done. Ever hear of the Roman Empire? Before its collapse, Rome had upwards of a million inhabitants and technically, no police force. If push came to shove, the Vigiles, who were more night watchmen and charged with watching out for fires, could call on the Praetorian Guard who were, you guessed it, a part of the Army."

"Ok, um, I'm not feeling better about this." Rachael was giving Karen the stink eye now.

"Oh, stop. I'm not saying we need to reinstate Imperial Rome!" Karen rolled her eyes. "Please, like I would stand for one second being a second-class citizen. Eric wouldn't even get to die in his sleep and he knows it. I said it hasn't existed quite like this. My point was that integrating a military and a civilian culture, having them live side by side, creating a new culture out of the two can be done. Regardless of what HBO would have had you think!"

Both of the women were laughing at that when Sheri walked up. "I have a feeling that either the ultimate good or supreme evil can come out of that. Do I get a peek?"

"Absolutely, but you can't be the virgin sacrifice. Sorry." Karen said.

"Shoot, one girls' night out too many. Oh well, more's the pity. So what's up?"

"We're recreating the Roman Empire but without all the gratuitous sex and pagan rituals--unless you want either or both. Come to think of it, they did have a decent sanitation system."

"Karen!" Rachael barked.

"Oh, all right! We were just discussing how we're going to integrate this group together into a functional community, and I was explaining how as far back as Imperial Rome, the military has been used for ad hoc police duty in a pinch."

"Ok, with you so far." Sheri nodded.

"Well, that's actually as far as we'd gotten," Rachael admitted.

"Ah, gotcha. So, it's certain feasible to have the Guard basically continue to be the guards." Sheri crinkled her brow into what the folks at work jokingly called her 'hound dog brow'. "So the problem is finding a happy medium, huh? Not everyone here is going to want to be in the military, and the military needs to maintain a certain amount of structure and strict discipline."

"She's a quick study. If Eric were here he'd ask you where you'd been all his life," Karen laughed. "Now if only we can come up with that happy medium, we'll be all set."

"Don't look at me," Sheri said. "I'm great at compromise so long as the give and take involves you giving me everything I want and you don't complain too loudly when I take something I decided not to ask for."

"And the problem with that is…?" Karen laughed. "I knew there was a good reason we got along! Seriously though, we all will have things to contribute to this, but I want to hear your take on this Rachael. Being married and a mom, I'm sure you've got some insight there that will be unique to our little command group here."

Rachael was gazing off into the distance as she thought about their situation, trying not to think about any one specific thing too deeply. It was a habit she'd developed in college when dealing with whatever big-picture problem had cropped up, either in class or in life. She'd found that if she focused on one aspect of the problem too much, it became all consuming, to the exclusion of all else, and the problem not only became insurmountable, but she simply lost sight of what she was supposed to be solving in the first place.

"What are we trying to do here then?" Rachael asked.

"Um, hello, earth to Rachael. Remember all the people running around with the pretty green and brown and black splotchy clothes, and the living side-by-side with people without the splotchy clothes we've been talking about?" Karen was squinting at Rachael now.

Still gazing at nothing, Rachael replied "That isn't what I mean, and I think you know it. What are we truly trying to accomplish? Are we trying to create a new kind of society? Are we planning on the electricity never coming back on like it used to be? Are we planning on the central government failing, and if not permanently then for a long time--as in a generation? Are we just trying to survive until someone bigger, stronger, more prepared, or just plain meaner comes along and tells us what to do?"

"What is the real point of this exercise? Do we plan on linking up with other groups eventually, and if so, what does 'eventually' mean? This is an awfully big country ladies." Rachael's gaze was back to Karen and Sheri, from wherever it had been. "We are a tiny, miniscule part of it. We haven't been thrown back into the Stone Age either; we've simply been cut off from the central supply of power and communication."

"Communication is already on the way back. We prove that every time we radio the Armory. How long will centralized power be out? I have no idea. Sheri, you can shed some light on that one. But it won't be forever, I'm sure. A lot will change before it comes back on, I'm sure of that too--but come back on it will, have no doubt."

"So, again, what is it we are really trying to do? 'Integrate the civilians with the Guard' is what we came up with, but that's not what Mallory asked us to do. She asked if we could take a concept and general instructions and flesh them out and make them work. She asked if we could be civilian analogs, and there's a reason I didn't say equivalents, to Sergeants under her."

"Karen, I think you were more right than you knew when you first said that this had never been done before, because it hasn't, not really. Yes, the Romans used the military for police work and guard duty. Now that I think about it, Knights would have probably served a similar role in England in the 13th and 14th centuries. They lived among the people as well, although they were nobility, and that system had its own flaws."

"I'm certain it's not an insurmountable problem, and I'm just as certain that it isn't what Mallory set us out to tackle. I have my suspicions, but I'm not certain, as to why she only put us on this, too.

It's not as though we're the only ones who are qualified to set up this new world order--if in fact that's what we're going to do."

Sheri looked at Rachael sideways for a few seconds before she said anything but was still the first to respond, "You, ma'am, are a little frightening. You just get all clinical and detached and matter of fact, like you're discussing some totally theoretical problem from an external objective viewpoint. That's just scary. No offense, I mean, we need that right now, I love you like a sister, but you're kind of a weird sister now." She grinned to try to take any sting out of the last comment.

"You know Sheri, Mallory said something very similar about Joel that night at the Armory, too," Karen replied.

"No offense taken, honest. I think it's one of the reasons Joel and I fit so well together. There are some things that either of us can step back and do that with. Neither of us can do it with the same subject, though, so at least we complement each other that way. The last thing we need is a bunch of people sitting around contemplating their navels while the world comes unraveled."

"Well, the first thing we need to do, I think, is determine how long this is going to last. In your opinion, Sheri, what is the soonest that the grid could be back up, assuming the worst?" Karen asked.

"It's not that simple, unfortunately. 'The grid' isn't an 'it', it's a, well, it's a bunch of its. Wow, my high school English teacher just turned over in her grave, assuming she's dead. There's so many pieces of the grid that are interconnected that have all been affected by this that, well, where to begin?" Sheri took a drink from her bottled water and went on. "Ok, start big and work down. I'll keep it limited to the U.S., even though we are tied in to the power distribution systems of both Mexico and Canada, which could theoretically keep us from getting things back online sooner.

"The big high capacity lines you see running along the freeway in the middle of nowhere, let's start there. Those lines are technically what did us in, or at least where it started. It's possible to take electrical current and convert it to a radio wave, obviously--that's how we get radio signals. What is just as glaringly obvious to an electrical engineer but not to most people is the inverse, you must be able to convert a radio wave back into power, or electricity." Sheri could see the 'aha' moment happen for both Karen and Rachael at the exact same time. This was a discussion she'd had more than once, and it never ceased to amaze her when people had their moment.

"Now, again, what most people don't know, or know and don't 'realize' is that the earth gives off a magnetic field that can be--and sometimes is-- converted into electricity. For example, if you run a suspended ½ inch diameter steel cable a long enough distance, say a half a mile, and you don't ground it before you connect each end to what you are terminating it to, and one device is grounded, there's a good chance that the arc of built up electricity will not only burn out whatever you are connecting it to, but that it'll kill you."

"That current is always being built up and bled off in the Extra High Voltage lines all across the country. In short, what happened is that because of the event on Thursday, that Geomagnetically Induced Current, which is the technical term for that electricity that magically appears on the wire, was upwards of eight times what the equipment on the ends of those lines were ever intended to handle."

"Eventually, the lines would have actually melted and broken, as passing current through them generates heat and the lines themselves were never designed to hold that much current. But before that could happen, the little guys, the power sub-stations and even the power plants, well, they shorted out. At the dam, we had two main gauges that I watched, among other responsibilities. The analog needle actually went to 200%, and it was buried. But there was a digital gauge that read 812% right before the power went out."

Sheri let that sink in for a few seconds before she went on. "Because of the nature of the spike, there was a dip of about 85%, which really caused everything to freak out. Because everything happened so fast, the spike was able to back feed through the substation, or at least our substation, and blew out two turbines in the dam. That's the damage that was done to the power plant, our power plant. Coal fired power plants, I'm sure, have suffered the same fate, as have nuclear power plants, but NO, don't look like that, there hasn't been a melt down!"

"A nuclear power plant uses steam to generate power you two! Nuclear power plants are even more redundant than ours was. Those are actually designed with an automatic secondary and tertiary power system and a completely isolated and manually engaged quaternary system. Push come to shove, they go into a room and literally start a generator practically by hand, and throw switches to get power back on to the plant to go into a controlled shutdown, and that's assuming that the power was out for more than six seconds to the control rod motor. I won't go into it but if the power went out, the reactions stopped. Game over."

"There's some cooling that still has to happen, and those folks would still have gotten their generators working to get the pumps going to get the water cooled off, they know their jobs. But we're getting a little far afield. Big surge burns out turbines at the power plants, regardless of the source of the motive power for those turbines. The next piece is the step up or step down transformer."

"The transformers are huge, they weigh tons, and when they go, they go big. I've actually seen one that blew up, and you'll notice I didn't use air quotes when I said that. The one I saw had a manufacturing defect that allowed for a small problem to get big, but it would have happened eventually anyway. It literally exploded like a 500 lb. bomb. It destroyed a large portion of the power substation, tore out power lines, took smaller transformers out, and resulted in power being out for an area with 2900 people for three weeks."

"They aren't field repairable and they aren't something that the power companies keep many of in stock. In fact, at last count, the really big ones…there were thirteen spares in the US and three in Canada, and they aren't necessarily interchangeable." Sheri had to chuckle at the look on Karen's and Rachael's faces. "Oh just wait, it gets better. Lead time on these things on the world market, assuming the factory or factories that make them has power," Sheri giggled, "is at least twelve months."

"No, seriously?" Karen whispered.

"I kid you not, and it isn't just anyone who can install them either. Assuming that we can find all thirteen of the spares, and that we get them installed as necessary, and we get the power plants back online so they can build more, AND we find the guys who can install them, AND we keep them busy installing them and teaching new people how to install them, *ten* years minimum. That's also assuming we close the borders and tell the rest of the northern hemisphere to go pound sand if they come calling looking for help. Like I said, Mexico has power plants and a grid too. So does Canada. They didn't have nearly as many spares as we did. Mexico actually didn't have any on the books."

"But that isn't all. There are substations as well, which are also step-down transformers, and there are tens of thousands of those nationwide. There are spares for those, but again, not for all of them, and they aren't field repairable, they have to be replaced. They are about half as large as the ones on the Extra High Voltage lines, which means they are still multi-ton devices, and lead time is still a year to get them built. And finally, there are the transformers on the poles out front of every two to three houses, or underground. Those might just be powering up the choir invisible and need to be replaced as well. Those, they have thousands of spares for, which is good, as there are hundreds of thousands of them across the country-- probably more like millions. It could be twenty-five or thirty years before we get back a grid anything like what we were used to, possibly even longer."

"Ok, so what do we know? The power is out generally for a long time. If we are successful, others will hear about it and will want to be a part of it because it is successful and stable. We will grow. The more we grow, the more the basics that we put in place will be stretched and something more will be needed to take its place. We're looking at a living document to be governed by. Hmm, where have we seen one of those before?" Karen crossed her arms and tapped her right thumb on her pursed lips.

"Question is, or I guess questions are, do we want to start with the US Constitution? If so, do we want to monkey with it? If so, *how* do we want to monkey with it? Are any pieces sacred and should never to be touched? Do we expand the 2nd Amendment? Do we prohibit smoking or drugs? Do we force the legal definition of marriage? Do we neuter the Supreme Court? Do we impose term limits in congress? I'm not saying yes or no to any of these things, I'm simply bringing them up."

"Well, let's see how much we can wade through before lunch. I do have a laptop that wasn't connected when the spike hit and I happen to have a copy of the entire constitution and amendments in a document. Let's pull it up and take a look…"

Chapter Twenty-Two

"Sergeant Ramirez reporting to Sgt Halstead as requested." Ramirez ducked into Halstead's tent.

"Come in, sit down." Halstead gestured at the chair behind Ramirez.

Ramirez sat down. "We have the parking situation completed and ready for both the group at the weigh station and the entire compliment from the Armory."

Halstead's eyebrows rose, "Already?" He glanced at his watch, "its 11:52; the only thing that needed to be ready today was parking for the semis and we weren't even planning on leaving until 15:00. Keep this up and you're gonna make Sergeant First Class." The comment was designed to get Ramirez's goat, they both knew he didn't want SFC.

"I'll be sure to be a tad late next time, Sergeant Halstead."

"You and I both know that would be a phenomenally bad idea, Sergeant Ramirez. I'll let Sergeant Jensen know you are ready far ahead of schedule, not just for the weigh station group but for all the vehicles at the Armory. How are we doing for barracks?"

"About 80% Armory personnel and family capacity. We will need to clear a little more land to meet full capacity but we should be done by Tuesday night."

"How are we set for water and power?"

"We have two more ROWPUs set up, one online, the other as a backup, ready to go in a matter of twenty minutes. We have a total of 2 MW generating capacity here at 'Promised Land' but our current draw is less than 3 KW so the majority of the generators are offline at present."

"Outstanding, thank you, Ramirez." Halstead said. "I know Top will be glad to hear about the prep for the egress as well. I think we'll probably end up heading out a little early for the weigh station group. Between you, me, and the fencepost, we're probably going to need a whole lot more room eventually, too. There's a lot of chatter on citizen band right now about the fact that the power still isn't back on, and now people are really starting to freak out about the radio and cell phones not working."

"Everything is second-hand so far, but that doesn't mean we should discount it." Halstead continued. "As things continue to come apart, I think we're going to start getting more and more folks looking for a port in the coming storm. That's going to be us--at least for some of them--and all those people will need a place to stay. Top is already thinking about that, and we aren't going to be some big charity case's wet dream, but not everyone is going to be able to jump in with both feet right away either."

"Understood. I've basically been operating under that assumption ever since I heard about the raiding party at the hardware store. I know Top won't just turn people away either, not unless they're the utterly worthless variety, in which case we'd all make them feel real uncomfortable and mostly unwelcome anyway." Ramirez's smile lit up his face, but never touched his eyes.

"Well, keep that 'planning ahead' under your hat, or you're going to find yourself in a desk job," Halstead said, again mostly joking. "Again, good job. Dismissed."

…

The same two Humvees that had been sent to meet with the group at the weigh station were sent to bring any who wanted to come with the Armory group in. They didn't go alone this time, however, as they would be escorting back over thirty semis. In addition to another day, the sunrise brought with it another caravan from the Armory, including a dozen Humvees, a half dozen Light Attack Vehicles, or LAVs, and a number of cargo vehicles. A number of the Humvees and all the LAVs were accompanying the original two Humvees to the weigh station.

Halstead and Wilson were in the lead vehicles, and before they were in sight of the group they made sure to make contact and let them know that more than two vehicles would be showing up. The last thing they wanted to do was spook somebody with a deer rifle. As they pulled into the weigh station, Wilson radioed to Halstead, "Looks like the same number of trucks, but it doesn't look like all the same trucks. I couldn't tell you which ones are different though. You catch that?"

"I was just thinking the same thing," Halstead replied. "It'll be the first thing I ask Tim when we stop. Good eye though."

Once they were parked, a little closer than last time but not too close, they walked halfway to meet a larger group of drivers. Halstead opened, "Afternoon, Tim, looks like you've got a few different folks with you today, who changed?"

Tim, to his credit, blushed a little. "Well, we weren't trying to pull a fast one on you. A couple of folks decided they wanted to head back home. One fella was from Memphis and another was from Little Rock. I don't know how he's gonna get diesel, but that's not my problem. A couple more wanted to head for elsewhere, too. I can understand wanting to get home. Everyone else here is either single or a team, so home is their rig."

"We figured that since thirty-four was the number we gave you yesterday, it'd be ok if we replaced 'em with folks we knew who'd cropped up recently. Overall, I think the trades were pretty good. We ended up replacing a half empty truck of tanning beds with a mostly full auto-parts truck. We also picked up another propane tanker, and if there're any kids where we're going, I think they'll be happy with the last acquisition."

"And that would be?" Halstead prompted when it became obvious that Tim wasn't going to offer until asked.

"We got a McDonald's truck. It's even got Happy Meal toys--not that they're really worth much, but they'll break the monotony for five minutes before they break." Tim was obviously pleased with himself. "I'll admit we deliberately hid it in the middle because it sticks out like a sore thumb. You can't miss it. We also pulled an inventory from everyone. If you'll still have us, we're all ready to pull out now." Tim handed over a sheaf of papers which proved to be the manifests from each of the drivers.

Halstead looked over a few of the invoices at random and then handed them to Wilson. "In that case, let's get this show on the road. The one thing we ask, although we can't enforce it, is that you not broadcast the destination yet. We're not asking for radio silence or anything like that, but we are requesting that you not broadcast where we're going for the time being. It'll be public knowledge soon enough, I'm sure."

"Fair enough. I'll make the formal request, as it were, once we all get saddled up, and, Sergeant Halstead, thank you. We all appreciate this."

"You're welcome, Tim. It's all in a day's work, but you're welcome."

Chapter Twenty-Three

Wilson took a few minutes to organize the invoices by type of vehicle and inventory, and put together a parking list which he radioed to the AA. The truckers didn't maintain radio silence by any stretch of the imagination, but unless there was some incredibly inventive and complex code being used, they also weren't trying to tell anyone where they were going.

The side road that had originally been crushed into existence by the Army vehicles and then re-graded once they'd gotten the bulldozer wasn't exactly 'smooth', but it was smooth enough; and the truckers who'd previously been to the park were impressed with the road that hadn't been there a week before. After about a mile, as the road didn't lead straight into the encampment, they pulled into the new parking lot.

Ramirez had outdone himself with the parking, as he had with everything else so far. There were a total of sixty-five parking spots for semis with up to 53' trailers, including a turn-around area. There were fifty spots for smaller military vehicles, like the Humvees and LAVs. There were one-hundred and fifty spots for larger military vehicles, like the 5 and 7 tons, and the towed artillery, and there were over five-hundred civilian-vehicle-sized parking spots. There were even parking lines on the ground. All of that had been done, in addition to everything else in the encampment, in three days.

Tim had to say something over the air about the parking lot, "I've been driving for almost twenty years, and I've been in dives and established truck stops from Chicago to Dallas, from San Francisco to New York. I have to say, this is a a far cry above many, and the equal of most. My compliments to the crew who put this lot together and especially on what had to be short notice."

There was a chorus of 'Amen' and 'You said it' when he was done. Ramirez, to his credit, who was in fact listening, kept his finger off the transmit button and his mouth shut. After all, he did feel a certain completely understandable sense of pride as his boys *had* done a pretty amazing job.

It still took almost twenty minutes to get everyone into what were essentially assigned parking spaces. They didn't want all the fuel trucks next to each other, for obvious tactical reasons--some habits were hard to break. And based on the invoices that had been handed over to Halstead at the beginning, they had decided to put some of the trucks closer to the camp than others simply to ease unloading.

By the time they were finished parking, word had gotten around that the trucks had arrived and Eric had made his way over to where Tim was talking to Sergeant Halstead. Tim noticed Eric after a few seconds and held out his hand. "Good to see you again, Eric. How's the Op-Sec training coming?"

"Nice, thanks, really appreciate that," Eric laughed. "How're things going with you?"

"Well, good, I think. Looks like things are shaping up nicely here. Just so you know, Eric, you were part of the decision to fall in with this crowd. One of the deciding factors was whether or not you were here--for me at least. I wanted to get that out in the open first thing. I don't know if anyone had mentioned that from yesterday's conversation or not, but I wanted to make sure you knew."

Eric nodded, "I'd heard that my name was mentioned. I appreciate that, especially since you really didn't have a whole lot to go on at the time. I understand the owner, Frank, closed down the truck stop on Saturday? How'd everybody make out when he ran everyone off?"

Tim grimaced a bit before he answered and made like he wanted to spit, "That's where most of this bunch came from. We were up to about sixty trucks by then, and I think ol' Frank was getting nervous with all of us just sitting there, though for the life of me I can't imagine why. He knew almost all of us by name, and has for years. Laurie pretty much had him pegged with 'skinflint' and 'prick' though."

"A couple of them were heading out to family, using either CBs or shortwave radios to keep in touch. A couple of folks wanted to stay put, though they had to be 'off the property', and Laurie came with us. She's been on again-off again with one of the other drivers, and it wasn't no big surprise that they got back together when Frank kicked us all out and closed the store."

"I really hope everybody does ok. They all seemed like good folks when we were there on Friday."

"That they are, and I think they'll probably be fine. They've all got folks they can turn to and band together with, just like we do now; I think they'll be ok."

"So, where in the world did you find a Golden-Arches truck? I mean, what are the odds?"

"Better than you'd think, actually. Those places go through a *lot* of food. I can't say for sure how much, but I'd be surprised if they didn't get deliveries of one thing or another every couple of days. That one is just about plumb full, too. Even though it's a refrigerated truck, there's a pallet of toys on the back end for Happy Meals as well, which we figured might break the monotony for some of the littler kids as they roll in. At least for a little bit."

Eric saw Rachael and Sheri walking up and took that as his signal to leave, "Well, it looks like the official welcoming committee has arrived. I'll hang around to make introductions as necessary, but I think you're probably going to be busy for the next little while getting settled in. Good to see you again, Tim," they shook hands just as the women walked up, "Ladies, you all remember Mr. Grace …"

…

"Ok, so we've grown, we're going to continue growing, and we're going to need to worry about feeding more for an unknown amount of time. The refrigerator trucks are going to help in a number of ways, but they don't actually produce food. Talk to me people." Mallory had what she was coming to think of as her think tank, which included her platoon Sergeants, Eric, Karen, Joel, Rachael, Chuck, and Sheri in what she assumed was the command tent. Having the group split like this was already getting old.

"Two things--getting food and keeping food," Joel answered. "You mentioned the trailers, and that's great for keeping it cold, but refrigerated and even frozen food only keeps for so long. We're going to need to can or preserve whatever we get somehow. I'm assuming that none of those trailers out there can do deep freeze, which could keep almost indefinitely. We're also going to have to build at least some structures to hold the food, as we won't be able to rely on the trailers forever. Plus, having a building with three or four of the trailer units working together would be more efficient and provide redundancy should a unit fail."

"Rachael, you're keeping him well fed? Making sure he gets enough sleep at night, every other Saturday off? I need him healthy; I can't afford to have him break!" Everyone could hear the smile in Mallory's voice and Joel was blushing slightly, but Rachael was beaming. She loved the fact that Joel had embraced his role as 'big-picture man' and was running with it.

"Oh yes, he even gets laid once in a while." Rachael said. Now Joel was turning bright red, and trying to look nonchalant, which just drew more attention to the fact that he was giving himself a second degree burn on the face...from the inside.

"Excellent. Anything you need Rach, you let me know." Mallory replied.

"You mentioned getting the food first. Explain that if you would please."

"Well, there are a number of places that we can get food. We are less than a week into this problem, and you are *the* military force in the area. Like it or not many existing food warehouses, suppliers ,or retailers would be happy to hand over their food supplies to you and make distribution your problem. That is not a problem you want to have, however. That, of course, assumes that the owners and managers of those supplies are even still in control of the supplies."

"It is possible that some supplies have been taken over by various groups who are incapable of or unwilling to manage it and will simply destroy it for lack of ability. People will die due to their inability to maintain the food supply and distribute it efficiently. If someone were to come in and 'liberate' it, leaving a certain amount for a new manager to be in charge of, but take the rest, well, there are Costco, Sam's Club, Wal-Mart, and Super Target stores all over within forty miles of here.

"And that's just getting the easy food in the short term. All of which could be gone, depending on how many people we get into the base, how hard they are working, what we can supplement with hunting and home gardens, in as little as three months. If we are able to get some really good refrigeration and freezing shelters together and make some massive runs on some of the big-box stores--again assuming there is something left to run on--I'm thinking we could conceivably put up almost a year's supply, though.

"But you have to think about things like milk; will it be powdered or fresh? We only have two cows so far. Eggs, very few chickens--and they need crushed oyster or clam shells in their feed to make decent eggshells. Ducks, if you like rich eggs. Fresh beef, chicken, or pork?"

"Now we step back and look at the big picture. We are surrounded by arable land that is being actively farmed, right now, even with the power out today. We need to approach those farmers, carefully, gently; find out what they need and what we can offer them. We need to build a relationship with them, including a work swap with them. If they need additional labor to get a certain amount of their harvest in or planted, or whatever done in a fixed amount of time, we cut a deal. Bread needs flour, salads need vegetables, etc, etc, etc. They may know someone with an orchard who knows someone with a dairy herd who knows someone with more chickens than they can coop."

"We just need to find slightly newer, slightly older, or just plain different ways of doing things that get the same job done. And frankly, with less and less people playing 'Blow up the Space Zombie Rocket Scientist Rock Star' for nine hours a day, so what if something takes a little longer to get done than it used to? We have a whole lot more hands and hours to get it done with."

"Hold that thought, Joel," Mallory said and opened an additional radio channel to the communications tent. "Delta Two, this is Alpha Six, over."

"Alpha Six, this is Delta Two, go ahead."

"Has there been any traffic from any of the farmers or the ranches in the area recently? Over."

"Roger Six, a little chatter, nothing major. Some seems to be routine, some to be expected related to 'the CME'... We have it recorded; would you like a dump to your device, Top? Over."

"Negative Two, I'd like to listen to it in a few with 15klic, over."

"Roger that, I'll have it set up and ready when you call, over."

"Six out."

"What's a 15klic?" Joel asked.

"Not what, who," Mallory replied, "we call you 15klic as you're the one with the 15 kilometer, or about 50,000 foot view, of the situation. I want to listen in on their CB chatter with you and see what they're talking about and if it can give us any clues on how to approach them and what they might need."

Chapter Twenty-Four

"Frankly, Mr. Tripp, Ms. Gharity, we're of two minds about the whole situation. We know we aren't fully self-sufficient right now, and we don't have a lot of the skills we might need in the long run, but we're not out in the cold either. One of the guys we keep in touch with has two-hundred and fifty acres of soybeans, for example, which works out to a little over 12,000 gallons of biodiesel every year.

"Now, I know that some of that has to go back into the plant to do the extraction and all, but when all's said and done we'll have enough to run the generators and tractors a fair amount, and all the land is irrigated from wells run on solar or those generators. We haven't relied solely on municipal power for a long time out here."

Randy Carlisle, the farmer they were meeting with, held up his hand when Eric looked like he was going to interrupt. "Hold on, I said we were of two minds. I'm just explaining. I'm not being rude, I promise, but I'm gonna finish, too." At Eric's nod he went on, "Alright then, there're a fair number of us around, and like you said, we do have more work than we can handle by ourselves. Folks seem to be staying home for the time being, which doesn't get much work done."

"Weeds still grow, machinery still breaks and needs to be fixed, plants need to be thinned out, and we're gonna have a harvest here eventually. Harvey's got a dairy herd that needs milking twice a day and he's literally going to kill himself, his family, or half his herd trying to keep it up by himself--and there is only so much milk the rest of us can drink and cheese he can put up. Cameron and Bill both have commercial egg ranches and are used to getting rid of tens of thousands of eggs a week. Paul is pretty lucky as he recently had a major slaughter and his pig herd is fairly small, comparatively; he's down to 3,000 head."

"My point is, well, I guess I already said it. We're of two minds. We've got a lot, but we don't actually need all that we have. Add in the fact that we're awful spread out for being as close knit a bunch as we are. We worry about each other. We can come to each other's aid in a crisis if we need to--we've got the CB's—but..." Randy stopped, realizing he was really going into too much detail about how many people there were and where. Everything seemed to be going well, but right now it was just him sitting here, and he needed to watch it.

"And to top it all off, we overheard some of the exchange over the CB yesterday between you and that group of semis. That seemed to go smoothly, and you all appeared to handle it well. There weren't any suddenly cut off transmissions or calls for help or anything. No distress calls, although it's only been a day, and I guess that doesn't technically mean anything--not that I'm implying anything either."

"Ok, I guess I'm done; I'll shut up now and let you go back to making your case. I've probably given too much away about our situation as it is," Randy grinned. "Wife always did say I talked too much for my own good. God rest her soul." "No, sir, I don't think you did, and there isn't much more I can say other than what I already have. If anything I think I've probably tipped *our* hand. I'm serious about what I said at the beginning though, we aren't here to 'appropriate' anything. The phrase most of us have taken to using is 'The lights will come back on eventually', and when they do, well, the First Sergeant, Sergeant Jensen, she doesn't want to have to apologize for or defend anything she or those under her command have done."

"I think the right thing to do, for all involved, would be to set up a working, equitable relationship where we can trade goods for labor, at the very least. We are looking to get power back up, slowly but surely, and that will include to the surrounding area. We'd like to include communication in that, and anyone we were working with would obviously be high on the list to get wired. I don't say that as an incentive or a threat, though, just a fact that should be weighed when making the decision.

"I'll be honest, we didn't expect to walk away from here with half a dozen trucks loaded up with supplies--which would be why we didn't come with half a dozen empty trucks," they all three laughed, "and I do appreciate your candor, because I think the last thing we need right now is people jerking each other around. If you can talk with everyone else you've been keeping in contact with and everyone can give it an honest, open chance, I think we can come to an agreement that will work for everyone."

"That much, Mr. Tripp, I'm willing to do."

They shook hands as they stood up, "I'll be in touch as quick as I can, and for what it's worth, I appreciate the lack of strong-arm tactics. Some folks don't realize that while they might look like they're working on the surface, they almost always backfire in the end."

"Mr. Carlisle, while I'm not in the Army anymore, I've been in a long time and in the position of needing to convince people to do what I thought was the right thing for too long not to have learned that lesson," Eric smiled. "We'll manage, one way or another, even if it means cutting down acres of that park and turning it into farmland, we'll manage."

"I believe you will, but I don't think it'll come to that."

…

"So, gentlemen, we are going to begin working for our daily bread," Sergeant Stewart said to the assembled Staff Sergeants. "No more of this lollygagging and laying about."

"Thank you, I was getting so bored," Kyle said half under his breath, with a hick drawl.

"Can it, Ramirez," Mallory said over the intercom.

How'd she know it was me? he thought to himself.

"I'm that good," Mallory said out loud.

"Right." Ramirez muttered.

"Top, all yours," Stewart said.

"Thank you, Sergeant Stewart. As you heard, we will be rotating through some of the farms and a couple of the ranches. Eric and Karen acted as my liaison with the representatives of the farmers and we've come to what we all feel is a very equitable agreement. There is one dairy, one pig ranch, one chicken farm, and a number of vegetable farms that we will be assisting with. Your initial assignment will be to identify those that may have any prior experience in any of these areas, and I do mean *any* prior experience."

"Of special importance, as in they will leave as *soon* as you identify anyone, as in I want them sent one at a time if necessary, is anyone with dairy herd and milking experience. Outside of that, shifts will start the day after tomorrow and will be squad in size, based around someone with prior experience wherever possible. I'm not going to gut the base, but we need to keep food on the table."

"We've already had two additional civilian groups radio in on the citizen band, one of which is going to be larger than the group of trucks we brought in. Assuming we allow them in, we're going to put them to work fairly quickly, both in the rotation at the farms and ranches and here at the AA--which I assume is going to start looking more like a town. I say that because I don't want anyone to start thinking that we're going to be doing all the work while the civvies get all the benefit. They'll be pulling their own weight, and I want that passed on down the line. I'm not going to keep you here any longer than necessary, though, because I'm serious about that skills inventory. If anyone already knows for sure about the dairy experience, talk to Sergeant Stewart now. Dismissed."

SergeantRamirez walked up to Sergeant Stewart as everyone filed out of the command tent, not that it was much of a tent with the walls rolled up during the heat of the day. "I already know the answer to one of Top's questions."

Stewart looked at Ramirez and just barely kept from slapping his forehead. "Crap, that's right. Grab the headset."

Once Mallory was back on the radio Ramirez started, "Top, we need to talk."

"I need to warn you, Ramirez, I don't handle break-ups real well," Mallory replied without missing a beat.

Ramirez did, in fact, miss a beat. If he'd been walking he probably would have stumbled, "Sorry, say again?"

"You said 'we need to talk'. Isn't that the girl's line when she's going to dump a guy?"

"Top, you know I'd never dump you! You'd kick my ass!" Ramirez had recovered a bit of his equilibrium. He wasn't used to Top being a smart-ass…that was his job.

"Exactly my point, anyway you were saying."

"Well," Kyle let out a noisy 'horse-lips' breath, "my aunt and uncle owned a dairy and I spent summers there growing up. I had hoped I'd never, *ever* have to do that again but needs must when the devil gives you lemons, or whatever."

"Great, not only have you threatened to dump me, you've gone and made a liar out of me too. I can't send you immediately because I need you to go through your squad first. Let me guess, this is yet another of the many, many reasons that you…" they were both laughing as they finished the phrase together.

…

"Would anyone care to hazard a guess as to the name of this particular beast?" Harvey Litton asked the three men from the base.

"It wouldn't be, by chance, 'Cow', just like the previous however freaking many there've been," said one of the two guardsmen that had accompanied Kyle.

"At least we used some imagination when we named them all 'Leather' back home," said the other.

"Knock it off, you two," Ramirez snapped, "Go on, Mr. Litton."

"Nah, we're just about done. I'm just being difficult now. You guys have obviously done this before. The next milking is in two hours. I can't tell you how much of a relief it is just to have some additional hands to help out, even if I'd had to train you from scratch. Once you've done this, even if you've done it by hand, you know the basics. It'll come back pretty quick, and heaven knows we needed the help."

"So, what do you need us to do first? You mentioned we've got a couple hours before the next milking. Is all the equipment working ok, anything needing repair, everything sanitized and ready for the next shift?"

"Actually, everything's ok for now, we haven't had any problems with any of the equipment recently and everything was serviced about a month ago. If you guys would like to start by going around and making sure you don't have any questions about the machinery, I think that would be a good place to start."

"Fair enough, you heard the man, move out." Kyle barked.

…

"Stupid, fat, ugly, smelly, can't even use you for steak, manure factory."

"That would be 'milk factory' Perkins," Ramirez corrected, "and if push comes to shove, you can in fact use them for steak, but it's far more likely that we would make hamburger as we can stretch that with filler. Other than that, nothing you said was incorrect--they are stupid, fat, fairly ugly, and they do usually stink, although how you can tell over your own foul stench right now is beyond me."

"However, I believe the problem has nothing to do with the cow, and everything to do with the fact that you haven't turned on the milking machine. It helps to have the vacuum running when you put the teat-cup on the teat son," Kyle said as he reached over and hit the 'On' switch.

"Sorry Sergeant, no excuse."

"Don't stress it. You do stink, though."

"Roger that, and I think the only reason I can smell her over myself is my nose is three inches away from, OH MAN!" Both Ramirez and Perkins had to jump back to keep from being, 'christened', as it were.

"Careful, I think she heard you. She was just reminding you that female cows are ladies too, and don't forget, they don't fart--they get the vapors." Kyle was having a hard time keeping a straight face, but he'd been crapped on by more cows during milking than he cared to remember.

"Thanks, I'll try to keep that in mind. Half a dozen more and I can start thinking about a shower," Perkins mused.

With the three guardsmen, including Ramirez, with experience identified, the immediacy at the Dairy had been lessened. Squads were being shuffled a bit based on who had what prior experience. Within the next couple of days they would be rotating people through what had been dubbed 'The Co-op', and would include about a third civilians in the mix. Ramirez himself had two civilians in the group at the Dairy right now who had at least worked with cows, although not with the automated milking equipment. So far, everyone was doing ok, and like he'd told Perkins just now, there really hadn't been any problems that time doing the job wouldn't fix.

It helped that everyone understood, and not just at an intellectual level, that food didn't come from the grocery store, it was stored there; which may very well be the root of the word in the first place. Nobody was slacking off, and the civilians who would be out working on the farms and ranches would all be volunteers.

With the immediate crisis over at the dairy, Kyle now had to get back to the base and make sure it was ready to receive the remainder of the troops from the Armory.

…

By early Wednesday afternoon, there was officially 15% more capacity than needed to empty the Armory, and the final call was made by Sergeant Stewart, who had accompanied the last group out on Tuesday. There were still one-hundred and sixteen people left, guardsmen and families, including the First Sergeant who was technically a part of Fifth Platoon, First Headquarters Unit.

"Attention all Nashville US Army National Guard Units still at location Romeo, this is Alpha Six." Mallory had agonized over what to say and how to say it when the time came for the last convoy to leave the Armory. Now that the time had come, she was going to wing it. "Location Romeo is now closed. All units are to proceed to forward base 'Papa Lima', Alpha Six out," she was *not* going to call it Promised Land! It had, however, graduated from Advance Area to Forward Base status.

With those few words, the final vehicles began rolling out from the Nashville Armory, loaded literally to the running boards. Mallory had decided that she didn't want to waste the time or the resources on empty vehicles for a return trip, so each truck, track, Humvee, and Jeep was loaded as full as it could be on the way out. They had ended up shuttling drivers simply because there were more vehicles than people qualified to drive them, but a few extra trips for a Humvee or two were acceptable.

They had stripped everything usable and portable from the Armory, but were forced to leave too much behind, in her opinion. They locked as much up as they could, knowing that if things went on as long as it looked like they were going to, it wouldn't be enough. The kitchen was virtually fully intact, though they had managed to pull out one oven and one stove. Almost the entire vehicle maintenance bay was left in place, minus tools and any parts they could carry.

Office furniture had been left, as well as most of the furniture for the squad bays, but the bunk beds had been disassembled and the mattresses shipped out. You don't leave a bed behind if you can help it. God gave you a padded butt so you could sit just about anywhere and be reasonably comfortable for a short period of time. He also gave us mattresses so we could be reasonably comfortable when we slept. You thank him for the food, and then show your gratitude by not turning your nose up at a bed, especially when you were going to be living in a tent!

And then there'd been the ordinance and heavy weaponry, which didn't necessarily go together. There were towed howitzer field guns and mortars that Mallory was not going to leave behind, even if it had meant leaving the beds. God would understand. They didn't have munitions for them, but that didn't mean that someone else didn't, or couldn't find some. For that matter Mallory knew exactly where to get it; they just hadn't gotten to that stage of the plans yet.

Then there were all of the personal weapons, rifles, handguns, bayonets, boot knives, tazers (yes, they had tazers), night sticks and the like, and all the ammunition that goes along with all of those firearms. Cases and cases and cases of ammunition, on pallet after pallet--literally tons of it. Small amounts of high explosive, C4, Willie Pete (White Phosphorous)--none of which would be left behind, period.

Ordering the egress out of the Armory had been as close to an exercise in futility as Mallory had ever experienced. It seemed that every time she began to get one thing under control or wrapped up, another area came completely unglued. What needed to be moved out to the AA first, and how quickly could it be moved out? Was the

AA ready? If we move too much at first, do we leave the Armory vulnerable?

There was some radio chatter as everyone pulled out of the Armory in single file, every vehicle mounting either a .50 or an M60, loaded and manned. So far there hadn't been a single incident reported by any Armory convoy meeting with any resistance or dealing with any problems along the way, but there was an SOP for a reason, and it didn't cost anything to follow it and be prepared just in case.

It was almost an hour and a half to the new base, and she would be coming up with questions with no real answers the entire time. She really needed to sit down face to face with some people, instead of over the radio, and hash some things out. It had been less than a week, but it felt like much longer, and she hoped that Karen, Rachael and Sheri had been able to put some time into the task she'd set them to. She also hoped that Joel had been using that frightening intellect of his to not only come up with worst case scenarios, but hopefully some solutions, or at least workarounds.

Chapter Twenty-Five

She knew that Ramirez had been holding back, not in a bad way, but not really 'being all that he could be', as it were. He was an excellent Staff Sergeant, probably one of the best she'd ever worked with, and she liked him on a personal level as well. She knew that he was capable of motivating his men and practically working miracles, sometimes with a crew of some of the biggest screw-ups she'd ever seen--but this was impressive even for him.

Some things in life you simply took for granted and a decent place to park was one of them. She'd heard the reports about not only the parking lot, but the AA, and then the base, and run them through her personal filter, as she usually did for things that got reported up the chain of command. Things got embellished, good and bad, every step of the way, and the more amazing the individual was made out to be, the bigger a dirt bag they probably were--or vice versa.

She'd figured, based on the reports, that the base and everything that went along with it would be nice. Better than usable, because Ramirez wasn't a slouch and he'd be living here too after all; but it wouldn't be, couldn't be, as nice as everyone was making it out to be. If the parking lot was any indication, she was about to be pleasantly surprised. "I can't believe I'm getting the warm fuzzies because of a freaking parking lot. " Mallory muttered to herself.

"I'm sorry, First Sergeant, I missed that," her driver said, ,wondering if he'd missed something important.

"Nothing, really, just chastising myself. Nice lot, huh?"

"Looks like it. I'd heard Sergeant Ramirez outdid himself on it, but then I've also heard the entire base is pretty well squared away too."

"Certainly looks that way. Let's get parked and see what home's going to look like for the foreseeable future, shall we, son?"

"Roger that, Top."

They were being directed to their assigned space, which actually had a "6" on the ground, in what looked like toilet paper. Mallory was trying to decide if she was offended by the fact that Ramirez had used toilet paper to designate her parking space or pleased that he'd used something that could be cleaned up afterwards so as not to identify where her Humvee was parked. Probably pleased. At least there wasn't a sign on a post.

Halstead and Jackson met her at the lot to escort her into the base proper.

"Stewart is trying to explain why it is imperative that everyone read the instructions on how to use the saw mills to a couple of overzealous E4 soon to be E3s. The fact that he isn't here is, I'm sure, adding to the exuberance of his explanation," Halstead apologized for Stewart.

"No apology necessary, but I appreciate it nonetheless. Not that either of you actually needed to be here to babysit me getting to my tent either. By the way, where is Ramirez?" Mallory asked. "I figured he'd want to be front and center for the grand unveiling of his masterpiece. After all, from what I've seen so far--and the further I get into it, it continues to hold up--the reports actually don't do it justice."

"Honestly, I think he's hiding," Jackson answered. "Personally, I think he's afraid that if you see him now, you'll promote him on the spot, so he's laying low for the first little while, at least until you catch your breath."

Mallory shook her head. "I'll have to find something to complain about and then call him to the command tent so I can ream him out. Make him feel better." They all chuckled at that as they approached the command tent.

"We all know you don't micromanage, but we also know you hate going without face-to-face interaction for more than a couple of days. Nobody's actually in the command tent right now waiting to have a meeting, but just about everybody that you've been on the radio with over the past week is within a stone's throw for the time being," Halstead said as he pulled back the tent flap.

"I appreciate that, as I was ruminating about that very thing for at least half the drive. I don't want to keep everyone on pins and needles waiting to be called into my August presence, but I do want to get a couple of things settled first, and at least find where I'm going to rack out and where communications are at. That and the latrines, showers, and the mess hall, though I can probably follow my nose to the latter in the morning."

"As you'd expect, everybody's keeping pretty busy for the time being, so take your time Top. You all actually made a little better time than expected, too. Not much traffic on the roads?"

"None whatsoever. I think people are starting to worry in a big way about gasoline and diesel and not driving at all if they don't have to. I know we've got it made for the time being, but even our supply is severely limited given how many vehicles we've got. How do things look for long term viability here, on this spot? It's still only June, but we need to start looking at long term structures because it does get cold here in the winter and I personally do *not* want to camp out in a tent all winter, but I also refuse to be in a house while everyone else is in a tent. We need to take a look at some type of barracks structure that can have multiple uses--all men, all women, families, etc. Either all in one building based on floors, or based in multiple buildings, depending on what we can get built. More like dormitories, I guess."

"So, here I am, dumping on you two instead of enjoying my guided tour and saving it for the command meeting."

"And today should be any different than any other day, Top?" Stewart chimed in, as he'd overheard the last little bit while he caught up to the group.

"Point. Stewart, what's our total power generating capacity right now?" Mallory asked.

"Total is 9.4MW, but that's not usable. Usable is 7.8MW." Stewart replied.

"We need to start looking at something other than gasoline or diesel-powered power generation though. We've only got so much of that available in the near term, and yes, if it's remotely liquid in form and mostly a petro-chemical, the vehicles will run on it, but I'd rather not be forced into a situation where I have to start running the rigs on transmission fluid."

"Fair enough."

"Ok, that goes on the list of 'Conversations to Have Soonest' I guess. Enough shop, time to gloat, and I can see that you're all three about to rupture. Who's first?"

The three Sergeants looked at each other and then made a show of doing 'Rock, Paper, Scissors'. "Oh for crying out loud," Mallory said, "I HAVE left you out here without adult supervision for too long."

With that they headed off towards the saw mills, for a couple of reasons. It hadn't been Ramirez's idea, and so he wasn't likely to be there, and because the men were starting to get into the swing of things, and so they wanted to show them off. The SFCs were NOT trying to downplay Ramirez and his contribution. In fact, they all three agreed, to a certain degree, with his assessment, and thought hiding was a good idea. They were going to try to track him down last, however, for the exact opposite reason.

Kyle had been killing himself, and to a lesser degree his men, for the last five days to get the base ready to take everyone in, and had done a truly amazing job. The base looked like something that had taken ten times as long to set up. It kind of rankled him that people mentioned the parking lot so much because, well, it was just a PARKING LOT! The base, however, looked like a small town, with tents where all the buildings should be.

The streets were narrower, and there wasn't a bank or a saloon or other such nonsense, but there was housing for everyone with room to spare. There was a firing range for practice, and hadn't the bulldozer been nice when it came time to set up the berm for that? Karen, Rachael, and Sheri, with the help of a number of the other parents, were looking to set up a whole slew of activities to keep the kids, of all ages up to 16, occupied, including school if necessary come the end of August. There was a mess hall that was large enough to feed two-thirds of the entire current population at once, and another was being constructed (you didn't erect a mess hall, as that is one of the few tents you do *not* want coming down) since the population was growing.

There was redundant water purification, and multiple latrines and bathing facilities (thank you backhoe, thank you, thank you, thank you). A number of the tents did have power, as their primary function required an attached generator, so the base was never really quiet or dark. And a number of tents were being re-erected over raised wood plank floors, thanks to the saw mills.

The point was that all three Sergeants wanted the tour to end with a First Sergeant who was as overwhelmed as she'd ever been and a completely surprised Staff Sergeant., The classic unflappable force meeting the imperturbable object, to thoroughly garble an otherwise perfectly good analogy. No, they didn't want him promoted on the spot, but they didn't expect him to be either, because they didn't think that authority had been handed down from on high, and Top wasn't like that even if it had been. They did want him recognized though, and this oughta be good.

The nickel tour took almost a half an hour, and ended almost back where they started. One of the husbands who'd gotten swept up in the ad hoc activation of the Guard and subsequent migration was a carpenter by trade, specifically cabinets and some smaller furniture. His wife's squad hadn't been shipped out to the Advance Area yet when Joel had had his epiphany about the saw mills, but he'd approved wholeheartedly when he'd seen what was going on.

He'd also proven invaluable a number of times when it came to identifying different qualities of wood, ages, a couple of diseased trees that they'd ended up burning, and how best to trim, square, plank, or rough cut the wood, depending on the end use. They'd come close to using some really soft wood for floor planks at first, which would have been really easy to nail into place but would have rotted and splintered and come apart after not a lot of use.

Ramirez was there with Terrence Holcomb, the carpenter, half a dozen others. When a couple of the guardsmen looked up, Stewart put his finger to his lips and they continued on with what they were doing, which appeared to be some sort of instruction. When they were close enough, and Mallory could see that nobody would die if Kyle either jumped, dropped, or swung whatever it was he was holding--she struck.

"Sergeant Ramirez," Mallory barked.

To his credit, Kyle only flinched a little. He'd been holding a metal file, and he was in the act of setting it down when Mallory called his name. *Man,* he thought, *I really thought I'd be able to dodge her longer than this.* With a flick of his wrist, he tossed the file down as he came to attention and did an about face.

"First Sergeant Jensen?"

"Front and center!"

Ramirez was no slouch on the parade ground; he'd been doing this for a long time. He was filthy dirty, covered in sawdust and, more recently, metal filings from sharpening a chisel, and had been sweating since he woke up. When he marched over to Mallory, however, he made it look like he'd just stepped out of the Army's version of GQ. The top of his head never bobbed, his eyes never moved from three inches above Mallory's head, he executed the quarter turn necessary to face her at the end flawlessly, and despite what he'd told Eric a week ago he looked like he could hold the perfect attention posture until Hell itself froze over.

The three Sergeants behind Mallory smiled to themselves, each for their own reasons. Yeah, they'd gotten him, and not in a bad way, but the man was good, he really, really was.

Mallory didn't release him to his ease, "I have just completed a tour of this facility, Sergeant, and I must say, I am shocked, Shocked at what I have witnessed." *How thick do I spread this on? He can't think I'm mad, not really. He knows I'm not stupid, and he knows how well he's done.* So instead she was just silent for a few seconds, and she watched him. *Wow, he isn't even clenching his jaw! He's not fighting a smile, he's not sweating anymore, he's blinking but just barely. I wonder if he's exhausted and just can't feel right now.*

"Sergeant, in my wildest dreams, I couldn't have expected you to get this much done with ten times the people and twice as much time." *Still no reaction, maybe he's broken.* "At ease."

Kyle changed his stance, and took a little deeper breath.

"Ramirez, how in the world did you get so much done?"

"Top, not getting it done wasn't an option. We had people who needed to be out of the Armory, and those people needed a place to come to. We had trucks and drivers who wanted and needed a place to' come to, and they needed a place to park. I've never believed in 'We don't have time to do it right the first time but we have time to do it again'. You and I know that's BS."

"In our line of work you do it right the first time or you die. I'll be honest with you, I can't believe we haven't lost a limb or a hand or even a finger to the chainsaws or the mills, but we haven't somehow. No fires, nobody crushed or run over, nobody fell into the holes we were digging or got buried under the piles we were pushing around. No, I'm not going to knock on wood either, because that's BS too. It's not luck, because luck is just skill and preparation meeting opportunity."

"We got it done because not getting it done wasn't an option. Every single person here has done some pretty amazing stuff, including the kids. Just the fact that the older ones are keeping the younger ones out of trouble is a huge help, and they are doing it without being asked. You know that Joel came up with the saw mills; Terrence here is a carpenter and is already working on what to do with some of this wood outside of flooring and plank siding."

"Those are just two specific examples based on where we're standing right now, and frankly everyone is doing their level best to do the same, all because it absolutely had to be done. Failure was, is, and will not be an option."

Mallory had kept her face impassive up until this point, and although her face didn't split in half with the grin, it was a genuine, teeth showing, happy smile. "Sergeant Ramirez, thank you. The job done here has been phenomenal, and you are to be commended."

"If you truly wish to remain a Staff Sergeant for the time being, I don't see any reason not to grant that wish, foolish though it may be. Although 'Them's that do the best in combat see's the most combat', as it were."

"Thank you, First Sergeant, I appreciate that. The 'thank you' that is, and the remaining a Staff Sergeant part too, I guess, although I think you were kidding about that," Kyle quirked an eyebrow.

Mallory made the universal 'You'll never know, will you?' face that all women are either born knowing or learn from that special book that only girls get to check out from the library.

Kyle started to roll his eyes and then stopped himself. Best not to push it, he was on her good side, maybe he'd try to stay there for the rest of the day at least. "Thank you again, Top. I'll absolutely pass it on."

"I know you will, Ramirez, after all, 'there must be some reason you're still a Staff Sergeant'."

Interlude Three

The fires in Washington DC started earlier than elsewhere, but not by more than a few days. It seems to be endemic to the human situation that when things don't go according to plan, people riot. Riots almost always lead to fires, either by accident or by design, and then things go from bad to worse when there's nobody there to put the fires out. In June of 2012, there was nobody there to put the fires out.

Mrs. O'Leary's cow cannot be blamed for the fire that virtually destroyed Chicago, although it took substantially longer to burn the second time around. Over one hundred and twenty separate fires were started inside the 'Loop' alone, and within twelve hours they had grown and merged with other fires throughout the city that would burn for almost two weeks.

Fort Worth, TX on the other hand, was gutted in less than eight hours by what was most likely a relatively small number of fires that started in the stockyards. The stockyards in Fort Worth were still actually being used as, well, stockyards for livestock. An untold number of cattle, horses, sheep, and goats were killed in addition to the almost literal burning to the ground of the entire city. Contrary to popular belief, a skyscraper *will* melt if the fire is hot enough.

Denver, St. Louis, Salt Lake City, New York City, Cheyenne, Tulsa, Minneapolis, Nashville--they all suffered the same fate as almost every other major city in the U.S. About the only structures that survived the fires were those made of stone or bricks. Even then, brick buildings didn't necessarily make it through.

To a lesser extent, the outlying areas surrounding the major cities were also affected by fires, but while entire neighborhoods were lost in many cases they were also spared in far more cases as neighborhoods aren't always right next to each other.

While the loss of infrastructure was staggering, the loss of life was even more so. Where the initial death toll was near 1% of the population or approximately 3.2 million people, the number of deaths caused either directly or indirectly by the fires during the first two weeks approached 13% of the pre-event population of the U.S., just over 41 million people.

On the heels of the destruction of what little infrastructure remained came the inability to get any type of clean water and the introduction of airborne illness. This was not a pandemic or a tailor made virus designed to wipe out the human race; it was simply the type of illness caused by things left to rot in the hot summer sun. As human beings we need food, water, and shelter to survive. As a civilized society, we've come to rely on a relatively clean environment and quick access to competent medical care as well. Without our anti-microbial soap, hand sanitizers, and antibiotics our bodies don't know what to do with the world around us and another 6% of the pre-event population was lost over the next month.

During that same month, more and more of those that remained began banding together for protection, to consolidate and conserve resources, to maintain a sense of community, and to attempt to restore some sort of order to the chaos. Anyone who had any sort of survival plan in place, regardless of how rudimentary, and had at least attempted to implement it early on, had made it out of the major population centers before things came completely unraveled. Those who waited longer found that they had waited until it was too late.

Chapter Twenty-Six

At about 10:30 in the morning on June 22nd, two days after the Armory had been mothballed, Mallory's portable radio squawked to life. "Alpha Six this is Delta Two, over?"

Mallory responded right away, "Delta Two this is Six, over."

"Six, your presence is requested at Comms for a discussion with a civilian group looking for a new place to call home. Over."

Wonderful. How many are there? What can they do? Do they bring anything with them or are they looking for a handout? Are they going to be a fit, or even made to fit? "On my way, be there in a couple, over."

"Roger, Two out."

Ever since the encounter with the group of semis at the weigh station, they'd been monitoring the citizen band, but this was the first time someone was sending out a specifically worded message for someone to pick up. A small group was broadcasting, looking for "the military group from Nashville", wanting to join up and consolidate. It was the first time the base was being approached but she was sure it wouldn't be the last.

Mallory walked into the tent just as the third repetition of the message finished. "What have you got for me Sergeant Yates?"

"Well, Top, like I said it sounds like we have a group that wants a place to call home. They aren't broadcasting a huge amount of information yet, including size of their party, current location, etc. but that just makes sense with too many other folks potentially listening in.

"We haven't responded yet, as it's not my call to make. We've discussed the eventuality but we don't have a SOP for it yet and you said you wanted to be called directly if it happened."

She'd really hoped to have more time than this, but it never seemed to work out that way. "Ask me for anything but time," Mallory said under her breath.

"Napoleon may have been a nasty little prick with an ego the size of the Alps, but he had a decent grasp of logistics…at least at the beginning."

"That he did, Yates. That he did. Get my platoon Sergeants to the command tent for a pow-wow, and reply that the message has been received and that an additional response will follow in one hour. If nothing else we'll tell them to hold tight for another hour. Now the fun begins…so much for boring."

A few minutes later, everyone was seated around a folding table in the command tent. "So," Mallory began, "the main question is how big a force do we send to meet with said group, and how do we bring them in, if we bring them in? We've already established the fact that we are going to require them to become productive members of our little community, and we'd like them to bring *something* to the table. We don't have hard numbers for ratios of men to women to children, that's why one of you needs to go along on the first few of these meetings to make that judgment call. Suggestions?"

Halstead was nominally senior, so he went first. "As this is the first group we've encountered, and we don't know how they are situated yet, I'm already operating under the assumption that they are all traveling in a group and don't have any leadership that would be able or willing to meet with a representative from us. I would personally want to find out how large they are, meet that with a 25% increase in numbers and a sufficient force multiplier in hardware, and arrive at the designated meeting place ahead of time, prior to letting them know where that place would be--after proper recon of course."

Mallory nodded, "Go on."

"If we did that, we could either determine what they had to offer and allow them to accompany us back on the spot, or we could reject the request, also on the spot, and have a sufficient force to deny any attempt to follow us. I really think the show of force would keep

them from trying too terribly hard when we told them 'No', too."
Stewart looked at Jackson, who took up the train of thought.

"The first several of these groups looking for a place to go are likely
to be fairly desperate, whether or not they have something to offer.
Picking the time and place, arriving ahead of time, and then letting
the group know where to meet us will protect us in the short term.
We'll need to let word get out that we aren't ambushing people
though, somehow. We'll also need to try to keep a lid on where we
are for a while, too, otherwise we'll just have people showing up,
which could get hairy real quick."

"So, exactly how much time have the three of you put into this
behind my back?" Mallory asked.

Halstead smiled and answered for the three, "Actually, none. It's
logical though, and it's really no different from an unplanned
evacuation of a friendly village or town in a hostile area. As things
start to settle down, groups will begin to coalesce, and we'll probably
have people willing to send ambassadors to meeting places to discuss
coming in as a group. We'll need to have our people scope out the
area beforehand, and we'll probably have a totally different SOP for
it, but I think we've got the basics for today or tomorrow ready once
we get numbers from the group who called in today."

"Sounds like a plan. Do we have a formula or are we going to make
that up as we go along too?" Stewart asked.

"We'll swag it. I told Yates to tell them we'd get back to them in an
hour and it's been all of fifteen minutes. I don't want to appear too
eager to meet with them."

"So you make us suffer. Nice. You sure you've never been to
OCS?" Jackson asked.

"Far as you know. I've trained more snot-nosed six-month wonders
than I care to recall though, that's for sure."

"Amen." All three platoon Sergeants chorused.

"So, numbers, how many of what…"

…

After the initial radio contact had been made and communications had been established, it was reported that the group only had twenty-five people. Although time had not been on Mallory's side, Mr. Murphy didn't appear to have paid a visit yet, as the group had four couples and five families. The youngest child was seven years old and the group at least claimed to have skills and a willingness to work and contribute. They could provide tents and clothing for themselves, and all but one of the men had a serviceable firearm they were willing to use in defense of the base.

Three squads were sent out to secure a meeting area, as the initial assumption that the group was unwilling to separate and send out an advance meeting group had been correct. Halstead, once again being nominally senior, drew the short straw and accompanied what he hoped would be a welcoming committee. He also hoped it would be a short meeting, as full 'battle rattle' was *hot*.

There were eleven Humvees and LAVs parked in a semi-circle when the nine cars, trucks, and SUVs of the group looking for a new home showed up. None of the heavy weapons were aimed at the incoming vehicles but they were menacing nonetheless. Once all the vehicles came to a stop, everyone got out and three men and a woman came forward. Halstead and three others met them in the middle of the slightly lopsided circle.

"Afternoon. I'm Sergeant Halsted, U.S. Army." Halstead held out his hand to the man in the middle and slightly in front of the rest. "I understand you folks are looking to possibly relocate." That brought a chuckle and eased the tension a little.

"You could say that," one of the men said. "Mike Parker." He didn't introduce the others, but Halstead assumed that would either happen later or it wouldn't, in which case it would be three names he didn't need to remember.

Mike went on, "It doesn't look like things are going to get back to normal any time soon. A couple of us have Police scanners and CBs and what we've heard isn't real reassuring. Most of us are from the same neighborhood, but we all know each other and we got together and decided we needed to do something.

"Tammy here," Mike pointed to the woman, who nodded, "mentioned that she'd seen a number of convoys heading this direction from what she assumed was Nashville, as that's the closest military base of any kind in that direction that she was aware of. We put what we thought were two and two together and came up with something between three and five and threw out the CB broadcast."

"We knew we were taking a bit of a chance doing it, but we also figured that we needed to do *something*, and you folks sure do look like the Army, so at least that part seems to have panned out."

"Oh, I guarantee we're U.S. Army. And I truly do hope the power eventually comes back on, because I'd sure love to see my pension when the time comes." That brought another laugh and, once again, eased the tension.

"I understand that you all have tents and general personal supplies for yourselves for a limited period of time, is that correct?"

"Yessir, we do. We're doing ok for food and water for right now…shelter and clothes aren't an issue yet either."

Halstead let out a breath; he really didn't like having to ask the types of questions that came next, not of civilians. "Please understand, I'm asking the next questions because I have to. Are you all, or are most of you, able bodied and willing to work--and I mean work hard? There's a lot of physical labor that needs to be done from the time the sun comes up until after it goes down every day. Not just the military folks, the civilians that are there already as well." That got a raised eyebrow. Apparently they hadn't thought anyone else was there but the military.

"Well, of course. None of us are looking for a handout. Like I said, it doesn't look like things are going to get back to normal any time soon, and there's going to be safety in numbers." Mike wasn't acting indignant, which was a good sign. It would make the next questions easier.

"I'm glad to hear that, because frankly not everyone feels that way. Next, how do you feel about having the military in charge for the time being?"

"You're the ones we called out to, Sergeant Halstead. In the long run, if a regular government can be set up, well, not exactly like it was, but like it was as in *was meant to be* was, that would probably be best, but you aren't looking at a bunch of people wanting to take over via a coup. All of us either have a family history with, or current family in, the military and we're proud of that fact," everyone was nodding, "which is partially why we went with calling out to you all instead of trying to hook up with just any other group out there."

"Fair enough. In that case, what additional skills do you folks have that you feel will be of specific value to the group as a whole?"

"Brick masonry, carpentry, weaving, sewing, gardening, and farming, hunting, architectural design, and structural engineering for starters. If the base--that's what your radioman referred to it as--isn't dry, we've also got a wicked awesome brewer, but if so he won't even distill 'medicinal brandy'."

"I believe we may be able to come to terms then. If you'll give me a few minutes I think we can probably be on our way shortly. It was my understanding that you wouldn't need to make any detours or stops, is that correct?"

"Yessir, we have everything we need packed up with us."

"I'll be just a moment then."

Halstead went back to his Humvee and radioed to base to confer with Mallory and let her know that they would in fact be bringing the group with them.

"We're all on pins and needles with this one. It's a little different than the semis. We'll see you when you get back. Radio when you turn into the park, over."

"Roger, out."

"We're all set," Halstead said as he got back to the group waiting at the center of the circle. "In a couple of minutes a number of Humvees will pull out behind you. If you would turn around and follow them, we'll bring up the rear. And one last request, we ask that you not broadcast where we're going yet, although eventually we're sure it will be common knowledge."

"Sure thing. I guess we'll see you back at the base then, and thank you, sir."

Halstead couldn't stand it anymore, "We save 'Sir' for the officers, I work for a living. Sergeant or Halstead is fine."

"Ah, yeah, I knew that. Sorry Sergeant, just nerves I guess."

"Not a problem, Mike, looks like the escort has arrived. See you back at the base."

Chapter Twenty-Seven

With the perimeter of the base slowly expanding and constantly under observation, the biggest problem they were encountering was the fact that they were deployed in the woods. Security in a wooded area is always an iffy proposition at best, no matter what anyone says. It simply takes more men, more equipment, and more time the keep a wooded perimeter secure, primarily due to visibility.

Sergeant Evan 'Sparky' Lake and Specialists Morris and Hook were part of the patrol to the southwest of the base on Day 12, June 25th. Now that the Armory had emptied out and everyone was finally back together in one place, things were starting to settle down into a routine. Lake wasn't looking forward to the time when he would need to tell his men to cut the chatter on the radios during patrol but it would also mean that everyone was finally getting comfortable with their new surroundings.

Morris was on point and just as Sergeant Lake was wondering how long it would be before he would have to start reigning in his men, Morris's hand went up in a fist, then went flat and patted down, and he sank to the ground. Lake and Hook stopped where they were and slowly followed Morris's lead, relaying the signal and sinking to the ground. Sudden jerky movements caught the eye, that's why they didn't just fall straight down--that and it would have been noisy.

Morris low-crawled back to Lake, "We have a group of unknowns about 250 meters north north-west. Unknown number but they're making enough noise to raise the dead and acting like they're trying to be quiet. I heard 'Shh' no less than three times." Morris was pitching his voice low but not whispering. It was a talent that you learned quickly in the military as a whisper, for some odd reason, carried farther than a normal speaking voice under certain circumstances. Saying 'Shh' was just about the worst thing you could do to maintain quiet, as anyone who'd been on patrol knew. It was like screaming, "Hey, look over here!"

"Papa six, this is Papa two, over," Lake radioed in to base.

"Roger Papa two, this is Papa six, what's up? Over." Corporal Pine had radio duty.

"We have an unknown number of individuals of questionable intent about a klick south south-west of the base. They sound like moose walking over bubble wrap but they're moving slow. Request coordination with Papa one and Papa five to assist in determining intent and neutralization of any threats should they arise. Over." I seriously hope no threats arise.

"Roger, wait one. Over."

'One' ended up being almost two minutes while the First Sergeant was located and brought into the Net. "Papa two, this is Alpha six. Confirm you have an unknown number of individuals headed towards the base. Papa one, Papa five report, over."

"Roger six, this is Papa one, good copy, we can be above the party in two Mikes. Over."

"Roger six, this is Papa five, read you Lima Charlie, we can interdict the party before the base in the same two Mikes. Over."

Ok, so both of the other patrols on this side of the base could assist to surround this party on three sides within two minutes. Assuming that nobody else was headed into the area where they should be patrolling, that would be fine. *Hope I didn't just make a really stupid suggestion*, Lake thought to himself.

"Roger Papas one, two, and five. Proceed to positions 100 meters in front and 20 meters above and below the party. Pace them until Papa five meets a heavy fire team, at which point they will announce themselves…"

…

The three squads that were on patrol numbered twenty-eight soldiers and, as such, they were currently outnumbered by the invading force. While quantity *can* have a quality all its own, the raiding party was outclassed in every way that mattered. Each of the raiders had at least one unique characteristic that allowed him to be distinguished from each other. Each guardsman had thus been assigned an 'Alpha', 'Bravo', and 'Charlie' target.

By utilizing this tactic, a small defending force can defend against a potentially much larger attacking or raiding force. There was some overlap and every target was covered at least twice--a few targets were covered three times. In the unlikely event that one or more guardsmen ran out of targets then it became a matter of 'don't let anyone kill me or anyone else on my side'.

The use of the term target for another human being may sound cold and clinical but in a kill or be killed situation being cold and clinical is what keeps you alive. It's also what these men and women had trained for, in some cases for years. They all hoped, to varying degrees, that the situation could be resolved without any shots being fired--but they weren't going to let indecision or reluctance result in one of their own being a casualty.

Lake was just wondering how close they were going to allow them to get to the base when the answer came in the form of a hastily constructed horseshoe PA system and Sergeant Wilson's not so melodic voice at 120db.

"Stop where you are. Put your weapons down and then put your hands up. Do not fire or you will be fired upon. I repeat, stop where you are, put your weapons down, and then put your hands up." Sergeant Wilson paused for two seconds and everyone in the raiding party went stock still. "We know how many of you there are and you are now surrounded." While not technically correct, they couldn't know that. The sound was coming from three sides at this point.

Then, someone did something stupid. Instead of putting their rifle down they brought it to their shoulder, aimed, and fired. What they were aiming at was irrelevant as they missed. As soon as they pulled the trigger, they were hit by no fewer than nine rounds--three different three-round bursts. Whether because of his show of bravado, the act of defiance in the face of resistance, or simply the movement of that first person, eight other people made the same stupid mistake. In less than five seconds a total of nine hostile raiders, who had not only not put their weapons down but had taken aim at something and fired, were now down and assumed dead.

Wilson was disappointed that it had come to this but he was far from upset with his men. That didn't mean he wanted the situation getting out of hand though. "CEASE FIRE! You have been warned! For your own sake stop where you are, put your weapons DOWN and put your hands UP! You've just seen what will happen to anyone else who fires!"

Over the Tactical Network, or TACNET, Lake heard Top call in for a Situation Report, "All Units, this is Alpha Six, sit rep, over."

"Papa one, all clear, no casualties…yet. Soon-to-be Private Price thought it would be cool to take a head shot."

"Papa five, all clear, no casualties. Be advised several shooters aimed this way and shots went high."

"Papa two, all clear, no casualties."

"Cease fire, do as they say. Put the guns down! We don't need to lose anybody else!" That came from the raiding party, hopefully from someone with the authority to make that call. There was also the sound of retching coming from the group.

"I repeat, stop where you are, put your weapons down and then put your hands up." Sergeant Wilson said again, thank goodness the volume had been turned down. It had been cranked pretty high at first for shock value.

"Do it! Now people, let's go," Again, from inside the group.

Slowly, which was good, the guns were placed on the ground and people stood up with their hands in the air. It wasn't good enough to put their hands behind their heads because you couldn't see what was in those hands, they had to be in the air. Within a minute, all the hands were up and two additional squads of guardsmen came out of the woods near the front of the group. Each had a bundle of zip ties in one of their thigh pockets, as they made great hand-cuffs, and there were a number of lengths of rope that already had loops tied into them. Somebody'd been busy.

There were forty-one people in the raiding party originally, thirty-two after the unfortunate incident, and with twenty-four guardsmen-- three to a prisoner--that meant eight at a time could be secured. It took almost two minutes to frisk, hand-cuff, and secure a prisoner to the rope.

It took a little less than eight minutes to get all the prisoners secured and Lake felt like he'd held his breath the entire time. "I hope we don't have to do that again anytime soon. I know we're in the Army, I know we train for this, but I really don't want to have to fight a guerilla war against American citizens."

"Roger that, Sergeant, I really hope it doesn't come to that. What did they think they were going to accomplish? Did they have any idea what they were up against?" Morris asked.

"Good questions Morris and I'm sure that Top will be looking to get answers from whoever ends up being in charge of this little parade." Lake looked up at a call from medics, who had also been on hand, and had come out to check for any survivors of the brief engagement. Lake shook his head and sighed. "I don't know whether to be relieved or not. It looks like we have a survivor. As it sits, we need to get out there and pick up some weapons and bury some bodies. Move out soldier."

…

Treat all guns as if they are loaded. The only true safety on a firearm is the one between your ears. Never pull a gun unless you are prepared to pull the trigger. Know what is behind your target. These are by no means the only rules of gun safety, but they are repeated over and over by anyone who knows anything about firearms to novices and old-timers alike. In the heat of battle, though, they can be forgotten by even the most skilled and combat-hardened veteran.

The members of the National Guard did not forget these or any of the hundreds of other rules of engagement or firearms safety that had been drilled into them over the course of years of military service. They were also prepared for the encounter and, as such, weren't surprised into action. The raiding party had none of the benefits afforded to the guardsmen. While every round fired by the guard found its target, every round fired by the motley crew they were up against missed completely.

The fact that the shots went wild was due not to the fact that they weren't aimed well, or that the shooter was a poor marksman, but that they didn't have anything to aim at and that they weren't used to being shot at. A total of nine shots were fired by the raiding party.

Seven of them were enough off the mark to eventually hit trees or drop harmlessly to the ground. One ricocheted off the exhaust pipe of a semi in the parking lot. One made its way all the way into camp.

Traveling at just under 1400 mph but with much of its kinetic energy spent and beginning to tumble, the final projectile had dropped nineteen inches from where it had been "aimed", which was at chest height. It hit Troy Patterson in the pelvis on the left side, just above the hip socket. If it had hit much lower and to the right it would have hit his femoral artery. If it had hit with much more force it would have shattered his pelvis. As it was, Troy was in for a world of hurt, hours of field surgery, and months of recovery. And someone had just made themselves an enemy for life out of one Staff Sergeant Rebecca 'Hammer' Patterson.

…

When conducting interrogations the questions can sometimes appear completely random and unconnected. That is, of course, the idea. The interrogator isn't actually the prisoner's friend, and by asking questions in such a way that the prisoner gets confused, backtracks, answers the same questions repeatedly, or is answering questions that seem innocent, the interrogator is able to cause the prisoner to slip up and reveal information.

When the interrogator is at least minimally trained and the prisoner is a civilian, simply asking what you want to know usually suffices and the mind games are just for the entertainment of the intelligence staff. Within half an hour a fairly coherent picture had been painted and corroborated by the few people who seemed to know anything about the raiding party. The bad news was where the raiding party had come from. The worse news appeared to be who its nominal leadership was, and that he had been holding on to the reins for as long as he had.

"So now we know who Earl acts as the right hand man for, and my, isn't he a pleasant fellow by the way?" Mallory said as she walked into the command tent, disgust and contempt warring on her face. "Unfortunately, Clint doesn't feel the need to lead from the front. I'm not happy about the fact that he was also able to determine where we are and convince forty-one men and women that a raid on us was a stellar idea. He also apparently felt that they were expendable."

"Before we get into what we're going to do about Clint, I want to know what went wrong, though." Mallory said.

"We waited too long to intercept," Stewart replied. "We tried to be cute and we let them get too close. That's all there is to it. We had them a klick out and could have stopped them almost that far away." Sergeant Patterson was in his platoon and he was dealing with a number of issues, not the least of which was her desire to immediately and single-handedly dispatch the remaining thirty-two members of the raiding party. Thirty-three if you counted the survivor of the gunfight who was undergoing field surgery to repair a punctured lung and laundry list of other internal damage done when he'd been hit seven times. Professionalism and training only went so far and Rebecca was *pissed* about her civilian husband.

"Is that all? Nothing else?" Mallory asked.

"No, First Sergeant, that isn't all. The perimeter should have been further out and they should have been detected far earlier." Halstead replied. "I can give you reasons but no excuses, and nothing I say is going to make recovery for Troy any easier."

"No, it won't, Sergeant. Give me the reasons though because I need to hear them from you so we can work on getting them resolved."

"Nobody expected anything like this so quickly. It's only been twelve days. Who else is this organized? Don't say it, Kyle, I swear I'll hit you if you do."

Kyle looked as innocent as a newborn babe but everyone in the room *knew* he had been about to say "Well duh, apparently Clint is this organized."

"But who could have *known* he was this organized and ready or willing to pull something like this? The last time we heard something about him a single guy yelling 'Hey' ran off his entire party for crying out loud! No, he isn't the only guy out there and yes, there have to be other groups but, well..." Halstead shook his head. "Assumptions, pure and simple. I can't even blame it on bad intel because we don't have any intel to blame at this point. We've been making assumptions based on swags that were based on guesses and wishful thinking."

"Now that your head is out of its rectal cradle, I'm going to *assume* you'll have a resolution for me by tomorrow morning?" Mallory made the order sound like a question.

"Absolutely." Halstead did an admirable job of not flinching, although the rebuke stung and he knew he deserved it.

"The next order of business then is, in fact, Clint. You've had a couple of hours to think about it; I'm open to suggestions. What are we going to do about this?"

Those present included both military personnel and civilians, as had become both the custom and the standard. Mallory wasn't interested in setting up a dictatorship backed by the military. Kyle, though technically junior to everyone else in the room, was the first to respond, "Well, we could always just head over in the middle of the night and kill everybody."

"Thank you, Sergeant Ramirez. Your suggestion will be duly noted in the minutes…oh wait, we aren't taking minutes, so I guess it won't be," Mallory smiled.

"It really depends on a number of factors at this point." Jackson added after it was clear that Ramirez wasn't actually going to add anything productive at this point. "First, how many people do they really have after the forty-one they sent? Second, how heavily armed are those that remain? Third, is it possible that they are being held against their will or being used as leverage on some of those who participated in the raid today? Fourth, is it possible to, if not directly remove this Clint person, assist in his removal indirectly? Those are the things that come to mind immediately."

"Keep in mind that we aren't set up for prisoners, Top." Stewart added.

"Valid points all. So, I ask again, what are we going to do? I'm asking because you are my command team, we make decisions. This isn't an autocracy and hasn't been for a while. We have a situation that affects the safety and security of everyone here. We've decided, more or less, that the Guard will fill the role of security or 'Police' but not with a free reign." Mallory looked at those gathered in the tent.

"We have to contact the group, no matter what. We have to make contact with them and possibly with Clint directly, assuming he will speak with us," Eric replied. "We've already spoken with him once and it was obvious he was in charge then, even if he didn't say as much."

"How do you propose we do that? Do you have suggestions on how to make contact?" Mallory asked.

"When we encountered them last time they had CB antennas on every vehicle, so we start there. Send out a broadcast on channel 19 and listen. I assume they haven't told us where home is yet?" Eric asked.

"Correct, but we haven't really asked very 'hard' yet either." Jackson answered.

"And we aren't going to," Mallory replied with an edge to her voice.

"True, sorry, Top, thinking in military terms and this group is definitely not that." Jackson was now also sufficiently reprimanded.

"I don't think that this group is going to need all that much persuasion to tell us whatever we want to know," Mallory continued. "Frankly, if we let them go to sleep and then wake them up every 45 minutes, after four or six hours they'll probably beg to tell us anything and everything just to let them sleep for a full eight. We did find their vehicles, and some of them are rather nice--almost new in fact. Unfortunately, the gas gauges are all over the place so we can't use that to give us even a rough estimate of where they might have originated from."

"So, how long do we give them to give up Clint and do we need to know where he is before we start broadcasting? I have my ideas but I want to hear yours," Mallory asked.

"I say we give them until this time tomorrow before we start spreading stories," Ramirez answered. Common interrogation techniques included creating a simple story that a prisoner or group of prisoners had ratted out another and simply letting the feeling of betrayal loosen the tongue. "As for waiting, it's your call. We need to have some sort of plan and something to say before we turn on the radio though."

"Anyone else?" Mallory asked.

"Anything we plan now is going to be, as Sergeant Halstead put it, a swag based on a guess," Eric said to the quiet tent after five seconds of everyone looking at each other. "The difference is that we'll know that going into it this time. We don't know anything yet aside from who's nominally in charge of this group and that one of the guys in the raiding party gave the girls in our group the willies." Rachael, Karen, and Sheri all nodded in agreement with the last sentiment. "Unless we're going to broadcast for a meeting with Clint, which I don't know that I can weigh in on the merits of, I don't know that we can really do anything until we get more information from the thirty-odd people we now have in custody."

"Always the pragmatic one," Kyle muttered. "Not that I have anything better, but I can't say I like it."

"That's about where I was at. I was hoping I had just talked myself out of being able to do something and I didn't want to poison the well, so to speak." Mallory said. "Because it's the only thing we have at the moment, I do want to try to open some sort of dialog with this guy and find out just what he thought he was going to accomplish this afternoon. Stewart, I'd like you to take that on. Eric, I'd like you to work with him as you have an intelligence background. Not a word about Military Intelligence, Ramirez."

"What? All of the sudden I'm the *only* one thinking these things?" Kyle asked with a wounded expression on his face.

"No," Mallory replied. "You're just the only one with a broken filter. Anyway, Eric, I can't order you to, but it would help."

"Glad to, Top. When do you want to start trying to make contact?"

"I'd like to begin trying before dark, but only if you two can come up with something coherent. Although it might be a good idea to let Clint sweat overnight--assuming nobody sent a broadcast that we've captured his crew."

"We'll get right on it. Eric, I've got a couple of guys to grab that you may have worked with before. Top, if it's ok, we'll get started now." Stewart got up at a nod from Mallory and he and Eric left, already discussing how to go about their newly assigned task.

Chapter Twenty-Eight

"My how things can change," Clint thought to himself as he looked around the small mobile town that had followed him out of Nashville. In less than a week he'd picked up eighty people and cleaned out an RV lot…literally. Once he'd left he'd picked up another fifty or so people. Other than trailers he couldn't pull, there'd been nothing left on the lot worth taking except the bulk propane tank, and they had left that less than a quarter full once they found someone who knew how to operate it without blowing themselves or the smaller tanks up. He wasn't using everything he'd stockpiled just yet but he'd been able to bring it all with him by having everyone who felt comfortable driving a truck with a trailer do so.

When he'd made the decision to pull out of the Nashville area three days ago and head west, he'd made sure to steer clear of the park because he wasn't sure how many people were holed up inside. Once they had settled down here on the west side of Beech Lake, just outside of Lexington, he'd figured it was time to go take a peek at the group that was causing such a commotion. It seemed like every other conversation that they had been picking up on the CBs had been about some group in Natchez Trace.

Now the party he'd sent out to probe the group in the park had been gone for a day without calling back in. Earl might be a letch and a thug but he was responsible and he should have radioed in by now. They weren't supposed to get in over their heads and up until now they hadn't. What was keeping them? What had gone wrong? I can't afford to lose that many people!

"Clint." The walkie-talkie at his waist squawked.

"This is Clint, give me some good news."

"Sorry boss, no can do," Cooper replied. "You need to hear the broadcast we're picking up over at the cruiser though."

"On my way." Great, now what?

Even with over seventy RV trailers, three full-size class A motor homes, and over eighty trucks and SUVs, it took less than a full minute for Clint to get to the other side of their mobile village. When he arrived he found almost a dozen people gathered around the former squad car. "So, the radio has started filtering water?" Clint snapped as he walked up.

A couple of the newer folks gave him sheepish looks and headed away with mumbles of some kind or another. A few of his original group ignored the implied rebuke and kept listening to the message being broadcast on the police radio. It sounded like it had just begun and Clint had missed the first few words so it took a few seconds to sink in.

"…States Army base located in Natchez Trace State Park calling the individual Clinton Baxter."

Oh. Shit. Earl, what have you done?

"Regarding the group sent to Natchez Trace on Twenty Five June Two Thousand Twelve, led by one Earl Brent Hanson. Request contact on simplex CB channel 39 upon receipt or duplex CB channels 33-36 after Twenty Eight June."

"Bad news, boss, they used Earl's middle name," one of the gathered hangers on said. "Nobody but the law and your momma uses your middle name, man."

Clint glared at the speaker, whose name he couldn't come up with at the moment. "Thank you so *very* much for that enlightening insight into human nature."

"On the plus side," Coop replied, trying to draw Clint's ire his way. "They didn't use *your* middle name."

"That's only a plus if you don't factor in that I don't *have* a middle name," Clint replied. "I can't even say it's a long story, because it's not. My mom named me after the neighborhood she grew up near in Brooklyn. My dad was nowhere to be found and she'd either exhausted her full store of imagination on my first name or realized 'Hill' would have been worse than no middle name at all."

When nobody said anything Clint snorted. "Oh come on people, you act like you've never met anyone without a middle name before!"

"Well, actually, no I haven't." Coop was the only one to reply. "The closest I can come is an old girlfriend's grandfather. He didn't have a first or middle name, just two initials. His legal name was W. D. Miller."

Clint shook his head and tried to get back on topic. "The point is that we seemed to have sent a raid against the United States Army." The radio crackled as the message started over. It was apparently recorded and broadcasting about every two minutes.

Clint either ignored or missed Cooper's raised eyebrows at the use of 'we'.

"I need to think and I can't do it standing here with that running every few minutes. Coop, turn it down some and have someone else man the radio for a while. Grab Tony and meet me over at my rig."

…

Clint had given up trying to pace inside the trailer as a lost cause, it was just too short and too narrow. He'd smacked his knuckles a couple of times turning around and instead of throwing a punch through the paperboard siding and ruining something that he couldn't easily replace he'd decided that he'd do his pacing outside. Tony and Coop showed up after Clint had made a couple of passes back and forth in front of the trailer and stood waiting to be noticed.

"How long ago did you first pick up the broadcast?" Clint asked when he noticed Cooper and Tony.

"About three minutes before I called you," Coop replied. "We were channel hopping and jumped in at 'request contact' the first time. Once we'd heard it all the way through we called you."

"How long had you been off of 19?"

"Four, maybe five minutes tops," Tony said.

Clint sighed. "That means they just started transmitting, which means they've been thinking about it," Clint trailed off.

"Come again?" Tony asked.

"Earl took that group out of here over twenty-four hours ago. He was supposed to radio in after three hours which means that the U.S. Army has had the entire group in their care for at least twenty-one hours. Do you sincerely think that whoever is in charge over there just now had the bright idea to transmit a meeting request after a day?"

Clint went back to pacing while he talked. "I don't think so. They wanted us to stew about our missing people. I know I have been." Clint was scowling again when he looked up and in the direction of the squad car which he couldn't see through his trailer. "And as much as I hate to admit it, Kenny's right. The only people who use your middle name are 'the law and your momma' and both of them only when you're in trouble. Hell, even I didn't know Earl's middle name."

Tony and Coop looked at each other.

"What?" Clint asked.

Neither former policeman answered right away.

"I said *what* and it wasn't in the rhetorical sense. One of you knowing something may be bad news, both of you knowing something and not wanting to share it sounds a lot like 'no good can come of this'. Spill it, like *now*."

"We actually both knew Earl's middle name already. He's kinda got a rap sheet," Coop replied.

Clint controlled his temper and kept it to making a fist that cracked the knuckles of his right hand. "Is it Brent?"

"Yeah," Tony answered.

"Sonofa…ok, the next time one of you two thinks of something like this, something that might be, oh I don't know, IMPORTANT! Let me know ahead of time."

"You got it boss, sorry. For what it's worth, I don't recognize anyone else in the group as having a prior history." Tony was the junior of the two and was taking the rebuke harder than Coop.

"I think I recognize one but if so it's minor and really nothing to worry about," Cooper added, letting Tony's apology apply to both of them.

"It's water under the bridge now. What matters is getting them back, if we can."

…

"Why are we screwing around, Top?" Halstead asked as he walked into the command tent.

"You want the short answer or the long answer?" Mallory replied.

"Will I like either one?"

"Probably not."

"Well then I'd just as soon have an actual explanation for our little Charlie Foxtrot in the making if you're willing to give it because I'm pretty sure the short answer is 'I said so'."

"Have a seat." Mallory gestured to a folding chair across from her 'desk' and once she wasn't looking up at her potentially insubordinate subordinate she continued. "We know who he is, we know where he is, we know how many people are there, and we have a fairly good idea of what resources they have at their disposal. What we don't know is what is going on in his head," Mallory tapped her own head to make the point.

"Ramirez already suggested going in and laying waste to the place in the middle of the night. He made the same suggestion as soon as we actually had a place to lay waste to." In a slightly softer tone she went on, "That man, I swear sometimes I think he would try the patience of Job."

"I'm with you, on both counts," Halstead agreed with a small smile.

"We aren't going to go in and play tornado to their little trailer park though. There are those who feel that the ability to make ethical and moral decisions is a luxury available only to those blessed with a stable, civilized society." Mallory paused for a second to let that sink in but continued before Halstead could interrupt or respond. "We may not have the same level of stability that we had a month ago but I'll be *damned* if we don't still have a civilized society." Mallory's fist came down on her desk at damned and it made Halstead jump because it had come out of nowhere.

"We could have killed every last one of the raiders yesterday with no warning whatsoever. One second they're sneaking up on us, the next people are literally dying left and right, and then it's over. Clint would never have known what happened. We send out a *real* scouting party, find his group, and wham, done."

Halstead wasn't stunned, but he was silent. Mallory leaned forward with both arms on her desk, "I won't invoke the almighty Murphy and his immutable law and say we wouldn't have suffered any casualties but I'd have been very surprised if we'd had anyone so much as injured on our side."

"Sergeant, you and I both know that this was probably at least partially a mistake on Clint's part. You don't have to agree with me openly or out loud but think about it." Mallory waited to see how Halstead reacted before she went on. He had the good grace to nod. "Nobody attacks a military base using forty-one civilians unless they have bombs strapped to their chests. It wasn't a feint--unless the other group got lost and this lot was kept completely in the dark about being the bait."

"You're keeping things close to the vest, though. Do you have a plan or are you playing it by ear?" Halstead asked.

"Yes," Mallory replied. "I'm not really keeping it close but I'm sure it looks like it from where you're sitting. I wasn't kidding yesterday about not running this whole deal like a military dictatorship. Not now, not ever."

Mallory leaned back in her chair and tried to stretch away some of the tension that had been growing for the last week and a half. Two seconds can only do so much though and she had to get back to the task at hand. "I have some general ideas of how to handle this but it depends on how Clint reacts to the situation. You aren't here to pick my brain, though you clearly have something you'd like to say--more than one something unless I've completely missed my guess. Permission granted to speak freely Sergeant, just not too freely."

Halstead took a breath to cover the second it took to gather his thoughts and then started with the most troubling aspect of this whole incident. "Top, what are we going to do with the thirty-three people we have here right now who weren't here yesterday morning? Are they prisoners and if so by what authority do we hold them? Is it a military matter or a civilian matter? How long do we hold them? Do we or can we even let them go? If we let them go, who do we release them to and under what conditions? That doesn't even get into the eight we have in body bags in one of the empty refrigeration trucks because we couldn't let them sit out in the sun for a day."

Halstead held up his hand when it looked like Mallory was about to begin answering some of those questions. "I'm not quite finished." At her nod he went on, "We're in the woods and we simply cannot secure the perimeter of this base like it should be secured, not like a real base. With the number of people here, the mix of military and civvies, and the likelihood that we are going to become more and more town-like, we just don't have the trained bodies. I guess I'm done for now."

"Good, because I was starting to lose track." That earned a grin. "Our guests are weighing heavily on my mind. I don't know if they're exactly prisoners or even enemy combatants at this point. It depends almost entirely on the reasoning behind their being here in the first place. Let me finish, we're discussing this but that doesn't mean we get to interrupt each other."

Halstead relaxed as he'd been about to protest the disposition of the captured party members. "Some things appear to be obvious to anyone with two brain cells to rub together. Point," Mallory held up a finger, "the group was most likely a raiding party and not doing scouting or recon. Point," another finger, "they were too heavily and similarly armed to have had *all* of those rifles until after the event and in fact we know that at least three of them still had pawn shop price tags on them. Point," finger, "unlike us they were willing to shoot first and ask questions later. With absolutely no idea of the tactical situation, nine of their party opened fire. Dumb, dangerous, and frankly a little bit mean if you ask me."

Mallory put her hand down, "I'm going to quit counting on my fingers now because you're a smart kid and at some point if I'm not careful I'm going to give you the bird. The point I was making is that they aren't prisoners or enemy combatants in the classical sense of the terms but they don't strike me as innocent either. Rules have changed a bit, I understand that, but this group appears to have already resorted to wholesale theft of firearms, ammunition, vehicles, trailers, food, water, and fuel."

"We need to talk to Clint first; we need to see how he couches this. How does he justify what he's doing and what he's done? Does he look at us and accuse us of doing the exact same thing but on a bigger scale? Does he claim that the ends justify the means or that the old rules don't apply anymore because they can't? We need to know what we're dealing with and more than that," Mallory paused and not just for dramatic effect but because once she said it out loud it always seemed more real, "we are going to have to choose our battles."

"Aren't we supposed to be the last bastion of hope and freedom and all that?"

"Yes, but we're also supposed to be realistic in the expectations we have of ourselves. We have *very* limited resources at our disposal with which to be that last bastion. There's a difference between guarding the gate and going out in search of the dragon."

Halstead was silent for several seconds and when he replied he seemed more his old self. "Point made, Top. I'm still mad about being caught off guard. I want to be able to put this to bed but I'm being active stupid."

…

"Now that's just active stupid, Coop!" Clint yelled.

"Why?"

"You really want *all* the reasons, fine." Clint turned on Cooper. "First of all it's not just my word against his; it's my word against theirs. Forty-one people to one. They were all volunteers and as a group they all heard me talking to Earl. Next, some of those people still have family back here. Do you *really* think they're just going to sit idly by while I hang their husbands or wives out to dry? C, or Three, or whatever I'm using to keep track of this list of stupidity, it's the *U.S. ARMY!* Maybe I should have listed that as the first, last, and only reason because that *should* have been enough."

"But they wouldn't be expecting it…"

"They wouldn't, huh? Really? And how long did you serve in the military? How many times have you been on a military installation after an incident that caused a heightened state of alert? Exactly what in your past gives you *any* reason to think that or qualifies you to make that determination?" Clint spat.

"I haven't but what makes *you* so sure that they will? What makes you the expert?" Cooper shot back with just as much fire and a touch of challenge.

"Fourteen months in the Army before an…unfortunate incident put an end to that. I was in Ranger School. I've been on a base during a heightened state of alert, several times. They *will* be expecting it."

"Oh," was all Cooper could come back with.

Clint wasn't ready to let it go yet, though. This was going to be a recurring problem and he needed to know just how big a problem as early as possible. "Yeah. So is there anything else you'd care to question while we're at it? The decision to send them out in the first place, perhaps? The fact that I put Earl in charge of the group instead of you or Tony? Work details, water rations, the women here not to your liking?"

"Hey, that's not where I was going man, honest," Cooper was backpedaling.

"Then make sure it's perfectly clear in the future you don't intend to go there." Clint and Cooper locked eyes until Cooper nodded and looked away.

"Ok, just so we're clear we are not going to pin the raid on the group as a rogue action and we are absolutely not going to plan another raid on what we now know is the U.S. Army. That having been said, I have no intention of rolling over and playing dead. I got us out of Nashville because there were too many people there for comfort in a crisis and nobody else was stepping up to take charge. The fact that we still aren't picking up any radio stations and the Army has set up a base in a National Park pretty much cinches the escalation from crisis to catastrophe."

Clint was pacing again and thanking his lucky stars or the fact that Venus wasn't in retrograde, or the fact that his mother had lived a mostly good Christian life, that the weather had been good for the last several days. "Madison was coming unraveled a little more quickly than I wanted to stick around for but Lexington looked to have enough rural area that we could hunker down and start to put things together again without too much outside interference."

So far that plan hadn't worked out too badly as they'd picked up some additional people on the way and found what had appeared to be a promising area. "I have a feeling that our independence here is about to be threatened, or at least questioned. I'm not going to hand everything over just like that. How was I supposed to know that the Army had set up shop there? Regardless of who was in there I wouldn't have sent my people in unarmed, right?"

"Of course," Cooper just nodded and agreed at this point for more than one reason. This wasn't the first time they had sent a raiding party out into what may or may not be an undefended small town or slowly depopulating or abandoned neighborhood. Each time, Clint would go through this same process, justifying it to both himself and anyone else who would listen. Technically the reasoning was sound; ethically it had more holes than a screen door.

Each time Clint would tell Earl to give anyone he encountered the opportunity to join up and come back with him but with fairly tight restrictions. None of the new folks could bring guns with them, although Earl could bring their guns for them if they were of the correct type. They had to have a skill that the group needed and be willing to work, *hard*. They had to bring virtually everything portable that they owned with them and it was pretty much a no questions asked, all or nothing agreement.

If people didn't want to join up then Earl should try to convince them to join up. Not like 'protection racket' convince but try to help them see the light if at all possible. Ultimately, the security of the group came first and anything that could threaten that had to be dealt with. Anything short of wholesale slaughter was Earl's call and there had been one time where a group didn't want to band together but decided to follow Earl and company back. That proved to be a very bad, very costly decision for the hold-outs. Of the four followers only one survived and that was by design--to tell everyone what had happened to the other three.

In another situation, Earl had confiscated all the firearms he could find and taken them with him when he left. It was part object lesson and part personal protection, as he was sure that as soon as his back was turned they otherwise would have put a bullet between his shoulder blades. To his credit he dropped all the weapons that didn't meet Clint's requirements, which was most of them, about a half a mile away. He'd then sent one vehicle back--with enough firepower to ensure its safety--to tell the group where they could find their weapons, but not to leave for five minutes.

Cooper was wondering what he'd signed on for when Clint turned to him and asked, "So, what do you think? Aside from another raid and passing the buck."

Eight years of being a beat cop was all that kept him from asking if there was any way out of this Mickey Mouse outfit, which is *not* a question that is limited to the enlisted ranks of the military. "I'm working on it. They did give us several days to get back to them. It sounds like they are going to set up duplex repeaters around the base and that's going to take a few days. Until we answer they can't know we've even heard them."

"You're way off base with that one as well, Coop. They didn't send out a broadcast until they knew who was in charge over here. They questioned, or interrogated, long enough to get Earl's middle name. That might not sound like much, but what doesn't sound like much to you and I is the chink in the armor that an interrogator uses to get inside your head."

Clint sat down for a minute to take a drink under the awning of his trailer. "Coop, we picked up the transmission, right?"

"Yeah, right."

"On what channel?"

"19."

"Which is a simplex channel, correct?"

"Yeah."

"Which means it has definitely not been sent through a duplex repeater, correct?"

"Yeah. I know how a CB works, Clint."

"Then *think* about how a CB works, Coop. Let's go back to when the FCC was still around and nobody wanted to go to jail. How far can you broadcast without skipping with the rig and antenna in your cruiser?"

"Oh, probably max out about sixteen miles. In country like this I'd be lucky to get that."

"And let's say that the Army knows this and they are, say, between fifteen and sixteen miles away from us as the crow flies. I'm making assumptions here but I'm trying to prove a point. If they sincerely didn't expect an answer until the repeaters were in place do you think they would be broadcasting now? Do you really think that nobody has told them where we are? Someone told them my first and last name and I'm willing to bet that they even still have their fingernails to boot."

Clint got up and started pacing again. "Coop, the term Army Intelligence is used as an oxymoron on purpose to lull the enemy into a false sense of security. I'm willing to bet they know where we are, how many people we have left, the layout of camp and even have a decent idea of our resources. Military brass may very well be incompetent but the guys at the pointed end of the stick are usually sharp as hell."

Chapter Twenty-Nine

"Joel, have a seat." Mallory indicated the folding chair in front of the makeshift desk she'd been using since the final move from the Armory and made yet another mental note to find something more permanent.

"You look kinda tired," Mallory laughed at the absurdity of what she'd just said and went on. "More so than I'd expect, I mean. Everybody is worn out by the end of the day but you don't look like you're sleeping well. You ok?"

"Yeah, I'm fine." Joel replied. He didn't snap at Mallory but something in his voice didn't sound normal.

"Bull, Joel. I'm not the barista at the corner coffee shop or the security guard in your office building. I didn't ask to be polite so you don't have to spare me the details and get the entire sentence out before you're two steps away." Mallory tilted her head a little as she looked at Joel, who squinted and frowned at her slightly.

"What's going on? If it's between you and Rachael then I don't want to know, but if it's anything else then I do," Mallory said.

"Well, that was blunt."

"You don't look like you're up to subtle right now."

"What if I don't think it's any of your business?" Joel asked.

"I need your help, Joel. You had some very good insight back at the Armory and I need some of that right now. Frankly, I have a civilian problem and you're my civilian point man."

Joel's shoulders had been relaxing a little from the defensive, slightly hunched posture he'd started to take when Mallory asked him what was going on. At this point, he put his elbows on his knees, his face in his hands, and let out a shuddering breath. When he looked up and ran his hands through his hair and then continued looking upwards, the only way Mallory could think to describe him was…haunted.

Joel was pale, with dark circles under his eyes that were even more noticeable now than they had been less than a minute before, almost as though he'd been keeping them away by sheer force of will. Now that she looked a little more closely he looked like he'd lost weight as well. Today was exactly two weeks after the event and the manual labor and constant physical exertion was beginning to tell in subtle ways on just about everyone. Food wasn't a problem, yet, and everyone seemed to be toning up, but Joel looked to be losing weight and not gaining muscle like most of the men.

"Joel, talk to me. What's going on?"

"I'm taking my own advice."

"Meaning? You've said a *lot* over the last two weeks Mr. Narrowing that down a bit without help is going to be tedious to say the least."

"Do you remember what I said about anti-depressants and bipolar medications? How those were going to eventually run out?"

"Oh no way, Joel. Tell me you didn't quit taking that cold turkey?"

"Ok."

"Ok, what?"

"Ok I won't tell you." Joel grinned.

"Joel Taylor! Does Rachael know? Do you have any idea what you could be doing to yourself? Have you never heard of titrating, perhaps by its more common term 'weaning'? For an intelligent person you can be an incredibly stupid man!"

"She says to someone who's been diagnosed as clinically depressed and bipolar *and* who hasn't been on his medication for a week," Joel replied with another slight smile.

"It's not funny."

"Actually it kind of is. I think this is the first time I've smiled in two or three days. If it makes you feel any better the headaches are gone and I don't get dizzy when I stand up anymore."

Mallory put her head down on her desk and covered it with her arms. "This is why I haven't gotten out of the Army. You people on the outside are just insane. You know it, you take medications for it, and then you *stop taking them on purpose!*"

"You do know you're taking this harder than Rachael, right?"

"So she does know. And she hasn't killed you, yet. Which means I can't kill her, yet."

"I'm functional, Mallory, I just look like hell and I have a short fuse right now." Joel shrugged. "If it gets really bad and it looks like I simply can't get by without them then we'll figure something out and somehow I'll get back on the meds. We'll stage a raid on a pharmacy while there's one still standing. We'll loop Tim in so we can take a semi and we'll grab *everything* they have so nothing gets ruined. Hell that might be a good idea anyway. People are going to get sick and need antibiotics and pain killers and pseudoephedrine and a thousand other things that you could only get behind the counter."

"See, that's what I mean, Joel. I don't need you doing something stupid like killing yourself because you got off of some medicines all at once. I'm not saying you can't get off them, not at all. I just think that stopping cold was a bit dangerous and rather stupid, and I know I keep using that word but that's because it fits."

"Ok, that's fair, but I did just come up with that on my own so I'm not completely broken." Joel was fighting to keep his temper now and Mallory wasn't used to his moods or the signs that he was swinging from one to the other and it wouldn't be fair to lash out at her with no warning.

"Alright, point made. As long as you've been off it would probably be a bad idea to jump back on all at once anyway, so you're probably better off to see how things go for a while at this point. I may take you up on the pharmacy raid in the near future, though. Right now I need to pick your brain about something else--specifically, Clint."

"Ok, shoot." Joel tried to settle back into the uncomfortable folding chair.

"That's the problem, I don't want to shoot," Mallory smiled. "I'd rather be a bit more diplomatic about this whole situation if at all possible."

"Nice. What do we know about him so far, other than the fact that he's still using creep factor for a right-hand man?" Joel asked.

"Well, let me start with that. Although Earl is creepy and I'm not arguing that fact, he does seem to be rather capable and intelligent. Don't let the fact that he gives you or the women the willies make you think otherwise. Clint's not the hick he made himself out to be when you ran into him on the freeway, either. Earl either couldn't or wouldn't shed any light on that little bit of playacting other than to say that Clint isn't like that and he has no idea where it came from." Mallory was afraid she was going to have to get used to doing briefings like this from memory and notes rather than reams and reams of paper.

"The day after you picked up the saw mills, Clint seems to have gotten his act together. That's when Earl says they appropriated the weapons, trucks, and RVs."

"They have RVs?" Joel blurted. Mallory closed her eyes and Joel could see her mouthing counting to ten. "Sorry, I'll shut up, continue."

"Thank you. Over the next three days, while they were still in Madison, they joined up with two other groups and raided another car lot for trucks and SUVs and grabbed more trailers. They actually have more than they can use right now, but that was the plan. Get as much as they could while it was available and grow into it if possible or simply use it as long as they could."

"How many people do they have right now?" Joel asked.

"If all thirty-three went back today they would have one-hundred and fifty-eight. We're holding nearly half of their adults right now."

Joel whistled softly. "Have we heard back from him yet?"

"No, nothing, but I'm not surprised. It took us a day to start transmitting and I wouldn't expect him to take much less than that to send something back. Once we've started talking I sincerely hope our communications pick up the pace though. I'm not accustomed to waiting a day for a reply during what amounts to a phone conversation."

"So, what exactly do you need *me* for again, then?" Joel asked.

"I need your take on this as a civilian."

At Joel's questioning look Mallory went on. "Put yourself in Clint's shoes as much as you can. You've put this group together and you've justified everything you've done up to this point. You now have forty-one of your adults out on a raiding, or reconnaissance, or whatever trip and it turns out that your objective was the U.S. Army. Now what? What's going through your head?"

"Aside from a slug from my own gun?" Joel chuckled. "Unless he's certifiable I've got to think that thought's crossed his mind. We haven't told him that he's inflicted any casualties on us, nor have we informed him of his ability to increase the food rations for his people. Frankly, that's going to piss him off."

"Explain," Mallory said noncommittally.

"Well, if he's justified everything he's done up to this point and all we *know* about is the theft, he feels he's in the right. A 1-for-8 or 1-for-9 trade in people is *not* going to sit well with him and Troy isn't even dead? Did we have to shoot all those people? Did we have to shoot to kill? If the one we injured dies did we really do everything we could to save them? Those are just the first couple of questions to come to mind."

"Ok, fair enough. Go on."

"Next he has to wonder if we are going to be looking to aggress him in the future. What is our end game? Will we be constantly watching him to make sure he doesn't get too big or become a real threat? If we're going to peacefully co-exist, how to we go about, oh, I don't know," Joel was at a loss for words, "recruiting isn't right, but bringing in the refugees that are going to be roaming around eventually. We really don't need to be bad-mouthing each other if we're going to be so close--not when negotiations are down to 'food and firearms'."

"Joel, you are so depressing," Mallory said.

"Duh, hello, clinically depressed," Joel waved his hand like he was trying to get her attention. "Was on medication up until a week and a half ago. That's life though, Mal. You didn't ask him to attack us and you *sure* as heck didn't tell him to shoot at us."

...

"I didn't ask for this, any of this," Clint said to Cooper, Tony, Shane, and Frank under the awning in front of his trailer. They were all sitting down, for once, after dinner on the 26th, the day they had received the broadcast from the Army.

"Maybe not but you stepped up and took the lead when it mattered." Shane said. "You've got it now and unless you're ready to step down and walk away, and I mean completely away, I don't think anyone else is willing to take over."

Clint stole a glance at Coop who didn't even flinch. Good, maybe he'll keep his head down for a while and I can deal with one mess at a time. Aloud he said, "We have to respond. If nothing else, they've got almost half the adults--and a bunch of them are parents." There had been a couple of cases where both the husband and wife were on the raiding party, but not if they'd had any kids. Clint had put his foot down when it came to the possibility of creating instant orphans if he could help it.

"I'm going to radio tomorrow morning and open some sort of dialog." Clint sounded resigned to the fact but still ready to put up a fight. "I still don't know what I'm going to say but I can't put it off any longer than that. I'd call tonight but I figure at least one person on the call should get some sleep beforehand."

"How bad can it be, boss?" Tony said.

...

"This is gonna be bad, I can just tell," Mallory said as she walked to the communications tent. All three of her platoon Sergeants were in tow, as were the civilian contingent that had accompanied the Armory to the park, and the now ever-present Ramirez.

"Why do you say that?" Kyle asked.

"When was the last time something like this went well?"

"There's always a first time."

"You'll forgive me, I'm sure, if I don't hold my breath while I also wait for the avian swine?"

"Oh I guarantee you, Top, given sufficient force pigs will most assuredly fly." Kyle replied.

"Judicious application and all that...well, here we are." Mallory looked over her entourage and shook her head. "We aren't all going to fit in there and frankly we don't all need to be here. Everyone but Sergeant Halstead and Joel is dismissed."

"Sergeant Wilson, I need a pair of headphones for myself and please put the conversation on speaker--no mic though." Mallory said as she walked into the tent with Halstead and Joel.

"Roger, already set up for you over here," Wilson pointed to another chair and headset and flipped a switch to turn on the monitor speakers once she had her headset on. "We got the first transmission at 8:30. He's transmitted twice at 5 minute intervals since. We should be getting another one in just a minute."

Right on cue the speakers came to life with the static-click common to CB transmissions. "This is Clint Baxter calling the U.S. Army base located in Natchez Trace State Park." Joel noticed that the voice was the same but, just as Earl had said, the speech wasn't. Whatever had been going on that day on the highway had been some sort of act. He nodded to Mallory. "Contacting as requested regarding the group sent to Natchez Trace on Twenty Five, June. Please respond."

Instead of letting the request linger, this time Mallory replied. "Mr. Baxter, this is First Sergeant Jensen, U.S. Army. Can you please verify your identity by providing the number of persons accompanying Mr. Hanson?" No reason not to at least be polite when telling someone you don't necessarily believe they are who they say they are.

"I don't know that I'd ever call Earl Mr. Hanson, but he was accompanied by forty others."

Good, the man can count, do simple math and follow directions. Mallory had dealt with a lot of people who would tell you how many people were in a group instead of answering the question you asked.

"And what color and make of vehicle did Mr. Hanson drive?" Mallory asked, not rising to Clint's bait about Earl's moniker.

"Burgundy Chevy Suburban, 2500."

"We need to talk." Mallory said.

"Isn't that what we're doing now?"

"Yes, it is. We need to talk face-to-face, though."

"I assume Murphy paid a visit at some point. How badly did it go off, if I might ask?" Clint asked.

"I'd rather discuss it in person."

"Top, I need something to take back to my people!"

Mallory's eyebrows went up as she glanced over at Wilson and Halstead. They had both caught it as well. "Very well, Mr. Baxter. We attempted to convince your group to surrender prior to any contact being made with the base as a whole. We were fired upon and took a casualty." Mallory had not wanted to say anything about the raid over the air but Clint hadn't left her any choice. She hoped that Clint would both understand what she said next and realize why she was saying it the *way* she was saying it and keep his cool until they could meet face-to-face.

"Of the forty-one in the group, nine fired on us unprovoked. Eight are currently Tango Uniform. One is recovering from wounds received at the time." T-U, Toes Up, one of the 'nice' but obscure ways of saying dead in the military. If he loses it he's going to do it now.

"They're WHAT! What the hell did you people do?"

"Mr. Baxter, we need to talk. Face-to-face."

"You've got that right! And I want my people back--all of them! I'll be in contact later. Baxter out!"

...

"What's Tango Uniform?" Sean asked.

"It means Toes Up, dead. Of the forty-one people we sent in eight are dead and one is recovering which means whoever it is probably got lucky and they missed the heart." Clint said absently as he started to pace.

"She said they had one casualty, so one of theirs died at least." Tony said into the growing silence.

"No, that's not what that means. A casualty can actually be an injury, regardless of severity. It just has to be sustained as a result of action, battle, whatever." Clint made a dismissive wave with his hand, not at Tony but at the fact that he wouldn't know the difference between action and battle.

"And don't take death lightly." Clint went on. "Are you happy they killed one of our people? Eight? Maybe nine if the last one doesn't pull through. We've been together two whole weeks; how hard did you take it when someone on the force got killed? An Army unit is the same way, Tony, so don't be so glib and free with the 'at least' when talking about killing people. It's not a numbers game."

"So somebody could have tripped leaving the scene and sprained their ankle and that could be their 'casualty' and we lost eight or nine people?" Sean asked.

"Yeah, that's exactly what could have happened, although First Sergeants don't get as far as they do by embellishing like that for long."

"Speaking of First Sergeant, why'd you call her Top?" Frank asked.

"What?" Clint spun and took a step towards Frank. "What did you say?"

Frank looked at the other three and swallowed. "You called her Top. You said 'Top, I need something to take back to my people' when all she would talk about was a face-to-face meeting."

"Son of a…" Clint's fists were turning white from lack of blood. "Top is a nickname for the First Sergeant in a Company." Clint was looking around for something to hit or kick. "It's something that you would know if you read a lot of military fiction or maybe science fiction but you wouldn't say it like I did unless you'd been in the military. Stupid."

Clint quit looking for something to vent his anger on and started pacing again. "It's not the end of the world. She probably knows I was prior military, big deal. I didn't tip my hand that much but it's one less advantage."

…

"So, Mr. Baxter is prior military and most likely Army. What else did we get out of that little conversation?" Mallory asked.

"He's less than pleased with the fact that you killed eight of his people." Joel replied.

"Now now, he didn't blame me specifically. He did say 'you people'." Mallory said.

"Ok, fine. He's mad at all of us then." Joel replied. "He went from sounding at least a little reasonable to totally irrational in a matter of seconds. He wants *all* of his people back. It was a good call to put the bodies in one of the refrigerator trucks for him, by the way."

"Thank you, that was actually Morris's idea but I agree it was a good one." Mallory had a small smile but it was sad. "We have no idea how long Clint holds a grudge and either way, it was the right thing to do. We have no idea how many of those people have families who will want the bodies for a funeral and burial of their own."

"Either way he's not taking it well. He focused on the dead and wants everyone back. Not entirely unexpected but not the best possible scenario either." Halstead interjected.

"What's he thinking, Joel?" Mallory prodded.

"I'd be getting advice. For as many people as he's responsible for, he has to be getting help. I would have had people listening in just like you were. He's probably explaining what Tango Uniform means and he may or may not be winding them up about it." Joel had his hands in his pockets as he walked in a circle in the tent.

"He wasn't taking any responsibility for the situation, either. The fact that things went wrong at all, he blamed that on Murphy. And then when shots were fired, it was like he ignored or didn't hear what you said about being fired on unprovoked. *We* must have done something wrong and then overreacted. He's looking for an obvious way to make us the bad guys here and in the absence of that I think he'll settle for a thinly-veiled excuse. He doesn't feel that he's at fault."

"How do you propose meeting with him?" Halstead asked.

"In the open but with a minimal guard," Mallory said. "I can't appear afraid of him, because I'm not, but I'm not going to do something overtly stupid either. It'll be a place of our choosing and when we get together I think it should be probably three on each side."

"There's no way you're going out with just two other people, Top!" Halstead snapped.

"That isn't what I said Sergeant" Mallory replied. "Nor did I get a chance to finish. I have no doubt that there will be a contingent on both sides and that we can field more and more heavily armed people should we choose. I meant for the discussion because more than that and we won't get anything done because everyone will think they have to get a word in edgewise. If we can keep the numbers that low then Clint and I will most likely do the majority of the talking."

"Sorry, good point."

"Forgiven. I won't push the man because he's been dealt a little bit of a shock but I'm not giving him more than eight hours to call us back before I'm going to call him. He's a grown man, he's most likely prior military and he needs to act like he's in charge, not sulk.

Mallory looked at the two men who'd accompanied her into the communications tent. "You two are who I'd like to come with me to the table. Halstead, you don't have a choice. Joel, you do, and I would think that Rachael would also have a say in the matter. Would you please discuss it with Rachael and get back to me as quickly as possible?"

"Of course I'll do it, er consider it. I'll go get permission right now." Joel was grinning like an idiot. "This is the most fun I've had in a week."

"To recap, insane," Mallory shook her head.

"Beats being depressed," Joel winked as he ducked out of the tent.

Chapter Thirty

"She isn't going to wait forever and we need to get it out of the way. They aren't going anywhere and frankly neither are we." Clint said. "Oh we might move around a little as we find a slightly better place to set up permanently, or grab a town that's been totally abandoned, but this area's nice."

Clint threw his arms out wide, "It's better than nice, it's perfect. We have water; we have a long growing season although it isn't quite year round. We have room to spread out, and if things get *really* bad we can always go crawling to the Army for help."

"How are you going to break it to the families?" Coop asked.

"I haven't decided yet. I want to find out what happened and who we lost first. If we lost couples and single people then it won't be an issue. If we only lost one or two family folks then I might be able to play it up and make heroes out of everyone. You know, big funeral, honors...something. Give the families bigger trailers, although that would be the exact opposite of what they need."

Tony snorted and almost had water come out of his nose.

"Something I say strike you as *funny* Anthony?" Clint asked with absolutely no humor in his voice.

"No," Tony said. "Well, yeah. I mean, duh. Give 'em a bigger trailer as an honor but they obviously don't need one because the family is smaller now."

"And what makes that funny? Because someone is dead? The fact that someone who obviously doesn't need more any longer is getting more of that thing?"

"Um," Tony was looking around for help and not getting any.

"Did you not hear me this morning when I told you not to make light of the dead or did you think I was kidding?"

Tony looked down at his cup.

"I asked you a question, Anthony, I expect an answer, or at least a response."

Tony looked up and flinched at the expression on Clint's face. "Neither, I guess. I guess I just forgot." Tony swallowed. "Won't happen again. Sorry."

"Last warning. Make sure it doesn't."

"I'm pissed at the Army. I'm pissed at whoever called for weapons free. I'm pissed at whoever pulled the trigger on both sides. I'm pissed at the First Sergeant for not letting people know there's a friggin' Army Base in the middle of a *National Park* and I'm pissed that we lost eight people." Clint was fighting the urge to get up and pace again. He was tired of walking in front of his trailer.

"I have to put the best face on this that I can, though, and honoring the dead *has* to be part of thatTelling the story in such a way that we don't play the part of the evil raider will be another part. Repeating that story often enough and with conviction so that everyone believes it without question is yet another part and doing it without starting a war with the Army is going to be half the problem."

"How long are you going to wait?" Frank asked.

"About another ten minutes." Clint said....

"Sergeant Jensen," Clint began, once Mallory was in the communication tent and on the radio. "I agree that we need to sit down and discuss some things in person but my initial stipulations stand. All forty-one members of the party are to be returned."

"As things stand I see no obstacles to that. One member is currently recovering from fairly serious surgery. It is entirely up to you when they are transferred back into your care."

"The specifics of the individual in question can be discussed during the in-person meeting," Clint replied. He'd forgotten about the wounded, he'd been so focused on the dead. Maybe he wasn't cut out for this leader crap after all.

"Is eleven hundred hours acceptable tomorrow? I suggest the airport outside of Lexington." Mallory prompted. Nothing substantial was going to be discussed right now so she might as well get the meeting set up and get on with the rest of her day.

"That should be fine. How many people do you want to limit it to?"

"I suggest no more than three people at the table from each side, including ourselves. I'm bringing one civilian and one military advisor."

"Sounds fair. Obviously everyone is going to be armed. I won't ask you not to be if you don't ask the same."

"Obviously. My Platoon Sgt's also won't let me out of their sight without an escort, which will be held back and out of the way so I wouldn't expect anything less from you."

"Of course," Clint replied with a small laugh. Add a few reporters and a camera crew and you'd think something important was going on. Throw in an Internet connection and some bloggers and they'd be set!

"Until tomorrow morning, then." Mallory said.

"Until tomorrow." Clint replied.

…

Mallory had every intention of not only being at the meeting first but being *obvious* about the fact that she was waiting for Clint to show up. That plan had been shot to hell when she got the radio call at 07:15 from the advance scout that she'd sent out the night before that Clint had just shown up.

Mallory instructed her scout to lay low, observe, and make sure Clint didn't do anything hinky. Apparently, Clint was planning to one-up Mallory in the showing up first game.

When Mallory arrived at 10:30, as though she had no idea Clint was already there, she was greeted with a 12x12 instant canopy under which was an 8' folding table with six chairs and a cooler at one end. She had planned to do something similar, including pads of paper and pens for everyone, but gave it up when the call came in as early as it did. Sometimes you just had to give the other guy the battle and hope to take the war in the long run.

"Mr. Baxter, I presume." Mallory held out her hand as she approached the table. She noticed that Clint had, in fact, provided paper and pens for everyone.

"Please, as far as I know my father is still alive. Call me Clint." Clint smiled. "Sergeant Halstead," Clint read the insignia and nametape from Halstead's uniform. "Mr. Taylor?" Clint quirked his brow at the lack of any type of insignia, including US Army on Joel's fatigues but the presence of a nametape.

"That's correct." Was the sum total of Joel's reply in that regard. "We met the day after the power went out, on the freeway. It seems your accent was a bit thicker then."

Color rose on Clint's face. Not in anger but sheer embarrassment. "Well, Mr. Taylor, as an old acquaintance of mine used to say, I got nuthin'. Let's just say it was so thick I cut it out by the roots."

Joel nodded and chose to let it drop. No use embarrassing the man any further. "Fair enough."

"As you deduced I'm Clint Baxter. This is Robert Cooper, a former Officer in Madison," pointing to Coop on his right. "And this gentleman is Dr. Ferris DeMarco," indicating the man on his left. "I asked him to come along to discuss the status of the wounded member of our group and whether or not we could provide adequate care yet."

"The sodas are cold and they're cans so they haven't been opened." Clint was playing the host but at least he was being realistic about what to expect from those he was hosting. They knew he wasn't being gracious; he was simply being the host and trying to make this *his* turf. At some point the gloves would come off.

...

"There's no reason to bring anyone anywhere en masse with the exception of the eight we've already discussed," Mallory said with a sigh. "They already know where we are, they are all healthy and perfectly capable of driving themselves. All the vehicles are fine as they are in our lot so they haven't been stolen. We'll escort them as far as Lexington but they can drive themselves."

Mallory leveled a glare at Clint, "They weren't in a prison camp for a decade. They haven't been mistreated. They've been sitting in tents, sleeping on cots, and eating the same food we've been eating for three whole days. I think they'll live."

"Ok, ok. How do you want to handle the transfer of the eight casualties?" Dr. DeMarco asked. "And thank you for using one of the few refrigerated trucks for a makeshift morgue."

"You're welcome. It really was the least we could do. Give us a day and we can have the truck driven down, with an escort, to deliver them. I can't have a handoff of the truck, I'm sorry." Mallory was shaking her head. "We won't come storming in and take over and we can even crank the temperature down to below freezing for a while so that you can get some additional time outside of the truck."

"We've got the names and only one of them had family still in the camp. I'll admit that's going to make it a *lot* easier on me." Clint said. "A couple of them might have been trouble waiting to happen but a few are going to be missed."

"Lastly, what about the weapons?" Clint had been waiting to ask about this. He knew that this, unlike the people, might be a sticking point. Everyone that had pulled the trigger was dead--except one, and he'd been torn up pretty bad and still might not make it. Everyone else was guilty of nothing more than brandishing a loaded firearm, and Mallory didn't have jurisdiction.

Not giving the firearms back, now that might be a problem. See, most of those people hadn't actually owned those guns three weeks ago. He was pretty sure some of them still had price tags on them from the pawn shops as a matter of fact. While he could make an argument that he needed them for protection and possibly for hunting, she could make the argument that they weren't his in the first place, that they had already been used in a raid against her people, and that if nothing else *she* needed them for self-defense and hunting. Finder's keepers and all that.

Mallory didn't reply right away, she simply looked at Clint for several seconds. Leaning forward, arms on the table, fingers steepled over her pad of notes she just looked at him.

Finally Mallory spoke and it was like a slap across the face. "Am I killing my own people?"

"How dare you! I'm the one burying eight, or possibly nine, of my people, not you!" Clint snapped.

"Spare me the outrage, sincere or otherwise, Mr. Baxter. Those deaths are on your conscience not mine," Mallory replied. "You sent them into harm's way, not me. You're the one burying people because you screwed up so you need to own it. Man up soldier!"

That caught him off guard but he covered it well by clenching his jaw and turning it into a sneer. Not since before they'd had the cause but not the proof and he'd taken the Less Than Honorable from the Army had he wanted to fire the gun at his hip in anger.

"So what do you want from me then, my word? Something tells me it's going to take more than that." Clint was almost fighting to get every word out.

"Unfortunately I have to start there." Mallory hadn't moved from her position at the table. "No treaty we could sign would be enforceable, and no declaration or truce would be binding unless we can trust each other."

"I don't trust you!" Clint snapped.

"And that's the crux of this whole charade." Mallory replied. "You planned on me not trusting you because I know you're pissed at me. That's why the sodas were in cans. You got here before me today not to show me up but because you don't trust me. You don't trust anything I say or any motivations I may have. At some point you might want to think about why you don't trust me but that's a topic of discussion for another day."

Mallory leaned forward, "I don't trust you because you aren't trustworthy. You've already proven that. For whatever reason, good, bad, or indifferent, you tried to raid my base. You've heard all the chatter over the Citizen Band, you knew someone was there, and you decided to try a raid instead of coming in through the front door like a good neighbor should."

Clint was clenching his jaw so tight he was going to be feeling it for a couple of days. Mallory leaned back and put her hands in her lap, keeping an open posture instead of folding her arms. "So, Clint, talk to me. I'll lay it out like I do with my Platoon Sergeants and say it just like I do to them. Give me just one single, solitary, good reason why I should give the guns back and I will."

She had him. All she had to do was squeeze, but she wouldn't, not yet. The first rule of an ambush is to give the enemy a way out and allow them to use it, or be prepared to fight them to the death to a man. He just had to humble himself, not only in front of her but in front of his own people. He couldn't even send Coop and the Dr. away first because that was how rumors got started.

Clint told himself he would get even one day and even believed it on some level, but that really didn't help. He started thinking of all the things he *wanted* to say and forced them down. Finally, he closed his eyes and took a breath to calm himself down--swallowing just enough of his pride to get through this.

"We need them, pure and simple, for self-defense and for hunting. Facts are facts and both Coop and the Doc can tell you that we've driven off our own raiders," both of the other men nodded and it wasn't the nod of someone going along with a story, "and the fact that we had weapons was one reason that another group chose to join with us. On the way here from Madison we stopped twice in some areas where guys had hunted previously and took down a couple of deer, and we've shot a number of rabbit, goose, and duck where we're at now to supplement the food we've got." The Dr. nodded again at the food comment.

Mallory didn't react right away but she didn't make Clint wait long. "Ok. And because I'm so nice I'm even sending back the ones you 'don't need anymore'." Clint relaxed. "However," Clint tensed again, "as the group is going to be escorted back as far as Lexington they will be disabled in some manner when they leave. I won't leave people unprotected, that defeats part of the purpose of escorting them, but I won't have them shooting at me along the way or as I leave them behind either. Most likely all the ammunition will be in a locked box which we will radio them the combination to once we are at a safe distance. That will be safest for all involved."

It was fair but Clint hadn't wanted fair, he'd wanted to win. *What* he didn't know--but he'd wanted to win *something*. He hadn't even surprised her by getting here early. "Thank you." He somehow managed to say it without gritting his teeth.

…

Turning her back on Clint wasn't the most difficult thing Mallory had ever done, but it was more nerve racking than she had anticipated when she first sat down. "He hates you. You do know that right?" Joel asked.

"Hate is such a strong word, Joel," Mallory replied.

"You're right, but in this case I don't think it's strong enough." Joel said. "He loathes you. He despises you. He wants nothing more than to destroy you and everything you stand for and have worked your entire life to build. If he had the chance he would erase all trace…"

"Fine. How big a thorn in our side do you think he's going to be in the long run?" Mallory asked Joel and Halstead as they walked back to their vehicles. Joel answered first, "Hard telling. He's so mad right now about being called out on the raid in general and having to eat crow and ask for the weapons back, I really don't know. He seems the type to hold a grudge though. It looks like he's developed a tic on the right side of his face, too. I don't know if that's new or not but it was really getting bad the more worked up he got without actively letting it show."

"I noticed that too," Halstead said as they got to the LAV they were using as their transport for the day. He held the door for Mallory as Joel went around to the other side and climbed in.

"Well, done is done. I'm not going to worry about it overly since I can't do too much about it and he needed to be called out on everything I brought up." Mallory was unapologetic.

"I'm not saying you were wrong, I'm just saying the situation isn't any better today than it was yesterday and it might be worse. The man really seems to have it in for you at this point and now it's personal." Joel wasn't sure what point he was trying to make or who he was trying to convince but he felt he needed to drive it home.

"He's been made to look bad in front of some of his people, regardless of the reason. He's lost eight adults and will have to deal with a grieving mother, again, regardless of the reason. He doesn't know what your motivations are and doesn't trust you--possibly because he's not the trusting sort, but maybe just because his situation is preventing it."

Mallory made the 'who knows' gesture and reached for a headset. "I think it's more a combination of a lack of honor among thieves and the fact that he never learned to keep his friends close but his enemies closer. He also needs to quit wearing his heart on his sleeve. Let's see, anymore lame clichés I could throw in while I'm at it?"

"We need to make sure everyone's ready to head out. I don't want to have guests any longer than necessary." Halstead said, ignoring that last remark. "They know where they're going and, assuming we can round up a lockbox in short order, I say we feed 'em one more time and show 'em the door."

"That was pretty much my thought. I'm not sending them back without warning, though, and if we can't get back in touch with Mr. Baxter and Co. today before dark then it will have to wait until tomorrow." Mallory was getting ready to call the base but held off for one more comment. "In fact, I'd be surprised at this point if we don't end up keeping them one more day after all. Clint would probably just as soon have us feed them all three more meals before he took them back."

"Bastard." Joel muttered.

"Possibly, but at this point I think it hardly matters."

...

"Sergeant Wilson, is your squad ready to move out?" Sergeant Jackson asked.

"Yes, Sergeant. We have the combination for the ammo cans. We'll be providing directions and changing channels randomly to minimize the chance of being intercepted prior to dropping off the detainees." Wilson said.

"Very good. Don't make a day of it but I don't plan on seeing you before lunch either."

The drive and drop-off were uneventful and when the time came to part company, Earl was even sincere in his gratitude.

"Sergeant Wilson, thank you for the treatment we've received while at your base. I understand that Clint and your First Sergeant aren't seeing eye-to-eye on most things right now, and I really don't know how bad it is between them. I hope things don't get worse between us." Earl held out his hand and shook Wilson's. "Thank you for giving us a chance and not just opening up on us. I'm sorry for the nine folks that didn't take you up on it, and I really do hope that the one who got hit recovers."

"Thank you for that, Mr. Hanson, and you saved a lot of lives when you got everyone to put the guns down," Wilson replied. "I hope we can keep it to a slow simmer for a while and let everyone cool off. I'd like to be able to give you the combination for the canisters now but orders are orders. We won't be too far away to protect you though if something goes wrong, that's why we're dropping off here and heading out in the direction we are."

With a final nod, Sergeant Wilson turned and trotted back to his Humvee and once they were a safe distance away they radioed the combination to the ammo cans. They watched through field glasses as the rifles and pistols were loaded and then the trucks and SUVs headed home.

Chapter Thirty-One

This was the second "meet and greet" Sheri had been involved in, but it didn't feel anything like the last one, and didn't sound like any she'd heard the others talk about either. It just felt...odd. There were a total of six people from the group that had broadcast a request to join up with the Promised Land group, four men and two women. The mix was pretty standard and the location, typical.

When the call came in over the CB or shortwave--usually CB--a site was agreed upon that was flat and open. In addition, the group hoping to join would arrive first; the number of representatives no more than six and armed with nothing more than handguns in holsters. They would already be away from their vehicles and standing.

When the ambassadors for Promised Land's group arrived, in this case Sergeant Keeler and Sheri, they reconed the area and determined if it was safe to proceed. There had been a couple of times where things looked odd but had turned out to be just fine. In this case, things looked ok so they parked the Humvee, got out, and walked to meet the group.

That's where normal took its leave and things started feeling really odd. They had been there for a little over half an hour so far; Keeler had checked in twice, and the women hadn't said a single word after the greetings. The majority of the talking had been done by two of the men, neither of them the older of the four present. They didn't have radios to relay any information back and forth with anyone else, but they acted as though they didn't have any authority to make any decisions on their own.

Decidedly odd.

"We have a number of the homes in the town with electricity already. Not everyone is going to want to move if they aren't going to have electricity where they are going. What guarantees will we have that we won't be going from what is, admittedly, not an ideal situation to a potentially worse situation?" One of the spokesmen asked.

Sheri was getting frustrated and a little pissed off at this point. It looked like this group was here just to get information out of Keeler and Sheri and not actually planning for a joining of their two groups. "I'm a little confused by your question, frankly. You are the one who requested this meeting initially about the possibility of joining up with us. We aren't asking you to move in and we aren't forcing you to do anything. We wouldn't expect anyone to move from a better situation to a worse one, that's absurd. But we're not providing guarantees either. What guarantee do you have that whatever power source you are using isn't going to dry up or go away? What guarantee do you have that you won't become prey to some crazy, power hungry, tin dictator wanna-be?" Did he just flinch? Interesting, I wonder if Keeler saw that.

"But we aren't just letting everyone in either," Keeler interjected. "People, groups, have to have something to offer, as we've said, and we don't mean money or possessions, we mean skills. It may sound cold but we don't have spare food, clothing, or shelter for people who won't contribute. I didn't say can't, I said won't. We've come across a couple of groups with folks who were in a really bad way, and we didn't turn them away, and nobody's complained. But we aren't going to take in a band of people who feel entitled to what we have but aren't willing to contribute to the community as a whole.

"What you've given us over the course of the last forty minutes is absolutely nothing. You've asked us questions, which we've answered, and dodged answers to our questions in return. If you are looking for guarantees, the only guarantees we can offer are the following; security, a place to sleep, food to eat, clean hot water, and a lot of work every day to ensure that the previous four things continue to exist."

"I think we're probably done here. It doesn't look as though you are actually in a position to make a decision, or at least not a binding one, so I suggest that you go back to those who can, discuss it, and contact us again so that we can do this again right."

Sheri was in awe at the dressing down she'd just witnessed. It wasn't really what Keeler had said, but how he'd said it, and the fact that he'd brooked no resistance. Twice the other group had tried to interrupt and he'd just run right over them. He was done, and he'd let them have it. They looked at each other for a few seconds, and then one of them said, "Thank you for your time, we'll probably be in touch." He held out his hand, and then everyone shook hands and said goodbye. Less than a minute later, they were driving away in their SUV and pickup truck.

"What a freaking waste of time," Sheri spat, "and after the last one went so well!"

"They can't all go well. After all, I'm in the Army ma'am, if everyone joins us, I won't have anyone to shoot at."

"That, Sergeant Keeler, is a very jaded view of life."

"The world, Ms. Hines, is a very jaded place in which to live."

"I'm sorry you've had the experiences in life that make you feel that way, I really am."

They were on their way back to the Humvee, and passing as close as they would be to the trees.

...

Pete wasn't a hunter, not really, much as he'd tried. There were, however, a few things he was really good at other than electrical engineering and baseball happened to be one of them. In fact, he'd been pitching since he was nine years old. He'd decided to watch the meeting from a distance, just to see how it went, and that turned out to be a very good thing when Sheri had shown up. It would not have done at all to let them know that he was involved with this group, not at all.

As they were walking back to their Humvee, Pete made a snap decision. He bent down and picked up a rock about the size of small apple. Keeler turned his back on Pete to open the door, and Pete pitched a breaking fastball at the back of Keeler's head. Between the distance and how hard he'd thrown it he was sure he hadn't killed Keeler, but he was gonna be out for a while, and pissed when we woke up…not to mention sore. He may have a concussion, and possibly a fractured skull--oh well.

As Keeler crumpled to the ground, Pete watched Sheri run around the Humvee to Keeler's side. Good, she didn't use the radio right away. That's the problem with playing things by ear; you don't get a chance to think things through. If she'd called for help he might not have a chance to get away. He had no idea how far away backup was, assuming there was any.

Sheri was engrossed in checking Keeler for obvious wounds, apparently wondering if he'd been shot by a silenced rifle, so Pete made his move. He was about ten feet behind her when Keeler's radio came to life.

"Tango Two this is Papa Two do you copy, over?" the voice on the other end asked.

Sheri just looked at the radio on Keeler's belt for the five seconds between the first transmission and the second. Pete kept moving the entire time, slower now that her focus wasn't as complete as before.

"Tango Two this is Papa Two do you copy, over?" the voice repeated.

Sheri apparently didn't want to use Keeler's radio for some reason, so she reached for the radio at her own belt. Pete reached her just as she pulled the radio free and finished standing up.

…

Sheri felt the press of cold metal against the skin behind her right ear and heard a familiar voice, "Put the radio down, Sheri."

In a fit of inspiration, she squeezed the transmit lock button as she slowly bent down to put the radio on the ground. The entire time the gun--she was sure that's what it was now--never moved. "What now, Pete, or should I say 'Peter the Great'?"

"I'm pretty sure I heard quotation marks there, Sheri, not a good start." The gun moved away and Sheri relaxed, that's when he hit her on the back of the head. Not hard enough to knock her out, but hard enough to make her see stars and drop her to her knees. "Don't do it again, ever." The fact that he simply said it, that he didn't yell, that he didn't threaten, that's what scared her.

"Yes sir, never again."

"Good girl, very good, now let's go, shall we?"

"May I ask where?"

"Why, *home* of course."

...

"Tango Two this is Papa Two do you copy, over?" Specialist Tyler Morris was manning the radio during this scheduled meeting. So far there had been a total of twenty such meetings and although they weren't yet commonplace, they were becoming routine. What wasn't routine was the fact that Sergeant Keeler, the military component of the team, hadn't reported in at his thirty minute interval as planned.

The thirty minute interval was Top's requirement, and it made sense. It was a compromise between only reporting in just prior to making contact and using a high bandwidth connection that would have higher micromanaging everything. It also made sense to check in fairly often and make sure that nothing had gone wrong.

Apparently thirty minutes was long enough for something to happen, and now it had. Morris switched to Sheri's frequency and just before he hit the send button got a transmission. It didn't sound like Sheri was holding her radio but she was the one talking, "Peter the Great?"

All transmissions were recorded on a 30 second loop which could be shunted to a permanent recording as necessary. At the mention of Pete's new moniker, Morris hit the record button and yelled for his NCO in charge, "Sergeant Bowersock! Could you please step in here?" While he waited for Sergeant Bowersock, the conversation continued and he heard a thump, followed by the sound of something or someone falling. Morris was swearing under his breath as KB ducked into the tent.

"Not quite the greeting I expected when you so politely asked for my company, Specialist Morris," KB said, knowing full well the comment hadn't been directed at him.

"No Sergeant, sorry Sergeant, no excuse."

"Oh give it a rest Morris. What's up?"

"I think we might have a problem with the "meet & greet". Sergeant Keeler didn't report in on schedule, and after I couldn't raise him I switched to Ms. Hines' frequency As soon as I did, I got the following."

He played back the recording, which transmission he'd been listening to as he briefed Sergeant Bowersock. By the end of the recording, KB was actually growling in the back of his throat. The community that had sprung up here at Natchez Trace had become very tight in the last five weeks, and the thought of someone doing harm of any kind to one of theirs was infuriating. "I'll be right back. Don't go anywhere and don't say a word about this to anybody else until I get back."

The order proved easier said than done as Morris was supposed to be relieved in three minutes and his relief showed up early. This presented a problem as Morris was unable to provide his relief with a situation report, having been gagged by Sergeant Bowersock prior to his departure. Corporal Alex Pine, being "Command Eligible" and therefore technically senior to Specialist Morris, didn't take kindly to "Negative" and "I'm truly sorry, but I'm unable to comply with that request."

"It's not a request, it's an ORDER! GIVE! ME! THE! HEADSET! NOW!" The shade of purple that Pine turned during the exchange was truly startling. Promised Land was still rather small, all things considered, and Corporal Pine had a good set of lungs. Bowersock and Jensen got to the communications tent at a run.

"Stand down, Corporal, he's refusing orders on my authority," Bowersock said. "And while you're at it sit down before you pop a vessel, or a nut for that matter. You look like a grape about to go all juicy on us. I assume you're his relief so you'd probably hear about it anyway but I told him not to talk to anybody about what's going on until I got back. I said sit down, I didn't mean when you got around to it."

"Has there been anything else since I left?"

"The sound of a vehicle leaving and it wasn't ours, which was just active stupid."

"Maybe, maybe not. I'll explain why in a minute. Please play it back from the time you switched freqs."

Morris played the recording up to the point that the car, it was obvious it was a car the second time through, was fading away. Mallory's normally olive complexion was turning redder by the second until she let out a breath she hadn't realized she was holding. Her jaw muscle was still clenched tight enough to be painful though. "KB, you said 'Maybe, maybe not' about leaving our Humvee being stupid. Explain."

"Well, he doesn't know if we can track it, at least that was the first thing I thought of. You and I know we can't but he has no idea what we can and can't do. I find it interesting that it doesn't even sound like he looked for anything in it but then again, maybe he plans on coming back for it." KB was squinting now, thinking about it from a couple of angles. "We have no idea how bad off Keeler is, that's why I stopped by and sent off two more Humvees to go get him with a couple of medics. I say we radio to them to leave the vehicle behind and try to tail him if he comes back for it."

"We have to assume that grabbing Sheri was a spur of the moment decision at the end of the meeting with what were obviously patsies, a crime of opportunity if you will. I think it was a setup from the beginning, like a couple of these have been, but not to grab Sheri." KB finished.

"I agree with a number of your points and most of your analysis, unfortunately. Morris, radio the group headed out to Keeler and instruct them to leave the Humvee and bring Keeler back," Mallory paused, "whatever his condition. And he better be functional eventually or I'm gonna be really pissed and not at my medics."

After the lead vehicle acknowledged their new instructions, the incoming transmission light flashed on the frequency that had been assigned to Sergeant Keeler. Morris switched to it and was greeted with an obviously pained "-apa Two. Repeat, this is Tango Two to Papa Two, over."

"This is Papa Two. Authenticate Whiskey Tree Niner, over."

"I authenticate Big Fat Bleeding Goose Egg Back of Head. Be advised; never drink nine year old whiskey in a tree. By the way, that's not nearly as funny when stopping to think about it, made my head want to split open and the world is spinning, and I think I'm gonna throw up, and Sheri's gone, over."

"It's him," Morris said to the others in the tent. "We read you Lima Charlie. We have two medics inbound. How bad is the head? over."

"I don't know for sure, but you did catch the part about the big fat bleeding goose egg, right? I can't look around too quick either or everything goes tilted like the old Batman TV show and I feel like I'm spinning. I feel like I was too close to an Abrahms when it let loose and I forgot to open my mouth and cover my ears. Did I mention Sheri's gone?" Keeler swore. "I knew we shouldn't have brought civilians along on these things. Over."

"Keeler, knock it off," Mallory broke in. She'd put on another set of headphones in order to have a microphone to herself. "We couldn't be meeting with groups of civilians without a civilian present, and we really couldn't meet with them with fewer than equal numbers of military and civilian representatives on our side. Everyone who has gone has been a volunteer, and it's something that's been discussed before--every single trip out. Don't beat yourself up over something that you couldn't have done anything about. Over."

"Yes, First Sergeant, I know all that, I understand, I'll do my best, but it'll be hard knowing that we lost the first person on my watch. I'm not saying I won't get over it, especially once we get her back. It just sucks is all, and I'm not too good at suck. Over."

"Roger that Keeler, major suck. For now, though, try to stay upright until the medics get there and let's get your head patched up. Over"

"Roger. Whoever did it didn't take my sidearm, and as long as I'm conscious I'd like to think they won't get the drop on me. Out."

To KB she said, "Please request that Jackson and Ramirez accompany you to the command tent. I'll be there in a couple of minutes." Mallory shook her head, "We've had it too easy for too long; I'm afraid this won't be the last time someone tries something like this unless we change our tactics."

"I concur, Top, but like you said, we have had it fairly easy as far as bringing other groups in. I'll be right back, by your leave." KB ducked out and went to find the other Sergeants.

"Morris, come with me. Pine, you cooled off enough to man the radio yet or do I need to dump a cooler of ice over your head?" Mallory asked.

"Sorry Top, I'm fine. Absolutely no excuse," Pine said.

"Go ahead and take the radio then, and if anyone comes asking send them to me please." Mallory said.

"Right away," Pine agreed.

When Mallory walked into the command tent, all three Sergeants were already there. "Who are we gonna go kill?" Jackson asked. "And no, KB didn't say anything. It's just that I've known him long enough that I can read the look on his face. He's gonna disassemble something and there's a good chance it's a biological."

"Well, good call then. Hold on a second and let me play something for you." She picked up the radio in the command tent and called over to Corporal Pine, "Pine, send the recording we've been discussing recently to this handset please." A few seconds later they were listening to Sheri and Pete; some for the first time, others once again.

Chapter Thirty-Two

When the recording was over, Mallory thanked Pine, cleared the channel, and looked at her present cadre. "Ok, protocol is suspended, advice?"

Ramirez didn't even hesitate a full heartbeat, "Personally, I'm this close to sending a Humvee out after this worthless meat-sack right now to prune the friggin' helix!" The string of creative uses for a human body that followed would later be referred to by those present or who overheard it as 'something that had to be experienced to be truly appreciated'; 'the reason I got into the military in the first place'; 'the funniest thing I've ever heard', and 'the single biggest reason that not a single teen pregnancy has ever been reported on base'.

"I can't fault your analysis or disagree with the general direction of your approach to dealing with the matter. I'm not, however, sure that some of those things you said are physically possible, dead or alive."

"If the body was still warm it would probably still bend that far, at least at first," KB interjected, and he didn't smile when he said it.

"Oookay, how about we move along then?" It wasn't often that you could make Top shiver. Going with her gut and getting these three together for this was probably the right move, but that didn't make it any less scary.

"I want to watch the vehicle, and try to follow whoever comes back to it, assuming someone comes back to it. Suggestions," Mallory continued.

"It needs to look like we simply showed up when our people didn't radio in and decided getting our wounded back was more important than getting the vehicle back. What did we have on the Humvee other than the .50, ammo, and the radio?" Jackson asked.

Ramirez responded to this, as Sergeant Keeler was in his squad. "Actually, we didn't send out a .50 on this trip because there wasn't a dedicated gunner. So we don't have to worry about that or ammo. There are two M-16s and ammo for them, but they'd be locked, and it's a combination lock, so we don't have to worry about someone losing a key. The medics will pick those up when they get there as part of SOP. The only thing they would get is a sweet ride and a radio, and all we have to do is have them pull the encryption circuit, again, SOP. At that point all they've got is a CB/shortwave combo unit."

"Ok, good to hear. What else?" Mallory asked.

"Just standard fare, five days of supplies for two people in two rucksacks, first-aid kit, tube tent, flare gun, etc. They weren't that far away and with the radio in the truck and two handhelds we were pretty sure they would have been able to get back in touch with us if necessary. It's actually only a two day hike from where they were, even under really bad conditions."

"So what are we going to do to get Sheri back? Somehow I don't get the feeling that Pete's the ransom kind of guy. KB, you mentioned that this struck you as a 'crime of opportunity', any more, well...ideas since I hesitate to use the word insight?"

"I appreciate that, I think." KB snorted. "Like I said, from what we overheard it didn't sound like grabbing her was the endgame of this little drama. It felt like it was designed to see how we would respond and possibly to set up another meeting and hopefully take more of our people and equipment at that point. Nabbing Sheri was a spur of the moment decision and it was done because he couldn't be sure she would be there next time. I do wonder if we'll hear from the group again and they'll deny that they had any involvement."

"Come to think of it, I'm almost sure we will," KB continued. Then his gaze snapped to Mallory, "We need to get three units out NOW. Far enough out that we can triangulate their position when they broadcast next time. We have no idea how long it will be before they contact us again and we don't have any time to waste. We need to make sure they are large enough to protect themselves, but small enough not to attract too much attention, and they need to leave literally as soon as possible."

"From here, let's see, they're going to need to be..." his voice trailed off for a few seconds as he muttered to himself and the fingers of his right hand flipped like he was typing and then, "four units would be better, put us at the center of a square twenty-one miles on a side. That way, no matter where they are coming from, we would have them surrounded geographically and should be able to triangulate almost perfectly, to within no more than half a klick."

"Nice." Jackson replied. "You really can set up a long wire in your sleep, can't you?"

"Not really, I think in feet in my sleep, not meters. Screws up the math." KB replied with a grin. "And no, I can't actually use the prosthetic for a resistor; the carbon fiber is way too conductive!"

"And we wouldn't have to watch the site either, no chance of being seen because we simply won't be there. If they take my truck and mess it up though I'm gonna be so pissed." Mallory was pragmatic about most things, but she loved her people and her equipment. She took them both personally and the thought of someone screwing around with either one made her blood boil. She was keeping her temper in check about Keeler right now but if she ever got her hands on Pete, he was not going to be a happy camper. You did *not* want to be the one who had clocked one of her boys on the back of the head.

"Next question, how do we break the news because *not* breaking the news is not the question?" This was one of the things that had endeared Mallory to her troops; she didn't hold back information, good or bad. "One, I'm sure a bunch of people either saw the medics leave or heard you send them off--or both. Two, Sergeant Keeler and Sheri should be back in about twenty minutes either way, but won't. Three, Keeler *will* be back in the company of medics in about forty-five minutes...without Sheri.

"On top of all of that, we have no idea if Pete is going to start broadcasting, not as part of this group they went out to see, but all on his own, to help prove his 'power and greatness'. After all, he just ambushed the U.S. Army all by his lonesome and made off with a hostage, did he not? He must be really brave and all that. You know, I'm developing a real distaste for this guy."

Jackson, having been SFC for a long time, piped up first with an oft-repeated axiom. "Seeing as how rumor is the only known phenomenon to consistently travel faster than light, we could probably just tell a couple of people and then tell them 'not to tell anyone else'. By the time we hit the third or fourth person, they'd be asking us to corroborate the story. The biggest downside to that is that by then we'd be wasting time correcting misinformation."

"Good points both. No, unfortunately we probably need to hit this one squarely. I think this is where Karen's "block moms" might come in handy. Kyle, could you please find Eric and Karen?"

"Absolutely, be right back." Ramirez replied. He also thought to himself, and only to himself, that she'd called him Kyle, not Ramirez. She hadn't done that, even with protocol suspended, since they'd both gotten falling down drunk the night his father passed away nine years ago.

"KB, organize the communications teams and get them on the road. I want them moving in thirty minutes or less. You will not be going, I need you here."

"Understood, they'll be on their way as soon as physically possible, sooner in some cases. I may need my other foot." With that, he was gone out of the tent, not that they couldn't hear him bark to one of the men in his squad.

It was almost five minutes before Ramirez came back with both Karen and Eric, as Eric had been both a little harder to find since he'd been on patrol and then he'd insisted on cleaning up. "Sorry it took so long, Mallory, Eric here didn't think he was clean enough for your presence apparently. He comes to bed without a shower but won't come to the command tent without changing clothes." Karen elbowed Eric in the side, but winked at Mallory.

"Tell you what, I'll order him to the command tent every night at about 9:30, maybe then you'll get a clean boyfriend in bed from now on."

"Deal!"

Eric was rolling his eyes in Ramirez's direction when he realized that nobody else in the room was really getting into the ribbing. "Ok, what's up? If Morris' jaw clenches any tighter he's gonna need new molars."

Morris made a concerted effort to relax is mouth, and commented that 'there was a reason he hadn't gone into intelligence', something about wearing his heart on his sleeve and his emotions too openly.

Mallory called over to Corporal Pine in the communications tent again and had him replay the recording for Karen and Eric. Hearing it again didn't do anything for anyone's mood, and Karen looked like she wanted to act out several of the more inventive ideas that Ramirez had come up with.

"Karen, take a breath. If you pass out, I *will* dunk your head in a bucket of ice water," Mallory said matter of factly. "Better. Now, this happened about fifteen minutes ago, and we need to address it, soonest. We aren't going to hide it and we aren't going to sugar-coat it. A bunch of folks out there had heard of Pete before they joined up with us, some even joined because of him. Everybody has heard of him since they came in.

"Word will get out no matter what, and we don't want to look like we're hiding anything because we aren't. What do you think of using the 'block moms', Karen?"

"That was actually going to be my suggestion once you got me thinking instead of reacting. We don't have phones, and we still haven't set up a radio station yet, so that was one of the things we figured they could be responsible for--passing on information reliably."

"Alright then, that's settled. Let's get to writing it."

...

Once the statement was finished and typed up, it was printed out and distributed. They had decided they would go ahead and continue to use laptop computers and inkjet printers as they both consumed less power than their desktop and laser counterparts. The statement was very simple:

"Today, July 28th, at approximately 15:19, or 3:19 pm, Sergeant Keeler and Ms. Sheri Hines, after meeting with a group claiming to have a desire to join the Natchez Trace Guardianship, were ambushed. At present, the following information is known or assumed:

- There appeared to be a single assailant who waited until after the meeting was over.

- Sergeant Keeler was struck in the head and rendered unconscious at the scene.

- Ms. Hines was abducted by the single assailant.

- Ms. Hines was able to transmit her conversation with her abductor.

- Ms. Hines tentatively identified her abductor as the individual calling himself 'Peter the Great'.

- Ms. Hines may have also been struck by the assailant, but that is not known for certain at this time.

- Sergeant Keeler was left at the scene by the assailant when he abducted Ms. Hines.

- Sergeant Keeler regained consciousness a short time later and radioed in, corroborating a brief portion of events. He has been treated by medics, and is being transported back.

- Everything possible at this time is being done, and more is being planned and will be done, to rescue Ms. Hines.

As soon as any additional information is known, it will be made available."

The reactions ranged from fear and anger to despair. Some feared for Sheri, while others feared for themselves. Some were angry at Peter, while others were angry at the Guardsmen who had failed to protect her, and in their own minds, themselves.

Some reactions were a bit deeper than those. One reaction in particular couldn't actually be classified. Chuck had helped organize the "block moms" when Karen first had the idea, and as more groups joined them they had proven their value a number of times.

He'd seen Paula, one of the original "block moms", waving the red and white checked flag-- that he was still sure had come from a tablecloth--so he headed over to the gathering group to hear what she had to say. It was amazing how quickly they could pass information without phones or a radio station when they needed to.

Then he'd heard about the ambush, about Keeler, Sheri getting hit by Pete. He was sure Sheri'd said something and he'd hit her, just as he was sure it was in fact Pete, and it was like a switch had tripped inside. Different people describe it different ways; for some, it's a physical sensation, and for others it's purely mental. Some people describe it as ice water running down their spine, or over every square inch of their body. Others say it's like an electric shock. Some people feel like every nerve is exposed or on fire. Some people say it's an incredible calm, and everything takes on an unnatural clarity, like the first time they saw an HD movie. Still others claim that they have a heightened sense of awareness, almost a fifth sense.

What is that ubiquitous 'it' that people talk about? Sometimes 'it' meant snapping, going over the edge, or losing 'it'--being the guy in the bell-tower, so to speak. Sometimes 'it' meant being in the zone; you could do anything, mothers lifting cars off of their children, or athletes becoming unstoppable on the basketball court for just one game. Chuck both lost 'it' and 'got in the zone' at the same time, in an instant. In the future, when he really thought about it, he would swear he heard a click and felt a rush of heat course throughout his body. He'd been pretty sure that was just adrenaline keeping his heart from stopping.

But the world slowed down at that point too, and unlike some people's experience, while edges were much sharper, colors were dull. And, oh yeah, he was furious; in a seething, white-hot rage. He had heard the term before, but never understood it until now. He'd been pissed before, plenty of times, but never so mad, so furious, so over the top that it threatened to take him over completely.

"ERIC!" Chuck called to get Eric's attention over by the Army command tent. When Eric turned around and saw Chuck he held up his hand to wait a minute, finished a brief conversation, and then came trotting over.

"Chuck, I'm so sorry, I was actually one of the last to know before they typed up the 'Press Release'."

"Man, I'm not mad at you, I just want to know if there is anything, and I mean *anything* I can do, right now, or later, here, there, over there, way over there, whatever, to get Sheri back. I don't want this to go on long. And if you can tell me anything to keep me from going off half cocked, please do Eric, because right now I'm wound about as tight as a cheap watch, and I've known for all of thirty seconds."

"Chuck, I don't know anything for sure, honest I don't. We really don't know where Sheri is, nobody does yet. But if I were you, I'd get a hold of a grid map and a radio, and listen in on CB19 and SAT46 so you at least know what's going on. What are you packing?"

"Taurus .45 1911, 8+1, Ranger SXTs, why?"

Eric closed his eyes and took a deep breath, "You know why, Chuck. Please don't do anything stupid. You're a grown man and she's a grown woman, and although neither of you has said anything most of us here aren't blind. I'm not asking you to stay out of it, because I know you won't, but don't do something dumb, please."

Chuck blinked, "Neither of us? C'mon, Eric, I really don't think it's a two-way street."

Eric snorted and shook his head, "Ok, you can go ahead and do dumb things as long as you limit them to phrases like that. Yeah, Chuck, neither of you, as in the two of you, as in Sheri and Chuck, the two people in the relationship who don't know they're in the relationship. Man, you need to settle down for a bit, nothing's going to happen for a couple of hours at the very least, possibly a couple of days."

"KB's got it covered if they try to call in again to set up another meeting. We should be able to pinpoint their position to within 500 meters and then swoop in like the wrath of God, or in this case, the wrath of Top. If you drink, find a drink, if you don't, go get a pill from the medics and try to get some sleep. You're a little closer to the situation than you're willing to admit and you're going to need your wits about you later on. I'm saying this as a friend, Chuck, please stand down man."

"Ok, ok, I'll take the day off, after I get that radio and the map. Not that I remember where I heard I should get one," Chuck nodded as he turned around and headed off to the quartermaster.

He is so gonna do something stupid and heroic...and stupid. Eric shook his head.

.

Chapter Thirty-Three

"What were you thinking?" The oldest of the three current representatives of the pothead group he'd attached himself to demanded. "Are you insane!? That's the U.S. Army you just pissed off, man!"

"Shut your mouth and show some respect," Pete said around a joint, which he was now chain smoking like gas-station cigarettes. "I don't have to explain myself to you or anyone else, ever. If you don't like something I've done, you are free to leave at any time." When he said that, though, his eyes got just a bit wider, and it was obvious from the gleam in his eye that anyone who left would be doing so feet first.

"Do you have any further plans, then?" The next oldest asked. He was in his middle thirties and a little less stupid, as he hadn't been doing drugs quite as long. "Just asking--not making any judgments."

"Yeah, you're going to call them tomorrow, just like we planned, and set up another meeting, just like planned, and pretend you had nothing to do with it, because you didn't. Roach-clip here can even go along and be all up-in-arms about how upset he is, just as long as he keeps his mouth shut about knowing anything about me. It'll make the whole thing more believable if it's sincere."

Sheri was handcuffed to what looked like a heavy-duty towel rack in the kitchenette area, but otherwise completely comfortable, and actually finding the entire situation rather amusing. Pete was stoned out of his mind, acting like he was the king of the potheads, and apparently thought that this was a good idea. She was literally biting her tongue to keep from laughing at the whole thing. When she wasn't thinking about how screwed up the situation was, that is.

He does have a gun after all, and although I haven't seen him use it yet, I don't know that he won't. Sheri was very careful to think to herself and not mutter. *I sincerely hope that tonight doesn't go like I'm afraid it might. One thing at a time girl, one thing at a time.*

"In the meantime, what are we going to do with her?" Less stupid asked.

"*We* aren't going to do anything with her. Like I said, you didn't have anything to do with bringing her here, and you won't have anything to do with her other than making sure that she gets food just like everyone else. Plausible deniability my friend. Speaking of food, what's for dinner? I'm hungry, I haven't eaten since lunch." Pete snickered, and then started to giggle, and within a few seconds he was yipping like a hyena. Pete was apparently a munchy-giggly pothead.

After almost a minute, tears streaming down his face, he stopped laughing and looked at the three still standing in front of him. "Well, what the hell are you still standing here for? I said I'm hungry!" Pete roared. He was also apparently an obnoxious-jackass-mean pothead too…great. Eenie, Meenie, and Miney, as Sheri had just decided to start thinking of them, filed out in reverse order of age. What a motley crew they made. How in the world did the little hippie societies like this that continually sprang up ever survive long enough to reproduce?

"C'mere Sheri."

"That's gonna be a little tough, Mr. Great, sir."

"Watch your tone, bitch."

"Watch your mouth, Pete. You don't own me and you have to sleep sometime. Call me bitch again and unless you do it from across the room and then shoot me dead, it'll be one of the biggest mistakes you've ever made, regardless of what it costs me in the long run."

"Fine, please come over here then, I want to look at you."

"Thank you for saying please Pete, but again, that's going to be a little difficult handcuffed to the wall as I am. And Pete, that's a little sick. I've been here for an hour. You don't really believe that I'm going to just roll over and be your little slave do you? I mean really?" Sheri said.

"This isn't a fantasy role playing game Pete! I'm a human being, and a strong willed one at that." Sheri wasn't sure why she was taking this tack with Pete at this point, but she didn't want to just let it go. She was starting to get mad again. "This is real life, and contrary to what you think, you can't do whatever you like. Not everyone is afraid of you, I mean think about it, only one of the three who just left was afraid of you, the other two are just keeping their mouths shut because they aren't as stupid as the one who *is* afraid. For heavens sake, Pete, you're using a *revolver* when everyone else is using a semi-automatic; assuming everyone in the world is an equal on the battlefield, everyone else has more bullets in their gun than you do! You aren't even playing it smart!"

Pete threw himself up out of the chair, at that point. That was the only way Sheri could think to describe it. He didn't get up, he didn't jump up, he looked like he had thrown himself up out of his own chair as he staggered when he got to his feet. "SHUT UP!" he roared, the joint flying from his mouth with little strings of saliva. "Just shut UP!" He had his hand on the butt of his gun, which he was no longer carrying slung low, but actually at his hip.

"Why, Pete, why should I shut up? What exactly have I said that isn't true? Which part of what I've said should I take back? The fear part? I'm not afraid of you. I'm afraid of pain, death, being shot, and I'm even afraid of spiders, but I'm not afraid of you. The slave part? Please!" Sheri made a dismissive gesture with her free hand and a little 'pffft' noise with her mouth. "Not a chance, not even with that gun to my head, literally. That bit about the hand cannon, I can't take that part back, and it isn't mine to take back." She did her best Scottish impression, which was, admittedly, pretty bad, "Ye canna change th' laws a physics! Your gun only holds six bullets, dude!"

The entire time, even when Pete had gotten up suddenly, Sheri had never flinched and never backed down. She'd been looking directly at him, and locking eyes with him as long as he'd been looking at her. They stared at each other for a full half a minute before Pete turned and stalked out of the house. To his credit, he didn't slam the door.

Sheri slumped back against into the chair and thought she was going to faint or throw up or both, neither of which would be a good idea right now. She was also sweating for the first time that day, which was odd, as the heat usually didn't bother her, which meant it probably wasn't the heat. When she'd gone on her diatribe, she'd specifically not said being afraid of being raped, although she knew that was on his mind. She just didn't want to let that genie out of the bottle.

Girl, that was dumb, though you might not have to worry about tonight now. Ok, now what? Sheri thought. *The town is apparently peopled with cowards, sheep, and potheads. I didn't see a single gun on the way in, but they didn't sound like they were actually going to join up with us either, so they probably have some somewhere.*

The handcuff was too tight to slip off, but not tight enough to chafe, yet. It didn't look like the 'novelty' variety either, which was disturbing in its own way. She could actually stand up and stretch, she just couldn't go anywhere. "This is gonna suck, and I am so sick of saying that!"

For the first time, Sheri could take stock of her surroundings. She could probably yank this stupid towel bar off the wall, but who puts a vertical towel bar…wait a minute, that's not a towel bar. Wonderful! Whoever had lived here in the past had either been handicapped in some way or had made the house handicap accessible. Her mom and dad had put these all over their house when she was growing up for when her walker-bound grandmother was visiting. Ok, so she was stuck here in the kitchenette.

I can't reach anything from here either. He took my Gerber tool, he took my sidearm, and he took my keys, although I don't know why I kept any of them except the one to the Explorer. I don't even have a coin to flip. The kitchen appeared to have been well stocked at some point, but had been cleaned out in the last couple of weeks. Too bad, too, the fridge looked almost brand new. It had been fairly well kept up since Pete had moved in, too, unless it had only been a couple of days ago, which she doubted. The three stoners had seemed too cowed for that to be true.

She could see the living room from where she sat; a dark TV sat in an armoire with a dark DVD player and stereo system. There was a couch, a love seat, a recliner, and a couple of tables and lamps. She got up and stretched as far as her arm would let her and then peered as far as she could down the hall. Then she jumped near out of her skin and wrenched her shoulder something fierce when the refrigerator kicked on.

What the...?! She tried the light switch, and got nothing, but sure as she was standing there, the fridge was purring away. Well, probably not almost brand new then, absolutely brand new. *I wonder where the generator is, since I don't hear it.* She shrugged, which hurt, and had to admit that, dumb as he's acting, Pete *was* an Electrical Engineer after all. *He's probably got a bank of deep cycle batteries in the garage, duh! Fridge is probably full of beer too, assuming any survived this long without being refrigerated.* Her mouth started to water at the thought of ice and she shook her head to push the thought away.

"How can one person be so smart and so stupid at the same time?" She said out loud and then laughed softly. "You are so one to talk, girl."

...

There were a number of problems with time slowing down, not the least of which is the fact that, well, time slows down. Chuck was losing his mind and it had only been three hours since he'd found out about Sheri. He was debating whether or not he could get away with going and seeing Mallory when Joel and Rachael came by his tent. "Hey, can you stand some company?" Joel asked.

"If you can stand me, yeah, I've been kinda distracted the last little bit. I know Pete and this is just so petty and," Chuck sighed, "I'd love to say that it isn't like him, but I'm afraid it is. Petty, and small, and typical, and I'm going to kill him for this. I swear I am Joel. I'm sorry Rachael, but I'm gonna kill that worthless piece of crap."

Rachael laughed, "Don't apologize to me; you're going to have to get in line bud."

Chuck didn't respond to the last part of what she'd said, although only Joel caught it. "Still, I'm sorry for my language. Sheri's always getting on me about it." Chuck ran his hand through his hair, "I can't believe he did this, though, you know? Whether or not it's like him, I can't believe he would actually do something like this."

"Yeah," Joel replied. "It's a real wake-up call though, for all of us. We can't just assume that everyone can keep getting along like they have been. As long as there are people like Pete out there, we're going to have to be more on our toes than we have been."

"Have they decided what they are going to do yet, I mean in the immediate future?" Rachael asked.

"Aside from not staking out the truck no, nothing new that they are telling us. It's just that the waiting is driving me nuts. It's like it happened a week ago already and I'm going crazy. If something happens to her, I don't know what I'll do." Chuck hung his head for a few seconds and when he looked back up his eyes were red, but he wasn't crying, not yet.

"The morning the power went out, I asked her if she had somewhere to go, somewhere safe, because I was really worried about her." He forced a laugh, "She said 'Yeah, I'm sure the house is still there', and then she told me she had you folks, and Eric and Karen."

"I was relieved, but I'll admit I was also a little jealous. I'd kinda hoped she'd, I don't know, need me? No, that's not right, that's not Sheri either. That's also the difference between me and Pete. He's been stung ever since she turned him down at the bar. But then she invited me to come with her and you all invited me to come along. Now, the reason I came along in the first place is gone because of that, that," Chuck caught himself this time, and just shook his head.

Rachael reached out and put her hand on Chuck's arm, "Chuck, I think she knows that…deep down. She's not stupid, she's just gun shy. She's had so many people trying to hook her up for so long with so many other people that she's just shut that conscious part of herself down. It doesn't matter though, because she still knows, and frankly, so does everyone else."

Chuck snorted, "Everyone keeps saying that. What's the old saying? The first time someone calls you a horse you punch 'em in the nose, the second time you call 'em a jerk, but the third time, maybe it's time you go get fit for a saddle."

"I don't know that we've had any saddle makers show up, but I'll let you know if they do. By the way, I think the term Kyle used to describe Pete was worthless meat-sack. Summed it up nicely if you ask me." Rachael replied.

Chuck couldn't help but laugh, which he'd really needed right now. "Thank you. We should probably go ahead and get some chow and I should try to turn in for the night."

"Good call. Hey, I hear we're having veal wheels," Joel jibed.

"Oh please, not those again!" Rachael made a retching sound. "Do me a favor guys, please take two each, even if you just throw them both away, please!" They were all three laughing as they ducked out of Chuck's tent.

Chapter Thirty-Four

Despite her best intentions, Sheri nodded off before Pete came back. Mostly due to the fact that he'd been gone for several hours. The screen door squeaking woke her up, and she was just barely sitting up when the front door opened. "I have *got* to replace the light bulbs now that I have power in this house. Keep forgetting to do that while there's daylight." Pete pulled out a flashlight and turned it on, the light temporarily dazzling Sheri's eyes. "Sheri, I brought you something to eat. If you promise not to kick me," he paused, "or do anything else that might cause me to do something either of us might regret, I'll bring it over and set it gently on the table for you. Deal?"

"Deal. Thank you." Sheri said.

"Don't thank me yet, they're a bunch of freakin' vegans out there. I went back to the Humvee and grabbed the backpacks from the back. I can't believe they sent you guys out there with only your sidearms. You'll be glad to know that they came and got your buddy though, apparently they felt he was more important than the truck, because they left it there."

You are such an idiot Pete, you have no idea. They didn't send us out without weapons you fool, they just took them with them when they took Keeler back to base. They left the Humvee, not truck, because they wanted you to pilfer it, probably wanted to make sure I had something decent to eat. Hopefully it's an MRE, you might be dumb enough to give me an actual fork. And last, and in this case also least, it's called a rucksack jerkoff. The comments were all completely to herself of course, but they helped her feel better.

"Anyway, like I said, don't thank me yet. I can't stand vegan, but I don't know if I can do these MRE things either. You want 'Beef Roast with Veggies', 'Chili Mac', or 'Meatballs Marinara'?"

"Chili Mac please, I like the candy pack that comes with it. Usually it's cinnamon candy and includes gum." When he handed her the packet and a water bottle, she shocked him by warming up the Chili Mac in the included warmer.

"So that's what that's for. How long have you been with that Army bunch?"

"Since day one. We actually hit the Armory on Thursday afternoon. One of the guys in my neighborhood was regular Army until about seven months ago, and we got together about ten minutes after I got home." She'd just barely stopped herself from saying 'once Chuck and I got home'. She didn't know why, but something had kept her from saying it.

"We had two normal meals at the Armory before we pulled out and then lived on these for almost two weeks." She toyed with the idea of *not* telling him the next part, but figured it would only do her harm in the short term, "Do yourself a favor if you've eaten one, Pete, drink a LOT of water, otherwise you're gonna be a bound-up mess. I didn't believe them when they told me and boy did I pay for it for a couple of days."

"Thanks for the tip. I believe it though, I'm pretty sure I've heard it before too."

Sheri figured she would try to keep the conversation steered away from any potential landmines. "How'd you get the house rigged? Solar? Generator? Is there an auto parts store within thirty miles that still has any deep cycle batteries left?"

Pete chuckled, "Yes, yes, and maybe but not for lack of trying. There are probably twenty houses here that are up and running with all the power they need. This place is no good for wind, but solar is fine. We have almost a dozen generators and a bank of switches set up. One of the guys here used to be a programmer, and another was a really sweet engineer. They set up a panel that monitors the levels of each of the battery banks when the sun is down and kicks on the generators as necessary to recharge the batteries. If it needs to, it will rotate the generators out to the different banks in series to keep everybody up and running. It's scalable too as we add more houses or generators."

"Wouldn't it be easier to keep all the generating capacity in one place and simply re-energize the town?" Sheri asked.

"Probably, but the problem is that there were already a number of folks with generators, alternators, and battery banks in their houses. These folks wanted to be 'off the grid man'", Pete said in a fairly passable Tommy Chong impersonation. "Short of killing half the town, which would probably royally piss off the other half, centralizing the power right off the bat wasn't going to happen. We could probably convince them to do it now, with two of us who know what we're talking about."

"You were always better at dealing with people than I was. You were the one that got everyone up out of the dam, even got me to help get Cathy up the stairs. I didn't even think about that. All we'd have to do is disconnect the town from the rest of the world, electrically, at the other side of any substations that feed us, and depending on the amount of power necessary, simply plug the generators into the line."

"They'd have to be wired right, and they'd need to go through some step up transformers, but I'm sure they haven't all been destroyed. Shoot, for the size we're talking, we could make ones that would last long enough to get some manufacturing going to build real ones."

"So, do you have any light bulbs floating around here? As long as this isn't a double throw switch it should be off. You can save the lantern batteries."

"Just a second, let me look. I was more concerned with the fridge and the A/C, I haven't looked for bulbs." The first place he looked was over the fridge, which held cookbooks and a number of pieces of elementary school art class pottery. Next was over the stove. Why is it that people always store their light bulbs over the stove?

"Bingo, 40, 60 and 75 watt. That's probably a 60 watt-max fixture, three bulbs. Sheri, please scoot away from the switch, dear. I know we've been having a wonderful evening so far, but I'm not stupid and I'm sure you remember that I smacked you on the back of the head and kidnapped you this afternoon."

"Fair enough, but in all honesty, the odds weren't high enough for a kill, so I was just going to let it ride."

"And here we were getting along so well. So much for letting my guard down. Now I have to weigh everything I do against the potential for instantaneous death."

"I didn't say it had to be instantaneous, Pete."

"Ok, this is really going downhill fast. Truce, or at least a cease-fire, ninety seconds while I screw in the freakin' light bulbs?"

"Truce, sorry. My head still hurts in all honesty, and I am still a little sore at being kidnapped."

"Ok, squint your eyes and try the switch," Pete said as he got down off the kitchen chair.

Sheri did, and to her immense pleasure, there were now 180 watts of soft-white electric light in the kitchen. "We've got electricity at the base, but we don't have a huge infrastructure yet. There are so many little projects that take up everyone's time; it's taking forever to get things completed. We have megawatts of generating capacity and nothing to run off of it, but we don't want to just move in and take over a town somewhere that already has an infrastructure."

"You gotta weigh your options. You can't make an omelet without breaking some eggs. Someone is going to have to be in charge in each of those little places out there. It's admirable that the folks at the Armory didn't just try to take over Nashville, but you've seen what happened to Nashville over the last couple of weeks."

"If you've been listening on the CB, you know that's happening all over, too. They couldn't have held it together there with the force they had, so getting out was smart. Starting over was smart. Starting from scratch, maybe not so smart."

"I guess that remains to be seen."

"Yeah, I guess it does. Moving on then, it looks like your dinner is done. Wish I'd known that's how those things worked. Yes the Chicken Chow Mein is edible cold, but just," Pete shivered for effect.

Apparently Pete was trying extra hard not to be a prick, to be human, trying to be, Oh My Word, ON A DATE! It struck Sheri almost like a physical blow, but one that she had to try not to laugh at lest he get the wrong idea. Yes, he'd been making a joke but she didn't want him thinking he was making any headway either. He really was that stupid!

"They tell me that's what the Tabasco sauce is for. I guess if you don't need it for one meal you hold onto it in case you need it for another one. With enough of the stuff you're supposed to be able to eat anything." Keep him talking and keep it neutral. Don't smile and no more joking. No more being friendly. He's the enemy, Sheri!

"Well, there are only about four more days' worth in the backpacks,"

Rucksacks moron.

"and there's a decent first aid kit in each one too. Is your head really still hurting, do you need something for it?"

Yeah, like I'm going to let you give me something to knock me out. The only reason I'm drinking this water and eating this food is because I broke the seal on both, freak show. "I'm actually fine, I was just being pissy." Calling him names in her head was good for her own frame of mind, but she was going to have to watch it before she slipped; some of the names she was thinking were already coming too easily.

"Well, I'll leave you to your dinner then. Give me a holler if you need anything." With that Pete got up and left. He might be stupid but apparently he could take a hint and had picked up on her change in attitude. What was he *on*, anyway? She'd seen metronomes that swung back and forth less frequently.

I wonder how he'd react if I yelled for him and told him I needed to be let go and dropped off back where he kidnapped me. Probably not a good idea, the man really didn't seem very stable.

Knowing that the group had picked up Keeler and policed the site, including securing the M-16s and the ammo that had been in the Humvee, actually raised Sheri's spirits quite a bit. She wondered whether or not someone had been watching the site so they could try to follow Pete back. It was possible, even likely, that they had. There were some former Rangers in the Guard. Then again they might not have, and Sheri didn't want to get her hopes up. She still needed to proceed as though rescue, if it was coming at all, was a ways off.

"I wonder if the radio was still on?" Sheri asked herself out loud.

. . .

Corporal Pine saw the frequency light for Sheri's radio blink and switched immediately back to the delayed feed and started recording. He grabbed a portable radio to call the First Sergeant and let her know that Sheri's radio had 'something' making noise around it again. "First Sergeant, Ms. Hines' radio is broadcasting again. It looks like someone is back at the site and moving things around. OW! Son-of-a…Sorry, Top, whoever it is just picked up her radio and either dropped it or threw it into their car."

"I'll be there in a minute, as soon as I find Chuck."

Chuck was lying on the cot in his tent looking up at nothing when Mallory called from outside. "Come on in First Sergeant. I'm decent, or at least dressed."

Mallory ducked in but held the flap open, "I need you in the communications tent, someone's at the site and I don't know why I didn't think of it before, but I want to play the tape for you to be sure it's Pete and then listen to see if he's come back. They also moved Sheri's radio, and Corporal Pine said it sounded like they tossed it into their car. If they did, they are going to take it with them." Mallory's eyes glittered.

"What are we waiting for, let's go," Chuck was up and gesturing Mallory out of the tent. "C'mon woman, move!"

Mallory grinned as they jogged to the communications tent. This might be one of the shortest abductions on record, she thought. "Any update, Pine?"

"Car's started and heading back, radio is definitely in the car. Sounds like they grabbed the rucks from the back as well. Good thing we cleared out the M-16s and the ammo."

"Good deal, keep the recording going and bring up the one from earlier today, please. I need Chuck to verify Pete's voice."

It only took a few seconds, as that recording was a shortcut right now. Within a few seconds Chuck was nodding his head, "Yeah, that's Pete."

"Ok, go ahead and stop it," Mallory started to say.

"No, don't, I want to hear the rest." Chuck interrupted.

Mallory nodded at the interruption, since Pine was not going to just take it on Chuck's say-so.When it was over, Chuck didn't say anything, he just nodded his head one time.

"Have they said anything yet, whoever they are?" Mallory asked

"Just some muttering. One second." Pine played back the most recent recording.

"That's Pete. He truly is that stupid; he came back himself. How dumb can one man be and still be alive?" Chuck asked.

"Pine, call Bowersock, please. Have him meet me in the command tent soonest," then she and Chuck left.

. . .

"Sooner than we had hoped or planned, but not necessarily a bad thing, not by a long shot. I'm glad we literally sent them out right away. Since we know what frequency her radio was on, we can just wait until they stop and triangulate on that frequency broadcast. It'll take a couple of minutes, assuming the battery holds out in the unit. It's got to be getting weak." KB finished up.

Corporal Pine added, "I did notice that it was a little weaker than it had been this afternoon, but the newer radios go into standby when they are locked in send mode and haven't heard anything above a certain threshold for ten minutes." He had been relieved early at Mallory's request and had joined them in the command tent.

"We know they weren't more than fifteen miles away when they contacted us originally, since they used a CB. If we assume they did so from their current home location, his drive time should narrow down their possible hidey holes." They had a map laid out with all the possible towns marked and the most likely candidates based on size highlighted.

"Realistically, there're only a half a dozen places he could have gone into and declared himself 'Supreme Overlord' for the duration of the current crisis. Everywhere else is too small and would have probably shot him on sight when he pulled that crap, or too big for someone like him to bully into submission." KB mused.

"Unfortunately we can't go storming into a half a dozen places hoping the five that haven't done anything wrong will give us a mulligan. We aren't Pete, we have to remember that. Everyone, we have to remember that. We moved out here into the middle of the woods and are building a town from the ground up instead of invading somewhere because we aren't Pete. People are coming to *us*, in some cases *literally*, because we aren't Pete." Mallory stopped.

"You're right Top," KB said. "But one thing I've learned, and it's never been proven wrong, is that you don't try to reason with a rabid dog. You put it down in the street, then you bury it and move on."

"We've been lucky all the way 'round so far. We haven't had a drinking problem, a theft problem, an abuse problem, or any sexual crimes of any kind. We've also only been here together for a little over five weeks. At some point crime is going to infest this little corner of heaven where everyone farts rainbows, and it won't be because of some puissant tin dictator wannabe. It'll be because of unrequited love inside the camp, or someone sets up a still and gets drunk, or someone wants to be the "block mom" this week, or one of a hundred different things for each person here."

KB looked around the tent and then went on, "Pete's not the problem, he's a symptom. I had a neighbor once who said 'Everything would be so much better if everybody would stop fighting and just get along.' I told her 'But I can't stand you. There, there's only two of us and your plan's already shot to hell, now what are you gonna do?' People will devolve without rules, so we need to put those rules in place, and prove we have the ability and the willingness to enforce those rules."

"Pete has broken those rules, both the old set and the new. If Pete was Army, UCMJ Article 134 provides for a maximum penalty of confinement for life without the eligibility of parole. I can't speak to the civil side of the law, but I'm sure that if we read it we could take letter of the law and put him away for 15-25 years with no parole. The question is do we have the will to do so? We've had a hell of a lot of will up to this point, but that was mixed in with survival mode and the search for the next batch of chocolate chip cookies. There's more at stake here though, and that's what Karen, Rachael, and Sheri have been up into the wee hours of the morning trying to figure out for us."

"A society of Laws, where men and women can protect themselves but not harass others, where the 'Castle Doctrine' will be in full effect. A Civil Society that also provides for the individual to protect themselves and take matters into their own hands, properly as necessary. BUT, we can't do anything until we find out where he's heading. How does the car sound, Pine?"

"Pretty good timing KB, sounds like he's winding down now. He's on paved roads, which is probably a good thing. I've heard a few other cars." Pine held up his hand for quiet, and wrote down a number on a pad of paper '15321'. "He just pulled in and stopped. He was talking to himself under his breath like he's not real used to the address yet. 'Fifteen-three-twenty-one'.

Chuck slowly ghosted to the back of the tent to let the people who knew how to plan get their jobs done. He wasn't going to miss this for the world though, and he wasn't going be any further from the door than he needed to be.

Mallory glanced over at him as he was watching the semi-madness in the command tent. She was trying to convey a sense of accomplishment and control, what she got back from him was 'just get me what I need'. Odd, that.

"Still broadcasting. Looks like we're picking it up on three remotes and us, almost due east of us, about thirteen miles. Up I-40 and off a couple of side roads. *Of course*, a brand new little town called 'Gratefille'. How do these people live long enough to reproduce?!?" Pine was disgusted. "I do not have specifics on the layout of the town address-wise."

"Jackson, Halstead, you two pick one team each to go in both ends of town at first light. Find and extract Sheri with minimal collateral damage." Mallory ordered.

"Pete?" Halstead asked.

"I don't recall giving any specific order regarding any individual other than Sheri."

"Roger."

Tomorrow is too long, it's too long, I can't wait that long, she can't wait that long. He could move. He could kill her. Stop it! Chuck was losing it. Get it under control man. Face calm, breathing regular, exhale. "I hate it, but it sounds like you have it under control. I'm just in the way, Mal, I'm gonna take off. G'night."

"Take it easy, Chuck, it'll be alright," Mallory said as he left.

Oh, I know it'll be alright, I just need my map. GPS don't fail me now. He walked back to his tent--thankfully they were all raised and on wood floors now--and grabbed the radio and the map. He already had his sidearm with a full magazine and one in the chamber with two extra magazines on his belt. He headed over to his truck with a water bottle, climbed in, and made sure that he was all strapped in and ready before he put the keys in. That way there was less likelihood of the dinging of the keys in the ignition catching someone's attention before it was too late.

Chapter Thirty-Five

Chuck had his truck started, in gear, and moving before anyone realized he was going somewhere. Nobody was forbidden to leave, but usually people had a good idea of when and where people were headed. Anyway, nobody went out alone, especially not at night.

Fifteen seconds later Mallory came running to the lot swearing, and not under her breath. "I am so gonna draft him when he gets back, *just* so I can throw him in the brig!"

She ran into KB and Halstead on her way back to the command tent. "Chuck just took off. I'm not taking odds on whether or not Sheri will be back here before morning because I hate to lose. We're still planning the Op though." Mallory said.

…

Chuck used the GPS to plug in the number portion of the address in the town and it came up with a single street address. He had an eleven minute drive if the thing could be believed. They were just on the other side of the Park for crying out loud. Pete, you are a real piece of work. Twisted, rusting, scrap metal--but a piece of work, nonetheless. A few minutes out his radio squawked at him. He was tempted not to answer, but really didn't want to have to ignore it for the next ten minutes.

"This is Charlie one, go ahead, over."

"Chuck, please turn around." Mallory paused, and then remembered to say "Over." It was a testament to how pissed she was that she forgot in the first place.

"Negative, I read you Lima Charlie but am unable to comply, over."

"Explain, over."

"Mallory, find Joel and Rachael and ask them what I said this afternoon, over."

"You said 'you were gonna kill that worthless piece of crap' and I told you that you would need to stand in line. You weren't speaking figuratively were you Chuck, uh, over." Rachael asked. Mallory had already pulled them into the communications tent.

"No, I wasn't. I think I saw that Joel had caught it, but didn't say anything. Pete gave up his rights to be a member of a society, our society, a while ago, and he died this afternoon--he just hasn't stopped breathing."

"Mallory, he's a rabid dog, just like KB said. No matter how nice he acts, you don't let him get close enough to lick your hand because he's gonna bite. He can't be fixed, he's sick. I'm going to get Sheri back. I'm sorry, I can't wait until tomorrow morning, and I don't think she can either. I'm sure that by now he's told her that he's gone back to the Humvee and scrounged for food and toys. She may be hoping for a rescue, may be planning for one. She may not be, too, but I'd rather that she under-plan and we, I, over-deliver.

"I need to focus now though, so I'm going to turn off the radio. I'll talk to y'all in a few. Chuck out." Then he turned off the radio and set it in the middle console.

"I'm coming for you Sheri, just give me a few more minutes."

...

Pete had been outside for about five minutes rolling a joint when he heard an unfamiliar engine coming up the road. He'd been in this town long enough to recognize most of the cars and the few trucks they used. This was not one of the local trucks. For starters, none of the local trucks were Turbo Diesels, that was anathema to all things 'groovy man'. Secondly, this truck was moving way too fast. Then he thought he recognized the color and the running lights, all of which were on, and dove back into the house.

...

There, up ahead, looks like someone just dove back into a house, and hey they have a Yellow Mustang parked out front. How convenient. This wasn't going to take as long as he'd thought. Then again, he just might die in the next six seconds, who knew?

Chuck put the truck in park, left it running, and got out. He'd parked the truck so the entire front of the house was illuminated by the running lights and headlights from the truck. As he walked to the front of the truck, he pulled out his Taurus. No use leaving a tool where you couldn't use it, and thumbed back the hammer.

As he reached the front driver's-side corner of the truck the front door opened and two people came out--actually one was pushed out in front of the other. The one in front was Sheri and she was wearing a handcuff dangling from her right wrist. You idiot, she's right handed. How did you expect her to eat you fool. Strike three, man, that's it. You're just too dumb to keep around anymore.

They didn't say anything. Pete stood with his arm tightly around Sheri's neck and the gun against her head. There were three things going for Chuck at this point. The first was that the .44 Magnum Pete was using had quite a pull on it and would require a lot more pressure to rotate the cylinder and pull the hammer back than if the hammer were already back. The second was that Sheri actually had quite a free range of motion with her head the way he was holding her. The third was that Pete wasn't pointing his gun at the threat.

Chuck had grown up with guns, and had been shooting since he was six years old. He'd probably put over 250,000 rounds of ammo through just the ones he currently owned. Unlike Joel, his .45 was new. Like Joel, he shot all the time. Chuck had put over 20,000 rounds through his .45 and knew exactly how it handled.

For Chuck, time had slowed down earlier this afternoon, to what felt like a crawl. Now it came to a screeching halt. Everything that happened took forever but that just meant he had plenty of time to do it. Thoughts raced through his mind at lightning speed, memories were recalled, surfaced, played out in entirety, and were re-stored in an instant. Super-slow-motion video replay would still be too fast compared to what it felt like was happening inside his head now.

He glanced at Sheri, who was looking directly at him. She was proud, defiant, and unafraid. She'd known someone would come, that they wouldn't leave her--least of all with Pete. She didn't look at all surprised to see that it was Chuck, either. In fact, there might even be the trace of a smile on her lips. She hadn't been crying, God bless her, she hadn't been crying. And then she winked at him.

Chuck looked back at Pete then, and didn't like what he saw. Pete was literally foaming at the mouth. He was furious, he was spitting mad. He couldn't make the words. "What, Pete, did you think we would let this stand? Kidnap a free member of society? Someone we have all come to respect and love? Did you think that would be OK? Did you think that *she* would be OK with that Pete? Because I'm pretty sure she's not." Chuck was very calm, very cool.

"That's not your call to make, Chucky!" Pete spat back.

"If it's not my call to make then it's certainly not yours," Chuck shook his head. "I'm a respected member of my community Pete. What are you? If someone kidnaps you, who is going to come get you back? Who has your back here? If you die, who is going to mourn you Pete? Anyone? Is there even a dog here that relies on you for food? No? I thought not."

"So what are you gonna do about it, huh, Chucky? Running around with all your play army friends! Sheri was telling me you don't even have lights yet. Five weeks and you don't have lights! Sounds like you made the right choice don't it, big man?"

"We have lights, Pete, you probably didn't let her finish or didn't hear all of what she said. We don't have lights in every tent but I didn't see lights in every home, either, driving in, so it looks like that point is moot." Chuck's stance changed.

Sheri had been watching him ever since he'd gotten out of the truck and he looked different now. She'd seen him in a bar fight one time and that's what he looked like now. The only way to describe it was 'ready'. Sheri didn't know what was going to happen next but she knew she was going to be 'ready' too. He'd won that fight in one hit come to think of it.

Chuck's voice was different too, maybe just a little deeper, almost like when he was being a supervisor over something really important and getting people's attention, but with even more depth to it. "Pete, you have five seconds…starting now. Let Sheri go."

Sheri started counting to five, which is actually a long time when a gun is pointed at your head.

"One," Chuck started walking to the front of the truck so that Pete would be looking directly at the lights.

"I have five seconds to let Sheri go? Or what, big man?" Chuck hadn't said 'You have five seconds to let Sheri go', there'd been two separate statements, but Pete had missed the very important distinction.

"Two," Chuck stopped and squared his stance on Pete.

"What are you gonna do, huh? All you've done is talk so far,"

"Three," Chuck relaxed his shoulders and rolled his neck.

"You're a coward. You were worthless,"

"Four," Chuck began bringing up the .45.

"as a manager and a...WHAT THE FU..."

At about four and a half, Pete began relaxing his left arm out of shock because he realized that either Chuck was taking a bluff *way* too far, or he wasn't bluffing at all. When that happened, he completely forgot about Sheri, who turned her head away from Pete, and ducked it down and to the side. It wouldn't have mattered. Pete's hand was completely paralyzed, and Chuck was, quite literally, a dead shot.

Chuck pulled the trigger. The bullet entered Pete's head just below and to the left of the bridge of the nose, mostly because Pete flinched. Pete's head snapped back and both arms flew wide open. Pete was killed instantly, and his body spun to the right as it fell onto the bushes to the side of the front porch. Thankfully, the door had still been open behind Pete, and the majority of the mess went inside--Chuck didn't want Sheri to see that. Still, Chuck had tears in his eyes when he safe'd the weapon.

When Chuck had told Pete he had five seconds, he wasn't giving Pete a way out, he was telling him how long he had left to live. Some people would call it callous and cocky, but he knew good and well that he'd be waking up in a cold sweat for a long time to come because of his decision. He walked slowly over to Sheri, who had crumpled to her knees when the gun went off. Chuck stopped a couple of feet away and whispered, "Sheri. Sheri?" He took another half step and then squatted down and whispered her name again,

"Sheri?" That's when he could see she was shaking. He couldn't tell if she was crying or shivering from shock. He started to reach his hand out and stopped halfway to her, not knowing how she would react, and pulled his hand back. He stood up to look around, then heard her say, "Don't, please don't go."

He knelt back down, and then in a rush scooped her up, one arm under her legs, the other arm behind her back, her arms around his neck. "Never, I'll never leave you, never." That was when she began to cry on his shoulder.

He knelt that way for a couple of minutes, until Sheri stopped crying and pulled her head back, and then cuddled her head into Chuck's neck. "Thank you. Thank you, thank you, thank you."

"All in a day's work ma'am." Chuck snorted.

"No, no it isn't, you risked your life to save me, and it wasn't in a day's work. You had no idea what you were coming into. Pete was a bully, but he was also obviously a nutjob. That was crazy, and heroic, and just a little bit stupid. Thank you." She then put her hands one on each cheek, and proceeded to thank him well and proper.

"Sheri," Chuck said, after he got his breath back, "you may feel free to thank me at any time, in any place, for any reason whatsoever going forward."

Sheri just grinned. "We'll see. Now go ahead and put me down, I need to rummage in his car and get my keys and my Gerber, and I want our Rucks before we head back. Please come with me though."

Her keys and knife were in the glove box, and the Rucksacks were in the back seat. She also saw her radio on the floorboard of the front passenger seat. "Is this how you found me so quick?"

"Yup, locking it on send was brilliant. Sergeant Bowersock had the idea to triangulate the signal as nobody else was on the channel. Smart move by a very smart lady."

"Glad it worked. Glad you came to my rescue. C'mere, let me thank you again." This time it was a short thank you, more like 'thanks'.

"Now take me home, Chuck, please take me home."

"Your wish is my command," Chuck shook his head. "I'm gonna have to radio ahead though, Mallory is pissed at me. I kinda just went off on my own." He helped her into his truck, and noticed the handcuff still on her right wrist.

"I figured as much, but I'm glad you did. It was you I was hoping to thank." Sheri blushed in the dash lights. Sheri followed his gaze down to her wrist and held up her arm. "We'll have to get this taken off back at the base. I can see it getting in the way after a while."

"I've got a pair of bolt cutters in the tool box in the back, we could get rid of it right now if you want," Chuck offered.

"No, I think we should leave it on until we get back. I think people need to see it on, for a couple of reasons. It will help people see what's out there and frankly, it'll help your case." She turned to look at Chuck and then threw her arms around his neck and hugged him tight.

Sheri shivered, "Chuck, I really think he was going to kill me. I don't know when, I don't know at what point, but I really do think he was going to kill me. You saved my life. You were defending me. More than that, you were rescuing me from what I truly believe was a life-threatening situation." She pulled back and looked him in the eyes. "People will need to see this," she pulled her arm back and let the handcuff swing back and forth, "to remember that. I think, I hope, people will be glad to see me and be relieved that I'm ok. In a couple of days, somebody's going to ask 'did you have to kill him'. This will help."

"Wow, do you ever stop? Not that I want you to, don't think that, but sheesh. I hadn't even thought of any of that." Chuck quirked a smile, "Not that it would have changed a single thing I did, not in the least. Ok, your call, let's get going." Chuck shut the door and got in on his side. Sheri lifted up the middle console and slid across the bench seat to the middle.

"I'm sitting next to you on the way back," Sheri grinned.

"I didn't say anything," Chuck grinned back, "but you are putting your seatbelt on."

"Yessir."

"And I'm going to need that radio, oh hell; your radio is still locked on send!"

Sheri turned pale, and then her stomach lurched, and then she giggled. "What's the matter, big man, afraid of getting a little good-natured ribbing when we get back? Should we give them a little something to listen to?"

"SHERI!" Chuck dove for the radio.

"Relax, Chuck," Sheri laughed, "I turned it off out of reflex when I picked it up out of the Mustang." Sheri didn't want to use Pete's name if she could help it. "Whose reputation were you trying to protect there anyway, huh?"

"Ours, ma'am, ours."

"Ok, that's fair." She leaned up and kissed him on the tip of the nose, then reached over and grabbed his radio and handed it to him.

"Thanks. Ok, here goes." As soon as he turned it on he got a call.

"Charlie One this is Alpha Six, over."

"Alpha Six, this is Charlie One, over."

"Chuck, we heard a gunshot and then heard Sheri's voice and then her radio went dead. Please tell me what the hell is going on, over," Mallory said. She'd been the one on the radio the entire time most likely.

"Alpha Six, I am returning to base with Sheri. There was an encounter with Pete, who was holding Sheri hostage with a gun to her head. Pete was killed during the encounter by a single gunshot wound to the head. Sheri is unharmed. Over." Chuck was keeping what Sheri had said about people questioning his actions later in mind while talking to Mallory.

"Was the gunshot wound self inflicted? Over."

"Ultimately, yes, actually, no. He made the decisions that ultimately lead to the gunshot wound. The bullet did not come from his gun, however, if that is what you are asking. Over."

"Yes, that is what I was asking. Ok, drive slow as you approach the parking lot, you're going to have a welcoming committee. Out."

"She's thinking the same things you were thinking, about me and my future."

"Which speaks well of her, she's not thinking about herself, or at least not only herself. She's concerned about you too." Sheri reached out and took Chuck's hand. "It'll be ok."

"I know. Whatever happens, it'll be ok."

Mallory hadn't been kidding about the welcoming committee either. With the exception of the military personnel who were on active patrol or duty, it looked like everyone at the base was waiting for them to get back and the applause started as soon as they heard Chuck's truck.

"Oh you have got to be kidding me!" Chuck said as they rounded the last curve to the parking lot.

Sheri was grinning from ear to ear when she looked at him and her eyes were glistening. "You, sir, are going to come around to my side and pick me up and carry me out of this truck. You are my hero, you rescued me, you are my knight in shining armor, and you are going to play that up. Understood?"

"Yes, ma'am." Chuck said with a small smile.

Chapter Thirty-Six

Getting back to his parking space was a slow process as the way was just a tiny bit crowded. Thank goodness the civilian portion of the lot wasn't as packed with vehicles as the military side, and there was actually room for him to carry out Sheri's plan. Chuck got out and made his way around the front of the truck, amid back slaps and the continued applause. When he got to the passenger side, Sheri had already slid back over and was really playing it up even though there weren't any cameras.

He picked her up the same way he had back at the house, and the arm with the handcuff came out first and went around his neck. She buried her face in his shoulder for a minute and then looked up, eyes legitimately wet, and waved--again with her right hand--and people saw the handcuff. Those closest to them murmured and passed it on, ensuring all the others saw as well.

"Don't lay it on *too* thick sweetheart; you don't want them to think it was rehearsed." Chuck murmured into her ear.

"K, go ahead and set me down when we get to a clearing in the crowd. I think we've made our point. That is, if it's ok with you." She hugged him. She was enjoying being close to him now that she was there.

"I'd completely forgotten I was holding you. Imagine that," he smiled. "Probably ought to take my own advice here though." Mallory was coming through the crowd and she had a couple of MPs with her. "I'll probably need both my hands here in a minute anyway."

Chuck set Sheri down just as Mallory got to them, turned to face her, stood up straight, and held out both of his hands (close enough together that handcuffs would fit on him). It was ironic in its own way. He'd just gotten back from freeing Sheri, who was still wearing a handcuff on one wrist, and he was getting ready to be handcuffed himself.

A ring of silence surrounded Mallory, the MPs, and Chuck and Sheri, and slowly spread outwards through the crowd. As the silence grew, Chuck noticed the wire-boom jawbone microphone Mallory wore. They had lights in the parking lot, and apparently some of the PA system speakers had been newly put up over the last hour as well, as Mallory's voice was amplified over the lot when she spoke, "Put your hands down Chuck, I'm not here to arrest you."

"Everyone," Mallory looked around at those nearest to them and above their heads into the crowd and repeated a little louder, "Everyone, please listen to me. Today we learned a very valuable lesson, and we were very lucky. One of our own was taken from us by force. Taken by someone that all of you have heard of and some of you have specifically been trying to flee. It was the first such occurrence, but we have no way of knowing, and frankly no way of guaranteeing, that it will be the last.

"Tonight, whether by luck, skill, divine intervention, or a combination of any or all three and something else besides, a potentially nasty episode has come to an end. Pete will no longer trouble any of us. It is my personal opinion that Chuck acted in the best interest not only of Ms. Hines, but also of the base, and our group as a whole--and that had he not, we may very well have been recovering Sheri instead of rescuing her."

"That is, however, my personal opinion and not my professional opinion." Mallory paused for a few seconds to make sure that everyone was still paying attention. "My professional opinion is this: Regarding the events of this evening, no military personnel were engaged, no military assets were used, including vehicles, firearms, or ammunition, and no military laws were broken. This is an entirely civil matter, and the military has absolutely no jurisdiction over it. I am here, right now, for two reasons."

"The gentlemen behind me have a number of keys to handcuffs, as they are all keyed to a very small number of keys. They are here to help Ms. Hines remove her encumbrance. The second reason is to give my personal thanks to Mr. Turner, and don't you dare correct me, Chuck, I'll call you whatever I please at this point." Mallory smirked to take the sting out of it, but she wasn't going to take any lip about the 'Mr. Turner' bit either.

"He did an incredibly brave thing tonight. I have an idea what his motivation was, but I won't go into that. I also plan on reading him the riot act and you will all probably hear me scream at him sometime tomorrow until I lose my voice, because it was also reckless, dangerous, irresponsible, completely unplanned, and borderline stupid." Chuck flinched at each adjective she threw at him, but stood there and took it because she was right.

"However, none of those things take away from the fact that it was brave, and Sheri is back, and I really couldn't be happier." Mallory's eyes were shining now as she stuck out her hand.

Chuck went to shake it and was startled to be pulled into a hug, and the applause started up all over again. "If you ever do anything like that again," Mallory whispered through a smile into his ear, "I will *start* by letting Ramirez and KB come up with something appropriate to do with you when I find you." Apparently she'd shut the microphone off before she'd said that. Chuck shuddered.

"Yes, First Sergeant, I mean, no, First Sergeant, I mean, it won't happen again. Promise. I have something to stick around for now."

"Outstanding, Mr. Turner, I'm glad to hear that." Mallory looked over at Sheri and winked. Sheri was all smiles. I sure hope that lasts and I'm guessing that smile means he got there in time. Good deal.

The third key the MPs tried worked and the handcuffs came off, and Sheri found herself doing what every newly un-handcuffed person did in every movie ever made, rubbing her wrist, even though it didn't hurt. It was just, what …instinct? Verify that you were free, check to see that the weight wasn't there anymore? See that the irritant was in fact gone? She didn't know, and as soon as she realized she was doing it she immediately dropped her hands to her sides.

"If you two would come with me, I still have an operation to plan. Although it no longer needs to go off by tomorrow morning, I'd still like it to. And since both of you have at least been there, I'd like to have you two included in at least the initial planning stages."

Making their way back to the command portion of the base was by no means quick, with all the well wishers and residual crowd, but it wasn't as slow as the first few steps away from the truck had been.

Evidently Mallory had distributed a brief statement to be passed on by the "block moms" about the incident, and it was sinking in that Pete was dead and not just 'not going to be a problem anymore'. They even encountered a few whoops and 'yee-haw's' on their way back to the command tent. Chuck sincerely hoped that was more a case of pent up frustration and nerves than anything else. He knew that he, while relieved, certainly didn't feel giddy about the situation.

The usual suspects were already in attendance when they arrived, and in the relative quiet of the tent, he realized that Mallory and Sheri had been carrying on a conversation most of, if not the whole way back. "I'm gonna have to keep an eye on that," he thought to himself. "The last thing I need is Sheri getting advice on how to keep me in line from Mallory."

"Jackson, Halstead, who's going in?" Mallory asked.

Jackson replied first, "First Platoon, First and Third Infantry Squads will be covering the east approach to the town. They'll be going in heavy so they can either be using AM or Satellite. We have no recon at this time, so we have no idea what to expect as far as resistance or capabilities in the town."

"Second Platoon, Second and Third Infantry Squads on the western approach to the town will be supported by Fourth Platoon, First Communications and Third Medic Squads split evenly between the east and west ends of town," Halstead had the next group. "Like Jackson said, we don't have any recon yet, and while Sheri and Chuck where only there for a short time, and Chuck was only there after dark, we'll take anything they can give us that will help prior to committing anything."

"All right then, I'd like to begin with you, Sheri, if you're ok with that?" Mallory asked. At a nod from Sheri she continued. "If you could start with everything you remember about the town, including layout, number of occupied buildings, number of people, anything that you can remember could be useful."

Sheri told them everything she could remember about the drive into town, descriptions of people and buildings, numbers of people, and anything she could remember that Pete had told her. The fact that there were some technically-savvy people there, but that they didn't seem to be in charge was interesting.

When she was done, Chuck went through the same process, filling in any blanks that he could, although he hadn't been doing nearly as good a job cataloging information as Sheri had. She just seemed to be a natural at this. "I did notice that although there were supposed to be a number of homes with power, only four of them had lights on when I came into the town and when we left. I don't know what that means, if anything, but knowing what I do now about how many have power, I just found it interesting.

"I also didn't encounter anyone outside, which I was grateful for at the time, but it seems more than a little odd now that I think about it. I'm pretty sure I remember seeing a couple of curtains move, but I didn't see anyone outside--nobody. No one challenged me getting into the town; we were able to get Sheri's stuff out of the Mustang without incident. Nobody even yelled after the gunshot," Chuck grimaced a little when he said that. The adrenaline was wearing off and he was starting to come to grips with the fact that he'd shot Pete. He had a sneaking suspicion he was going to be violently, noisily sick in the very near future.

Sheri grabbed Chuck's hand and stepped into what could have become an awkward silence, "I mentioned it to Pete, but at the time I thought I was just trying to piss him off to leave me alone. The three guys that were nominally in charge, or at least that were in the group that came to meet with Keeler and I, didn't act like they were happy to have Pete around. They certainly didn't act deferential to him--not in front of me. I'm not surprised that they didn't come to his defense or make any effort to stop us."

"Ok then, we aren't going in with guns blazing, but now that Pete's out of the picture, we need to talk to these people. I've got a couple of suggestions…"

…

After about thirty minutes of discussion, it was obvious that Chuck and Sheri didn't have anything more to offer, and Mallory called for a break. "Sheri, have you had anything to eat? I can't believe I didn't think of that before, but do you need anything?"

"No, I'm good. Pete actually brought back the ruck's from the Humvee and I had a #5. The adrenaline is wearing off though."

"I think we're good then. If either of you thinks of anything else that you feel would be helpful, let us know though, k?"

"Roger that," Chuck said with a small smile.

They both got up and walked out of the tent, and by mutual assent took each other's hands as they left.

The first awkward moment came as they were approaching the more-or-less civilian side of the base where both Sheri and Chuck had their tents. They were still holding hands while they walked, Chuck on the left, Sheri on the right, and they each proceeded to walk in those directions towards their own tents when the time came, each assuming the other was coming with them. Neither of them, however, let go.

They didn't actually get to the point where their arms were sticking straight out before they looked at each other, but it was obvious that they were headed in two opposite directions. Sheri was the first to blush, but not by much, and then they were both giggling, and then they were chuckling, and pretty soon they were sitting on the ground laughing, all without saying a word.

After a couple of minutes it was Chuck who asked the question that both of them had had written all over their faces while they blushed. "So, um, ma'am," just not eloquently, "I absolutely didn't mean to presume anything, not at all, really, but um…"

He was saved from terminal embarrassment by Sheri launching herself from her sitting position at him and bowling him over. "Your place is fine, big guy," kiss, "although I really am tired," kiss, "and this is all so sudden," kiss, "and that's all you're getting tonight," kiss "Now let's go get some of my stuff."

Interlude Four

Societies, communities, and civilizations are different things, and people post-event were finding that they weren't necessarily complimentary sides of the same three-sided coin. Not every group of people who'd had the presence of mind to get out of town early had an ethical leader in charge of their group. Not every town that had been sufficiently removed from a population center had been sufficiently prepared to provide for itself long term. Not everyone who had a plan to keep civilization intact had a society or community with which to surround themselves, and not every society that remained had civilization at its core.

What remained of the U.S. Government, for example: the President, Vice-President, Cabinet, fifty-seven Senators and one-hundred and fifty-three Representatives from the House, had a plan to keep civilization intact. They had a society that numbered less than 2,500 people, however. Without a much tighter command and control network and the ability to communicate with more than just a handful of military entities, there was no hope of implementing the plan on the books. They did have a society, though, and it did have almost 2,500 people. Those people were currently located at an Air Force base, and they were doing as well as anyone could expect to be doing under the circumstances, they just weren't running the country anymore.

There were other societies and communities now, too--some not more than one-hundred miles away from where the President currently called home. Many wouldn't have been at all opposed to what the former U.S. Government would have proposed had they been able to hear it, but they couldn't, and so they went their own way. One group of less than three-hundred people, just up the road, would continue to farm on their land, milk their cows, gather the eggs from the chickens, and slaughter the pigs. Simply put, they would continue on as they had been for the last couple of generations, if a little slower now that it was all done by hand.

Of course there were other groups, calling them a society really would be going too far, who were nothing more than roving bands of modern-day marauders and land pirates. Their only concern with civilization was that it seemed to have come to an end. If they happened to encounter it they would take advantage of it as long as it lasted, feast on the corpse until even that was gone, and then move on again. They couldn't really be said to be anarchists as many of them didn't even know what anarchy was. They were just hooligans who'd finally gotten a free rein.

There were the rare groups, however--true communities—which, regardless of their size or location, were determined to maintain civilization. They were few and far between but they did exist. In Massachusetts, a group that came to be called the Freemen finally proved they weren't all wacko's and established law and order in an area that encompassed almost 4,900 square miles and had towns begging to be brought into the "Freemen Coalition". In San Antonio, Texas, using the Alamo as the center of operations, a group calling themselves the New Texas Rangers kept a rough circle sixty miles wide peaceful, orderly, and civilized. The Freemen did it with 1,800 people; the Rangers started with only two-hundred and eighty-five.

Chapter Thirty-Seven

Just as the sun was peering over the horizon, fourteen fully loaded, combat ready Army vehicles came roaring into Gratefille from both the East and West sides. As Mallory had said, there were no guns blazing, but Humvees and LAVs are not quiet at the best of times, and when you deliberately downshift, they can wake the dead.

It took about three minutes for the newly reinstated leadership of the town to present themselves in response to a very politely phrased request, albeit phrased at a fairly high decibel level, at which point parlay could begin. Everyone from the "meet-and-greet" was there-- from the town, that is. Neither Sheri nor Sergeant Keeler was present. Sheri wasn't there since Mallory had put her foot down and declared this a purely military operation as the security of the base was entirely the province of the Guard. She'd been tempted to use the excuse that Sergeant Keeler had been the only one physically injured until Halstead had reminded her that Pete had slugged Sheri in the back of the head as well, just not left any permanent marks, which both cooled her down and pissed her off all over again. Keeler wasn't there because he wasn't quite seeing straight yet and, frankly, in his shoes, Mallory wasn't sure she wouldn't have just shot all six of the "front men" and been done with it. Screw permission, forgiveness was usually easier to come by and required less paperwork.

"Before you say anything, we're going to get a few things out of the way," Sergeant Jackson began. "My name is Sergeant Jackson and the first thing you need to know is that we are, *I am*, pissed. Sergeant Keeler is, and I say is because he is still with us thankyouverymuch, under my command, he is in a squad in MY platoon. That means you dicked with one of MY boys. I don't care who threw the rock. I don't care that he's dead. No, I take that back, I do care that he's dead. I'm *glad* HE is dead but the point is MY boy was there because of YOU people. YOU people are DIRECTLY responsible for what happened to him yesterday. Period. End of discussion."

The group as a whole flinched at every capitalized word, and they were very obviously capitalized when Jackson said them. He let the silence hang for a few seconds before he continued, "All of that aside we are not here for reprisals." The group from the town visibly relaxed at that and the two women let out a slow breath. "I'm not done, and I'm still not happy. This isn't The Hague, you aren't on trial, and I think we all know that the, well, mastermind certainly isn't the right word, but the individual ultimately behind yesterday's joke of a meeting is no longer around to be a thorn in our sides."

"Our sole purpose for being here is to find out just what yesterday's little production was all about and what it was supposed to accomplish. We aren't going to take anyone back to the base and water board them and we can't and won't force anything from anyone but today won't go like yesterday. Is that understood?"

After a few seconds and a few head nods Jackson just couldn't help himself, "I CAN'T HEAR YOU!"

A chorus of 'Yes, sir' and 'Yes, Sergeant' was the reply. "At least I know you heard me. There's a reason we have a protocol in the military and not all of it is to stroke the Officer's egos. So, just what was yesterday all about, anyway? And I'm not talking about the little drama that got resolved last night, because we've already been told that you didn't have anything to do with that so save the 'righteous indignation' and 'moral outrage' for some other time. I'm talking about the waste of time, energy, man and woman hours, and resources--not the least of which is the fuel which could have been either saved or put to better use."

The townspeople looked at each other for a few more seconds and then the oldest one of the bunch, the same one who had originally stood up to Pete the afternoon before, took a half step forward and became spokesperson for the group. "Frankly, we aren't entirely sure. Pete was keeping his cards close to the vest, what few cards he had left, and I think he was making things up as he went along. He started out drinking and in just a couple of days started smoking weed like it was cigarettes. I know that he wanted us to get as much information about you all as a group as we could but without committing to anything, and then try to set up another meeting-- outside of that, not much else."

"I think he had some grand design that only he knew all the details to, and like I said, I doubt he was playing with a full deck there near the end. He was threatening people for no reason, swinging his dick, trying to act like some combination magnanimous ruler and cruel overlord, and nobody had the guts to call him on it or stand up to him after the first day. I think that's when he snapped, actually."

"What happened the first day?" Jackson asked.

The old guy ran his hands through his hair and looked over at the sunrise through partially closed eyes for a couple of breaths before he continued, "The first morning, when Pete showed up, he pulled in here in that hotrod of his about 10:30. He'd apparently been listening in on the CB, since we'd been using it to communicate with each other since Friday after the power went out. He had that ridiculous antenna on his car that let him pick up from farther than he could transmit and he'd evidently been driving around, listening to the signal as it got weaker and stronger, sort of a poor-man's triangulation, trying to find a population center that wasn't falling apart outside of Nashville."

"So he pulls in and asks, fairly politely, who's in charge. We don't have a police station in town, we were covered by the county; and we don't have a Mayor, we had a City Council. He drives over to the Municipal building, where the library and City Council are--and the one remaining councilman was, since the rest took off within a couple of days of the power outage-- and asks to speak to him. When Mike comes out he doesn't think anything of the fact that Pete's wearing a gun as there's probably ten or twelve people in town doing the same. Too bad, because after Pete asks if Mike's all that's left of the City Council and Mike says yes, Pete hauls off and shoots him. Bang, right there in front of the library.

"There were a half a dozen people there who saw it, including me. Didn't bat an eye at the time, just turned to us on the sidewalk and said 'I'm in charge here now. You all might want to run along and let everyone know, and if I see anyone else with a gun in town, they'll end up just like Mike here. No questions asked.' Then he turned around, got a good look at Mike, turned green, and threw up all over himself--didn't even make it to the bushes or the gutter."

"He grabbed me before I could turn away and asked me where Mike had lived--what the address was--and then he moved in. After he did what he did to Mike, even the few of us who had some sort of gun didn't dare try to do anything. Nobody knew when or where he'd show up or what he'd do. That evening he saw some of the kids, um, smoking... and when he asked them where they got it, they didn't answer because they didn't know if he wanted some or if he'd be pissed that they were getting stoned. When they didn't answer, he beat the crap out of my nephew, broke his nose, gave him a black eye, and cut up his face pretty bad with the butt of his pistol. "Turns out he wasn't opposed to the idea of taking a hit or two himself, and when he finally got his joint he cooled off for a while. But I swear, I've never seen a chain pot smoker before and I've been smoking it all my life. The man was a natural."

"Correction," Jackson said, "Pete was a coward, blight on the human race, and a dozen other choice colorful metaphors that I'm choosing not to use right now. He may have been an adult male human being but he was absolutely, definitely not a man in any sense of the word. I have very little respect for you but given what I've heard so far and the fact that you are even talking to me means you are more man than Pete ever was." Jackson decided to leave it at that, he could have gone on about the fact that they were surrounded by prime examples of Men right now, and Women for that matter, each of whom embodied the finest ideal that Manhood or Womanhood could hope to attain but he could always rub the salt in that wound later if necessary.

"I stand corrected and I see your point. To get back to your original question, I don't really know what the end game of yesterday was all about but I can guarantee that it won't happen again. To put it bluntly, that crap ended last night."

"Well, I'm glad to hear it, Mr.?" Jackson asked.

"Lawson, Lyle Lawson."

"Like I said, I'm glad to hear it Mr. Lawson but please understand where I'm coming from when I say that I'll believe it when I see it."

"I do, really. Basically because, well, some of the folks in town want to be part of the group at the base, but a few here that don't want to leave the town for the base, they would basically like the town to be 'occupied'."

Jackson raised his left eyebrow at that. "Excuse me?"

"Those that would like to stay here figure that if it's occupied, it has a better chance of being defended if necessary because it's home to those doing the defending," Lawson finished.

"Makes sense, sort of. Which do you prefer, between joining the base and occupation?" Jackson asked.

"I'd actually prefer to stay here--partially because I've been asked to but also because the folks who stay are going to need someone to be in charge on the civilian side, and I know everyone here. It would make more sense that I stay than just about anyone else."

"Well, I'm authorized to OK just about anything. That, however, was never even considered, frankly. This is going to take some discussion above my pay-grade, not that any of us are getting paid for this right now," Jackson finished in a mutter.

...

"They want what? Over." Mallory asked, trying and failing miserably to keep the incredulity out of her voice.

"That's about what I said and they know we're in the park, even if they don't know specifically where we are. That, in and of itself doesn't surprise me, so I think either bringing a couple of them in to talk to us or having you come somewhere where they can talk to you would be a good idea. This group is going to need a little more administrative involvement than the others have, I'm afraid, over."

"That's probably a fair assessment of the situation. Give me a minute, over."

"Take all the time you need, Top. We were the ones pushing here. I don't think they were expecting an answer right away and I don't think they are even expecting to have anyone come back with us today. We surprised 'em pretty good this morning. They figured someone would be coming around sometime, but not nearly so many of us and certainly not at the crack of dawn, over."

"Point. Ok, we need to talk to them. If they are willing, and frankly they better be, bring back Lawson and one or two others of his choosing. We aren't leaving anyone there though, period. We'll stay in contact with them over the radio, which is only fair. There's too much to think about to make a snap decision on this and I refuse to do it unless I absolutely have to, over."

"Roger. I'll let you know how many are coming back on the way in. Jackson, out."

Jackson walked back to the group from his command truck after closing the connection with Mallory. "Mr. Lawson, as I said it's a decision that needs to be made at a higher pay-grade than mine. It also needs to be made after a bit more discussion than we've had so far. First Sergeant Jensen is willing to meet with you and one or two others if you'd like, back at the base." Lawson was nodding his head as though he had been thinking along the same lines already. "We would obviously provide safe conduct for you; however Sergeant Jensen has not authorized me to allow anyone to remain behind at this time."

"As long as someone here in town would be able to radio in occasionally and talk to one of us who went with you I don't see there being a problem with that. I can think of a number of potential issues that would need to be worked around off the top of my head if this is going to work out at all and I would be happy to meet with your First Sergeant. If she is willing to meet with us today, can you wait while I and two others get ready to go?"

...

"I'm trying to be cool and rational about this," Sheri was clenching and unclenching her fists at her sides, "honest I am, and I know that none of the people who will be coming into the base were at the meeting with Keeler and I, but I'm having a real hard time here. I can't believe that none of those people saw Pete walk me into the house at gunpoint or that the story didn't circulate after the 'elders' left and none of them did a single thing to try to help me."

"I think you're doing a fabulous job but I'm probably a little biased." Chuck said, but wisely didn't try to hold her hand or rub her shoulders or try to get her to calm down.

"Sheri, I know you are pissed about this which is why I wanted to be the one to tell you." Mallory said. "Lawson and I hammered this out for most of the day today and this was a sticking point. It wasn't until I threatened to tell him to go to pound sand and all but declare open season on his town that he backed off. He understood that you would be upset but he also figured that you would 'understand the situation that they had been put in'. I'm not going to come to his defense but he did watch a man get his heart all but blown out of his chest from about two arms lengths away, Sheri."

Mallory paused and then asked. "I'm not asking if it's fair, I'm asking if it's the right thing to do."

"Yes, alright, yes it's the right thing to do. There, are you happy now?"

"No, I'm not happy. I'm not as pissed about this as you are but I'm not happy either. Sheri, in a very real sense, whether they knew it or not, they ended up being the bait in a trap that could have caused me to lose not just one of my soldiers but two friends as well. This does not make me happy." Mallory said.

"They won't be coming in for at least a couple of weeks because everyone needs some time to cool down and come to grips with their arrival. There are also a lot of logistics that are going to need to be worked out surrounding putting either a permanent or rotating detachment there in the town. It will take time and with time things will get easier. I won't say you will forget and I don't expect you to forgive but I do expect you to live with it. Am I asking too much?"

Sheri was silent for a good half minute before she answered, "No, you aren't, and I wasn't just pouting. I hold grudges though, I can't help it, I have all my life." She turned to Chuck and said with a small smile, "You'd do well to remember that Mr." Then she took a deep breath and looked squarely at Mallory, "I can deal with it, it just came as a shock and a bit of a blow. This whole thing just happened so fast. Yesterday morning we were talking about going out to meet with these people for the first time, then yesterday afternoon I was abducted. Last night Pete gets blown away less than a foot away from me," she put her arms around Chuck, "and then I fall asleep in this man's arms and now this. It just seems so surreal. You're taking it much better than I am."

"That's because I've had twenty years of being told to dig a hole so that I could fill it back up, both metaphorically and literally. Oh, believe me, I'll scream into my pillow tonight most likely-- but you aren't allowed to see that, so you won't."

"You're very weird, and a little bit scary," Sheri replied.

"Better than being like Joel. He's a lot scary and only a little weird. And on that note let's go get some chow."

Chapter Thirty-Eight

Morris had the radio detail again. He was sure everyone else was pulling their fair share, but it seemed like he was always in this stupid tent. Then again, there was that old saw that 'them's that did the best in combat, saw the most combat'. Not that manning the radio was really all that tough.

It was 19:14, or 7:14 pm, on Saturday, August 18th. Morris had forty-six minutes left in his shift and, frankly, he was bored. The number of groups in the area wanting to join up had all but dried up and communication was down to routine traffic with the local farmers. So it came as a complete and utter shock when a totally unfamiliar voice came over his headphones, and on the secure channel, no less. No, it wasn't on a secure channel--it was on THE secure channel. The first inbound communication from higher in over two months!

"Promised Land Two this is Lima Alpha November Charlie Echo Romeo Six, over," the voice on the other end said.

Usually, in the interest of maintaining proper radio discipline, and to keep transmissions short, both parties start with their entire call signs and then respond with only the last two or three letters and/or numbers. There is one exception. Training kicked in and Morris replied, "Lima Alpha November Charlie Echo Romeo Six this is Promised Land Two." That one exception was currently LANCER or the current call sign for the President of the United States.

Morris hadn't had to do the next part, seriously, in over two months, as he'd recognized every voice over the radio and they'd verbally decided on authentication and duress codes prior to departure. "Wait one, please, over." He needed to grab the code book as it wasn't close by since they weren't using it. Bad practice, Morris, and this is what you get.

"Take your time, son, it's OK. Over."

That stopped Morris in mid reach, "Say again, over."

"I said take your time Morris, it's OK. Over."

Morris blinked, ok, whoever this was knew him by name. Interesting. He got the code book and turned to the current page. "Authenticate Bravo Niner Delta Whiskey Alpha Foxtrot Four. Over."

"I authenticate Five Zulu Echo Yankee Lima Tree Papa. Over."

At this point a truncated call sign was permissible, "I authenticate, go ahead Romeo Six. Over." *I can't believe I'm having this conversation.*

"Critical message follows, repeat, critical message follows. Critical message to be archived, over."

"Roger, I copy critical message to follow. Critical message to be archived, archiving active, over." Why they couldn't just say 'record the stinkin' message' was beyond him. But they couldn't, so they didn't.

"As of 5:00 hours GMT, 19 August 2012, procedure ARCLiTE, repeat Alpha Romeo Charlie Lima Tango Echo is in effect. Critical message ends." There was a sigh on the other end, but he hadn't said over, so he wasn't done.

"Specialist Morris, we've never met in person. I'm Colonel Spencer Olsen, and this is the thirty-first time I've relayed this message. There are a few things I want you to know. First, you are not alone, although you are a little unique in how quickly your group got their act together. The National Guard and full-time military all over the U.S. and northern hemisphere are in the exact same situation you are."

"Some of them are at their bases & forts, some of them are still in their Armories and some, like you, have moved out either by choice or by circumstance and had to set up elsewhere. Some are doing a little worse than you all seem to be, some are doing as well, and few, frankly, are doing better. We've been monitoring anyone utilizing the satellite systems, including yourselves, which is how I knew it was you manning the radio. When contacting your group, for example, it had been decided that it would be yourself, Pine, or Wilson manning the radio."

"When I transmitted the critical message, a download was also initiated to your system that can only be accessed by your First Sergeant, Sergeant Jensen. In a few moments, you'll be bringing her into the 'net. Before then, I want to say how proud I am of what we know of, from what we've gathered, about what you all have done. One day, I'd like to meet Chuck Turner too, sounds like a hell of a man and damned good shot. You've all done a truly incredible job under some very difficult and stressful circumstances."

"From the decision to leave the Armory, to the location you chose, to the integration with the civilian population, everything we've been able to gather has been the absolutely exemplary ideal of a United States Soldier. I am proud to know that I have served with such honorable men and women up to this point and I know you will continue to be such--and Morris, this isn't a script. I'm not saying the same thing to everyone. There's a whole bank of people here monitoring communications and some folks have stood out. You people are one of those groups and I want you to know that, and I want you to share that."

"Now, I need to speak with First Sergeant Jensen. If you would please get her, I would appreciate it, over," Colonel Olsen was done and the praise had been sincere. You could tell when an officer was just blowing sunshine. He wasn't finished though.

"Wilco, wait one. Over." Everyone that Mallory had been relying on for her command meetings had started wearing a radio a couple of weeks ago, so now it was a simple matter of calling Top on her radio.

"Alpha Six, this is Papa Two, over."

"Papa Two, this is Alpha Six, go ahead, over." Mallory was a little taken aback as she was usually Mike Six inside the base, and Alpha Six when talking to someone outside the base.

"Six, I have a call for you, please proceed to the communications tent, over."

"Go ahead and send it to my radio please, over." Mallory was on the other side of the base and really didn't want to head over to the communications tent to deal with a farmer right now.

"Negative, Alpha Six, your presence is required in the communications tent, over."

"Say again, over." What was so important that her presence was required in the tent?

"Repeat, the physical presence in the communications tent of ALPHA SIX for a call from someone with a very long call sign is required, over."

Really? "Roger, be there in a minute, over."

"Papa Two out."

Less than two minutes later, she was in the tent. "Who's on the radio?"

"A Colonel Spencer Olsen. He called in from higher, duh, obviously, sorry. They've been monitoring communications for a while; he knew who I was by my voice. He authenticated, he's on *the* secure channel, not just *a* secure channel. He authenticated LANCER. There's also a data dump that is "Eyes Only" for you. I haven't even tried to touch it, much less get into it. He had a critical message that as of 05:00 ZULU tomorrow morning something called ARCLiTE goes into effect."

"That and they're proud of us, specifically us, and we aren't alone in this. We've done at least as well as everyone else and better than many. And he'd like to meet Chuck some day, so apparently they were monitoring the feed when he made the world a better place." Morris usually didn't babble and had to clamp his mouth shut.

For Mallory's part she was doing her best to keep emotion off of her face. She had no idea what ARCLiTE meant, officially, but ever since boot camp there had been unofficial ARCLIGHTs and none of them had been 'good'. "Alright, get me a pair of headphones. Let's see what he has to say."

A few seconds later, Mallory identified herself on the radio. "This is Alpha Six, go ahead, over."

"Specialist Morris, is this transmission still being archived? Over." Col. Olsen asked.

"Yes, Sir. Over."

"Then with all due respect to First Sergeant Jensen, please remove yourself from the 'net." Although it was phrased as a request, it was still an order. Morris was already reaching for the switch as he glanced towards Top, who nodded to him as she slowly blinked.

"Dismissed, Morris."

After Morris was disconnected and had left the tent and it was just Mallory and the Colonel, he continued. "First of all, I assume that Specialist Morris filled you in as much as he could in the very limited time available to him. Secondly, he probably left you with more questions than answers. That's simply in the nature of the situation."

"Third, I'm going to dispense with some of the protocol, as the link we've got established is fully bi-directional and supports you and I arguing at full speed and talking over each other if we want to. Have you been informed that ARCLiTE will go into effect at 05:00 ZULU tomorrow?"

Mallory waited a second, and realized that this is what the Colonel meant by dispensing with some of the protocol, before answering, "Yes, sir, although I don't know what that means."

"In a nutshell, ARCLiTE is Autonomous Regimental Control, Long Term Engagement. It was initially designed for a situation where either communications were going to be unavailable for an extended period of time or could compromise a unit, up to a Regiment in size, or some sort of short-term catastrophe disrupted centralized command and control. In this case, it's a bit of a combination of things."

"The communications capabilities, i.e. the satellites, are there, but not everyone has the power to run the gear and centralized command and control is not possible at this time. As Morris may or may not have told you, we have been monitoring all satellite based communications but have not been interfering or communicating until now. We'd hoped to have things back on track and put back together by now but obviously we don't and we don't know how long it's going to be."

"ARCLiTE puts each isolated unit under local command and control under some well defined but very broad guidelines. That's part of what was downloaded. The briefing is actually one-hundred and eighty-four pages with an additional five-hundred pages of 'useful information'. The legal part is in the one-hundred and eighty-four pages though. It officially puts your group in control of what it's doing instead of hoping you're doing the right thing and waiting for us to get in touch."

"From a 10,000 foot overview it may even look like the military is being disbanded with the exception of any base or fort responsible for securing nuclear, chemical, or biological weapons. Those will stay on station and that is what the remaining centralized command and control has to focus on, which is why we are releasing control to the local level."

"Any questions so far?"

"Actually no, for once it makes sense, sir."

"Fair enough. The next part is gonna be a kick in the pants. Control of the local unit, regardless of size, cannot be relinquished to an NCO. I just heard you take a breath, do not interrupt me Major; I am still your Superior Officer."

"Yes, you heard me right. You have been reviewed; you might feel that Captain would be more appropriate, and then again, you might feel that First Sergeant was just fine too. It was, up until about thirty seconds ago. You do, of course, have the option of refusing the commission, but I don't think you will. I've had the honor of promoting seven people and so far none of them have refused, although one of them was a near thing."

"You may now speak freely."

"Sir, I choked on my original objection when you said Major. When you said it couldn't fall to an NCO, I assumed there would be a field promotion to Second Lieutenant, just to get the Officer rank. Frankly, I'm still trying to process that. I'm not sure, sir, I," Mallory stopped for a second. "Let me try that again, sir, I've never been to OCS, I don't know that I'm ready to be an Officer. I won't say that I don't know the first thing about being an officer, because that's patently false, but stripes to a Gold Oak Leaf? Sir, that's an awfully big jump."

Olsen laughed out loud, "Indeed it is Major, but official in every way, shape, and form, and is effective as soon as you accept it. All branches of the United States Military still exist, but you will soon be, literally, under completely autonomous local command and control. Additionally, there is an extension that had to be added to ARCLiTE, which is why it hasn't been called sooner."

"The change won't be nearly as difficult for you and yours to accept or internalize, but it basically allows for a much tighter relationship between you and the civilian population. In fact, it almost requires it. Some folks might even read it as a requirement that the military begin to operate more as a militia that reports to whatever civilian government is being put into place. We're obviously not omniscient, we don't know everything that's been going on, as we've only been able to monitor what's gone over the satellite links, but from what we've observed, your group is set up at least as well as many and better than most." Olsen paused.

"Thank you, sir, that's due in large part to the civilians and the ability of everyone to work together. I've been blessed, frankly, with a very good group of people who are not only very capable, but incredibly motivated. That goes for both civilian and military." Mallory took a deep breath.

"Colonel Olsen, Sir, I hereby accept my commission to the rank of Major in the United States Army. As a Major, and under the terms outlined in ARCLiTE, having not yet read them, am I granted the authority to either promote from within my ranks, and/or accept for enlistment into my ranks, civilians under my area of influence and protection?"

"Major Jensen, I am uploading additional orders that cover that specifically, but which had to wait until your acceptance of your commission, as they aren't actually covered directly under ARCLiTE. To answer your questions, yes on both counts, based on guidelines you have just received. Congratulations, Major. As a side note, do you in fact have any Gold Oak Leaves in stores?"

"Thank you, sir, and yes, sir, we do, we should be good for a while at least for ranks."

"Very good. In that case, I'll let you go. I assume you'll need some time to adjust, but congratulations again, and good luck. Olsen Out." And with that, Mallory was alone in the tent. She reached over and pressed the button that stopped recording the transmission.

After a few minutes, Mallory chuckled to herself. "After all these years, it looks like Ramirez is going to have to stop saying there's a reason he's still a Staff Sergeant." Mallory leaned forward and put her face in her hands, "What in the world am I going to do? I can't gut my entire existing command staff with promotions. I'm going to need a First Sergeant, and I'm going to need other officers. Time to see what the orders say."

She wasn't overly concerned with the details of ARCLiTE, she could get into the nuts and bolts of it later and she had a feeling that it wouldn't be changing their day to day much based on what Col. Olsen had said. She was actually more interested with what her additional orders said and how much leeway they were going to give her. Autonomous was all well and good as far as it went but the lights would eventually come back on and she would not put her people in a position to be hung out to dry. She was a Soldier after all, well, actually now she was an Officer in the U. S. Army but the sentiment was the same.

...

Eric and Karen were seated across the table from Mallory in the command tent, which would soon be replaced by an actual building. Mallory's hands were clasped in front of her on the table to keep them still. She wasn't nervous exactly, but she was still feeling her way around in this new arena of 'officerhood'.

"Eric, I need your help, don't interrupt please. Before I begin I need to share some information with you and Karen that you cannot share with anyone else for the time being. This is not the beginning of a rumor tree, this is serious. If you cannot assure me that what I tell you, regardless of what you decide to do, will remain confidential no matter what it is, we can be done now. It is something that both of you need to know, though."

Eric's face was stone; he'd been in this position before and knew exactly how to handle it. Karen, not so much. Her eyes were huge and her face was pale as she turned to Eric and grabbed for his hand. When she turned back to Mallory and asked, "What's going on?!" there was more than just a little panic in her voice.

"Karen, the answer to that question isn't going to be forthcoming until we can convince First Sergeant Jensen that whatever she tells us will remain between us for as long as she sees fit." There was a slight tremor at the corner of Mallory's mouth when he called her by her title. "I will say that if you and I are here, I doubt it's all bad, or even bad at all. I'm guessing she needs me to do something, and she wants you to know and/or wants your blessing. I'm also guessing that she just doesn't want it to get out before she has a chance to let everyone know."

Eric turned back to Mallory, "I won't ask if that's right, Top because you won't answer, but you have my word. You know my security clearance level and, active or not, you know I mean it when I give that word. Anything we say here stays here until you give the go ahead. You also have my word for Karen that if she says the same thing its good but I think you know that already too. If you can ease her mind as far as 'we aren't all gonna die in the next ten minutes', I think she'll give you that word too."

"Fair enough. Karen, I promise that to the best of my knowledge, we aren't all gonna die in the next ten minutes." Mallory smiled.

"Oh screw you and the horse you rode in on!" Karen laughed. "Ok, ok, but Mal, you really need to work on the delivery, girl. You could have started with the whole not gonna die part, you know?" Karen took a breath, as she was calming down and getting some color back in her face, "Yes, I swear. Give me a Bible if it would help, but I'm not going to make light of it by crossing my heart. Anything we discuss stays here. I won't even discuss it with Eric."

"Good enough for me." Now it was Mallory's turn to take a breath. "Some time later this evening, next couple of hours at the latest, you can quit calling me Top." Neither Karen nor Eric could keep the surprise off their face this time, and Eric almost stood up until he got a look from Mallory that made it clear she wasn't finished and that he better not make a scene.

"You will finally be able to refer to me as ma'am and not incur my wrath as I've been promoted to Major, God help us all. Eric, before you retired you were a Master Sergeant and therefore senior to everyone here but me, and I'm going to need a Captain…"

…

"Ramirez, have a seat."

"Top, everything ok?"

"That remains to be seen, but I have a little problem, which means you have a little problem," Mallory said. This of course was a euphemism, and one that senior NCOs and Officers have been using time without end. It also just about made Ramirez stand back up.

What did I do, who screwed up? Usually I have some idea why I'm getting called on the carpet ahead of time!

"Gotcha," Mallory grinned.

"Top, don't DO that! You're gonna have to get this chair redone. There's a one inch hole missing in the fabric in the seat now!"

"Oh settle down, I haven't given you grief in weeks, you were due-- and besides, I really do have sort of a problem and it really does concern you, but not in a bad way. I saved you for last because I knew you were going to give me the most flak about it. As of right now, Sergeant Ramirez, while you will still be Sergeant Ramirez, you will just be Sergeant First Class Ramirez. And while you can no longer call me Top you will finally be allowed to call me ma'am as I am now Major Mallory Jensen."

"Of course you have to accept, technically, which I guess you could refuse to do, technically, but I sincerely doubt that's going to happen." Mallory waited a few seconds and then chuckled, "Close your mouth, Kyle, you're gonna swallow a fly."

…

It was 23:13 by the time Mallory had her staff assembled, which included herself and the newly promoted; Eric as a Captain, Halstead as a Lieutenant, Jackson as a 'Butter Bar' Second Lieutenant, Stewart as First Sergeant, Wilson, Bowersock, and Ramirez as Sergeants First Class, and Morris, Keeler, and Pine as new Staff Sergeants. She had also assembled Joel and Rachael, Karen, Chuck and Sheri, and all the "block moms" (which also included more than a few dads now).

"Ladies, gentlemen… First Sergeant Stewart is now Top. I'll forgive you for a couple of days," Mallory smiled, "he probably won't," a chuckle rippled through the 'room'.

"Now for the briefing. Morris, good job keeping a lid on this," heads turned to Morris as nothing had leaked, including the fact that higher had called in the first place, until Mallory had called each of them in to talk to them. For some of them, this would be the first they were hearing about what was going on.

It took just under forty minutes to describe ARCLiTE to those who had assembled and Mallory handed out a 'Press Release' for the "block moms" for the inevitable questions after the morning announcements via the radio, which had been up and running for almost three weeks now.

"Are there any questions?" Mallory asked.

Rachael raised her hand and at a nod from Mallory stood up and glanced down at Joel. "Do we have any idea how much longer it will be until we have a maternity ward? I think I'm about six weeks along."

--The End--

332

Coming September 2012
DARK ROAD

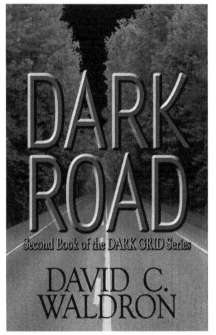

Chapter One

"Day 64," Dan Clark wrote in his journal. The entries were getting shorter but he'd made sure to put something down every day since the power went out on June 14th. When they had all come together at

the cabana and Ms. Hines told everyone what had happened to the power plant at the dam…well, he just hadn't wanted to believe it.

But then the next morning she was gone--along with the Taylors, Eric and Karen, and that guy, Chuck, her supervisor from the plant. Carey, the jumped up HOA President, had a broken nose and didn't want to talk about it, and the Neighborhood Recreational Activities Committee was suddenly the "Food Police". Practically overnight they were living in some bizarre feudal society and nobody could remember how Carey got put in charge, or why they allowed him to stay there.

Now, *"Day 64 – We had another suicide today, the last of the single folks. An older gentleman by the name of Rolland Brandt. He took a handful of allergy pills, the kind that make you really drowsy, and drank most of a bottle of 80 proof rum. I hope it was peaceful."*

Dan closed his journal and put it in the drawer in the nightstand by the bed. The same nightstand that used to hold a lamp, alarm clock, iPod, cell phone, and CPAP machine but now held only a candle and a picture of his son, Danny Jr. His only son, who would have been two tomorrow. Dan closed his eyes.

Three weeks ago Dan had come home to find his wife Marissa rocking their youngest and trying to keep him cool with a damp washcloth. Danny Jr. had come down with a fever out of nowhere and nothing that they tried could bring his temperature down. Even alternating toddler ibuprofen and acetaminophen did nothing. They did their best to keep him cool and tried to keep him hydrated, but later that evening he quit drinking.

Dan and Marissa took turns taking care of their two daughters—eight-year-old Bekah, and six-year-old Jessie--and then stayed up together with Danny. In the middle of the night they had both fallen asleep over their fitfully sleeping, and now also wheezing, toddler. Dan couldn't remember when he fell asleep…but he knew that he woke up at 4:22 am.

Marissa had her arm over Danny's legs and was holding Dan's hand. Dan was an EMT, so he knew what he would see even before he looked at his son. He heard no wheezing, felt no heat coming from his side, and sensed no stirring from the small body between himself and his wife. When he turned his hand to look at his watch it woke Marissa up and they both looked at Danny at the same time.

"No!" Marissa said with a sort of half yelp, half sob.

"Rissa, sweetie, it's too late. I'm so sorry, honey, he's already cool to the touch."

Marissa was crying freely, but keeping it quiet--because even in grief she was thinking of the girls in the next two rooms. She was stroking Danny's hair and looking back and forth between Dan and her son. "Dan?"

"I don't know." Dan said--not knowing what the question was but sure he had no answers, regardless. He was having trouble seeing and wondered what was wrong until he realized he was crying too.

They sat there together, with Marissa cradling Danny and rocking him for several minutes until they could compose themselves enough to think about what they must do next. As the only person in the neighborhood with any medical training, Dan had been involved in dealing with just about every death in the neighborhood so far. He didn't want to have to deal with this one, though. Dan wanted someone else to deal with this one.

Dan opened his eyes. Marissa and Dan had still not come to terms with the loss of Danny Jr. They had dealt with it to a degree, and Marissa had "put it behind her" for the time being. They didn't discuss it, ever. The picture on Dan's nightstand was the only concession she had made, and if either of them had been willing to hit the other they would have probably come to blows over even that. Neither of them had truly dealt with the grief, and the house hadn't been the same since.

"I miss you Danny, I'm so sorry." Dan said out loud as he reached towards the picture.

"What was that?" Marissa asked as she came into their bedroom.

Instead of the truth, Dan covered what he felt was a moment of weakness by lying to his wife. "Nothing, just lamenting our fate," Dan said. Something they had agreed on less than a week into the crisis was that they wouldn't keep bringing up the things that they missed as it just made it worse.

"Go ahead, what are you missing this time?"

"I don't want to say, it's stupid. I mean it, it's really stupid," Dan said, hoping she would drop it because he really didn't have anything to say other than Danny.

"Try me. I'll even go first. I miss chocolate. Chocolate brownies, chocolate chip cookies, Hershey's chocolate bars…with almonds, mint Milano cookies, chocolate cake with chocolate icing, I miss eating Nutella right out of the jar with a spoon!"

"Ok fine, my turn. I miss stupid time-waster video games on my phone. I miss Bejeweled Blitz. I miss downloading the monthly update for Bloons Tower Defense 4 and just losing three hours to Plasma Monkeys and then going to bed. I miss being smarter than the Pig in Angry Birds!"

Marissa sat down on Dan's lap and gave him a hug, putting her head on his shoulder. "Oh honey, you will always be smarter than the pig. You don't need your phone to prove it to me," and kissed him on the cheek, for which she got tickled.

After just a few seconds, Dan stopped with a worried look.

"What?" Marissa asked.

"Take off your shirt."

"Honey, the kids are still awake." Marissa said, playing coy.

"Rissa, I'm not kidding," he walked over and shut and locked the door. "Take off your shirt, right now." His tone of voice was worrying her and she started to untuck her shirt as he walked back to the bed.

"I've been so busy with everyone else that I haven't been paying attention to my own family. How much weight have you lost?"

She stopped in mid motion.

"I didn't say stop. I could feel your ribs when I was tickling you, Rissa, and not in a good way. You are too thin! The scale is a spring type and it still works, how much have you lost?"

"I'm not sure," she paused, "I stopped weighing myself over a month ago."

"Why?" Dan was trying to remain clinical but this was his *wife*!

"Because I knew I wasn't eating enough but it was me or the girls."

Dan pinched the bridge of his nose and closed his eyes to hold back the headache that was forming, and now the tears that threatened. Not the kids…the girls. Even now she wouldn't mention Danny.

"Come to think of it, Dan, take off *your* shirt," Marissa said.

"What?" Dan started and looked at his wife.

"Oh come on. Take it off, we're all losing weight and I've seen you put extra on the girls' plates at dinner too. I know, I know, you're supposed to be the provider and the protector and all that but just do it, ok? Take off the shirt."

"Fine," Dan complied and then they both had their shirts off. Dan realized that his wife wasn't wearing her normal bra but a sports bra, and even that wasn't all that snug anymore.

"How much weight have *you* lost, Mr.?" Marissa asked.

"I don't know, I haven't weighed myself in a couple of weeks either, I just feel like I'm in OK shape."

"OK shape? You are skin and bones! Get into the bathroom, I'll bring the candle."

In the bathroom they were confronted with the harsh reality that they were starving to death; or more accurately, they were starving themselves to death for the sake of their children.

Chapter Two

"Day 65 – August 17, 2012. Today would be my youngest child's birthday. Dan Jr. should be turning two. There will be no cake, there will be no presents. I miss you, son, and I know your mother misses you, too. She's just in denial."

Dan hung his head after putting the diary away. "I know the stages of grief. I've seen them thousands of times. I really am an idiot—her first word *was* 'No', after all."

Marissa was already up and making some Cream of Wheat for the girls. Dressed for the day, he helped make some powdered milk for Jessie and Bekah, and then they both took the multi-vitamins that he and Marissa had hidden in the air-return vent when the first attempt at a food collection came around. The vitamins were in the garage, initially, when the HOA board first tried to inventory everything. They simply hadn't been brought into the house from a previous trip to the warehouse store. Thankfully, they'd bought a couple of bottles of kid's chewable gummy vitamins the day before the grid went down.

They were lucky that all of their kids were on solid food and weren't still nursing or, worse, on formula anymore. Not that formula was in and of itself a bad thing but when there wasn't anymore, well, there wasn't any more and one of the families in the neighborhood had run into that situation less than a week after the power went out. Thankfully she had just been supplementing with formula while they were getting ready to wean the baby off of nursing completely and onto more solid food. They just made the transition a little sooner-- and more abruptly--than they had originally planned.

It was one of those things that still crossed Dan's mind on occasion--more frequently than he'd like to admit, actually. How was the rest of the world dealing with the loss of the grid? It was a foregone conclusion that there were families out there that hadn't had enough formula, or enough to feed a nursing mother. What had happened to the baby? It was just one more thing that Dan had to set aside and simply not dwell on or he would go mad.

The original plan to consolidate all the resources in the neighborhood had been a miserable failure—that is, until Carey and what remained of the HOA board decided to enforce their edict, and collect all food, at gunpoint going forwards…for the good of the community. What Carey didn't seem to understand was that people were already helping each other out. Pantries were being opened. What backyard gardens people had were being worked by everyone who was able and the harvests were being shared. The problem was that the typical garden was about twenty feet by ten feet and the seeds were all hybrids. But pantries were running bare and no amount of communal planning could or would change that. In fact, if Carey *had* been in charge of it things would have probably been wasted or ruined in the long run.

Dan was in an enviable position because he had the only medical training in the neighborhood. He could have been trading help for food, but he just didn't feel right about doing that--not yet. If it came down to keeping his children fed then he would consider it; but nobody was going hungry yet, so he simply felt he was doing his part for the community.

They couldn't stay here forever, though, because the neighborhood wasn't *producing* enough food to survive, and they hadn't seen or heard anything--or any*one*--from the outside since the power went out. The government wasn't going to come in and help; which meant no relief, which meant they needed to help themselves. The neighborhood was teetering on the ragged edge, and looking around… Dan could see that it wouldn't take much to push it over.

"What're your plans for today?" Marissa asked before their oldest came downstairs.

"I'm going to poke around the Taylor's old place," Dan said. At the sidelong look his wife gave him, he went on, "I know it's been picked over pretty good, but they had to have gone somewhere and I'm guessing that they were fairly well prepared. Eric was in the military so he probably had some idea how to live out of a tent, and we saw how packed Ms. Hines' supervisor's truck was when it came back. They were obviously prepared to go and not come back. Maybe we could find them, join them?"

Marissa shook her head, not in denial but in resignation. "Maybe you're right. It's getting to the point that anywhere would be better than here."

...

After breakfast, most mornings started with the two and a half mile round trip to get water from the Cumberland River. Dan had rigged the baby trailer for his mountain bike to hold a couple of the three-gallon frosting buckets the neighborhood had scrounged from one of the grocery stores and now used to transport water for the community. He was lucky he had both the bike and the baby trailer, otherwise he'd be making the trip multiple times to bring back his share of water.

During his ride and while he was filling the buckets, he paid closer attention to the state of the world--both in the neighborhood and on the other side of the river. The process had become such a routine that he hadn't thought anything of it in weeks; ever since he'd convinced Carey that people needed to quit doing it on their own so they could establish and maintain a central supply of clean drinking and cooking water. People had been getting sick because they were either drinking the water straight from the river or they weren't filtering it *or* boiling it correctly, which amounted to the same thing.

Their section of riverfront, while not heavily fortified, was guarded at all times with some of the rifles that just about everyone in the neighborhood, excepting he and Marissa, apparently owned. There were twenty-four hour patrols of the neighborhood as well, and the only reason that Dan wasn't on them was that he didn't know how to use a gun of any kind, and they didn't have the extra ammunition to teach him.

Not quite directly across the river, but near enough as made no difference, was a house with a boat slip that another neighborhood seemed to be using for the same purpose. The main difference in the neighborhood across the river was that the bulk of the houses were closer to the river so they used a bucket brigade each morning to get the water up to what Dan assumed was some sort of cistern--or possibly a converted water truck? *"If only we had all been closer to the river,"* Dan thought to himself and then chuckled. *"If only the power hadn't gone out in the first place."*

At least twice that Dan was aware of the guards had...thwarted... attempts to breach the security of the neighborhood --but the amount of gunfire along the river had made it sound more like a full-scale invasion. Dan had patched up one of the guards with a gunshot wound to the lower leg after the first firefight, and ended up using most of his ready supply of antibiotics.

As it was, Dan finished his compulsory chore in a little under half an hour, which he thought was pretty good given that he hadn't had more than 1,200 calories a day for the last six weeks. As he dropped off his full buckets he was told they needed him to report for firewood duty later that afternoon and then there were always the sick to look in on. The meager medical supplies he had on hand--the ones the neighborhood knew about anyway--were running thin.

...

He'd been to the Taylor's house a number of times over the past couple of months, but always with someone else, and always looking for something specific. Now he was here alone and he had no idea what he was looking for. The front door was closed but unlocked. It smelled musty inside as Dan walked in. Apparently it had been some time since anyone else had been here and nobody had been leaving windows open. Dan closed the door behind him and started walking through the house one room at a time.

The formal dining room at the front, which had been turned into an office or library, had been stripped almost to the walls. The computers, books, furniture, and rugs were all gone. The only things remaining were the built-in shelves. Nothing to see here, move along...across the entry way was another formal room--a den by the looks of it. There was still a recliner, and a flat-panel TV on the wall, with a Blue-Ray player and Xbox sitting on the floor. The shelves had been pulled down and burned several weeks ago, as had everything else that would burn once fuel got scarce.

The kitchen had been pretty well picked over and now held mostly just appliances. The first time he'd been through the house, only the doors had been taken off the cabinets--because they were easy to remove, but pulling the cabinets down would have been too much work. As easy fuel grew more difficult to find, the cabinets had finally been deemed "easy pickings". Interestingly, the cork bulletin board was still on the wall next to the fridge, with a couple of notes and postcards still tacked to it. They looked to be your typical vacation postcards with "Wish You Were Here" from a couple of regional, State, and National parks.

The living room was about half empty, with only the really large pieces and leather furniture still in place, again because it was more work to disassemble something to get to the wood than it was worth...so far. The remaining downstairs rooms were just as disappointing. As Dan climbed the stairs, he wondered why he'd bothered to come in the first place and hoped he'd find something useful.

The first two rooms had been kids' rooms--he could tell by the paint scheme on the wall if not by the furniture, or lack thereof. It had apparently all been wood furniture, as it was all gone. One was a boy's room; he had clearly been into cars. Plastic models didn't burn real well so they'd been left strewn on the floor. The closet was mostly hangers but there was one of those 'space bags' that you compress by pulling all the air out of it on the top shelf. Dan grabbed it and headed into the other kid's room. No telling what was in the space bag; he'd look at it later.

The girl's room was just as picked over and with nothing to find in the closet. The third room was an empty guest room. The last room was the master bedroom and Dan almost didn't go in.

This room had no furniture, except for the bedframe, a stand mirror, and a couple of under bed Rubbermaid boxes which had already been gone through. He didn't feel like going through the picked-over stuff. He was already feeling a little uneasy about going through the house on his own and he'd only been here for ten minutes. It wasn't that there was any rule about picking over the empty homes by yourself; it was just that this was Carey's neighbor and everyone knew that Carey and the Taylors didn't get on well…and now he was starting to have second thoughts about being in here for too long on his own.

Dan did a quick check under the sinks in the master bathroom to be sure nothing was missed and found a bar of Irish Spring, still in the box, and a disposable razor. Next was the closet. He turned on the flashlight that he'd only turned on three other times since June, to make sure it still worked. The Browning gun safe was still there; Carey still hadn't tried to pry it away from the wall. Mr. Taylor had done too good a job of bolting it to the studs and the floor and it just wasn't moving. Too bad, maybe Mr. Taylor had left some of his guns behind.

Dan looked up at the ceiling and the dangling cord for the pull-down attic stairs. Dan had been with Carey on almost all of the initial walkthroughs of empty houses after people had either left or passed away. For the first six or eight homes, Carey had gone up into the attic himself, or had one of his lackeys do it, to see if there was anything worth "collecting". The vast majority of them had held empty suitcases, if anything at all, and after another half dozen or so, Carey had called off searching them.

It was Dan's hope that Carey had neglected the attic of the Taylor's house as well. Dan grabbed the cord, pulled down the folding stairs, and got a smattering of dust, pink fiberglass, and grey, papery insulation in the face. Most likely he was going to be the first to go up.

The creaking of the springs and metal joints sounded incredibly loud in the otherwise silent house. Like his own attic there were a dozen or so sheets of plywood lain down between the rafters to walk on and support the odd bits of junk that you didn't want to leave in the garage but just couldn't bear to part with.

There were the two heating units and the light switch that didn't do anything anymore and of course a couple of suitcases that hadn't been taken. There were, however, what looked like a couple of sleeping bags in stuff sacks that appeared to have been up here for a couple of years and forgotten about. Those could come in handy. They were on the far end of where the plywood was in the attic, where Dan had to stoop down to keep from hitting his head as the roof was sloping down, and he was about as far from the opening back down to the closet as he could get.

From this vantage point he panned the flashlight back and forth across the attic again to see if there was anything else that he'd missed, or couldn't see while standing on the steps. On the third pass he caught the brief reflection of something on the back of the rafter that held the light switch for the attic. He carried the sleeping bags back to the stairway, set them down, and examined a nail driven into the rafter. Hanging on the nail was a single key--a key with the word "Browning" on it.

Acknowledgements

First and foremost I must thank my wife. She has put up with a lot, and I do mean a LOT, while I did what I did to get this thing done. She made sure I stayed fed when I would have just kept writing when I was 'in the zone', went to bed when I had to get up in the morning for the job that actually pays the bills, and spent time with the family so my kids didn't ever say, "Who's the guy taking off in Dad's car?". I was even accused, tongue in cheek--I'm pretty sure, of having an affair with one of my main characters because of the amount of time I was spending writing, and she stuck with me through it all. Thank you, hon, I love you.

An additional *huge* "Thank You" goes to my wife as editor. She took this challenge on for the second edition and I have to say that it was a Herculean task. Neither of us knew what she was in for when she signed on but I think the results speak for themselves. Words alone don't do justice but thank you, from the bottom of my heart.

Second goes to my kids. I have the greatest family in the world, bar none. Daddy was grumpy when he couldn't write but he really wanted to or felt he needed to but was stuck. Even though the first draft was done in a relatively short amount of time, there were some rough patches. Then there were the times when Dad just wouldn't...shut...UP about the book. Again, they were great. I'll make it up to you, and we'll go get ice-cream!

This has been a long time in the making. If I'm really honest with myself, I've been toying with bits and pieces of this since 1988 and my "Writing Science Fiction" class with Mr. K at Lake Forest High School (you will always be "Ken" to me, sorry). For good or ill, I actually started a story back then with--I kid you not,--"It was a dark and stormy night". As God is my witness, I didn't even know it was a cliché at the time. After I graduated, I toyed around with writing the dust jackets for the books I eventually hoped to write but never got around to even starting, and eventually, life got in the way.

Fast-forward twenty years and a co-worker introduced me to an author who is going to hate me for describing him this way, but so be it. This co-worker (who shall remain nameless at this point but appears as a character in Dark Grid) hands me a book by one John Ringo, and I like it. I read another one, and another, and then I got this wild hair to start writing. Don't get me wrong, I didn't want to compete with John but I got, no foolin', a little inspired. After about a month of hammering on the keyboard I decided to email John and ask him for advice and lo and behold, he responded...within like fifteen minutes! This is where I use the word he'll probably hate...since then, he's been a bit of a mentor. He's been supportive in a way that I don't think anyone else could have been with advice, insight, and blunt honesty.

Then there's a whole cast of additional characters, some based more in "reality" than others, but all of them just as real to me in many ways. I work with a bunch of really great guys, many of whom are Veterans (capital "V" people, that wasn't a typo) and a lot of them show up as characters in the book. I have never served in the military but several members of my family have, and I have the utmost respect for ALL members of our Armed Forces. Those that I know personally proved to be an invaluable resource, allowing me to tap into their knowledge and past experiences. It's a culture that I can only glimpse from the outside and only understand at the most basic level, but it is one that I am grateful for nonetheless.

Debbie Kolstad, who did the final cover treatment for the book; it looks great, thanks, Mom.

Finally, but certainly not lastly, or least, all of the many proofreaders and first readers who not only helped make corrections and suggestions but also gave me the confidence to go through with seeing this through to the end. I couldn't have done it without you and for that you have my undying gratitude.

--David

http://www.davidcwaldron.com

http://www.facebook.com/AuthorDavidCWaldron

14414040R00187

Made in the USA
Charleston, SC
09 September 2012